"Come here and kiss me, baby. I need to taste that sweet mouth of yours," Titus growled playfully.

Paris braced her hands on his broad shoulders and made a soft noise of surprise as he pulled her close and covered her willing lips with his eager mouth. The *ooh* that came out of her turned into a sigh of rapture as the kiss deepened into something erotically beautiful. His lips were firm but pliant and they molded to hers, while his tongue sought hers and the mutual stroking and sucking excited her in a way she'd never before experienced. Her hands left his broad shoulders as she wrapped her arms around his neck, the better to feel the warmth of his skin through the thin shirt he wore. His hand was tangled in her long hair as he held her gently, prolonging the sensual exchange. The kiss turned into more kisses, long, passionate ones that had Paris's heart pounding and her pulse racing in every part of her body, especially the most private parts that were becoming drenched with her desire for Titus.

They finally pulled apart and Paris's head rested on his shoulder while she tried to remember how to breathe normally. They held each other for a long time, until Titus kissed her forehead and tilted her face to his. Looking at her with an expression she'd never seen on any man's face before, a combination of intense desire and seduction, he uttered the words that would change her life forever.

"Let's make love."

The Closer I Get to You

Melanie Schuster

ARABESQUE®

THE CLOSER I GET TO YOU

An Arabesque novel

ISBN 1-58314-521-4

© 2006 by Melanie Woods Schuster

www.kimanipress.com

Printed in U.S.A.

Dedicated to
The memory of my mother,
Virginia Mae Hunter Woods
A strong lady and brave in spirit,
A gracious and loving woman
Who enriched everyone she encountered.
If I become half the woman you were
I'll be a success.
I owe you everything.

It's a great life,
If you just don't weaken.

Acknowledgments

Thank-you really doesn't begin to express my gratitude for everyone who prayed for me and with me during this last year. You have no idea how encouraged and uplifted I was because of your caring.

Special thanks to Betty and Regina, to Nicole and my wonderful Janices; Janice Sims and Janice Cochran and to Leslie, Beverly Jenkins, LeSonde, Kim, Yolanda, Stephanie, Debe, Brenda Jackson, Brenda Woodbury, Angela Griffin, Missy, Robert, Jamil, and Clint, Linda and Faye and Juanita and Susie. You all showed my family and me so much love and support; I know I couldn't have made it without you. And a very special thank-you to Mrs. Shirley Bady for her unstinting love and caring.

And my sincere and lasting gratitude to the skilled and compassionate nurses and doctors who cared for my mother as she made her final transition. Your kindness made all the difference.

Prologue

The wedding of John Flores and Nina Whitney was like something out of a fairy tale. It was beautiful, festive and very romantic. So romantic, in fact, that Paris Deveraux felt like she was close to passing out. "Swooning" was how her state was referred to in the romance novels she loved. Swooning, as in trembling with anticipation as she looked into the eyes of the man she'd adored for years. As luck would have it, both she and the object of her affection, Titus Argonne, were part of the wedding party. She'd managed to get through the wedding without expiring from his sexy gaze, but now that the reception had begun she was very close to a total meltdown.

They were seated at opposite ends of the bridal table in the vast ballroom of the hotel, and no matter where she tried to focus her attention, it was Titus who drew her like a magnet to heated steel. Paris had tried everything in her power to remain cool and poised, but Titus was too compelling, too sexy and thoroughly male to be ignored. She tried to talk to the other bridesmaids, to take small measured sips of champagne and to observe the beautifully clad guests who were enjoying the reception, but it was fruitless. Every time she looked his way, Titus was smiling at her, his fabulous blue-gray eyes lit with admiration. The heat he was generating in her body increased to the point where Paris couldn't keep still any longer. Suddenly she stood and left the table, not even picking up her small evening bag. Her destination was the ladies' room where she could hide out and regroup quickly; there was no way she could spend the evening trembling and quivering at every glance from the handsomest man she'd ever seen.

She made it to the hallway outside the ballroom and her getaway was at once revealed as being either the smartest or the dumbest thing she'd ever done; Titus had apparently read her mind and anticipated her every move, because he was waiting for her. He looked down from his impressive height and gave her a smile so sweet she could actually feel her resistance shatter like spun glass and land tinkling around her feet. He held out his hand and she put hers into it, so taken with the feel of his warm, slightly moist skin that her trembling stopped.

In minutes Titus had led her into a secluded atrium and her other hand joined his in a warm clasp. He looked down at her and his smile changed. His whole expression changed. He was looking at her as though he'd never seen her before. His eyes took on a deep, brilliantly blue hue as he looked deeply into her eyes. "Paris, you're looking good, baby," he said softly. "I've never seen you looking so beautiful." And before she could think of a reply, his lips were on hers and they were kissing madly.

They'd kissed before but nothing like this. His lips were

hot, sweet and totally mesmerizing; Paris couldn't think, she could only feel, and the feeling was remarkable. She could taste his essence, the smell of his skin filled her, and the warmth of his big hands as they encircled her waist filled her with desire. There was no one else in the world but the two of them and the sensation was incredible, it was passionate and heady and…suddenly she was jerked from his arms by two strong hands.

"What the hell is going on here?" a rough voice demanded.

Paris groaned and her eyes, which had flown open in shock, closed again in resignation. It was a voice she recognized, just like the familiar feel of the hands on her shoulders. It was her wildest brother, Lucien. She glanced quickly to the left, then the right. Oh yeah, they were all there in force. *How the heck did they find me?* she thought before issuing a huge sigh. Titus's eyes had darkened to a charcoal gray and he looked anything but amused; he looked quite lethal, as a matter of fact.

Even as she spoke, Paris recognized the farcical nature of her words. Like every well-bred southern woman in her family she remembered her manners while her world was crumbling around her. She politely introduced the hulking brutes on either side of her. "Titus, have you met my brothers? Lucien, Wade, Julian and Philippe, this is Titus Argonne."

The five men glared at each other intently, and Paris could have sworn she heard the sound of hooves being stamped like stallions about to challenge each other for leadership of the herd. She stared at her feet and took a deep, steadying breath. It was going to be a long and bumpy ride.

Chapter 1

Things were about to turn really ugly in the atrium. It wasn't just Paris's active imagination, she knew her brothers well enough to know when a fight was about to erupt. The Deveraux brothers were known throughout Louisiana as hot-tempered brawlers even though they were all well educated and had been brought up with an excess of home training. They'd all had what was referred to in the South as a "gracious plenty" of etiquette, something their genteel father had insisted on, although no hint of it was apparent at the moment. There was a running joke in their hometown that the only reason all four of them practiced law was to keep each other out of jail, a place where one or more of them might be headed that very evening, from the looks of things.

"Paris, what the hell do you think you're doing, letting him paw you all over in a public place?" This was from Julian, her oldest brother. Before she could answer, Wade jumped in.

"I don't know who you think you are, but if you touch my sister again I'll rearrange your face for you," he growled at Titus.

Titus gave the furious man a half smile that was completely at odds with his icy cold stare. "You're welcome to try," he invited in a quiet, dangerous voice.

At those words Philippe began removing his suit coat. "You ain't said nothin' but a word. You want some of this, come on," he said roughly.

Paris had quite enough of their antics by now and stepped in front of her brothers, grabbing the two nearest, Philippe and Julian, by their expensive silk neckties. "Cut it out! What in the world is wrong with you men—have you lost your minds?"

Wade, her second oldest brother, took issue with her question, shoving Julian out of the way so he could face her. "*We* haven't lost anything, Paris Corinna. I think *you're* the one that's gone crazy lettin' this here clown wallow all over you. We didn't raise you like that," he said, his voice rising with every word. His southern accent came out whenever he was enraged, and tonight was no exception.

Paris's face turned bright red, an ugly contrast to her rose-colored gown. "You didn't 'raise me' at all," she countered. "You're my brothers, not my daddy."

"A statement with which I must concur," a deep voice without a trace of humor intoned. Paris turned to find Julian McArthur Deveraux, known to all as Mac, standing behind her with a look of utter disgust on his handsome face.

"Daddy," Paris breathed with a sigh of relief.

Mac acknowledged his daughter with a comforting pat on her shoulder and a kiss on her cheek. He turned to his sons, however, with the lowered brow of censure plain for all to see. "Why is it that I'm still breaking up your brawls? At your ages, with your educations, why can't you find it in your hearts to imitate civilized adults, at least when you're in decent society? What's gotten into you people?"

Philippe and Julian were busy straightening their ties while Lucien tried to justify their behavior. "Judge, we saw Paris leaving the ballroom and this…person followed her, so we followed them. And you won't believe what he was doing to her," he added angrily.

The elder Deveraux looked Titus over and seemed to take his measure. "He was probably doing what any man with sense would be doing when he's alone with a beautiful woman. What you all would be doing if you fools could leave your sister alone long enough to find someone to tolerate you." He turned to Titus and extended his hand. "Mac Deveraux, young man. And you are?"

"I'm Titus Argonne, sir. I assure you, sir, I have nothing but respect for your daughter," he said quietly.

The two men gave each other a long stare as they shook hands, and were apparently satisfied by what they saw. Mac nodded to Titus and suggested he take Paris back into the ballroom. "I seem to need to have a quiet word with some members of my family." He winked at Paris and said, "Don't forget to save me a dance, Cupcake."

Paris couldn't trust herself to speak, but she nodded weakly. Titus put a strong hand on her waist and guided her in the direction of the ballroom while her brothers stared after her, all of them scowling and mumbling as the couple took their leave.

They were about to follow the two of them when their father's voice stopped them cold. "Where do you lunkheads think you're going? I'm not through with you, not by a long shot," he said in the voice they each knew meant business. He looked at his four sons one at a time, his expression growing more and more morose. "I've told you over and over again,

Paris is not a child. She's a grown woman, a very intelligent and accomplished woman and she can run her own life. She doesn't need you hanging over her shoulders, nosing around in her business and acting like her father. That's my job, one I think I accomplished quite well, thank you. You all need to butt out of her personal life. This is not a suggestion, it's an order, in case you were wondering," he said sternly.

"Yeah, but Judge, look at her!" Julian frowned, making him the mirror image of his handsome father. "When did she get to be all…all…" His words stopped and he used his hands to approximate a very curvy woman's frame. "All of a sudden she's like this…um…" His voice faltered and he looked to his brothers for aid.

Lucien chimed in at once. "Look, Judge, I don't know if you've noticed but our Paris has turned into a real hottie. Out of nowhere she's gotten gorgeous and sexy and she's gonna have men hanging all over her like that fool was tonight. We just don't want anything to happen to her, that's all."

Philippe and Wade agreed. "You know she's been sheltered, Judge. That's the way you wanted it, the way we all wanted it," Philippe pointed out.

Wade concurred, saying, "She doesn't know enough about men to handle all this attention, that's all. We just don't want her to get hurt."

Mac shook his head. "You'd do well to remember that the road to hell is paved with good intentions. I'm sure your hearts are pure and your motives are, too, but you've got to leave your sister alone. Paris has indeed grown up to be a stunning woman, something you obviously haven't noticed until now," he said dryly. "But she's also a very smart and self-reliant one and she can handle herself. It's time for you to let your sister handle her own affairs. Now, why don't we go join the party before these nice people regret inviting us?"

Without another word he left them standing there with their mouths open, walking away from them with the stride of a man who's in complete control of his universe. His oldest son broke the silence he left behind.

"I don't care what Judge says, Paris is headed for trouble with this guy and I'm keeping an eye on this situation," vowed Julian.

"You got that right, brother," Wade agreed. "This is something that's going to need our attention."

The four men exchanged their customary handshake, which was more like a dap and pound ritual. Whether she liked it or not, Paris had four guardians who took their job very, very seriously.

Titus took Mac Deveraux at his word, and as soon as he and Paris arrived in the beautifully decorated ballroom, he led her out on the dance floor and they danced several times before they returned to the bridal table. He sat next to her, pulling his chair closer to hers and smiling down at her. He could tell she was still embarrassed by what had taken place earlier and he wasn't having it. He ran a long finger down her cheek and turned her pretty face so that she had to look at him. "What's on your mind, Paris? I can tell you're deep in thought."

Paris made a face as she gently moved Titus's hand. She didn't let it go; she continued to hold one of his long fingers and unconsciously stroked it up and down with her soft, supple hands as she answered him. "I'm trying to think of a time when I was more embarrassed than I am right now," she said glumly. "There was the time the top of my bathing suit came off at the family reunion, but I was three at the time, so it's not quite the same thing, I guess."

Titus tried not to smile, but she looked so pretty and so flustered, he felt his lips turn up in a grin. She kept talking, trying not to meet his eyes. "Once on the first day of school my slip fell down. It was a fancy half-slip and I just had to wear it even though it was too big. Well, down it came and landed around my ankles right in front of God and everybody. I mean that literally, too, I went to a Catholic school. Of course, I was only seven then, so I managed to live through it. But this performance is the very limit, it really is. This just passes all understanding. I've always known they were protective, but this…" Her voice trailed off as her head went down a notch.

"Listen, Paris, you don't have to apologize for having protective brothers. As fine as you are they'd be crazy not to be concerned about you. You're a very sexy woman and they're smart enough to know that all kinds of men are going to be after you," he said honestly.

Paris hadn't released his finger and the touch of her hand was having an odd effect on him. Her delicate strokes gave him a heightened sensitivity as sensual as it was unexpected. Titus wasn't prepared for the sudden arousal that grew as she continued to play with his finger, with a sweet and unaffected sensuality that came from the fact that she didn't realize she was doing it. She was totally unaware of the effect her touch was having on him, her mind was focused on the words he was saying. He cleared his throat and gently retrieved his finger, kissing her on the forehead as he did so. He was pleased to hear a little throaty giggle as his lips touched her soft skin.

"That's better," he said with satisfaction. "Don't let your big brothers get you down, they're just showing you love."

"The sad thing is, only two of them are my *big* brothers. Philippe and Lucien are younger than I am," she said, making a face. "And every single one of them thinks he's my daddy, which is ridiculous. I have a perfectly good father and I don't

need four bodyguards. I can take care of myself," she added
with flashing eyes.

Titus loved the look of determination on her face. He liked
all her expressions; Paris wasn't the kind of woman who
could hide her feelings. Whatever she was thinking was reflected on her classic features and made her even more attractive. He was about to tell her that when the DJ called for the
bridesmaids to dance with the bride. They had a big disco
number planned and Paris went to join the other women on
the floor.

Titus settled back in his chair to watch Paris as she and the
other bridesmaids danced energetically to "Boogie Wonder-
land," the old Earth Wind and Fire classic. Nina Whitney-
Flores loved disco music and he could see why; she was
incredibly adept at the kind of dancing that went along with
it. But so was Paris, matching Nina step for step.

Her creamy skin was aglow and her rosy lips were parted
in a smile as she tossed her long thick black hair out of her
eyes. All of the bridesmaids looked fantastic in their dresses,
but Paris looked the best, in his opinion. Each dress was
slightly different from the others, something he'd never seen
before, not that he'd ever really paid any much attention to
the outfits worn by bridesmaids. Paris's dress had a sweetheart
neckline that extended into a sexy halter and it curved to her
body in a way that really accentuated her figure. The skirt of
the dress flowed out to a matinee length that allowed a
provocative glimpse of her trim ankles and suddenly he was
consumed with the desire to see more of her stunning legs.
Paris was built just the way he liked his women; she was tall
and stacked with a nice full bosom, small waist, big hips and
a lush, rounded behind that swayed when she walked. And she
had big shapely legs, too. Titus had a serious weakness for a
big thick woman. He was six feet six inches tall and muscular

and he had no use for a petite little thing. His eyes continued to follow Paris on the dance floor and he smiled in satisfaction. This was an affair he couldn't wait to begin. He'd been flirting around with Paris long enough; it was time for the real thing to start.

Angelique Deveraux Cochran looked at the smiling face of her cousin Paris and returned the happy look with one of her own. The two women were in Angelique's bedroom in the big Palmer Park home she occupied with her husband, Adonis, known to all as Donnie, and her little girl, Lillian Rose, known as Lily Rose. They were lounging after breakfast before getting ready to go to a cookout at the home of Alan Cochran, one of her brothers-in-law. Lily Rose was spending quality time with her daddy, who had gone to walk the dogs and get the papers, and the cousins were going over every detail of the wedding, reliving it with glee.

"Nina looked just beautiful, didn't she?" Paris sighed. "She looked like a doll in that dress. And John looked like he was ready to grab her and run out of the church!" She laughed.

Angelique agreed. "I'm surprised he made it through the ceremony. Any fool could tell all he wanted to do was be alone with his bride. It was so cute. And the way he kissed her after the vows, ooh, honey, I have to say it inspired me," she said with a wicked giggle.

"Oh, so that's why you and Donnie disappeared from the reception," Paris said knowingly. She was reclined on a chaise in the corner of the bedroom, pointing an accusing finger at her cousin. Angelique was sitting at her antique vanity table, a recent gift from her husband. She put down the big sable brush she used to dust loose powder across her nose and gave Paris an arch smile of her own.

"Yes, we left early and yes, it was for the very reason you

imagine, because we couldn't keep our hands off each other another minute. I'm surprised we made it all the way home, to be honest. But," she drawled, "we didn't leave before we saw you and Titus Argonne making love on the dance floor. We definitely didn't miss that, cuz."

Paris threw a small satin pillow at Angelique, protesting the whole time. "Angel! We were just dancing, that's all. You don't have to make it sound like we were dry-humping out in front of everybody. I have more class than that," she sniffed.

Angelique deftly caught the pillow and tossed it back. "Okay, I apologize. I didn't mean you were a-bumpin' and a-grindin', I just meant you were so caught up with each other it looked really sexy and romantic. It was like a tango without movement, if that makes any sense. And I'm not the only one who thought so. Your brothers were staring at you so hard they could probably see what color underwear y'all were wearing. How did they all manage to be here together anyway?"

Paris stifled a scream by pressing her face into the poor pillow. "Girl, don't get me started on those lunkheads! They're all going to some legal conference in Chicago and they decided to come to the wedding since Detroit is so close by. The four of them hardly ever get to come to family affairs together because if one of them isn't on some big case, another one is out of the country or has to give a speech or something. I think the last family wedding they all attended was Bennie and Clay's," she reflected. "Anyway, they performed in true Deveraux fashion. If it hadn't been for Daddy, somebody would have ended up in the county lockup last night," she said in disgust before filling Angelique in on the details.

Angelique didn't help matters by laughing as Paris recounted how her brothers had practically thrown down a gauntlet for Titus. "I'm sorry, girl, I didn't mean to laugh, it's just that I'm picturing the whole thing in my head and it's pretty hilarious. They just don't want to admit their little sister is all grown up. How did Titus react?"

Paris's face turned dreamy as she recalled how Titus had acted coolly disinterested in her siblings' histrionics. "Honey, it didn't bother him in the least. You know how he is, relaxed and in control all the time. So very different from some other men I might mention but won't. Sometimes I think our fathers wound up with the wrong sons," she said wryly. Both women laughed at the truth of that statement.

Their fathers were brothers. Angelique's father was the late Clayton Arlington Deveraux Sr., and before his death he'd been a most formidable man. Tall, handsome, charming and ruthless, he was hot-tempered and impulsive and made as many enemies as friends. His sons, however, were calm and rational, all of them wealthy and successful but none as flamboyant as their father. Paris's father was the opposite of his brother. Not physically, as both men were tall and handsome. But in every other way they were poles apart.

Julian Deveraux was quiet, refined and considered to be one of the leading legal minds in the country. His name was often on the short list for the Supreme Court, an appointment he refused to consider. He preferred his life as a justice in the State Supreme Court of Louisiana. He was levelheaded, persuasive and was never known to raise his voice in anger; he had other ways of getting his point across. His sons, however, were brilliant renegades, all with fiery tempers and aggressive personalities, who had already garnered reputations that bordered on legends, not just in Louisiana, but everywhere they traveled.

Angelique looked thoughtful as she pondered the truth of Paris's remark. "It's true. My brothers are more like your daddy than our own father. They're much more easygoing and laid back than your brothers. But you must admit those boys are *fun*," she pointed out.

Paris laughed as she recalled how they had danced the night away. Her brothers were excellent dancers and they made it their business to see that every lady in the place danced as often as she liked. "Yes, they are," she said fondly. "Once they stopped pouting and trailing me around the reception like bloodhounds, it was a good time being with them. They all apologized before we left the reception and we made up before they left for the airport. I really do adore all of my brothers and you know that. They were my rock when I was growing up. They always made me feel like I could do anything, they treated me like I was Superwoman. Hard to live up to sometimes, but it made me the woman I am today."

Angelique glanced at the small digital clock on her dressing table. "We'd better get dressed if we're going to get to Grosse Pointe for the cookout. John and Nina are going to be there, too. They spent the night in some posh hotel, but they said they'd be at the party today. Now when are they actually going on their honeymoon? Nobody seems to leave right after the wedding anymore," she said reflectively.

"They're leaving next week, going to the Caribbean for a couple of weeks," Paris said. "They planned it so it would coincide with John's semester break. And you're right, the norm used to be to take off the day after the wedding, but people have to work in a long vacation where they can these days. One of my production assistants got married on a Saturday and was back to work on Monday because her husband couldn't get a vacation until the next week. Doesn't seem as romantic, I guess, but that's modern life for you."

Both women turned to the door as Donnie's Aunt Ruth tapped on the doorframe. "Good morning, ladies. I was just about to make a pot of coffee and wondered if you wanted to join me?"

Angelique smiled brightly. Her husband's aunt had become one of her very favorite people and she always loved entertaining her. "We'd love to, Aunt Ruth. Give us a couple of minutes to throw on some clothes and we'll be down."

Paris took note of Aunt Ruth's shapely figure in a chic and casual outfit consisting of a FUBU jogging suit in cream with red lettering and red K-Swiss running shoes. "You're looking awfully good for this hour of the morning. Have you been out already?"

Ruth nodded with a smile. Her honey-colored complexion was smooth and youthful and her silky hair was cut in an audaciously smart style with a long tail accenting the nape of her neck. The tail was even tipped with a gold highlight. Her clear green eyes sparkled as she answered Paris's question. "I took my usual walk after breakfast. Even though I'm away from my gym I wanted to get in a little exercise so I stay nice and limber. So I did my yoga and walked a few miles. This is such a lovely neighborhood, it's always a pleasant walk. Come on down when you're ready," she invited as she turned to go down to the kitchen.

Soon they were all seated at the breakfast table enjoying Ruth's excellent coffee and the cinnamon toast she'd made to accompany it. The wedding was still the main topic of conversation, naturally. Ruth was particularly happy that John Flores had found love with Nina Whitney; in a roundabout way John was a part of her family. She considered him a nephew, even though they didn't share the same blood. John's father, Big Benny Cochran, had been married to her late sister Lillian when John was conceived and Ruth had arranged for the baby to be adopted by her dear friends Consuela and Nestor Flores. No one knew about it except Benny and Ruth, although the burden of secrecy had taken its toll on Ruth. She was extremely relieved to have the story out in the open at last, and truly grateful that Benny and Lillian's other children didn't despise her for helping Benny cover up the proof of his one time infidelity. And the fact that his half siblings had accepted him into the family was something else that brought joy to Ruth's heart.

"I'm very happy that all my nephews and my niece have married so well. A wonderful marriage is the cornerstone of a happy life. Marriage can be a great adventure," she mused. "Angelique can tell you all about it, Paris. You can look at her and see how happy she is. I'm telling you this because I have a feeling your turn is next," she teased.

Paris's eyes got huge and she almost dropped her cup. "Umm, what do you mean, Aunt Ruth?" She stopped and covered her mouth with an apology in her eyes. "I'm sorry, I shouldn't call you that, should I?"

Ruth waved her hand to indicate it was of no importance. "Honey, you can call me Ruth, Aunt Ruth, or whatever you feel comfortable with. We're family, aren't we? I mean with all these Cochrans and Deverauxes marrying each other we're all just one big happy family, so don't worry about it. And don't change the subject. You and that young man seem quite involved. If you aren't now you will be soon and you make a beautiful couple. Why are you being coy about it?"

Angelique laughed at the look of surprise on Paris's face. "Aunt Ruth doesn't hold back. What comes up comes out, so be prepared. And she's right, you know she is."

Paris sighed and gave both women a bashful grin. Then she moved her cup out of the way and leaned forward onto the table. "Okay, Aunt Ruth, this is the scoop. I've had a mad thing for Titus for a few years now. When I was interning at the Deveraux Group I saw him for the first time and I went for him big time but I was so shy around him I couldn't put two words together. He's always been really sweet to me. He never acted like I was a moron even though I always managed to behave like one when I was around him. Anyway, I guess it was at Adam and Alicia's wedding that I was able to just talk to him like a normal person. That's when we started really talking and getting to know each other and we've been dating ever since. Not as much as I'd like because I've been really busy with the show and he's been doing a lot of work out of the country. But—" She smiled and the color in her cheeks intensified "—things do seem to be heating up."

Before Ruth could comment, the back door opened and Donnie entered with the dogs, Pippen and Jordan, and the couple's little daughter Lily Rose, who made a beeline for her mother with her usual bubbly smile. "Mommy, we're home! I missed you, Mommy!"

Angelique gathered the little girl up and kissed her soundly. "Mommy missed you, too! I'm so glad you're home. We're going to see Uncle Alan and Aunt Tina, doesn't that sound like fun?"

Ruth was watching Paris's face and smiled into her cup at the expression she found there. Paris was looking as though she was just realizing that marriage and motherhood were real possibilities in her life. Ruth started to tease the younger woman but decided not to say a word. *She'll figure it out on her own. It's always better when it's a surprise*, she thought sagely.

Chapter 2

"Okay, I'm ready. How do I look?" Paris asked. She was turning around so that Angelique could inspect her outfit.

"You look fabulous. That color is wonderful on you," she approved.

It was a delightful shade of deep peach that flattered Paris's creamy skin in the same way the outfit highlighted her best assets. The top was a gauzy linen and rayon blend, cut on the bias to flow gently over her curves. It was strapless but it fit so well there was no cleavage visible. And there was a clever necklace-like attachment that circled her neck and added additional stability to the top, which flared out into a handkerchief hem. It showed off her sculptured collarbones and firm, toned arms and it also flattered her waistline. She wore it with a pair of low-rise ankle-skimming slacks in the same shade of peach that were just snug enough to emphasize her figure and not disguise it. On her feet were flat leather sandals in bronze that showed off her perfectly pedicured toes. Her thick hair was worn in loose waves and she had on chandelier earrings with tiny gold beads that drew the eyes to her face with its high cheekbones, flawless complexion and the tiny freckles that danced across her nose. She looked wonderful and she smelled very feminine and romantic. Angelique repeated her earlier compliment.

"You look even prettier than usual. Titus is going to be knocked out, girl. We'll be ready to leave in about ten minutes," she said as she recombed Lily Rose's hair.

Paris cleared her throat discreetly. "Umm, Titus is actually going to pick me up," she said shyly. "He should be here in about five minutes."

Just the then the doorbell rang and Paris's eyes got big again, but she was smiling. "I think my date is here," she said. "I'll see you ladies in a few," she added as she went down the stairs to greet Titus.

He was talking to Donnie in the living room when she made her entrance. He immediately stood up and held out his hand to her, a hand that she took with no hesitation as she walked towards him.

"Paris, you get more gorgeous every time I see you," he said in a voice only she could hear.

The look in his eyes was so sincere she had no choice but to believe him. She gave him a very private smile and they chatted with Donnie for a few minutes before leaving in Titus's rental car. As they approached the car, Paris impulsively told him how nice he looked, which was true. He was wearing well-worn jeans that nevertheless bore a knifelike crease, and a long-sleeved patterned rayon shirt that was untucked. It was in a shade of blue that really brought out his eyes and almost made up for the fact that she couldn't see his butt, which was one of her favorite views in the world. Besides being very tall, Titus had a gorgeous body, hard and muscular and with his tawny skin, oddly colored eyes and sandy brown hair, he was just too handsome for words. His face was hard and masculine with high cheekbones and his eyes had the slightest slant that gave him an oddly Asian look at times. Right now he just looked sexy, so much so Paris could feel it in the pit of her stomach. It was a strange tickling feeling that seemed to be snaking its way around her body. It wasn't an unpleasant sensation, but it was unsettling.

Titus seated her and made sure she fastened her seat belt before getting behind the wheel. He reached for his sunglasses, giving her one more devastating look before putting them on. "Paris, you really do look tempting in that outfit," he drawled.

"I do?" she murmured.

"You surely do. You look good enough to eat; all sweet and pretty like a bowl of peach ice cream. Makes me want to taste you, just to see if you're as sweet as I think you are," he said, leaning toward her with a trace of a smile.

Without realizing she was moving, Paris was drawn toward him, leaning in just enough so that their lips met. It was a gentle, tender kiss, but it was enough to triple the sensations that were rippling over her like the pattern left in a pond when a pebble touches its surface. Her eyes flew open when she heard him groan.

"Even sweeter. We'd better get going before I lose all my self-control around you. You're too tempting for my own good, Miss Paris."

He started the car and they took off, but not before he reached over and reclaimed her hand.

By the time they reached Grosse Pointe, Titus wished he had on anything but the jeans in which he was attired, because his body's interest in Paris was overwhelming. He was way too aware of his unruly male anatomy in the confines of the jeans, and the only thing that would keep him from total exposure was his loose-fitting, untucked shirt. His reaction to Paris was so strong he had to exercise even more control than he normally did. If there was anything Titus was proud of, it was his discipline. He had more resolve and steely determination than ten men and these governed every aspect of his life. He didn't make rash decisions; he made coolly calculating ones that always paid off in his favor. In his line of business he couldn't afford to be careless. Titus was a graduate of West Point, and after his tours of duty in the army he parlayed his training in military intelligence and his law degree into a firm that specialized in investigations and corporate security. Everything about his work required precision, deliberate procedures that resulted from intense research and observation. But right now, alone with Paris in the relatively close quarters of the car, all he could think about was her.

She was chatting away about something but at the moment he couldn't have said what it was because she was stroking his hand while she was talking and it was driving him crazy. He was holding her left hand in his and she was caressing the back of it with her right hand, a gentle, tender touch. He knew without being told that she wasn't deliberately trying to arouse him. God help him if she ever decided to do that; he'd lose his mind for sure. But the soft pressure of her fingertips against his skin was heightening his awareness of her and creating sensations in his body that were impossible to ignore. Titus glanced over at her, thankful for the camouflage his sunglasses offered him; he could only imagine the raw heat that was in his eyes as he devoured her with a look.

They finally reached their destination, the big brick home of Alan Cochran and his family. He was relieved to be able to park the car and get out, because the light, sweet fragrance of Paris's perfume had assailed his nostrils during the entire ride and was bringing him to a dangerously high level of arousal. He lectured himself as he went around the car to open her door; he hadn't felt this crazy since he was a teenager. Then he opened the door and held out his hand to Paris. She turned to the side and gracefully got out of the car, tilting her head up to smile at him. He stared down at her, looking so carefree and sensual he had to kiss her, had to feel her luscious lips under his mouth. That would be enough to bring him back to his senses. It was just a quick kiss, their lips touched briefly and that was all. But the innocent little caress didn't have the effect he'd planned; instead of dousing his desire it heightened it. He turned abruptly to get the bottles of expensive wine he'd brought out of the backseat, glad to have something to distract his attention even for a moment.

He picked up the bag from the wine store and locked the car door, then held out his hand to Paris. She took it easily and naturally and they walked up to the house where they could hear the sounds of festivity from the huge backyard. "It sounds like things are getting started already," she said happily. Giving him the look that never failed to send a tingle through his body, she added, "I'm glad you were able to stay over for this, Titus. I thought you'd have to go right back to Atlanta after the wedding."

Titus gently released her hand and put his arm around her bare shoulder, trying to ignore the lure of her smooth, silken skin. "I scheduled some meetings in Detroit and Minneapolis. I was hoping to be able to spend some time with you," he told her, enjoying the pleased look she gave him.

Before she could say anything they were greeted by a chorus of happy voices coming from the assorted Deveraux and Cochran children in attendance. Clayton Deveraux III, called Trey for short, came around the corner of the house with a smile on his face and his younger siblings on his heels. He gave Paris a hug and a kiss on the cheek, which was repeated by his twin brothers, Marty and Malcolm, when Paris stooped down to their level. He offered his hand to Titus, who had to hide a smile while they exchanged a manly handshake. Trey was so much like his father it was eerie. He had a calm maturity that was unusual in a boy his age, but it was totally natural for him; there was nothing put on about it.

"I'll take that for you, T," Trey said, taking the bag from the older man's hands. By now they'd reached the backyard where family and friends were already enjoying what was going to be a fantastic party. Trey turned to Paris to ask where her brothers were.

"Daddy and the boys went to Chicago this morning, Trey. They had a law conference to attend," she told him.

"That's too bad," Trey said thoughtfully. "I hardly ever get to see the Judge and the cousins. Maybe they can come visit you in Atlanta when we get back," he said innocently.

Paris's eyes widened as she tried to think of something diplomatic to say. She loved her brothers and enjoyed their company, but the thought of them all piled up in Atlanta running interference while she tried to date Titus was unsettling to say the least. She looked at Titus and felt the heat rise up to her cheeks because his look of amusement told her he knew exactly what she was thinking. She was rescued, however, by the greetings of the friends and family who'd already gathered in the huge backyard.

Some of the Deveraux family had already flown back to Atlanta, but Bennie and Clay Deveraux were still there, as were Martin and Ceylon Deveraux and their children. Bennie and Ceylon were both from Detroit and always tried to maximize their visits to Motown so they could spend time with their families. After hugging the two women as if she hadn't seen them in a week, Paris made her way over to Lisette Alexander, who was sitting next to her husband, Warren, on an old-fashioned glider. The two women had become close friends while Paris completed an internship with Cochran Communications in Detroit two years earlier. Paris gave Lisette a perfunctory greeting and wiggled her fingers at Warren; her real target was Warren Frederick Alexander Jr., the young son of the doting couple. She cooed happily as she took the adorable little boy from his mother's arms and kissed his irresistibly chubby cheek.

Warren laughed good-naturedly. "I can see you're not interested in me in the least, so why don't I get out of your way?" He rose from the glider and offered Paris his seat, which she took without hesitation.

"Thanks, Warren," she murmured absently while she admired the toddler. "Lisette, he's beautiful. And he's so sweet," she added as Warren, Jr., gave her a big smile and started wiggling. He loved the ladies, but he wanted to hang out with his father.

Lisette smiled proudly and agreed with Paris. "I shouldn't say this, but you're absolutely right. He's very handsome and good-natured, just like his daddy." Her expression changed as she looked at her big teddy bear of a husband. Paris had reluctantly released Warren Jr. who was running to his father as fast as his chubby legs would allow. Lisette couldn't hide the fact that she was still madly in love with Warren, even more so than when they first married. She'd once told Paris that it was love at first sight for her, and her feelings hadn't changed one bit, they'd only gotten deeper.

"I haven't told Warren yet, but I'd like to have another one soon. I want them to be close in age so they'll be great friends," she confided.

Paris raised an eyebrow. "That's a done deal then, because you know Warren can't refuse you anything. Do you want a boy or a girl this time?"

"I don't care which. I just want another baby," Lisette smiled. "There's something wonderful about making babies with the man you love, it's like being under a magic spell or something," she added dreamily. "You'll find out what I mean pretty soon."

Paris felt her mouth fall open but she couldn't seem to close it. She must have looked positively panicked because Lisette patted her hand comfortingly. "I'm sorry, sweetie, I didn't mean to shock you like that! But the way Titus looks at you tells me it won't be too much longer before you're planning your own wedding. Honey, that's just how Warren looked at me when we were dating." Lisette stopped talking and smiled, a warm beautiful smile meant for one person only. She put her lips together and formed a discreet little kiss, directed at Warren, who was staring at his wife as though this were the first time he'd ever seen her.

Paris had to laugh at the two of them. "Lisette, I think he's still got the look. You are Warren were just meant to be together, that's all. Titus and me, well, that's different. We've just started going out, it's not that deep," she said, trying to sound convincing.

Lisette dragged her eyes away from her man long enough to give Paris a look full of mischief. "Oh really? Then why is he looking at you like he wants to eat you up, hmm?"

Against her better judgment, Paris looked over where Titus was chatting with her cousins Martin and Clay. Sure enough, Titus was staring at her. He'd removed his shades and she could see his eyes, their color once again radiating a warm shade of blue. His expression was warm and relaxed and it suddenly turned blatantly sexy as he acknowledged her observation of him by giving her a slow wink and touching his mouth with his forefinger as he sent a silent kiss her way.

Paris blinked her long lashes and stifled a gasp as a hot tremor started in a place she'd never felt before. A soft "ooh" escaped her lips as Lisette laughed with delight.

"Not that deep, hmm? Not for long, sister. Your day is coming very, very soon," she vowed.

Paris tried to think of a witty response but failed. Her mind was too full of the possibilities engendered by Lisette's prediction and her own intensely passionate reaction to the man who was still watching her. Her rescue came in the form of Aunt Ruth and Angelique as they joined the two women. Thanking a higher power, she happily joined in conversation with the others as they made themselves comfortable in lounge chairs. *Hallelujah, I'm safe for now*, Paris thought gratefully. Then she made the mistake of glancing up once more to lock eyes with Titus and felt the same tremor, this time stronger and deeper. *Oh, who am I kidding? I'm not safe. I'm in trouble, deep trouble. But for some reason, I don't really care.*

Chapter 3

After the afternoon spent pleasantly in the company of her friends and family, Paris was relaxed and happy as she and Titus drove through the streets of Detroit. She was so relaxed, in fact, that she didn't jump and tremble when he reached over to stroke the side of her face.

"You're awfully quiet. You're not getting shy on me again, are you?" he teased.

"No, I'm not," she assured him. "I was just thinking about what a nice party that was. I really enjoy my cousins and their friends," she said.

"You do have a wonderful family. You're very fortunate to have a family like that," he said quietly.

Paris laughed out loud. "Even the lunkheads? You think I'm lucky to have four pit bulls for brothers?"

Titus laughed with her. "Actually, yes, I do. If they're going to keep the players and poseurs off you, I'm all for them as a matter of fact."

"I take it that doesn't include you. You would be the exception to the player-poseur rule, is that it?"

Titus brought the car to a stop. "Absolutely. I should be the only exception because I don't fit in either of those categories," he said confidently.

Paris was so taken with the look on his face she didn't register the fact that the car wasn't moving. "Really? And what category do you belong in?"

Titus unfastened his seat belt and leaned closer to Paris, close enough to savor the fine essence of her fragrance and marvel again at the purity of her beauty. "I don't have a category, baby. I'm a one-of-a-kind item, totally unique. I just happen to be a man who recognizes your exquisite quality and who just has to have you," he said softly, so softly Paris wasn't sure what she was hearing.

"You have to…" she murmured.

Titus leaned in closer, touching her lips with his own, talking to her as he did so. "I have to, Paris. I want you so bad it's turned into a disease. I think it might be terminal," he breathed as he sucked her lower lip, then her top one, feasting gently on the juicy and tender flesh of her mouth. "I think if I don't touch you soon, I might just die from wanting you, baby."

Paris was dizzy with sensation and longing for more. "You're crazy, Titus, you know that, right?"

"Yeah, I know. It's because you've *driven* me crazy. Those lips, those hands, that skin…damn, you've got beautiful skin," he sighed as he first stroked her shoulder, then ran his hot tongue over it.

She gasped and began trembling, which made him unfasten her seat belt and attempt to pull her into his arms. "Okay, this vehicle isn't made for this, at least not for us. Let's go inside and get comfortable," he suggested.

That made Paris realize they weren't moving anymore. "Go inside where?" She looked out the window to see where they were but all she could see was a parking lot.

"We're at my hotel. I thought we could go up to my suite and be alone for a while. Since you're staying with your cousins, you don't have any real privacy, and I won't be back in Atlanta for another week. So, if you're not put off by the idea, I thought we could have some much-needed solitude. Are you comfortable with that?"

A voice she didn't recognize as her own said, "Yes, of course." It was true, even though she was having a little trouble making her voice work, Paris didn't have a problem with what Titus suggested. It sounded like the perfect plan to her. She waited for Titus to open her door and pivoted on her seat to put her long legs out of the car as she took the hand he offered her. He smiled down at her with admiration.

"Paris, you do that so well. Most women don't know how to get out of a car that elegantly. You have an amazing style and grace, baby."

Paris gave him a big smile as they entered the hotel. "Thank my aunt Lillian for that. From the time I was about eleven I spent every summer with her in Atlanta and she did her best to make me a lady. I was a real tomboy, believe it or not. My mom died when I was five and it was just the boys and me. I was just one of them, one of the rowdy Deveraux boys," she said with a smile of remembrance. "Nobody had the time, inclination, or skills to teach me how to be a girl. I learned to hunt, fish, ride, play football, poker and fight. If it hadn't been for Aunt Lillian, I might have grown up to be a lumberjack." She laughed.

Her laughter stopped as she looked around the lobby of the

hotel. It was serene and elegant, with tables that held arrangements of fresh flowers almost as big as she was. She barely
had time to take in her surroundings as Titus put a big warm
hand to the base of her back and guided her to the elevator.
They were alone in the car and Titus took full advantage of
that fact, pulling her into his arms for a long sweet kiss that
left her breathless. The doors opened and an older couple
stepped in just as they were ending the embrace. Paris's face
heated up as it always did when she was embarrassed, but the
couple's smiling faces somehow put her at ease.

"Oh, look, dear, they must be newlyweds! Reminds me of
when we were on our honeymoon," the woman said with a sigh.

Her husband winked at Titus and gave him a conspirator-
ial grin. "Just keep kissing her that way, son. One of those
every morning and every night is the secret to a happy
marriage."

Just then the elevator came to a stop and they made their
escape while waving goodbye to the friendly pair. The merriment that had been building up escaped as both Titus and
Paris succumbed to a fit of laughter. Paris was giggling so hard
she didn't realize they were in the suite until Titus closed the
door behind them. Her laughter died away as she looked
around the spacious area. It was nicely furnished, looking
more like the living room in someone's home than a hotel
suite. There was a comfortable-looking sofa that faced a faux
fireplace and was flanked by two wing chairs. A small desk
was between the two windows and an armoire held a stereo
system and a flat-screen TV. The coffee table and end tables
were made of rich honey-colored oak and the furniture was
upholstered in blue bargello-stitch fabric that matched the
draperies. Restful-looking abstract paintings enlivened the
walls and an area rug highlighted the luxurious navy blue car-
peting. Silk plants increased the ambiance of the room and

made it even less hotel-like. Paris took the hand that Titus offered her and allowed him to lead her to the sofa to sit down.

"Would you like something to drink? A glass of wine or something?" he asked solicitously.

"Not right now. Some ice water would be nice in a little while, but I don't need anything right now," she answered.

While she was speaking, Titus used the remote to start some sultry jazz playing. "You don't need anything? That's good to know, although I'll get you anything you want, anytime you want it," he said quietly. "But I do want something. Something I can only get from you."

Paris swallowed hard before speaking. She was alone at last with the man of her dreams and she had no idea what was coming next. She dared a look at Titus, who was lounging comfortably with his long legs extended and one arm along the back of the sofa. He was smiling at her, an intimate, sexy smile. His pretty eyes were flashing bright blue, that way they did when he was relaxed or amused. Even if she'd wanted to, Paris couldn't have imagined a more good-looking man. He wasn't conventionally handsome, but there was something about him, with his high cheekbones, his juicy, tender lips, his broad shoulders and his hard, muscular body that spoke to Paris in a language she was just beginning to understand. The early summer sun had done its work and given him a light golden tan that promised to get darker and richer as the months went on and right now he was truly the most compelling man Paris had ever seen. And he wanted something from her that he couldn't get anywhere else. Without realizing she was doing it, she daintily moistened her lips with her tongue before speaking.

"What is it, Titus?" she asked demurely.

"I want you to come sit next to me," he said gently, indicating the space next to him.

Paris stared at him for a moment, and then put her hand into the one he extended to her and slid over so that she was nestled next to him. She froze for a minute, and surprised herself by the ease with which she relaxed against his body. He put his arm around her shoulder and his free hand around her waist, giving her a soft squeeze.

"That's better, isn't it?" He inclined his head to rub his cheek against her hair, and then kissed her temple, letting his lips trail down her cheek to her sensitive ear. "You smell fantastic, Paris. What are you wearing?"

Paris let out a soft sigh before answering. He felt so good next to her; it felt so right for him to be touching her like this. "It's called Amazing Grace," she murmured.

"That's the perfect name for you, baby. You're so graceful and sexy when you walk. It makes me nuts," he admitted. He started exploring her neck, first rubbing his face against her soft skin, then spreading soft, nibbling kisses where his face had been.

She began breathing harder as his hands began to move. Before she knew what he was doing, Titus had scooped her up so she was sitting in his lap with one arm locked around her waist. "Ooh! I think I'm too heavy for you," she began only to be cut off by his deep laugh.

"Sweetheart, look at me. I'm six feet six inches tall and I probably outweigh you by a hundred pounds. If you weren't so warm and sexy I wouldn't even know you were here." His free hand caressed her thigh softly but firmly and he squeezed gently, making her sigh with pleasure. "Come here and kiss me, baby, I need to taste that sweet mouth of yours," he growled playfully.

Paris braced her hands on his broad shoulders and made a soft noise of surprise as he pulled her close and covered her willing lips with his eager mouth. The "ooh" that came out of her turned into a sigh of rapture as the kiss deepened into something erotically beautiful. His lips were firm but pliant and they molded to hers while his tongue sought hers and the mutual stroking and sucking excited her in a way she'd never before experienced. Her hands left his broad shoulders as she wrapped her arms around his neck, the better to feel the warmth of his skin through the thin shirt he wore. His hand was tangled in her long hair as he held her gently, prolonging the sensual exchange. The kiss turned into more kisses, long, passionate ones that had Paris's heart pounding and her pulse racing in every part of her body, especially the most private parts that were becoming drenched with her desire for Titus.

They finally pulled apart and Paris's head rested on Titus's shoulder while she tried to remember how to breathe normally. They held each other for a long moment, until Titus kissed her forehead and tilted her face to his. Looking at her with an expression she'd never seen on any man's face before, a combination of intense desire and seduction, he uttered the words that would change her life forever.

"Let's make love."

Paris had no idea how luscious she looked to Titus as she perched in the middle of the king-size bed. He'd carried her into the bedroom as though she weighed next to nothing, because to him she really was the perfect size. Their clothes had been dispensed of quickly and efficiently and now she was ready for him, her bountiful curves exposed to him in the way he'd wanted for months. He loved looking at her, touching her and now he was going to make love to her, something he'd been looking forward to for a long time. He moved behind her so that she rested on his big chest while his hands began to explore her body with long, sensual strokes, as he talked to her in a deep, sexy voice.

"You are so beautiful, Paris," he whispered as his hands

caressed her breasts, fondling them for the first time and loving the feel of the firm, luscious globes. "Your body is gorgeous, baby. I love the way you're made, you're just right for me. And I'm going to love you all over, every single inch of you," he vowed as the soft sounds of passion began to issue from her throat. He smiled as Paris relaxed into his embrace, her nipples hardening and growing big with anticipation as he worked his magic on her.

He turned her so that she was on her back and he moved over her body, kissing his way down to her breasts and taking her nipple into his mouth for the first time. It was hard to say who derived the most enjoyment from the erotic gesture; he experienced an erection as hard as tempered steel while Paris trembled and moaned as he applied a gentle but intense pressure to the tender tip, sucking and nibbling as he kneaded the other one. She tasted as good as she smelled and the lush bounty of her body was making Titus hotter than he'd been in years.

There was something about the feel of her body that was driving him into a frenzy of desire; she was soft yet firm and totally inviting. The way she reacted to him also fueled his fire. She looked beautiful and exotic, lying beneath him while she let him know in every possible way that he was exciting her, too. He treated both of her breasts with his hands and his mouth until her breath was coming in soft pants and he knew he was giving her as much pleasure as he was getting. Only then did he continue his exploration, kissing and licking her torso, loving the firm roundness of her belly as his hands stroked her hips, learning the curves of her thighs and parting her trembling legs to find the treasure within.

The thick curly triangle that adorned her was a special delight to Titus; he loved the silky feel of it as he began to explore that which made her woman. He began to stroke her moist folds with his long fingers, only to find her wet and throbbing for him, so fragrant and yearning he couldn't resist, he brought his mouth to those lips and plundered her sweetness. He parted her legs and groaned deep in his throat as she put her long legs over his shoulders while he paid her the ultimate erotic tribute. Her response was more than gratifying; he could feel the powerful tremors that racked her body as she cried his name, over and over. When he finally made his way back up her body she was still sighing his name.

He kissed her thoroughly, their mouths pleasuring each other as he reached for the condoms on the nightstand and quickly and expertly put one on. "Paris, baby, this is going to be so good," he promised. He positioned himself between her magnificent thighs and joined their bodies in one swift movement, or he tried to. Paris's hands clenched on his shoulders and in the late afternoon sunlight that streamed through the windows, he could see her face contorted in pain. His eyes widened in shock and he realized for the first time that Paris was a virgin. *How the hell is this possible? This is crazy*, he thought frantically. *This is all wrong.* For a split second he thought about leaping off the bed and calling a halt to this, but he couldn't do it. Instead he changed his technique, making his movements slow and gentle so he could initiate Paris into the art of lovemaking the right way.

"It's okay, baby, it's not going to hurt anymore," he said soothingly. "We're going to take it slow and easy, Paris, nice and slow and gentle until you're ready for more," he whispered as he kissed away the tiny trickle of tears from her face. "Open your eyes, sweetheart, and look at me," he crooned and was pleased when she did. Still moving against her, he rocked slowly, bringing her closer with each gentle push. "It's just you and me, baby, and we have all the time in the world. Just relax with me and we'll get there, Paris, just take your time," he breathed as he stared into her face, which was flushed

with passion and wearing the most incredible expression of
innocent trust and adoration he had ever seen. That look,
coupled with the feel of her around him, hot, tight and exquisitely moist, was almost his undoing, but she surprised him yet
again.

Her eyes widened suddenly and she began moving against
Titus, matching him move for move until she gasped his name
and her hands tightened on his huge biceps. "Ooh, Titus…"
she moaned. His gentle movements had brought them to the
place they needed to be, he was inside her fully and she was
able to experience everything she should, every thrilling sensation as her body clenched and released his in the rhythm of
love. The passion continued to build as Paris began to experience the release of her body into Titus's strong thrusts. They
were both damp with perspiration and breathing erratically as
the final climax began. Titus tightened his arms around her
as his body began to empty itself into her tender heat and it
was his turn to cry her name. "Paris, oh damn, baby… Paris!"

Paris was awash in a sea of the same ecstasy and she
returned his passion with all the emotion she could muster as
she sobbed, "I love you, Titus. I love you."

Minutes later, they lay spent, still wrapped in each other's
arms, neither one wanting to end the intimate connection.
They didn't speak, they just stared at each other for long
moments and by mutual consent, their mouths connected for
another long and passionate kiss.

Paris was awake for some time before she opened her
eyes. She was so sated and so euphoric she didn't want to
move a muscle. She was still feeling the aftermath of Titus's
incredible lovemaking and that's all she wanted to feel. After
that first time, when Titus had made her his woman in the
most profoundly passionate way, they'd made love for the

rest of the afternoon and into the evening. He'd carried her into the shower and they bathed each other slowly and lovingly. Then they took turns drying each other. The constant rubbing and stroking with the soft thick towels began to turn them on until they couldn't stand any more sensation without completion. Titus had put his big hands around her waist and walked her backward to the bed while kissing her as if it were their very first time. They fell onto the rumpled bed and continued kissing until the kisses weren't nearly enough.

She sighed softly, remembering every moment with the unerring clarity of a woman who'd experienced love for the very first time with the first and only man she'd ever loved. Her rosy lips turned up in a smile as she thought about her reaction to seeing his body; she'd probably never completely recover from it. When Titus had taken off his shirt to reveal the most magnificent chest she'd ever seen, Paris forgot how to breathe for a few moments. He was like a bronzed Colossus, smooth and hard with sculpted definition that was amazing to behold and irresistible to touch. She had shyly put her palms on him, amazed by the feel of his skin. "Titus, you are…beautiful," she'd whispered. He'd laughed in delight and grabbed her hard, kissing her over and over. It was then he said the words that made her believe that he had the same impassioned love for her that was making her heart pound like a thousand butterflies.

"Paris, you're the one who's beautiful. You're as pretty to look at and you have a beautiful spirit. You're gorgeous, you're sweet and you're so damned sexy you need to come with a warning label." They lay facing each other, looking at each other's body, touching each other and kissing gently, a subtle prelude to their next round of lovemaking. "If I'd only known, sweetheart," he murmured, pulling her closer to his body and stroking her possessively.

"If you'd known what, Titus?" she said softly as she kissed his neck, his shoulder and his chest.

Titus had risen up on one elbow so he could look down at her, taking in every inch of her body. He caressed her with his eyes and his hand as he touched her reverently but deliberately. He circled her breast with his palm, then leaned over and took her nipple in his mouth for a brief, hot salute. Then he raised his hand to stroke her face before lowering his lips to hers. "If I'd known how sweet you are, Paris, I couldn't have resisted you as long as I did, and that's the truth, God help me. I'd have come after you a lot sooner," he said solemnly.

And with those words he urged her on top of him and began to show her yet another way of making love. Until then Paris had considered herself fairly well educated in the ways of love. Untried, yes, but she hardly considered herself untutored. She'd had many frank talks with her aunt Lillian, her cousin Angelique, and her close friends both male and female. Besides, there was so much reading material available on the subject of sex it was rather impossible to be uninformed on the process. In addition, Paris also had a secret arsenal of very well-written romance novels that were frank and uninhibited besides being captivating stories. So on one level, she knew all about sex, but the depth of what she was feeling now was a revelation. Her naked body was still throbbing, her nipples tingled and there was a lovely warmth emanating through all of her erogenous zones. She sighed again and reached for Titus, only then realizing she was alone in the bed. Her eyes finally opened, and she smiled shyly as she became aware of the fact that he was in the room. He was standing next to the bed looking down at her and she was so glad to see his beloved face she didn't feel the least bit self-conscious.

Pushing her hair away from her face she smiled again, radiant and welcoming. "Good…is it morning?" she asked curiously.

"Not really. It's about midnight," Titus said quietly.

"Why are you standing there? And why are you dressed? I like you much better naked," Paris said mischievously. As she spoke she took a peek under the sheet at her own body and yes indeedy, she was quite devoid of clothing. Titus didn't answer her at once, but he did sit down on the side of the bed. Paris scooted over to make more room for him, but he stayed where he was. His face was completely serious as he addressed her.

"Paris, you should have told me you were a virgin," he said solemnly.

She flashed him a wicked grin. "I think you're missing the big picture, Titus."

"And what would that be?" he asked, still using the dull, unemotional voice she'd never heard from him before.

"I'm not a virgin any*more*. I am *so* not a virgin. So it's kind of a moot point, really."

"You should have told me. I had a right to know before this happened. Fine as you are, as old as you are how in the world did you manage to never have sex before this?"

Paris looked at him strangely. "You had a 'right to know'? Virginity isn't a communicable disease, Titus. And how was I supposed to announce it to you? Virgin pins went out of vogue a long time ago."

It was Titus's turn to look puzzled. "What's a virgin pin? Never mind, it doesn't matter. The point is it never occurred to me that this was your first experience. I just can't believe someone as sexy and sensuous as you are never made love before. How is that possible?" His growing frustration was evident in his voice.

"Titus, come on now, you've met my brothers. There isn't a man in the state of Louisiana who would touch me with a ten-foot pole," she said with wry humor. "I didn't even go to my prom because they scared off every potential date I ever had. And before you ask, I went to an all-girls' high school and a women's college. I didn't have all that many opportunities to meet men. When I was in law school the only men I had any interest in were my professors because I was there to get a law degree, not a husband. And it was the same way in graduate school. Besides," she added, and her voice lowered and took on a soft, dreamy tone. "I don't have the gene for promiscuity, apparently. I wanted my first time to be with someone I love. And I've been in love with you for a long time, Titus."

Titus groaned and stood up abruptly, clenching his hands into fists and pounding his forehead lightly with one as he spoke. "Paris, you don't know what you're saying. This is all wrong; this is… Look, how old are you anyway?"

Again she stared at him oddly. "I'll be thirty on my next birthday. What does that have to do with anything?"

"I'm almost forty, Paris. I'm too old for you, baby, way too old. I don't know why I didn't realize it before. This is all wrong, sweetheart, it's not going to happen for us," he said with finality, the regret was plain in his voice.

Paris sat up, mindless of the fact that the sheet slipped away to reveal her round, enticing breasts to his eyes. "I'm confused, Titus. From my perspective it's already happened between us. Several times, I might add, or are virgins also unable to count? What are you talking about?"

He paced back and forth a few times before coming back to sit on the side of the bed. "Paris, you're a beautiful woman, a magnificent woman, as a matter of fact. You're everything a man could ever want, but I'm not the man for you. You need someone who's going to want to settle down, marry you and give you some pretty babies and I'm not that man. That's just not how I roll. Every relationship I have is finite. We meet, we flirt, we go out a few times and if we're both agreeable, we have sex. It lasts as long as it lasts and we part with no regrets. That's why I've never dated anyone as young as you are. It's just not fair to you."

Paris didn't say anything for a long moment. Finally she spoke, sounding as serious as Titus. "I see. So the flirting and the dating and all the attention, that was like step two of your master plan, is that it?"

"I wouldn't put it like that, Paris, you were—"

"Don't say I was different," she warned in a low, ominous tone. "Don't say I was different or special, please. You had enough respect for me to show me some honesty, so don't start lying now. It was just step two of the plan, that's all." She let the words hang heavy in the air for a few moments, then asked him a question, in the same expressionless tone of voice. "So why didn't you jump up and run? You had to realize I didn't know what I was doing, why didn't you cut your losses and scamper? We wouldn't be having this horrible conversation right now if you had," she said, not bothering to disguise her bitterness.

Titus, to his dubious credit, met her eyes and answered her honestly. He stood and walked away from the bed, staring blankly at the picture on the wall, and then turned to Paris, his face taut and rigid. "I should have and a part of me regrets that I didn't. But I couldn't for two reasons. I didn't want you to despise sex or be afraid of it and I had to make it a beautiful experience for you. That's the main reason why I didn't stop. And the other part is, well…" He hesitated for a moment, seeming to weigh his words before continuing. "The other reason I couldn't stop is *you*, Paris. I don't know how to say this without sounding like even more of a jerk, but you're incredible, baby. Once I felt that beautiful body of yours I couldn't stop touching you any more than I could stop breathing and that's the truth. I couldn't get enough of you, Paris."

She raised an eyebrow. "And yet, you seem to have done that very thing. Odd how that works, isn't it?" Without warning she flipped back the sheet to reveal her nude body and slid out of the bed into a standing position. "If you don't mind, I'm going to get dressed. I don't suppose you could scare me up a cup of coffee? Is there a Starbucks around here?"

Titus seemed thrilled to have something to do and offered to go find out. He took off as though propelled by a jet pack to find Paris a cup of Starbucks coffee. She gathered her clothes and her dignity and went into the bathroom to put herself together. By the time he got back to the suite, she was gone.

Chapter 4

Paris paid off the cabdriver, overtipping him and ignoring his effusive thanks. She was just happy to have found a cab in which to make her escape. To have been sitting there looking like Boo-Boo the fool when Titus came back would have been way too much for her to deal with, so she went into action as soon as he'd closed the door behind him. She'd dressed hastily and almost cried with relief when she was able to get a taxi right in front of the hotel. Now her only concern was getting inside without waking anyone. She slipped out of the backseat of the cab and stared at the big brick home owned by her cousin, Angelique, and her husband, Donnie. It was a really late hour for a houseguest to come stumbling in, even if the guest had her own key, the way Paris did. Making a face, she tiptoed up to the side door, praying that she wouldn't disturb anyone. Dealing with what she'd just been through was hard enough. She didn't want to compound the angst by having to share her humiliation with Angelique; she was just too raw emotionally for that. The door opened and Paris came in stealthily, turning to close it as quietly as possible. With a soft sigh of relief she turned to enter the kitchen.

"Keeping some mighty late hours, aren't you?" The voice that made Paris jump straight in the air held a tinge of laughter. She turned to find Aunt Ruth sitting at the breakfast table in her robe and slippers, enjoying a cup of tea.

Paris gamely tried to play off the fact that she was skulking in like a thief in the night. "Umm, I, ah, umm…" Her voice faded away and she tried again. "Hello. I hope I didn't scare you," she said politely, ignoring the flaming heat of her face.

"I'm wide awake. I'm afraid I'm a night owl. Just having a little tea while I catch up on the latest fashions and gossip," Ruth said with a smile as she gestured to the thick fashion magazine she was perusing. "Have some?"

Paris shook her head to indicate no, but her face wasn't co-operating. She looked bedraggled and forlorn as well as embarrassed. "I'm, umm, going to turn in. I've got a flight tomorrow, an early flight, so I should get to bed," she said hurriedly. She was about to take off for the guest room when Ruth's voice stopped her.

"Paris, honey, the last time I saw you, you were looking very put together and absolutely radiant on the arm of that ridiculously good-looking man. Now here it is, a few hours later, and you're tipping in here looking like who-did-it-and-ran. Are you sure you don't want to talk?"

Ruth's face didn't look condemning or amused; on the contrary she looked wise and comforting. Without even questioning her actions, Paris found herself going to the breakfast table and sitting down across from Ruth.

"This has been the worst night of my adult life," she admitted. "I told a man I loved him after making what I mistakenly thought was mad, passionate love with him. Unfortunately, as soon as it was over he politely informed me that we're all wrong for each other and going to bed together was a mistake," she said in a dull monotone.

Ruth surprised her by reaching across the table to pat her on the hand.

"You poor child. You must have really laid it on him for him to act a fool like that," she said in her disarmingly frank way.

Paris's lower lip trembled briefly but she bit down on it hard; she wasn't about to dissolve in tears like some sniveling soap opera queen. "I wouldn't know. My experience in that arena is limited to this very evening," she said dryly.

Ruth put her elbow on the table and propped her chin in her hand as she stared at Paris. "I see. And I take it your young man had no idea he was your first love. Probably scared him witless," she said in an aside. She moved her head slowly from side to side. Her big green eyes were full of concern as she addressed Paris.

"Are you okay, honey? The first time at sex can be rather traumatic if it's not handled right. Quiet as it's kept it can take years for a couple to get it right. Great sex doesn't always just happen. He didn't hurt you, did he?"

Paris was shocked, not by Ruth's blunt words, but by the ease with which she could talk to the older woman. She answered her honestly, not even blushing as she told her. "At first it hurt, just for a minute or so. But he was so gentle, so loving he made everything good. And then it just got to be amazing! Now I know why people are so obsessed with sex— it's wonderful," she confessed. She covered her face and dropped her head as Ruth laughed gently.

"Look, don't be ashamed of enjoying sex. Sex is a major part of life. You wouldn't be here right now if somebody hadn't engaged in the art of making love. And it's not just for procreation, either. A healthy sex life is a beautiful thing, especially when it's with your partner, your soulmate. Lovemaking is a precious gift to a loving couple, it's something to be gloried in and it shouldn't make you feel shame."

Paris raised her head and looked bleakly at Ruth. Her eyes filled with tears, which she dashed away with the heel of her hand. "Yes, but that's just it, Aunt Ruth, I'm not part of a loving couple. I shouldn't have gone to bed with Titus because he was right, we're all wrong for each other. We're not soulmates, or some perfect couple, and we never will be. I made a huge mistake, thinking he cares about me." She looked stricken as she uttered the words.

Ruth patted her on the hand again. "I'm making you some tea right now," she said as she rose from the table to fill the kettle with water. "You sound awfully convinced of what you're saying, Paris. What exactly did he say to you, if you don't mind telling me?"

Paris ruffled her hair, which was still a tangled mass, as she hadn't taken the time to comb it properly. With a deep sigh, she told Ruth word for word what Titus had said after their interlude. "So, the bottom line is that he's this loner who gets together with women for no-strings sex and that's all he wants. He doesn't want marriage and children and the whole family life thing. And I'm not going to settle for anything less. If I was made differently, I suppose I could just have a pointless affair with him but the fact is that's not how I plan to live my life. So it's over. Over before it got started, really."

Ruth busied herself making the tea, bringing a steaming mug of it to the table along with a plate of Lily Rose's arrowroot biscuits and a small jar of cherry jam. Placing the tea and cookies in front of Paris, she smoothed the younger woman's hair and gave her a comforting pat on the shoulder before resuming her seat. "Honey, you sound so final and fatalistic about the whole thing! I wouldn't count Titus out. He's confused, that's for sure. I'm sure that finding out that he was your very first lover was a startling experience for him. There aren't a lot of women who have enough self-respect to remain celibate these days. It had to be a shock to his system, for one thing. For another, I think he's probably stunned at how deeply he cares for you. I've been watching the two of you and in order for him to fake the way he reacts to you he'd have to be a better actor than Jamie Foxx or Denzel Washington. The way he looks at you and touches you, just the way he smiles when he's around you, all of those things tell me he's quite smitten with you and he's just handling it badly. Give him a little time, he'll come around, I promise you."

Paris took a grateful sip of her tea. It was Constant Comment, one of her favorites, and the spicy orange flavor was soothing to her throat. She put the mug down on the table and smiled sadly at Ruth. "I wish I could agree with you, Aunt Ruth, but I don't think anything remotely close to that is going to happen. One thing I've learned is that people don't change, not unless they really want to. He is the way he is and there's not a thing I can do about it," she said firmly.

"I believe anything a man tells me," she said, smiling at the reaction on Ruth's face. "I do. If a man says he's not good enough for me, I believe him. If he says he's not the man for me, I believe him. If he says he's going to hurt me and I should stay away from him, I believe him and I do what he says. I'm not getting sucked into that trap of thinking I can change a man, once he sees how good I can cook and how loving I am or whatever. Everybody is entitled to have what they want out of life, if they can get it, and that includes me. I want what my cousins have. I want a happy marriage to someone who loves me and I want lots of babies. So I need to have a man who wants the same things and Titus has made it abundantly clear that he's not that man. At least he had the decency to be honest with me," she said bravely, even though she was unaware that her voice was shaking.

Ruth couldn't hide her admiration for Paris. "I have to say you're the most levelheaded young woman I've known in some time. You remind me of Benita in that way," she said thoughtfully. Benita Cochran Deveraux was married to Paris's cousin Clay Deveraux and the comparison was high praise to Paris's ears. But she was too honest to accept it without sharing something with Ruth.

"I'm not all that levelheaded. I was lucky enough to have a very calm and steady father, and since my brothers were such firecrackers I always had to be the voice of reason," she said with a fond smile. "But right this minute I'm doing a good job of fronting. I'm going to bawl my eyes out as soon as I get in the shower. The only reason I'm not doing that right now is that I can't stand for anyone to see me cry. And I'm seriously considering calling my friend Chastain back home to make me a little voodoo doll. Chastain's into all that crazy stuff and she'd be happy to supply me with a Titus replica complete with those danged eyes of his," she said defiantly.

Ruth laughed, but Paris couldn't even muster a smile. "I really do feel like a prize fool, you know. If I'd had any real idea of how this would turn out, I never would have gone near Titus Argonne, not in this lifetime or any other." She looked bleakly at Ruth and to her intense shame, the tears started to flow.

After Titus left the suite to get Paris a cup of coffee, he stopped cursing himself long enough to take a deep breath. Punching the button for the elevator, he still couldn't believe how badly the evening had gone. He entered the elevator and gave the lobby button a vicious jab. Badly, that was putting it mildly. It was also inaccurate; the events of the evening, while unexpected, were stupendous. An involuntary tremor rippled its way through his body, so strongly that he had to stop pacing in mid-stride to shake off the feeling. This was positive proof that strange things were afoot. Titus couldn't remember the last time he'd reacted to a woman the way he had to Paris. The feel of her silken skin, the taste of her, the look of her, the explosive way she'd responded to him all blended together in an erotic haze that rendered him unable to think clearly. Surely that would explain his behavior afterwards. The elevator doors opened and he stepped out into the lobby. Looking around in vain for an open restaurant, he exited the hotel and walked to the rental car. As he crossed the parking lot, he glanced at the upper floors of the building where Paris waited.

Opening the car door he slid into the driver's seat and started the car, pulling out of the lot into the late-night traffic, scanning the well-lit streets for an open café. He still couldn't believe how stupidly he'd reacted to the fact that Paris was a virgin. If anything he should have been honest enough to tell the truth, that he was stunned and ridiculously pleased to be the first man to touch her beautiful body. He should have told her that she was the first woman to confess love for him so freely and honestly, without an agenda of any kind, and he should have told her how those words made him feel, how they excited him almost as much as feeling her surround him, hot, moist and yielding. And he certainly should have told her that she was the most passionate partner he could ever remember being with in his life. No one had excited him like Paris in years. He laughed with bitter irony. If she could arouse him like that on her first time, there's no telling what she could do when she got in some practice. Paris Deveraux was an incredible woman; it was as simple as that. She might be young, but she knew how to handle herself.

He spotted a Tim Horton's, the ubiquitous coffee and

doughnut establishment that blessedly was open twenty-four hours. While he was waiting in line at the drive-through, he leaned back against the head restraint and continued to rake himself over the coals. He'd been an idiot, a total fool about the whole thing. For one thing, he should have realized that Paris was inexperienced. For the past few years all she'd ever done was blush and stammer every time she was around him. He'd known she was shy around him and he should have realized the source of that shyness. He'd seen how open and outgoing she was with other people; Paris was only tongue-tied when he was in the vicinity, and he thought it was cute, never bothering to try to figure out why. Besides, since she'd embarked on her new career, she was like a new woman. He'd seen the change in her at the wedding reception of Alicia Fuentes and Adam Cochran. It was the first time she'd been relaxed and comfortable around him, the first time she was able to converse with him without turning puce with embarrassment. From that time on, they had been enthusiastically flirtatious with each other. The dates they went on were thoroughly enjoyable and seemed the perfect prelude to passion. If he was going to be honest about it, he'd had a lot more fun with Paris than he had with any of the women he dated and there had been plenty of them in the past.

He thrust a twenty-dollar bill through the drive-through window and took the large café mocha and the small black coffee he'd ordered, along with his change. His mood got even worse as he recalled with unerring clarity the way Paris had reacted to his pompous postcoital statements. She didn't scream, cry or rail at him; she didn't beg him or argue with him. Instead she looked at him without batting an eye, looking more seductive than any woman he'd ever seen with her incredible breasts bared and her hair tousled and tossed. When she got out of the bed and calmly walked across the room completely nude, the image had burned itself into his brain. He couldn't recall ever seeing a woman, especially one as young and inexperienced as Paris, behave with such elegance and dignity. *She let me off light. She should have thrown something at me, screamed at me, threatened me, anything but that,* he thought morosely. He knew, even as he formulated the thought, that if she'd done any of those things it would've been easier to forgive himself. If she'd started howling and blubbering it would have instantly confirmed his notion that she was too young and they weren't right for each other. But no, she didn't do any of these things.

She was upset, that much was obvious. And she should've been upset. I was being a total jerk. No, I was being a pompous jerk, a pontificating, proselytizing jackass. She showed me, though. She's a hell of a woman, he admitted. She was, after all, a Deveraux, and they didn't put up with much crap from anybody. They knew, and she obviously knew, how to deal with idiots. Suddenly he groaned aloud, remembering, as though for the first time, that Paris was the first cousin of his best friend, Martin Deveraux. He and Martin had been friends since law school and he knew for a fact that Martin and his brothers loved Paris like a little sister. *What in Sam Hill is wrong with me? When I decide to lose all control with a woman, why do I decide to pick the one woman in the world I need to keep away from?*

By now he was back at the hotel, taking the elevator back up to the suite, where he was both longing to see Paris's beautiful face and dreading another confrontation. When the elevator doors slid open, he had to acknowledge two inescapable facts. One, he'd behaved badly to Paris and he owed her a huge apology, and two, she meant more to him than any other woman he'd ever known. Somehow she'd slipped past his radar and gotten deep inside him before he

knew what was happening. Carefully balancing the small
black coffee on top of the café mocha, he used the card key
to open the door. He pushed it open, his lips starting to form
the sincere apology he owed her. Paris deserved that and
much more from him, from any man lucky enough to be
blessed with her company and he at least needed to tell her
sincerely how sorry he was for his behavior. The door had
barely closed behind him before he realized the true meaning
of the phrase, "too little, too late." The suite was empty. Paris
had left him.

True to her word, Paris had a long, awful cry in the shower.
A few tears had escaped while she was having tea and
sympathy with Ruth, but she meant it, she couldn't stand for
anyone to see her cry. But when she had parted from Ruth and
made her way to the guest room where she was sleeping, she
got into the shower and bawled like a small child. She hadn't
felt pain like this since her mother died. The tears fell faster
and harder until she thought she might not be able to stop.
Leaning against the ceramic tile of the shower stall, she forced
her breathing back to normal and made the tears slow down
to an occasional trickle. The one thing she didn't want was to
wake her cousin Angelique. She and Angel, as almost
everyone called her, were as close as sisters and if she were
to see Paris in this condition it would mean death and destruc-
tion for Titus Argonne. The thought of Angel's retribution
actually put a smile on Paris's red, swollen face. It wasn't
much of a smile, but it was better than the alternative—more
tears. Angelique Deveraux Cochran didn't play when it came
to her family and friends. If someone she loved was hurt or
wronged in any way, Angel would go after the transgressor
like a juggernaut. Paris shuddered at the idea of Angel seeking
vengeance on Titus and turned off the shower.

Wrapping herself in a big bath sheet, Paris got out of the shower and made a horrible face as it dawned on her how very messy the situation could become. Titus wasn't just the man in front of whom she'd humiliated herself; he was the best friend of her cousin Martin. If that weren't enough, his firm was in charge of corporate security for The Deveraux Group. Even worse, his offices were in the complex owned by The Deveraux Group. It was a huge complex, but it wasn't big enough to keep their paths from crossing. There were bound to be times when they'd see each other, just like they had in the past. She sat on the side of the bed and sniffed, remembering how much she'd loved the times when she'd seen him around the complex. He would come to her office once in a while, just to say hello. And a couple of times she'd spotted him in the back of the studio when her show was taping, something that always gave her a special thrill. Well, those days were over.

She patted herself dry and applied a generous layer of her favorite lotion. The soothing pearberry scent comforted her senses as the thick, emollient substance soothed her skin. She only hoped that Ruth was right. It had occurred to Paris that her friends and even her family knew she was dating Titus and in very short order, it would become obvious that they were no longer involved and they'd wonder why. Ruth had put her hand over Paris's and given her the best advice she'd ever heard.

"Honey, one thing about getting older is the realization that you don't have to answer a question just because someone asks it. Your personal life is your own business and you don't owe anyone an explanation of anything you do."

She finished applying the lotion and added a light misting of the body spray. Her aunt Lillian had taught her to always go to bed smelling nice because it made for sweet dreams. After slipping on a short cotton gown with spaghetti straps and a tiny floral pattern, Paris brushed her hair and got into bed. She wasn't counting on any sweet dreams tonight though. She reached into her tote bag, which was on the floor next to the bed and pulled out her journal. She never went to bed without writing in it and tonight was no exception. In her beautiful handwriting, courtesy of the nuns from her Catholic school days, she began to write.

This was the best day of my life, and the worst. I found out two things today that I'm never going to forget. One is that making love is the most wonderful, most intimate experience two people can share. And the other is, when your heart breaks you can actually feel it. There's a horrible sharp pain and then a little "pop" that feels like something ruptured. Then there's a gush of hot agony like someone spilled acid into your bloodstream, and you know you'll never feel anything again.

Chapter 5

Paris looked up from her computer screen into the face of her dear friend and art director Aidan Sinclair. He was looking at her with a mixture of exasperation and concern, which was borne out by the first words out of his mouth.

"Don't you ever go home? This place can get along without you for ten minutes. You need to start getting out of here earlier. What do you pay all these people their ridiculously high salaries for if they can't handle things for you?" he asked acerbically.

Paris looked at the time and yawned, "Oh, excuse me, I'm didn't mean to do that in your face. I'm going home right now as a matter of fact. It really isn't my intention to spend every waking moment here, but there's been a lot to do. Planning the new season, restructuring the staff, taping the promos. You've been a part of most of that so you know how much work's been involved." She yawned again, delicately.

"Restructuring the staff? What do you mean?" Aidan asked innocently.

Paris narrowed her eyes at her friend. "You know what I mean—don't sit there and try to pretend otherwise."

Aidan continued to look blank as he probed. "You added a new staff member? Why was that?"

"Because someone left the show," Paris said with a tiny edge in her voice.

"Someone left? Was it anyone I know?"

"Aidan, why do we go through this? Gayle Rodgers left my staff as you well know." She closed her eyes in resignation as Aidan began singing "Ding-dong the Witch is Dead" from *The Wizard of Oz.* Everyone who worked on her show, which was simply entitled "*Paris & Company,*" was so thrilled with the fact that Paris had terminated the woman that they all started singing the tune the day the announcement was made two months ago. They had finally stopped singing it all day long, now they only burst into song when they could trick Paris into saying her name.

When his musical interlude was over he grinned at Paris with no sign of repentance. "She's a miserable human being and you know it. She was tearing this place apart with her incompetence and her laziness and when you let her go it was like sealing up a hole in the ozone. You can see for yourself how much better the atmosphere is around here. People can't wait to come to work in these halcyon days post Witch Rodgers. Best thing you could have done, absolutely."

Paris stretched, standing up from her desk and picking up the few papers that covered its surface. While she was preparing to leave the office she reflected on Aidan's words. Gayle Rodgers was an assistant producer who'd had good qualifications coupled with a rotten disposition and an aversion to hard work. She was gossipy, temperamental and dictatorial and caused nothing but trouble. She often didn't complete projects and would blame so many others for her ineptitude that internal strife and bitterness followed her everywhere. Paris had inherited her, as she was part of the show that had preceded "*Paris & Company.*" She'd tried everything to make the woman more productive and bring her into line but it was fruitless. The woman had a particular hatred for Paris and felt that she, not Paris, should have been tapped to headline the show, absurd as that concept was.

Paris was nearing the end of her patience with Gayle and had rightly concluded that the relationship was not salvage-able. Gayle Rodgers actually sealed her own fate when Paris overheard her in the ladies' room. She was saying some vicious and patently untrue things about Paris to a couple of other staffers when Paris emerged from her stall with a cold look in her eye that no one had ever seen before. Paris had calmly washed her hands while advising the other two women to leave. "And for the record, ladies, it's always a good idea to make sure the object of your scorn isn't within the sound of your voice when you decide to trash her verbally. Gayle, come with me."

She took the woman into her private office and offered her a seat while she retrieved a file from a locked drawer in her desk. Placing the file in front of her, she looked at Gayle with a carefully bland expression. She picked up her phone and pressed a preset button, talking quietly into the receiver before hanging it up. Steepling her fingers, she looked at the woman whose attractive but petulant face was mottled with red.

"Gayle, for some time it's been evident that you aren't happy here. You're obviously intelligent and capable, but this position doesn't seem to be fulfilling to you, so I'm going to give you the opportunity to find the kind of career that will challenge as well as satisfy you. As of today, your employment is terminated. You may leave now and your personal belongings will be delivered to your home by end of the business today. I wish you all the luck in the world in your future endeavors," she said calmly.

The woman stuttered and stammered for a minute, then proved Paris right by snapping at her. "I know you're not trying to fire me because you were eavesdropping on a private conversation. You can't fire me for that. I'll sue you!"

Paris didn't even blink. "I am terminating your employment because of a pattern of behavior that indicates an employee who will not perform to expectation. You have been counseled on a number of occasions about not finishing assignments, botching assignments, about your attitude towards the other members of my staff and nothing seems to make a lasting change in your behavior. If there'd been the slightest indication that you were willing to improve your performance it would be different, but nothing changes. You're still doing, or *not* doing, the same things you were warned about six months ago. Therefore—" Paris spoke with a slight inflection ignored by the other woman "—you will be leaving my employ today. The director of Human Resources is bringing your coat and purse to my office now, and will escort you out of the complex."

The other woman's attractive but petulant face shone with perspiration as the realization of the humiliation she was about to suffer dawned on her. "So you're just Miss High-and-Mighty, aren't you? You just can't wait to make a fool out of me, because you're jealous of me, that's what your problem is. You know I'm better qualified for your job and you can't stand it. The only reason you have this job is that your cousins own the company and you're their favorite," she sneered, oblivious to the fact that her anxiety was making her nose run.

Paris looked at Gayle with exasperation and pity. "If that were the truth you'd have to be criminally stupid to alienate me, wouldn't you? It just so happens I have this position because I have a bachelor's degree in journalism, a law degree and a master's degree in leadership. I also interned with The Deveraux Group and their partner, Cochran Communications, for three years. I learned how to do everything in this company from sorting the mail to simple elevator maintenance. And you had an opportunity to do the same thing because you could have gotten tuition reimbursement for advanced study as well as opportunities to intern the same way I did."

Gayle was sputtering with rage by now and could barely speak. "I don't need any damned internship to do what I do! I can do anything you do and do it better," she spat out.

Paris's exasperation left and she felt nothing but pity for the woman. "I'm giving you the opportunity to prove that somewhere else. In the right environment I'm sure you'll blossom."

The scorn and anger left Gayle's face, replaced at once by desperation. "I can do that right here. Just let me go to another department, to another division and I can prove myself," she pleaded.

Paris's face grew resolute. "Unfortunately, this situation is too far gone for that. I don't believe in moving problems. I believe in solving them. A new start in a new environment outside of The Deveraux Group is sure to provide you with the opportunity to prove yourself in ways you haven't imagined and I do wish you luck with that."

By now the head of Human Resources for the corporation had made a discreet entrance and was waiting quietly with Gayle's coat and purse. Something about the sincerity of Paris's words seemed to make Gayle snap because her rage returned, louder and shriller than ever. "You think you're something, don't you?" She stood, making a swipe at Paris's desk that dislodged a large crystal globe, a gift from Vera Jackson Deveraux. Luckily, it was so heavy it rolled across the carpet instead of breaking. "You're going to regret this, Paris Deveraux. If it's the last thing I do, I'm going to make you pay for this!"

With the help of a burly security guard and the director of Human Resources, Gayle was restrained and escorted from the building in a much more public fashion than Paris would have liked. She'd planned to have them leave very quietly through a little-used exit that would have shielded her from prying eyes, but the woman made that impossible. Even though she was doing the right thing, Paris still felt bad about the manner in which Gayle reacted. Clay, Martin, Marcus and Malcolm, her cousins, all assured her she'd acted in an appropriate manner, though.

They were actually proud of her for terminating the woman, as she had become so disruptive that if Paris hadn't taken the step on her own, Marcus was going to address the situation in his capacity as CEO of the corporation. "One of the hallmarks of a good manager is to know when employees have to be let go. If they can't, or won't, conform to the culture of the company, it's time for them to move on. This woman has been a major problem in every department she's worked in but no one had the guts to fire her. They would just transfer her somewhere else until the turmoil would start up again and then she'd go somewhere else. It's too bad, because she's not stupid and she has some talent but she's got issues," Marcus reflected. "Just don't worry about it, sugar. You did the right thing and you did it correctly. It's all part of the process of running a company."

The ugly scene was now relegated to the mental tapestry that comprised the last five months of Paris's life. She'd made an admirable adjustment to not having Titus in her life, a remarkable adjustment, really, considering how badly he'd hurt her. Her pain had been replaced by anger, a slow-simmering rage that she kept at bay only because she rarely laid eyes on the critter. Paris had thrown herself into work with a vengeance and refused to allow one monkey to stop her show, that monkey being Titus. She'd also started dating quite a bit. There were a lot of men in Atlanta and other places who were, it seemed, dying to get to know her and her social calendar was quite full. And she now had a roommate, albeit a temporary one. Aidan had come to her on New Year's Eve and asked if he could bunk with her for a couple of weeks while his house was being remodeled and she agreed.

She was living in the two-story carriage house occupied by Vera Jackson before she'd married Marcus Deveraux and there was plenty of room for two adults and one cat. Aidan had brought his Russian Blue, Merlin, with him. Luckily, Paris liked animals and Merlin was an especially beguiling feline. Aidan moved in the day after New Year's Day and his presence, while unexpected, was a pleasant diversion. He was wonderful company, funny and supportive. Aidan was the one responsible for Paris revamping her look some years before. He'd not only insisted she get a wardrobe of fashionable clothes that fit correctly, he'd gotten her on a program of healthy eating and exercise and she'd gone from a size twenty-two to her current size sixteen, although she was looking like a size twelve these days, something which concerned Aidan very much.

He continued to stand over her as she prepared to leave the office. "Hurry up, woman. I'm starving and you need to eat. That skeletal look you're sporting is not happening. You've been doing an excellent job of pretending that you don't care about Voldemort, but I know better. You have to start eating more, Paris, you're starting to look downright gaunt," he scolded.

"Voldemort" was how Aidan referred to Titus, as in the "he-who-must-not-be-named" character from the obscenely

popular *Harry Potter* series. Aidan had pried the whole story
out of Paris when she returned to Atlanta after John and Nina's
wedding looking wrung out and overwrought. He was furious
with Titus and wanted nothing more than to kick his teeth in,
something he assured Paris he could do. "Please, please,
please let me! I have two black belts in martial arts and a really
twisted imagination, as you well know. I could hurt him in
ways no one's ever thought of before. Let me avenge your
honor," he'd pleaded.

Paris had tearfully laughed him off at the time, but it wasn't
so easy to ignore the fact that she was looking right peaked.
Studio makeup and a fabulous wardrobe could only go so far;
her frame wasn't meant to be this lean and she was on her way
to looking haggard. "Okay, okay, I'll eat! Are you cooking?
And can I have some chicken or shrimp or something?"

Aidan shuddered theatrically before agreeing. He was a
vegetarian whose views on the subject bordered on the
militant. "Fine, I'll give you some dead animal to chew on,
but only because you're looking practically anorexic. I'll
make a stir-fry and you can have some grilled chicken with
yours. But you're eating the rice, too, sister, and dessert. *Car-
nivore*," he muttered under his breath as they left the office.

Paris rolled her eyes at him. "Yeah, well explain to me why
you wear a leather coat. Since you're such a dedicated vegan,"
she said dryly.

"My mother gave it to me," he answered without a trace
of irony. "How can I not wear a gift from my *mami?*"

It was Paris's turn to mutter. "I give up."

Unbeknownst to Paris and Aidan, someone was observing
them in the parking garage under the compound. Titus was
about to get out of his car when he saw the two of them emerge
from the elevator. Paris was laughing and looked very happy.

She also looked very pretty, although she looked too thin. Thin or not, she was still gorgeous and desirable. Five months of carefully scheduled avoidance hadn't lessened the impact she had on him. He got the same rush every time he looked at her; it didn't make any difference if it was up close and personal, across a parking garage or even looking at her on television. He couldn't look at her without remembering how she felt in his arms, the sweetness of her lips and the warmth of her body. And it wasn't just her beauty and sensuality, he loved the sound of her voice and the long conversations they once had. Paris could talk about anything and she always had something interesting to say. He liked talking to her more than any other woman he'd ever been involved with, and he missed it. They hadn't really talked since the Detroit debacle.

When Titus realized Paris had managed to leave the hotel, he was furious. He at least had enough sense to be angry with himself, because it was his stupidity and selfishness that had caused her to flee. He called her on her cell phone, but she didn't answer. He paced around the suite for a minute or two, and then he took off. For some reason he couldn't stand the thought of being there alone. He left the hotel, this time driving straight to Greektown. His destination was the casinos, brightly lit and alive with people twenty-four hours a day. He needed the noisy, impersonal anonymity of the casino to give him some equilibrium. The controlled raucousness of the place served to calm him down, although he wasn't ready to admit how wound up he really was, nor the cause for his mood. He called Paris several more times but she apparently had her cell phone turned off or she was just determined to ignore him. *How can I apologize if she won't talk to me? Maybe I shouldn't apologize. Maybe I should just let it go.* He'd no sooner entertained the notion than he realized how fruitless it would be. This was something he was going to have to live with, the fact that he'd taken advantage of a beautiful and innocent young woman who fancied herself in love with him.

When he'd finally had enough of the casino, he left without even cashing in his chips. He beckoned to the nearest cocktail waitress and when she approached him with a smile on her face he told her to hold out her hands and he dropped the stack of chips into her palms. "Get yourself something nice, you deserve it," was all he said before he walked away. By the time he got back to the hotel he was reeking of secondhand smoke from the casino and the smell turned his stomach. He stripped off the offensive clothing, rolled it up and put it in the plastic bag the hotel provided for guest laundry. After a long, punishing shower and needlessly brisk shampoo, Titus got into the bed he'd shared with Paris and groaned as he detected the light sweetness of her fragrance. It was a long time before he slept, and when he finally drifted off he was cradling the pillow that smelled of her essence.

He continued to stare at Paris and Aidan as they got into her car, the sporty little Thunderbird with the custom pink paint job and the black interior. He recalled her saying that her brothers and her father had given her the car when she got her MBA. He knew how much she loved it and he could see why. She looked perfect in the car. *She looks perfect, period,* he thought glumly. Against his will, he remembered again what her declarations of love had done to him, how they made him feel. No woman had ever shared herself with him so freely and completely with such true adoration. He still felt a harsh, twisting pain when he remembered the sweet surrender on her face as she admitted her love for him.

The guilt consumed him at times, but it was tempered by the knowledge that he was right; he wasn't the man for Paris. She was beautiful, smart, ambitious and adorable and she deserved the world. A man who could marry her, make a life with her and give her all the babies she could possibly want. Titus's face grew stony with resolution. He wasn't that man, there was no way he could ever give Paris the things she merited above all the other women he'd ever been with and he had to remember that or it would spell disaster for both of them. He almost started his car, and then grimaced as he remembered that he was coming to the office, not leaving it. He'd spent so much time out of the country avoiding Paris over the past several months he now didn't know if he was coming or going. He laughed bitterly as he got out of the vehicle and walked to the elevator. What he needed right now was some hot, mindless recreation with a willing partner. And he knew just the person. A lot of things may have changed, but the important things remained the same.

Chapter 6

The next morning found Paris in a good mood, as always. Oh, it wasn't always like that; in the early days after the night she spent with Titus, she'd wake up every day in tears. At first she would schedule a good cry every morning. First it was fifteen minutes a day, then she tapered off to ten and gradually the ten minutes became five a day. These days it wasn't necessary to set aside time to nurse her pain. The pain was gone, replaced by a coolly disdainful anger. She had nothing about which to mourn these days. She'd made a colossal error in judgment with Titus, but life had to go on. There was something to be said for doing the stupidest thing a woman could do with a man and doing it early in the relationship before some sort of precedent was set. She'd screwed up, she knew better now and she'd never, ever fall into the same trap again. And that was that.

She was really happy with her living arrangement; her life was a lot easier these days. Aidan was the perfect roommate as he was not only much neater than she was; he also derived a bizarre satisfaction from cleaning. Her house was always immaculate and she only had to cook three days out of the week, unless she had a dinner date, which was quite often now. Aidan cooked the other three days and they ate out at least one day a week.

Merlin was also very companionable. He only had two flaws as far as Paris was concerned. He was obsessed with her pantyhose and she often had to chase him through the house to retrieve them from his sharp little teeth. His other obsession was anyone Paris dated. Merlin had designated himself protector of the house and he did his level best to dispatch any potential suitor from the door. He would pretend to hack a hairball on someone's Italian loafer, or go into a frantic spasm at the feet of a new swain, or just resort to the age-old cat trick of staring. Since Russian Blues have very large eyes and he accompanied the stare with a hypnotic swaying of his long body and a low growl in his throat, it was the most successful of his maneuvers. Luckily, Paris wasn't that attached to any of her dates and secretly found his antics quite amusing. She was actually laughing with her secretary, Deirdre, about something he'd done the night before when her intercom rang and her cousin Clay asked her to come to his office.

She was there in minutes with a smile on her face; she adored all of her cousins and was always glad of a chance to chat. He greeted her with a hug and a kiss on the cheek as usual, and she thought, as she always did, that he was just like a really exceptional vintage wine—he was getting better and better with age. Clay was about six feet seven with the light golden complexion that was shared by most of the family. He was still lean and muscular with broad shoulders and a truly captivating face, highlighted by long-lashed, heavy-lidded eyes, a thick mustache and topped off by a thick head of wavy hair that was turning prematurely silver, courtesy, he always said, of his wild brood of children. When he asked her how she was doing, she had to hide a smile at his deep, sonorous voice. His wife, Benita, had often said that Clay's voice was the thing that really got her going when they first met.

"I'm just fine, Clay, and you? How's the family?"

"Everyone is fine, better than fine, in fact. We want you to come over for dinner tomorrow, if you can manage it."

She accepted happily and asked if Clay had been keeping up with the show. He raised an eyebrow in surprise. "Of course I am. Even if you weren't my cousin I'd be keeping abreast of *Paris & Company*. You're doing a fine job, Paris. Your ratings just keep climbing and your show is becoming a real powerhouse. The syndicators are going to be pounding your door down soon, mark my words. You're destined for great success, Paris. I'm proud of you."

"We're all proud of you, Paris. You make us look good." The deep voice was that of Clay's brother, Martin, who'd entered Clay's private quarters followed by his twin brother, Malcolm, and their younger brother, Marcus. All three men hugged Paris, and Martin guided her over to the sofa and sat her down with him on one side and Clay on the other.

"Wow, all my handsome cousins in one room on a workday," she teased. "To what do I owe this singular pleasure?"

Martin kept his arm around her shoulder and the four men glanced at each other before Clay spoke.

"Paris, there's no easy way to tell you this, so I'm just going to say it outright. Your life may be in danger."

She stared at each of the men in turn, trying to detect a smile or other expression that would let her know they were joking, but none was forthcoming. They all looked completely serious as they returned her stare.

"Clay, what are you talking about? Is this some kind of practical joke, some kind of prank or what? How am I in danger?"

This time it was Marcus who spoke and his voice was as grave as Clay's.

"We're not sure yet, Paris. All we know for sure is that there have been threats made against your life and we're taking them literally. Someone is after you, Paris."

Titus's mood was the opposite of Paris's. She might have been feeling sunny and warm that day, but he was overcast with storm clouds on the horizon. The previous night should have been relaxing and fulfilling, instead it had been the most humiliating one he could ever recall. He'd called an old friend, a woman with whom he'd had a very pleasant relationship some time before. He knew she wasn't seeing anyone exclusively and they'd always enjoyed a prolific and energetic sex life. Best of all, she was no more interested in settling down than he was and wasn't averse to the proverbial booty call. She'd initiated quite a few of them herself, as a matter of fact. She referred to them as "late dates." That was how he'd posed it to her when he'd called.

After a little chitchat, he got right down to business. "So how about a late date?" he'd asked in his sexy voice.

"But of course, sweetheart. I'll chill the wine and you come on over," she'd purred.

He arrived at her townhouse about forty-five minutes later and within a very short time they were in her bedroom, going at it with gusto. Neither one of them liked to waste much time; they knew what the deal was and they both wanted to maximize their enjoyment of each other. It didn't take long before his partner, Suzette was her name, noticed that something was amiss. For one thing he kept repeating something strange, and for another, what started out so well had now fizzled out completely as it was apparent that Titus Jr. wasn't feeling it that night. To his utter horror it was the first and only time in his life he hadn't been able to perform. The fact that Suzette didn't seem to be devastated by his anatomical indifference was also galling. She tried to be philosophical, which annoyed him to no end.

"Hon, it happens to the best of us sometimes. It even happens to women, quiet as it's kept. You start out with the best of intentions and somewhere along the line your body just won't cooperate." She was putting on a silky black robe as she spoke, looking at Titus over her shoulder as she did so. "Maybe you need a vacation. Maybe you really should go to France," she suggested.

Titus had been lying on the bed staring at the ceiling with his arms crossed behind his head. Her words made him sit bolt upright. "Why would I want to go to France?" he asked with a deep frown.

She raised an eyebrow as she answered. "You said 'Paris.' You said it a couple of times, like you had this need to be there or something. Does that make sense?"

What made sense to Titus was to get out of there as fast as humanly possible, which is what he did. He bolted. Now, after a restless night with little sleep, a long run, a brisk shower and a protein shake for breakfast, he felt like a new man, albeit an angry, frustrated one. It was bad enough that he dreamed about Paris with a regularity that bordered on nocturnal stalking; now she'd gotten to him in an even more personal way. He set his jaw grimly as he maneuvered his Hummer through the morning traffic. The oversized vehicle was his special play toy; he didn't drive it every day, he used it purely for fun. But this morning he had a need for the raw machismo of the ultimate man machine and walked past his Chrysler 300 to the highly polished black vehicle. He arrived at the office compound looking like something out of a glossy men's magazine: tall, impeccably clad and undeniably sexy. He strode into his office while mentally renewing his vow to keep his distance from the one person who had the ability to turn his world upside down.

His secretary, Denise, widened her eyes at the sight of her boss looming into the office wearing a glacial expression she'd learned over the years meant that he needed some alone time. She held out a pink slip of paper to him while she switched her gaze to her computer screen. "Good morning, boss. Your presence is requested," she murmured as he took the slip from her outstretched hand.

"Hold my calls. I'll be back soon," he said, staring at the request to come to Clay Deveraux's office.

After his startling announcement, Paris's eyes locked on Marcus's. She stared at him like he was suddenly speaking in tongues. The sound of someone else entering the office broke the spell and she looked around at all of her cousins and, inexplicably, Aidan, who'd just entered the room. "Aidan? What are you doing here?" she asked with a truly puzzled look on her face.

He cleared his throat and tried to look nonchalant, but failed miserably. His pale skin, courtesy of his Irish father and Mexican-American mother, bore a slight flush along his cheekbones as he took an available chair. "I'm here because I'm the one who's responsible for this little soiree," he admitted. "I accidentally got some of your mail about three weeks ago. It was pretty bad, Paris. Whoever sent it has a definite agenda. They're out to get you at any cost," he said quietly.

"You got one piece of mail that had something nasty to say about me and you decide my life is in danger?" Paris's incredulity was plain in her voice. "Honey, I get crap like that all the time. Don't be ridiculous!"

Clay's thick brows knit into a single line of concern. "What are you talking about, Paris? You mean you've gotten things like this before?"

All of her cousins were staring at her with intense, piercing looks that showed how serious they were. Paris looked around helplessly and shrugged. "Yes, sure, I've gotten my share of weird mail. People don't like my hairstyle, or they hate my outfit, or they don't like the sound of my voice, the size of my butt, whatever. I've gotten plenty of weird mail, guys. It's not that big a deal."

Martin's voice sounded so loud she jumped as he demanded to know how long she'd been getting that kind of mail and why she never told anyone.

"Martin, I don't get a lot of it, and when I do I throw it away. I'm just not that sensitive, I guess. I never thought I was going to be the end-all and be-all to every viewer. I knew there were going to be people who hate me and my show and who wouldn't have any problem letting me know that. And there're a few crackpots out there, too. I get marriage proposals, requests for money, and invitations to join folks on the mothership. The list is endless and I don't get upset about it, so I don't think you should either. I think it's just par for the course," she said reassuringly.

She was startled again by the intensity with which Aidan spoke. "Paris, this is not just some harmless crackpot. The letter I received was a deliberate threat. It was specific, very nasty and deviant and it wasn't the only one."

Malcolm turned his eyes on Aidan and demanded details. "How do you know this? How many letters were misdirected to you?"

Aidan met the man's gaze without a hint of remorse. "Only one. But I got nosy and started intercepting her mail from the mailroom so I could check for more and there were three more from the same person. Same postmark, same writing, same message."

Marcus exploded. "So why didn't you do something? Why are we just finding out about this?"

"I did do something," he countered. "I moved in with her so she'd have some protection and then I told you. I had to do it that way because, well, you know how stubborn she can be."

Marcus had to agree with that assessment. "Yeah, you're right about that. It runs in the family. I'm assuming you still have the letters for the investigator," he said. He looked from Paris to Aidan and then at his brothers. "Okay, we're getting a little bit of a late start, but it's better than nothing, and at least she has someone looking out for her at home."

"Yeah, that's true. Good looking out, Aidan, we appreciate it," Malcolm said. "So what's the next step? What's the first thing on the agenda?"

Paris had had enough. "The first thing is we stop talking about me like I'm not in the room. What's wrong with you people? You think you can just run roughshod over me because some lunatic is making crazy noises out there? I'm a grown woman and I can take care of myself. And as for you, Aidan Estevez Sinclair, I'm too through with you. How dare you move into my home under false pretenses? You're supposed to be my friend," she said angrily.

"I *am* your friend," he assured her. "And that's why I'm not going to let anything happen to you. I'm going to be there for you whether you like it or not."

Clay concurred with Aidan. "Sweetie, whether you like it or not, we have to take care of you. You're like our sister and there's no way in hell we're going to let some lunatic harm you in any way. So until we're convinced that you're not in any danger, you must be protected. There's no room for negotiation here, Paris. It's either our way or no way at all."

"But Clay, that's ridiculous. I'm perfectly capable of taking care of myself, I don't need Aidan and you guys hovering over me," she said fretfully.

The men exchanged a look before Clay assured her they weren't going to be hovering over her. "But there is going to be someone taking care of this situation. You need protection, sweets, whether you know it or not."

A new voice from the doorway sent a chill down her spine. "He's absolutely right, Paris. I'll be taking over from now on."

She turned her head to see Titus standing in the doorway looking like the wrath of God. Slumping against Martin's shoulder she closed her eyes and uttered a silent prayer for deliverance. *Please let this be a dream. A really weird dream,* she pleaded.

Chapter 7

Titus entered the office and stood towering over everyone, looking stern and uncompromising. "Sorry about just barging in but your secretary told me I was expected. I overheard enough to get the general idea of what's been going on and I agree totally with your cousins. Until we find out who's doing this and bring him down, you need round-the-clock protection. I know you don't like hearing that, but there's no other option." He crossed his arms and waited for the explosion he was sure would follow his words. Sure enough, Paris had plenty to say.

She stared at him balefully for a second, and then she stood to face him. "Look. I appreciate the fact that my cousins and Aidan are concerned about me, but I can't live like a victim. Has anyone been paying any attention to my show at all? The theme this year is 'Living without Fear.' The whole purpose of my show, the mandate for this year, is to empower people to take control of their own lives. How am I supposed to do that if I'm cowering in a corner somewhere?"

A long lock of her hair fell in her face and she pushed it behind her ear, all the while looking daggers at Titus. Suddenly the mere sight of him filled her senses in a way that made it necessary for her to look away from him and she turned to her cousins. "Clay, Martin, come on, guys, you can see how this is impossible! In order for me to maintain integrity with my viewers I've got to walk the walk. I can't just spout platitudes and do something entirely different in my personal life. I'd lose all credibility and you know it. This is really important, not just to me, but also to the show and to my viewers. I'm structuring the entire season on the idea that we can take control of our lives, that by facing up to our fears and dealing with them effectively, we can free ourselves to be the best we can be. How can I do that if I'm living with a bunch of keepers? Traitorous keepers," she added with a pointed look at Aidan.

There was a respectful silence that lasted almost thirty seconds before Clay's game face descended and Paris knew she was doomed. "Paris, I agree with what you're saying and I'm sure that Titus will be as circumspect as possible in his investigations, surveillance and protection. But let's not get it twisted in any way. If you don't cooperate fully, if you do anything to thwart anything he does, I'll have Judge and your brothers here within two hours. I know you think we're being unreasonable, but that's how much we care about you. That's the way it has to be, sweetie. No arguments."

With the sure knowledge that resistance was futile, Paris crossed her arms and resumed her seat on the long leather sofa. Martin's arm around her shoulder didn't make her feel one bit better; she was furious, as well as feeling smothered. Martin sensed her rage and tried to comfort her. "Look at it this way, sweetness. Titus is the best investigator in the business and he'll have this all taken care of before you know it."

She finally dared to look Titus directly in the eye and what she saw reflected there was anything but reassuring. She'd never seen his eyes that particular color; they were a light, icy gray, almost silver, in fact. He met her gaze steadily and suddenly she felt as cold as his eyes looked. *Heavenly Father, please help me. How could this possibly get any worse?*

Titus looked down at Paris's lowered head and had to remind himself harshly that all bets were off. She was now under his protection and therefore she was completely off-limits. The reminder was necessary because for the first time since his days in Special Forces where his career in investigations had begun, his personal feelings were encroaching on his professionalism. When he arrived at Clay's office and Clay's longtime, long-suffering personal secretary, Annie, told him he was expected and to go on in, Titus heard everything that was being said for two reasons. One was that a Deveraux voice carried. All the men had deep ones and they all had excellent lung capacity, so their voices were easy to hear and distinguish even when they were in good moods. The other reason was that when they were emotional about something, their voices got deeper and louder. Since Paris was offering resistance and they were all totally impassioned by what they were saying, it wasn't at all difficult to hear every word. Titus wasn't surprised by their reactions, but his own feelings stunned him.

When he heard Clay telling Paris her life was in danger, a white-hot rage descended on him with an intensity he couldn't equate with any feeling he'd ever experienced. As he heard the details about the letters, his anger didn't dissipate. It merely fused into an intense weapon with the force of a guided missile that lacked a clear focus. The target was whoever thought they could make Paris uncomfortable, much less put her in jeopardy. When he found out who was behind this, they'd pay, that went without saying. Right now his most important job was to make sure Paris was safe because if anything happened to her, if she so much as broke a fingernail, the person responsible would face a lifetime of hurt at Titus's hands. No one in the room could detect this intensity, at least Titus hoped they couldn't. No one could know how personally he was taking the situation. To the outside he had to present his usual stoic face that meant he was taking care of business. As far as the rest of the world was concerned, this was another job, nothing more. The fact that he would never do anything more important in his entire life was entirely his own affair.

It had been a couple of hours since Clay's announcement to Paris and the time hadn't been kind to her. They were now alone in her private office and she was seated at her desk with her head lowered and her face in her hands. She looked exhausted and the sight of her appearing so stressed and unhappy was tearing Titus up inside but he successfully disguised his feelings with a mask of professional indifference. She wasn't making it easy for him, though. "Paris, we can be as discreet as we need to be unless a time comes when the harassment escalates, at which point our efforts will show a corresponding growth," he said quietly. Paris looked at him with little liking and graciously invited him to sit down.

"Quit hanging over me, would you? You're working my last nerve," she said bitterly. "And can you also shut up for a minute? I don't want to hear about any of this mess for a while."

Titus recognized the fact that she was close to imploding and he honored her request by sitting down, but he had a few more points to make. "Paris, I'm sure this is difficult for you, but it has to be done. We can't afford to let any more time pass on this," he told her.

"Well, let's circle the wagons and protect the helpless womenfolk," she returned with sarcasm dripping from every syllable. The look in her eyes reflected her disdain. "Titus, how can you expect me to take this seriously? Aidan intercepts a couple of crank letters and all of a sudden I'm in some kind of mortal peril? Come on now, even you have to admit that's kind of a stretch. I think everyone is overreacting. I don't think anyone is after me and I certainly don't think I need anyone standing over my shoulder to protect me from someone who's not there."

She sat back and stared at Titus defiantly, waiting for his response. He returned her stare, his glacial eye color suddenly softening to a temperate blue. "Let's go," he said.

"Go? Go where? Are you putting me on a tether or something?" she asked, her eyes widening with apprehension.

"Let's get something to eat, Paris. I'm starving and you look like you are, too. We'll talk about this over lunch."

He rose and came around the side of her desk, holding out his hand to her. She stared at it for a long moment before taking it. In minutes they were out of the building and on the way to his Hummer. "Where are you taking me?" she asked.

He smiled down at her for the first time. "Someplace you'll like. Trust me."

Paris looked around the small restaurant with great interest. It was homey and charming like its name, Aunt Sister's. The dining room was sweetly old-fashioned, with small flowers on the wallpapers, starched white lace curtains at the windows and snowy white napkins and tablecloths. The floors were made of hardwood that looked old, but were buffed to a satiny patina. There were green plants in the windows and on stands throughout the room, and each table bore a small vase of black-eyed Susans and Queen Anne's lace. Even though the flowers were silk, they were very realistic and enhanced the warmth of the décor. The background music was perfect; Billie Holiday, Ella Fitzgerald and Sarah Vaughn serenaded them in the nearly empty room. Despite her turmoil, Paris felt herself begin to relax.

She looked at Titus and felt something else, too; her traitorous heart began to melt. She gazed at his handsome face and her eyes locked on his, which had turned back to their usual warm color. Her heart started to do its usual Titus dance, the happy little flip-flip that always started when he was around. Goosebumps sprang up on her arms as a well of common sense overflowed and she was reminded of that fateful night. She didn't know it, but her thoughts made her face go from relaxed and content to stern and wary. She wanted to say something aloof and scathing to show Titus she was in control of the situation, but she couldn't trust her vocal cords at the moment. A snit was brewing inside her, predicated by the fact that Titus was being so matter-of-fact. Obviously, being in her company wasn't having any effect on him whatsoever. It didn't seem to register with him that this was the first time they'd been together for more than two seconds since that night. To her it was just more proof that she was right, he couldn't possibly have any feelings for her, then or now.

Her jaw tightened and her throat constricted as the memory of how he'd touched her, how he'd made her feel came back to her with an unerring accuracy as vivid as it was unwelcome. Her body began its inevitable response to his proximity just as "The Nearness of You" floated out of the hidden speakers. Heat radiated up her spine and down her thighs and she wanted to run out of the restaurant, just get up and leave the big stupid overbearing oaf sitting there. A couple of things prevented this, though. One, she didn't have a ride back to the office, and two, she wasn't sure her legs would support her right now. She refused to look into those compelling eyes again and stared out the window instead. A hostile silence began rearing its unsociable head, but the arrival of their meal put an end to it.

Paris brightened at once as their pretty server put their plates in front of them. The food looked and smelled so delicious all thoughts of how much she disliked the man across the table vanished and she smiled for the first time since Clay's office. She reached into her purse for a small bottle of antibacterial cleanser and quickly rubbed it on her hands. Without thinking about what she was doing, she automatically offered the bottle to Titus, who took it and applied some while she placed her napkin in her lap. Later she decided it was those dratted good manners of hers that accounted for what happened next. She held her hand out to Titus and they said grace together, the way they always did whenever they dined. It was such a part of her, so natural that she'd forgotten momentarily that he was the enemy. But by now she was too hungry to care.

Grace over, they both attended to their meals with good appetite. Succulent, golden brown baked chicken with savory cornbread dressing, fresh green beans cooked with onions and tiny red potatoes, sweet potato fritters crusted with chopped pecans, sliced cucumbers and tomatoes in a tart vinaigrette and piping hot cornbread made for a feast as good to the tongue as it as was to the eye. It was all Paris could do not to moan out loud as she daintily but thoroughly cleaned her plate. She did sigh in repletion as she dabbed her lips with her napkin. After taking a sip of the aromatic iced tea, or "sweet tea" as it was known, she made herself look Titus in the eye. "Thank you so much for the lovely meal, Titus. It was absolutely delicious and just what I needed. I feel much better," she said honestly.

Titus smiled at her and asked if she wanted dessert. "They have a bread pudding here that's incredible. You want to try it?"

"I couldn't. I'd pop out of this dress if I did," she demurred.

"Well, I have a real craving so I'm going to order some. You can taste mine, how about that?"

In minutes he was holding out a spoonful of the warm pudding. It was rich and light and smelled deliciously of cinnamon and nutmeg, and was covered in a heavenly wine sauce. Paris leaned forward and allowed him to put the spoon in her mouth, her eyes closing in ecstasy as the flavors oozed down over her tongue. "Mmm, that's wonderful," she sighed. Her tongue darted out and touched the corner of her mouth. "Thank you, Titus."

Their server approached the table with reverence in her eyes. "Umm, Miss Deveraux, I hate to impose, but I'm a big fan of yours. And my mother is, too. She tapes your show every day. I was wondering if you could sign this for her."

Paris gave the young woman her best smile. "You bet I will, gorgeous! Thanks so much for watching. I'm glad you enjoy it. I loved my lunch here, this is a wonderful restaurant," she said warmly.

The young woman blushed and smiled shyly. "Thank you for saying that. This is my family's restaurant. My mother and her sisters opened it and we all work here. We may have to close in a few months if business doesn't pick up, but we're praying that doesn't happen," she said quietly.

"*Close?* This wonderful place? Oh, I don't think so," Paris said emphatically. "This place is too good to go out of business. Is your mother here now, or one of her sisters? I'd love to talk to them," she told the astounded young woman.

She accompanied the girl, whose name was Susy, to the office in the back of the restaurant, leaving Titus at the table. "Susy, if your mother and your aunts don't mind, I think we could do something to prevent this place from ever closing. Any place that serves food like this needs to stay open for a long, long time," she said confidently.

Titus expelled a huge breath of pure relief as Paris left the table. Of course as he watched her lush, shapely body walking away his passions returned fiercer than ever, so it was a very short respite indeed. Paris had been driving him to the brink of madness all afternoon and he needed her to be out of his sight even for a few minutes so he could calm down. Paris looked gorgeous. She always looked beautiful, but today she was especially delectable. She was wearing a wrap dress in a pink color that brought out all the warmth of her skin while making her glow. The dress was really showing off her beautiful curves without being vulgar. It wasn't low cut, but it made her breasts look spectacular. And it fit her body in a way that showed off her small waist and curved hips, plus it had the added benefit of displaying her legs. She didn't wear dresses often so it was always a treat to see her legs and Titus took full advantage, staring after her hungrily.

He wiped his hands on the napkin almost viciously. Taking her to lunch seemed a good idea at the time, but it was more difficult than he planned. After he'd discovered that Paris had left the hotel, he was furious with himself for mishandling the situation. He knew he'd hurt her and that was the last thing he'd ever want to do. He'd blown up her cell phone, calling her over and over to leave messages, which she ignored. He finally managed to get her and wasted no time in apologizing, an apology she all but ignored. Even today he could recall her exact words to him. "Titus," she'd said in precise and final tones, "there's no need to prolong this. As you so accurately pointed out, you and I made a mistake. We got caught up in the moment and while being together was enjoyable, it was regrettable. But being the mature adults we are, we can live with that, don't you think? Seeing each other in the future is inevitable and it needn't be torture. We can just forget anything ever transpired between us and life can go on."

Titus took a long drink of tea to extinguish the pain those words caused him even now. It didn't make any sense for him to feel like this because this was the way he wanted it. He was the one who'd set the rules, he was the one who said he was wrong for her and they shouldn't be together, so why was he tripping because they were of one accord? Why did it bother him so much that she was accepting what he'd said calmly and maturely?

He watched her closely as she returned to the table with two smiling women who had to be the owners of Aunt Sister's. He could finally admit why her words tortured him even now. *Because she said she loved me.* With Herculean effort he ignored the twisting pain in the pit of his stomach as he rose to acknowledge the women.

Chapter 8

Paris was so animated and excited on the way back to the complex that Titus didn't have the heart to reiterate the things they'd discussed earlier. She was full of plans for helping the Summers sisters make a success of their restaurant. The women had come out to the dining room with her while she checked her planner to set up a time for them to come to her office and talk about an appearance on *Paris & Company*. She had a regular cooking segment on the show and it was the perfect venue for showcasing their incredible culinary skills. Paris hadn't stopped talking from the time he helped her into her coat and led her out to the parking lot while he seated her in the Hummer. She was like her old self, bubbly, enthusiastic and utterly charming.

"There are three of them, the sisters, I mean. Dorothy is a nurse and Lena and Carmen are both teachers," she reported. She looked directly at Titus and flashed him her brilliant and familiar smile as she explained the origins of the sister's names. "They were named after Dorothy Dandridge, Lena Horne and Carmen McRae, isn't that something? They're looking for a way to secure some financial independence for their families. Dorothy, they call her Didi, is a widow, Lena's husband disappeared and Carmen is still single. Lena and Didi have children, though, and they want to be able to provide for them and make sure they go to college and not have to worry about expenses. They all love to cook and they're very creative, that's how they came up with this place, which is just wonderful, but they could certainly use some exposure which is where I come in."

When she finally stopped for air Titus looked at her pretty flushed face and smiled. She looked so pretty it was all he could do to keep himself from leaning over to take her lips in a hot, binding kiss. Luckily, they'd arrived at the complex and there was work to be done. He escorted her into the building and they went directly to her offices. The excitement faded from her face and the look with which he was becoming familiar returned. It was an expression of pure Deveraux stubbornness that meant she wasn't going to acquiesce to his plans meekly. It was okay, though, he figured he could lull her into cooperation.

While he was helping her remove her coat, he reminded her of the work they had to do. "Paris, I'm going to need one of my people to go through your mail every day, your mail and anything else that you receive here," he told her.

Paris merely raised a brow. "You might need more than one person," she said dryly.

Titus asked curiously, "How much stuff are we talking about?"

"Come with me and I'll show you," Paris said with a beckoning finger.

They left the office and walked down a corridor to an

unmarked door. "Welcome to the Closet," Paris said as she opened the door. Titus was amazed. It was a large conference room that had been pressed into service as a storage space. Deep shelves lined all the walls and a waist-high storage unit with shelves centered the room. The shelves were full of merchandise of all kinds, from shampoo and hand lotion to expensive cosmetics, small appliances and food items.

"What's all this, Paris?"

She looked embarrassed and wrapped an arm around her waist while she twirled a lock of hair around her forefinger. "This is the result of me opening my big mouth," she admitted. "If I mention a certain shampoo, the next day I get a case of it. If I say I use a certain brand of makeup, I get a huge assortment from the manufacturer. Then I get an even bigger supply from their rival in the hopes that I'll like it better. If I wear an identifiable piece of jewelry, the maker will send me a special design, well, you get the idea. I get gifts from viewers, from sponsors, from everywhere you can imagine. I try really hard to keep a low profile because I don't want to solicit this kind of thing," she said sheepishly.

"We call this place the Closet. I give the stuff away to the staff or to a women's shelter or any place that can use it. During the holidays I let the staff do their Christmas shopping in here and the proceeds go to charity. It's kind of embarrassing, but it ends up as a good cause, so I deal with it," she said with a modest shrug.

Titus looked around the room and realized how complicated this particular assignment was going to be. With an influx of goods like this it could be relatively easy for something deadly to get to Paris. This was going to require round-the-clock surveillance and that would mean keeping several of his agents on-site, something he knew Paris would hate. Furthermore, it would mean changing the way she did things, something else she was going to despise. His eyes once again took on a silvery cast as he thought about the alternative. Paris might be right; there could be a chance they were over-reacting, that no one was after her. But if there was even the remotest possibility that her life was endangered, they had to be prepared.

"Okay, Paris, I get the idea. If you don't mind being in my company a little longer, I have one more thing that needs to be checked out," he said without looking at her.

"What would that be?" she asked, barely hiding her irritation.

"Your house."

Titus followed Paris in her sporty little Thunderbird, shaking his head at the personalized license plate. "That's got to go. The Barbie Dream Car draws enough attention, but the LUVPARIS license plate is just too much. To a sick mind that looks like advertising. Or an invitation," he said to himself with gruff concern. A pithy bit of profanity escaped his lips as he imagined the look on Paris's face when he told her she'd be chauffeured to work until it was certain she was safe. "I guess I'll be on her hate list permanently," he muttered. They arrived at her brick town home in the Ansley Park area of Atlanta. Paris was renting the house from Marcus Deveraux's wife, Vera. It had begun life as a carriage house at the turn of the century, now it was a charming two-story house with a small front yard and a spacious backyard. Titus parked in front of the house as Paris pulled into the driveway. He was slightly annoyed that he didn't get to her in time to open her car door, but he made no comment. A mere tightening of his jaw was the only indication anything was amiss.

Paris opened the door and stepped inside, taking off her cashmere overcoat and putting it away in the hall closet. She turned to Titus and held out her hands for his leather coat. He started to say he'd keep it on, and then realized that would be slightly ridiculous. He took off the full-length lambskin coat but hung it up himself while Paris watched with a remote expression on her face. She led the way into the living room and sat down in a comfortable looking chair, indicating Titus should do the same. He was about to take a seat when something thudded down the stairs and flew past him, landing in Paris's lap. It was a large shorthaired cat in the weirdest color Titus had ever seen on a cat. The big feline was *blue*, a deep velvety blue, and its fur was tipped with silver that gave it a sort of iridescence. It was beautiful, no doubt, but without question it was the most unusual cat Titus could remember seeing. The creature leaped onto Paris and she giggled madly as he put one paw on each of her shoulders and stuck his nose in her ear.

"Thank you, Merlin. That was a lovely hug. Did you have a nice day? Did you sleep on Aidan's bed all day or mine?" she asked as she scratched his ears.

Titus watched the scene with amusement. Having been to Paris's house several times, he knew this cat wasn't hers. It had to be the property of her temporary roommate, Aidan, although the cat was obviously fond of Paris. The fondness didn't seem to be universal as the cat took one look at Titus, hissed and fled the room. Paris smiled apologetically.

"Merlin doesn't take to strangers much," she said. Suddenly her smile vanished. "Okay, you're here. So what did you have to see?"

Titus responded in a calm, professional voice, "I need to take a look at the layout of this place to see if there are places where you might be vulnerable." He tried to soften his words when he saw her scowl. "Let me just take a look around, okay? Then we'll talk."

The house was well lit and airy, with multi-paned windows

all around and French doors that led out to the patio and garden. Even now, in January, he could see that the flower beds were laid out precisely and the perennial plants were neatly prepared for winter, the rosebushes and other delicate plants wrapped in burlap. He was walking around the perimeter of the house, looking for places where an intruder could conceal himself, or where it would be easy to gain access. He could see Paris watching him through the kitchen window, and he could only imagine what she was thinking. She wasn't going to like what he had to say; of this he was perfectly aware. But it was better to err on the side of being too cautious than to risk her coming to harm in some way. He retraced his steps and went back into the kitchen through the French doors. Paris was standing near the work island in the middle of the room, looking at him with borderline hostility. Rather than letting her anxiety build, he wiped his feet thoroughly on the mat and suggested they go through the rest of the house.

Paris dutifully led him from room to room, although she had a comment. "It's not like you haven't been here before," she said acidly.

Titus didn't answer at first, although he thought about the times he'd visited Paris while they were dating. He'd always enjoyed coming to her home. The décor reflected her warm and loving personality and it was a pleasure to bask in her hospitality. Seeing how tensed and uneasy she was now he had to say something. "Yes, Paris, and you always treated me like royalty. I don't know if I ever told you how much I liked coming over here."

Paris looked utterly shocked by his words. "All we did was watch DVDs and talk," she pointed out.

"Some of the best conversations I've ever had," Titus said, his deep voice warm and caring. *And some of the best kisses I've ever tasted in my life,* he thought, remembering the sweetness of her lips and the fragrant warmth of her body. He had to remind his libido who was the boss and with great effort pulled his head back into the here and now. It wouldn't do to remember the last time he and Paris had been alone here, sitting on the big comfortable sofa with her curled up next to him. They would make a cursory effort to watch a movie, but they always ended up doing more talking than watching and eventually, more kissing than talking. Titus liked kissing Paris more than any of the women who'd preceded her. Her lips were soft and sweet and her mouth tasted like roses and strawberries, for some reason. It was like being a teenager again, without the angst. It was just so satisfying, so sensual…

And there I go again, he thought angrily. What was it about this woman that made him so crazy? He forced himself to pay attention to the rooms Paris was showing him, embarrassed that he'd lost focus. Again.

"This is the kitchen," Paris said briskly, waving her hand at the brick walls, the high, multipaned windows and the French doors that led to the patio. The room was accented with dark green and had tall cupboards with glass fronts. There was a work island in the center of the room and a small table with two chairs in front of the biggest window. The stove was stainless steel, as was the Subzero refrigerator, which was decorated with a magnetic poetry kit. It consisted of little rectangles in white with black printing and each one had a different word on it. The words could be arranged to form poetry and Paris loved playing with it, writing whimsical little poems, some of which were actually quite good. Titus frowned as he took in the lack of curtains in the room but didn't comment. He indicated a wooden door next to the patio doors. "Where does that lead to?"

Paris followed his gaze. "The pantry and the laundry room," she said, walking over to the door and opening it.

There were shelves of canned and boxed foodstuffs neatly arranged on shelves, along with an array of oversized pots and pans and things like slow-cookers and woks that weren't used very often. The laundry room was entered through the pantry and it was small and unremarkable except for another door, which Titus inquired about. "That leads into the garage, but it's always locked."

Titus said nothing, but walked over and tried the doorknob, frowning as the door came open at once. Paris blushed bright red, mumbling, "How did that happen?" She tried to save face by leaving the laundry room and heading back to the dining room. It was another bright and airy room with French cream walls and the mahogany Duncan Phyfe table Paris had inherited from her grandmother. Chippendale chairs with thickly padded seats upholstered in a pretty floral chintz surrounded it. There was a matching buffet with a china hutch filled with part of Paris's collection of fanciful teapots. Paris had been collecting teapots and water pitchers in unusual shapes and colors for years and the evidence was in this room, as well as the living room. Titus always smiled when he saw a teapot because it immediately reminded him of Paris. She didn't see his expression soften as she was still conducting him through the house like a tour guide.

"Now we're back in the living room," she said tonelessly. "The sofa and chairs are Vera's but the other stuff is mine. Nothing much to see, really."

Titus looked around and disagreed mentally. This room, like the dining room, kitchen and the solarium where they had spent a lot of time watching the sunset and smooching, was full of the plants Paris had grown and nurtured so carefully. She had a real way with plants; even the most delicate thrived under her care. They were lush, green, and full of vigor and they looked positively sensual as well as imparting an earthy fragrance to the air. There was also a curio cabinet full of her water pitchers in crazy shapes like a rose, a toucan, a pineapple and even a leopard. They added a touch of whimsy to the room, just like the family pictures lent an air of warmth and charm. Titus took in everything about his surroundings, especially the solarium doors that led to the patio and the fact that there were no window treatments in that room, either.

Without a word he went to test the solarium doors and heard Paris's little sound of triumph when he found the doors really were locked. The triumph turned to a gasp of dismay as he gave the handle one good shake and it released at once, letting the cold winter wind into the house.

"I guess a locksmith is in order," Paris said without meeting Titus's eyes.

"That and a few other things," he answered in a dry voice. "So much for downstairs. Let's go to your bedroom."

"Excuse you?" Paris looked at him then, her eyes full of indignation, which turned promptly to fury as Titus laughed in her face.

Paris entered the back door of Clay and Bennie's house, walking into the kitchen with a smile on her face that disappeared as soon as she saw her cousin. Making a great show of ignoring Clay, she hugged his wife, Benita, tightly and told her truthfully how good she looked. Benita, or Bennie as almost everyone called her, was not only a raving beauty, she was the epitome of grace to Paris. Nothing seemed to bother her; she was a calm, happy and very loving woman whose greatest loves were Clay and her children. She hugged Paris back, and then stepped back to take a good look at the younger woman.

"Poor Paris. I know this isn't easy for you, but you know they love you or they wouldn't be going through all these changes."

Paris sighed resignedly as she acknowledged the truth of Bennie's words. She went to the kitchen sink and washed her hands so she could help Bennie get dinner on the table. Drying her hands on a paper towel she turned around and leaned on the sink. "I know my cousins love me and I love them, too, but Bennie, if you knew what Titus Argonne is putting me through you'd feel the same way I do, which is miserable!" She glared at Clay who was smiling down at her from his towering height. "This is all your fault," she said with a frown. The frown disappeared and she dissolved in laughter as Clay, ignoring her accusation, wrapped his arms around her and rocked her back and forth, saying "poor baby" over and over in his deep, gravelly voice.

"Poor little Paris, I'm sorry I got all up in your business, but you're my baby cousin and I can't let anything happen to you," he crooned.

Paris hugged him back and tried for a stern look, at which she failed miserably. "I understand, Clay, I really do. But you have no idea what that man is doing to me!" She pulled away from his arms and started counting off the various indignities to which she was being subjected.

"I can't drive my car, for one thing. And you know how much I love that car. Daddy and the boys gave it to me when I got my MBA. Titus says it attracts too much attention. He says it's like baiting a bear, whatever that is. He says it's like having a big red arrow pointing at me wherever I go, so until this whole thing is wrapped up he says I have to ride to work with Aidan or he'll send a car to pick me up. He put outdoor lights and motion detectors all around Vera's house, and he replaced every single lock in the place. He also had me put up curtains in the kitchen and the solarium. He says I'm too exposed without them. He has someone reading all my mail at work and he has people going through the Closet, tracking the origin of every single thing that comes to the studio and I'm pretty sure he has someone following me!" she said indignantly. "It's bad enough that I'm going to have to drive that ol' granny-looking company car on the few occasions I'm allowed to drive anywhere, but to have someone tailing me is just too much." Paris tried to take a stack of plates into the dining room, but Braxton, the Deverauxes handsome and capable house manager, waved away her help.

"You just relax, I've got this. Sounds like you've had a really rough day," he said kindly.

Paris gladly accepted his warm sympathy. "You're right, Braxton, I have. I'm trying not to be a spoiled brat about this, but I'm beginning to feel trapped. I just hate it, I really do."

Bennie went to Paris and hugged her again. Keeping her arm around Paris's shoulder, she led her into the family room. "Paris, I know how you feel. I'd hate being in your position. And yeah, they're probably overreacting, but you know how your cousins are. They protect their own. Imagine what your daddy would do if something happened to you."

By now they were sitting on the extra-long sofa that sat in front of the huge window. Paris made a face before answering. "It's not Daddy I'm worried about, it's the boys. My father is an elegant and civilized man, but my brothers are primal life forces, you know that."

"Elegant and civilized? Sounds like my kind of man," a teasing voice said. Paris turned her head and smiled as she saw Aunt Ruth entering the room. She jumped up from the sofa and went to give the older woman a big hug. "What are you doing here? It's so good to see you," she said, as they held on to each other in a tight embrace.

"I'm just visiting for a few days. I love to travel and I do a lot of it since I retired. And I don't get to see enough of my favorite niece and her beautiful family, so here I am."

They sat down on either side of Benita, who couldn't resist teasing her aunt.

"Umm, I'm your *only* niece, Aunt Ruth, or did you forget that little fact?" Bennie said with a smile.

"Of course not, darling, that's why you're my favorite," Ruth answered with a wicked grin. She looked at Paris with concern. "How are you doing? Benita told me what's been going on. Is there anything I can do to help?"

"Can you make Titus Argonne disappear? I'd like that a lot," Paris admitted. "And can you keep my daddy in New Orleans? I called him to let him know what was happening and he reacted quite well, considering. He agrees that the boys need not be informed of anything at this point, but he insists on coming here this weekend to make sure I'm okay. That's like the last thing I need in this life, another overprotective male hanging over me. How am I supposed to enjoy the wild debauched lifestyle appropriate to my age group if I'm surrounded at all times?"

All three women laughed and the sound of their merriment brought the Deveraux children into the room. Marty and Malcolm, the twin boys, came in, followed by Trey, the oldest son. Trey had one of his little sisters on his hip and the other one was holding his hand. Kate and Bella were twins, too, and very fond of their big brother. Paris was both touched and amused by their devotion to him; they followed him around like little kittens and he was always sweet and patient with them. They gladly let go of Trey to give Paris big wet kisses because they loved her almost as much as they did their idol. Bennie smiled as she watched them shower their cousin with affection.

"So when is your daddy coming to town? You know you miss him," she said gently. "I'm the only girl in a big family, too, so I know how that is. No matter how grown you are, you're always the baby girl. And I'm the oldest child, too," she said, shaking her head as the little girls made their way to her lap for more hugs.

"He'll be here this weekend," Paris sighed. "It'll be wonderful to see him. It seems like Christmas was such a long time ago although it really wasn't. I just don't want him to start worrying about me. Daddy needs to start living for himself. He needs more in his life besides his family and the law. He needs something more," she said thoughtfully, watching Ruth, who was now sitting on the floor romping with Marty and Malcolm. She looked happy and relaxed and at least ten years younger than her real age. *Daddy definitely needs something more in his life and so does Ruth. This could be perfect. Absolutely perfect,* she thought with a smile. *Something good is going to come out of all this after all.*

Chapter 9

After the dinner at Clay and Benita's house, Paris put her plan into action. She loved nothing better than seeing deserving people get the love and happiness they desired and had quite a reputation as a matchmaker. She even referred to herself as Martha May Matchmaker and no one was safe from her desire to make suitable couples, including Aunt Ruth. As she had explained to Aidan that night, it had suddenly dawned on her that Aunt Ruth would be perfect for her dad. Aidan had come in late that night after having dinner with an old friend from college. He stuck his head in her bedroom to say goodnight and she regaled him with her plan for putting the two of them together.

He had to smile even as he was shaking his head no. "Woman, why do you do these things? Why can't you let people alone to make their own mistakes instead of trying to put these perfect couples together? It's getting to be an obsession with you," he scolded her playfully.

Paris was sitting cross-legged in the middle of her bed writing in her leather bound journal. She was wearing long-sleeved flannel pajamas in a soft pink plaid and she looked like she was about sixteen. She gestured with her ink pen as she waved away his objections. "I have an excellent track record in these matters," she reminded him. "Look at Marcus and Vera. If I hadn't interceded they might not be together today and look how happy they are. And they are the perfect couple—even you have to admit it. Daddy needs someone like Ruth. She's smart, funny, energetic and gorgeous, besides being age-appropriate. And he's a good match for her, too. He's kind and caring and absolutely brilliant. And I might be biased, but he's still got it goin' on."

Aidan nodded absently because it was true; Mac Deveraux bore a startling resemblance to the late Adam Clayton Powell, another charismatic and very handsome man. "Okay, I can admit they'd certainly make a striking couple. But what makes you think they want to be paired up with anybody, much less each other?" He grunted as Merlin, who'd been attacking Paris's toes, suddenly launched himself off the bed and cannoned into Aidan's arms.

Paris finished writing with a knowing smile. "Daddy needs someone in his life. Whether he admits it or not, he's been a lonely man since Mama died. He goes out once in a while, but he's never had a real relationship with anyone. And I think Aunt Ruth is tired of being a nomad. I think she's ready to have some stability in her life, the kind that comes from having a wonderful relationship in her life. You just wait and see. She's going to think it's a great idea."

The next day her theory was put to the test as she had lunch with Ruth. When Paris blithely brought up the subject of Ruth coming to dinner when Mac Deveraux was in town, Ruth said no, politely but emphatically. She had to laugh at the look on Paris's face. "Don't look so stricken, darling. I just don't do blind dates, that's all."

They were having lunch in the nicely appointed dining room in the complex. Ruth had come at Paris's invitation to watch a taping of the show and stay for lunch. Today's show had included a segment on exotic animals and a keeper from the Atlanta Zoo had brought several creatures to the set. Ruth adroitly changed the subject from blind dates back to the ease with which Paris had handled the animals. "I still can't get over you with those snakes! The way you let that thing wrap around your wrist and crawl up your neck! Eww!"

Paris laughed as she speared another piece of avocado from her Cobb salad. "It's like I told that zookeeper. I grew up in Louisiana with four brothers. I have no fear of snakes, lizards, spiders, frogs or any other kind of slimy thing. You either learn how to deal with critters or your brothers will make your life a misery."

"I take it you learned how to deal, because the way you handled that tarantula was amazing. I don't even like to look at the creatures, much less touch one." Ruth looked appraisingly at the younger woman. "How did your father handle your being the only girl? Did you have to become the little woman of the house, the surrogate mother of your siblings?" Her eyes were full of curiosity and concern.

"Oh, no, not at all," Paris answered earnestly. "My daddy was way ahead of his time as far as that was concerned. He hired a housekeeper to keep everything in order. Just because I was a female he wasn't about to enslave me. I had no more chores than anyone else. We all had to keep our rooms clean, feed the pets and things like that and that was about it. I learned to cook from Aunt Lillian because the housekeeper did all the cooking and she didn't want us underfoot."

Paris paused to sip iced tea. She had a far-off look in her

eyes when she spoke again. "My mother was a real individualist. She wasn't the typical Southern bride, she was tough and independent and very smart and my father wanted me to be raised in her spirit. So he let me run wild with my brothers and get feminine with my aunts. First it was my mother's sister, Gertrude," she said, making a dreadful face. Then she smiled. "But after a few summers with Gertie, I got to spend my summers with Aunt Lillian and Angelique, thank God. I'd be a big burly tomboy if she hadn't intervened."

Paris laughed to herself while Ruth looked out the window with a thoughtful expression. She turned back to Paris with a smug grin on her face. "Tell you what, darling. I'll be more than happy to have dinner with you and your father on one condition."

"Of course, anything you say," Paris agreed eagerly.

"You have to invite Titus Argonne, too." Ruth sat back with a satisfied smile and watched as Paris turned hot pink with shock.

Titus took a final look in his bedroom mirror before leaving his condo. He decided he looked at least presentable. He was anything but vain and paid a minimal amount of attention to his appearance, but he did like to look nice. He was wearing a cashmere crewneck sweater in a shade of blue that really brought out his eyes and charcoal-gray pleated trousers with a pair of black Italian loafers. The only jewelry he wore was his watch. He'd never admit it, but he was looking extra sharp in a casual sort of way. Turning off the light in the bedroom, he went to the hall closet and got out his full-length black lambskin coat, putting it on and picking up his black leather gloves from the console by the front door. He exited the condo and went to the Hummer, once again bypassing the Chrysler 300. He started the SUV and waited a few minutes for it to warm up before pulling out of the parking lot. While it warmed up he selected a mellow CD and wondered again what had possessed Paris to invite him to dinner.

She'd called him at his office on his private line and without any preliminaries, issued a perfunctory invitation without a hint of cordiality. "Titus, this is Paris. If you don't have any plans I'd like you to come to dinner on Saturday. My father will be in town and I'm cooking for him." She didn't say anything else, waiting for him to respond and giving him the distinct impression that she wanted him to refuse. Titus wheeled the Hummer through the early evening traffic and smiled as he recalled how crestfallen she'd sounded when he said he'd be happy to come. "Oh. Okay, fine. Saturday at eight. See you then," she'd said dully, and then hung up the phone.

He turned into the parking lot of his favorite wine shop. He selected two bottles of very fine vintage champagne, reasoning that champagne went with anything, including dessert. In addition, it was the only spirit he'd ever seen Paris consume. She just wasn't a big drinker, but then again, neither was he. Other than an occasional glass of good wine with a fine meal, Titus didn't indulge much either. He stepped out into the cold night and looked down at the small shopping bag in his hand. For some reason it seemed inadequate; it didn't seem good enough for Paris. He looked across the street and spied a small flower shop with the name Blossoms by Betty on the striped awning. Miraculously, it was still open. He quickly crossed the street and entered the shop, which had an old-fashioned brass bell that tinkled to signal the presence of a customer. Titus went into a kind of sensory overload as soon as he crossed the threshold.

The shop was pretty and charming, even to Titus's untutored male eye. It looked like a miniature jungle with plants of every description and exotic blooms of rich and rare color.

There was a wonderful scent in the air from the flowers as well as from the scented candles and incense that were sold in the shop. A large white parrot in a brass cage whistled at Titus and a big black cat sprawled on the counter, enhancing the atmosphere. Titus looked around with doubtful eyes, growing uneasy at the prospect before him. He was completely out of his depth here. He'd sent virtually no flowers in his dating life; his brand of courtship didn't dictate that kind of behavior. He was pretty sure he was totally inadequate to make a good selection. Maybe he should just forget his ill-advised impulse and take his chances with the wine. He was about to leave when a voice stopped him.

"When in doubt, carnations are always nice."

Titus turned to the source of the remark and faced a tall, older woman with a spectacular head of hair that may or may not have been hers. It looked almost too perfect to be her real hair, but she was so attractive it was hard to believe it was fake. She looked at him over the top of her reading glasses and smiled. "I could fix you up a nice selection of carnations I'm sure your young lady would enjoy. We have several different colors, what do you think she'd like?"

"Ah, umm, I'm not sure," Titus muttered. He stared helplessly at the glass fronted refrigerated units that housed the cut flowers.

The smiling woman gave him a knowing look and stroked the big black cat as she asked Titus another question. "What kind of flower is she?" Titus stared blankly at the woman, who chuckled quietly. "All women are like flowers, you know. We all have an essential nature that's evocative of a specific bloom," she told him. "So I ask you again, if she were a flower, what would she be?"

"A rose," he said without any more hesitation. "Definitely a big pretty rose."

The woman's smile got even bigger. "Well, then. What color?"

"Something warm," he answered. "Pink or something like that. Something very feminine and romantic, but really sexy at the same time." He felt his face grow warm at the deeply personal response, but he stood by his answer.

The lady gave the cat a last long caress and moved around the counter. She walked to the unit and opened the door. Reaching into a vase, she took out a rose of an unusual color, a deep bronze with a pink undertone. "This is a cinnamon rose. How about I make up an arrangement of these with a few lighter ones for contrast and some nice greenery? And what about a nice vase? If she's making dinner for you she might not have time to look for something to put these in. How does that sound?"

Titus nodded, even as he wondered how the woman knew Paris was making dinner for him. He didn't have time to dwell on it too much as the black cat took a great interest in him and walked down the counter to begin a minute inspection of Titus's hands, which were resting there. The parrot added several comments in French, which would have compounded his unease but in mere minutes the woman was finished. The result was so beautiful even Titus could see it for a work of art. He thanked the woman effusively and assured her it would be much appreciated as he handed her one of his platinum cards with which to pay for it.

"Thank you, dear. When you need anything else, stop and see me again. I'm Betty and I have a feeling I'll be seeing a lot more of you in the near future." She chuckled.

Titus wanted to tell her that she was wrong, that this was a spur-of-the-moment thing, a one-time occurrence, but she looked so pleased he didn't want to burst her bubble. He just nodded and made his escape. As he was crossing the street,

Betty watched him go. She looked at the cat and said, "Pyewacket, I believe I'll be doing a wedding for that young man."

The cat meowed in agreement and even the parrot chimed in. "True love, true love."

"You're so right, Penelope. He may not realize it yet, but that man has the look of love all over him. Now let's lock up, shall we?"

Despite her vows to remain calm and wittily sophisticated this evening, her heart jumped when she realized it was Titus at the front door. It had to be Titus, since her father had arrived on Friday afternoon. Ruth was also already there as she had come over at seven to help, even though Paris had protested she didn't need any assistance. She was actually glad of Ruth's presence for a couple of reasons. For one thing, Paris had seen a light go on in her father's eyes that she hadn't seen since her mother died. As young as she'd been when that tragic event occurred, she could remember vividly how much in love her parents had been. They had been warm and affectionate with each other every day and Paris could remember them kissing all the time, although she couldn't remember a single argument. The looks on Mac's and Ruth's faces when they met was something Paris wasn't going to forget for a long time and she'd see to it they remembered, too. Aidan might scoff, but Paris just knew when a couple was meant for each other, even though she'd been totally wrong about Titus.

When Ruth had arrived, Paris had opened the door and greeted her, complimenting her on her appearance. Ruth looked fabulous in a dark green merino jersey dress that fit her body like a glove and barely skimmed her knees, leaving her long legs on display. It brought out the clear jade green of her eyes, but she didn't look too dressy, thanks to the very chic and expensive leather flats on her feet. Then Mac walked into the living room to greet the new arrival. Paris made the introductions and Mac took Ruth's hand in his for what was supposed to be a handshake but neither one of them seemed to want to let go. They started a conversation that showed no sign of ending. At the moment Ruth was snuggled into one end of the sofa while Mac sat on the other end, regaling her with his wit while he stole glances at her slender, shapely legs.

Paris was so happy that her plan seemed to be working she momentarily forgot they were expecting a fourth until the doorbell sounded. Now she stood in front of the big oak door with her heart in her mouth, wondering again what had possessed Ruth to force her to invite Titus. She tucked her hair behind one ear, took a deep breath and opened the door. There he was, looking better than he had any right to, with shopping bags in both hands. "Hello, Titus, come on in out of the cold," she said with a forced smile.

He entered, towering over her in a way that made her want to scream. The sheer size of him drove her mad; she always felt so dainty next to him. She offered to take the bags from him and he shook his head no. He set the smaller of the two bags on the floor and handed her the large one, a dark green one with the words Blossoms by Betty in a stylized gold script on the front of the bag. "Is that for me?" she asked softly.

"Of course it is. Open it," he said patiently.

Paris set the bag on the round table next to the front door and gasped when she took out the contents. There was a round amber bowl like a fishbowl filled with the most amazing looking roses, all bronze except for a few ivory ones and a dusky pink one in the center. There were feathery green ferns and the combination of the greenery and the unusual spicy scent of the flowers temporarily rendered Paris speechless. She stared at the bowl in her hands, and then at Titus, who was looking at her with an expression that was difficult to read. If it had been anyone else she would have said he was looking at her fondly, but that was just crazy. Still, looking into those eyes of his made her remember her manners.

"Titus, what a lovely surprise. Thanks so much," she murmured. "I'm going to put these in the living room so we can all enjoy them. Do you mind hanging up your coat? I seem to have my hands full," she said with a smile. Her words were somewhat superfluous as he was already removing his coat and heading for the closet, since he knew where it was. Paris tried hard not to gape at him as she gazed at his mighty shoulders encased in the fine knit of the sweater, but it was darned hard not to as he looked like a fashion spread in a men's magazine. She tried to maintain her equilibrium as she led him into the living room, bearing her floral treasure. Carefully placing the bowl in the center of the coffee table, she reintroduced Titus to her father and Ruth.

"Daddy, you remember Titus Argonne, don't you? Titus, this is my father, Julian Deveraux. And of course, this is Ruth Bennett, Benita's aunt. I think you may have met her a time or two," she said.

The older couple greeted Titus, with her father reminding him to call him Mac. "Nobody calls me Julian," he said. "I'm so used to being called Mac or Judge, I don't know if I'd answer," he joked.

Ruth looked disappointed. "That's too bad. I love the name Julian," she said with a little sigh. "It suits you so well," she added.

Mac turned a glazed look on her. "You can call me anything you like, Ruth. Whatever pleases you." They smiled at each other and for a moment Paris could have sworn her father was purring, and then she realized it was Merlin who was draped across the back of the sofa basking in Mac's aura.

"Daddy, Merlin really likes you. And he doesn't like many people, so you should be flattered," she told him.

"Merlin smells Bojangles, that's what he likes about me," Mac said. He explained to Ruth that Bojangles was a cat who'd been abandoned by the courthouse and who had adopted Mac, going home with him and taking over the house. "Now he rules the premises with a paw of iron. No decision of any importance is made without his approval. Luckily he's a benevolent despot and allows me the illusion that I'm still the master of my fate."

Just as Paris asked Titus what he wanted to drink, Merlin caught sight of him and hissed. Paris scolded the big cat. "Merlin, stop that. He's not a date, he's just visiting, and you don't have to go all territorial on him." She said she'd be right back with the drinks and left the room without noticing the look on Titus's face. Ruth excused herself to help Paris and left the two men alone.

They sat in silence for a moment while Merlin decided to escalate the hostilities between him and Titus. Made bold by the presence of his new best friend, Mac, Merlin slithered down from his perch on the back of the couch and presented himself before Titus. He sat up in front of the big man like an Egyptian deity and trained his large green eyes on Titus's blue-gray ones, emitting a low vibrato. It was one of the strongest weapons in his arsenal, the one that unnerved even the most stalwart of Paris's dates. Titus leaned forward and whispered, "Boo." Merlin jumped straight in the air and flew out of the room while Titus leaned back in his chair and collapsed in laughter.

Mac laughed as well, but then he addressed Titus with utter seriousness in his voice. "You're good at keeping cats at bay, but how are you with humans? Are you sure you can keep my baby girl safe? She's my only daughter. I can't get another one and wouldn't want one. I wouldn't trade my baby for her weight in gold. Paris is very, very precious to me and to her brothers. I need your assurance that you can protect her," he said with a lethal calm.

Titus sat up straight and gave the older man a steely look of confidence and commitment. "I'd lay down my life for Paris, sir. I have the best investigative staff in the country and I want you to understand that we're going to find the person who's making these threats before they escalate into something else. However, you have to know that no one is going to touch her, not while I'm alive to protect her. If she were my daughter I'd probably be just as concerned as you are, but you have my personal assurance that no one can harm Paris and continue to live. You have my word on that."

Mac seemed to relax slightly after hearing those words. "Tell me the truth, son. What's really going on here? Has anything happened other than someone sending a couple of crank letters to the studio?"

Titus nodded his head. "Yes. There have actually been seven letters sent, three that Paris isn't aware of and I want to keep it that way. I brought photocopies of them for you to see, sir, I had a feeling you'd want to be more aware of the true situation," he said. "I'll be right back," he added, rising from the chair and going to the hall closet. He retrieved the copies from his coat pocket and handed them to Mac.

"I have to warn you, sir, they're graphic in the extreme. This is what got Aidan's attention in the first place. He recognized them as being the work of a sick mind and moved in here with Paris to protect her."

Mac quickly perused the letters while his face paled and his expression showed how the contents disturbed him. "This is a sick bastard," he said quietly. "I've been an officer of the court for a long time and I've seen and heard all manner of depravity over the years. But to see something like that directed at my own child…" His voice trailed off and for a brief moment he looked old and haggard. It passed so quickly it was like a trick of the light. The real Mac was back, resolute and determined, demanding answers. He insisted on knowing every detail of the investigation to date and what the plans were to flush out the culprit. He leaned forward, placing his elbows on his knees. "Do you have any leads, son? Do you have any idea at all who could be doing this, and why?"

Titus admitted the going was slow so far. "We're keeping a careful eye on some prospects who've been known to do this to other celebrities. There are some people who form bizarre attachments to people in the public eye. We're also investigating any people who might have a personal grudge against Paris for reasons real or imagined." He gave the older man a quick smile. "That part is a little more difficult, frankly. Paris is very well liked by everyone. We're having a hard time finding anyone who has a bad thing to say about her. She's a wonderful person, sir. You raised a beautiful and remarkable young woman," he said without realizing how much he'd revealed in those few words. "There's the matter of an employee she had to terminate recently. We're actually having a little trouble tracking her down. She seems to have disappeared, but we'll have her run to earth in a day or so."

Mac looked down at the floor while he considered Titus's words. "She hasn't seen this filth, has she?" The older man indicated the discarded letters next to him on the sofa. When Titus said no, Mac looked at them and sighed. "That's probably a good idea. I wouldn't want her to see them, they're too disgusting. But you've got your hands full with my girl. I don't imagine she's making this easy for you."

Titus grinned. "She doesn't like all the precautions. She

hates them, as a matter of fact. But she's gone along with everything so far."

Mac looked at Titus and leaned back against the sofa cushions. He looked Titus over carefully and then leaned forward again. "This isn't any of my business, and the timing of this question couldn't be worse, but I have to know. What happened between you and my daughter?"

Chapter 10

Titus was doing his best to look cool and controlled but it was difficult in the face of Mac's pointed question. And the older man wasn't finished, either. "You seemed quite taken with my daughter a few months ago. From what I could deduce, there was a great deal of affection and interest there and now the two of you are acting like you're strangers. What happened?"

At that moment Paris and Ruth returned with wine, cheese straws and crudités. "Dinner will be on the table shortly. In the meantime, please help yourselves. What are you fellas talking about?" Paris asked cheerily as she and Ruth sat down.

Mac smiled wickedly and raised an eyebrow at Titus. "We were talking about you, Cupcake, and how beautiful you are."

Paris almost choked on the long spear of cucumber she'd just begun to nibble. "Daddy," she said reproachfully. "Don't go there," she added with a frown, not daring to look at Titus. She sighed in relief as the oven timer went off. "Saved by the bell. *You,* that is," she said giving her beloved father the same look many a recalcitrant attorney had seen in his courtroom. "Behave yourself if you want dessert. If you'd like to freshen up, everything will be on the table in about ten minutes."

She excused herself, unaware that she really did make a very pretty picture. She was wearing slim-fitting black velvet pants and a matching top with a portrait neckline. Her feet were in little leopard-print leather flats and she looked sophisticated and sexy without being blatant about it. Soon everyone was seated at the table with heads bowed as Mac said grace. When Paris looked up it was to find Titus staring at her with a heated look that was as arousing as it was disturbing. Determined to get through the meal with her dignity intact, she ignored the hot flush that assailed her body and smiled gaily. "Daddy, will you do the honors?" she asked, indicating the carving knife and fork next to the plump, golden brown capon in the center of the table.

Mac carved the bird expertly and quickly and soon everyone was dining on the moist, tender capon stuffed with wild rice, dried cherries and toasted pecans, sweet potatoes a l'orange, grilled asparagus and hot cornbread muffins, followed by a spinach and pear salad with a balsamic vinaigrette dressing

The conversation was light and amusing and the food and wine were superb. Paris, thanks to her aunt Lillian and her own vivacious charm, had the gift of exquisite hospitality. Coffee and dessert, which was intensely rich chocolate brownies with *crème fraiche* and raspberry sauce, was served in the living room. It was the perfect ending to a lovely evening, an evening that turned out much better than Paris could have anticipated, given the presence of Titus. She was relaxed and mellow, or at least she was until Ruth announced that it was time for her to leave.

"Paris, darling, it was wonderful. Thanks so much for having me. But I've got to get back to Benita and Clay's house before I fall asleep," she joked. "The food was delicious and you're a fabulous hostess," she added warmly.

Mac rose and insisted that he would follow Ruth home to make sure she arrived safely. Ruth tried to refuse, but one look at the determined look on Mac's handsome face made her acquiesce graciously. Paris was mentally clapping her hands with glee at what she considered her latest triumph in matchmaking. Then Titus announced he would remain with her until Mac returned. Her eyes met Ruth's as Mac was holding Ruth's ivory cashmere coat for her. Paris's eyes were full of panic, while Ruth's green ones were full of merriment.

"Titus, that's a good idea," she said calmly. "I'm sure we won't be long, Paris, and you'll have good company until your father gets back. Since Aidan is out of town it's the best thing, really. I'll call you later." She kissed Paris on the cheek. And before Paris could protest, they were out the door and she was left alone with Titus. *I am* so *going to get her,* Paris thought furiously. *Traitor*.

She crossed her arms tightly and took in a deep breath before turning to face Titus. "Look, you don't have to stay here. I'm a big girl and I don't need a keeper. It's bad enough that your people are hovering around and poking into my life. I definitely don't need a babysitter while Daddy's away. You can leave now," she said tightly.

She turned away from him to go into the dining room and to her dismay he was right on her heels. "I'm not leaving, Paris. We need to talk," he said, his deep voice pouring over her like hot honey.

Paris tried to ignore him, making sure that everything in the dining room was returned to its normal pristine condition. Finding nothing out of place, she went into the kitchen, hoping to find something to do, but she and Ruth had been too thorough in their post-dinner tidying up. Looking vainly for a task, she ended up leaning against the sink, arms still crossed. She refused to meet Titus's eyes as she denied his assertion that they had something to discuss. "I can't think of a single thing we have to talk about, Titus. All the security issues have been hammered into my head a thousand times so what else is there to say?"

Titus moved so that he was standing in front of her, putting one big hand on either side of her. "There's a lot left to say, Paris. We need to talk about us," he said softly.

Paris's breathing turned shallow and fast as the closeness of Titus's big body overwhelmed her senses. His smell still had the same unique power over her, his personal pheromones aroused her, touching off sparks in every erogenous zone she possessed. "There is no 'us,' Titus. You made that…abundantly clear," she murmured. She moaned softly as he leaned even closer and his hands moved to her hips and squeezed gently. "Stop it, Titus." She sighed. "This isn't right. We're not right together, remember?"

He answered her by touching his lips to the corner of her eye, then moving down to her cheekbone. "The only thing wrong is the timing, Paris. We have a lot of things to talk about but we have a big obstacle blocking our path. I'm supposed to be protecting you, so that means you're off-limits to me right now."

Paris sighed raggedly as his hands moved up her hips to encircle her waist and pull her into his body, his arms enfolding her and holding her closer than close, so tightly she could feel his every breath. Before she knew what she was doing, she slid her arms around him to return his embrace. "You shouldn't be…holding me like this," she whispered.

He maneuvered her lush curves even closer and tightened his arms around her warmth while rubbing his cheek against her hair and inhaling her beloved scent. "Look at me, Paris," he crooned. "Look at me just once, baby."

She turned her face to his and was instantly mesmerized by the passion she found there. "I had to touch you, Paris. Even if it makes you hate me more, I had to feel you one more time, taste those lips." He paused and kissed her gently. "Oh, damn, Paris, I can't—"

"Lucy, I'm hoooome!" Aidan's cheerful voice could be heard as he opened the door that led from the garage to the laundry room. "Miss me much?" He walked into the kitchen to find Paris and Titus still locked in each other's arms. "Guess not. My bad, people. See ya," he said with ill-concealed amusement as he walked through the kitchen without breaking stride.

Paris was scarlet with embarrassment and anger as she pushed Titus away. "Okay, you can leave my sitter is home. Good night," she said hotly and left the room.

Titus leaned against the sink until his steady, slow breaths returned his pulse to normal. If it had been anyone else he'd have laughed at the situation but right now he wasn't amused in the least. *You're not getting away from me that easily, Paris. This isn't the end, baby. It's just the beginning.*

The ride to Benita and Clay's suburban home didn't take long. Ruth looked into her rearview mirror and smiled. There was something comforting in knowing that someone cared enough about her well-being to make sure she arrived safely, especially when that someone happened to be tall, charming and very handsome. It was almost enough to make her reverse her stance on blind dating. *I owe Paris something very, very nice for this,* she thought. *Maybe a diamond tiara or a Rolls Royce or a trip around the world, some little trifle to show her how glad I am she thought of this.* She laughed softly to herself as she parked the car in the big turnaround at the top of the driveway. She was still laughing when Mac graciously opened her door and held out his hand to her.

"You're obviously amused by something," he said in his deep voice. "Care to share?" She placed her hand into his and gracefully exited the car. Smiling up at him brilliantly, she confessed that she wasn't amused at all.

"I'm happy, if you really want to know. I can't remember when I enjoyed an evening as much as this one."

Mac tipped her head up so he could look into her luminous eyes more deeply. "I'm glad to hear that, Ruth. I'm glad I'm not the only one who's thoroughly excited by our meeting." He bent his head and gently touched his lips to hers. He smiled ruefully and apologized. "I shouldn't have done that without asking."

Ruth raised an eyebrow and smiled as she pulled his head down to hers. She kissed him back, softly but firmly. "Now we're even. I didn't ask either. Would you like to come in for coffee? Then we can talk about our lapse of manners and what we can do about it."

Mac smiled and kissed her on the cheek. "I'd love to." He put his hand at the small of her back and they entered the big house, using Ruth's key. He put his hand over hers to stop her. He'd stopped smiling and looked completely serious. "I may as well tell you now, Ruth, I intend to kiss you again before I leave."

Ruth tried to look equally serious but failed. She reached up to cup her hand around his cheek. "And I intend to let you. Would you like decaf or regular?"

Chapter 11

The next week was so hectic Paris didn't have time to dwell on the events of the weekend. She was hard at work on a new project for *Paris & Company*, one that had come up unexpectedly. Her best friend from college had called her with an amazing announcement. He was a major jazz artist and he'd been nominated for not one but two Academy Awards. Not only had he been nominated, he was going to be performing at the award show and he was taking Paris as his guest. She was still stunned by the news. It was frankly unimaginable to her. She tried to explain it to Aidan over lunch at the Pleasant Peasant. The restaurant was an Atlanta institution they both enjoyed and they were savoring a leisurely meal while Paris gloated over her projected stroll down the legendary red carpet with her friend.

"I met Billy in college when I was going to Mount Holyoke and he was attending the New England Conservatory of Music. We got to be really good friends. We were like brother and sister," Paris reported. Her eyes were sparkling as she took another sip of tea. "To be honest, I had a huge crush on him, but it didn't go anywhere. I wasn't exactly a man magnet back then," she said ruefully.

Aidan scoffed as he helped himself to more bread. "If he didn't view you romantically it's his loss. You're beautiful inside and out and if he was too dense to see that, he didn't deserve you."

Paris blinked. "Aidan, that was so sweet. Thank you."

He rolled his eyes in mock irritation, saying it was stupid to thank people for telling the truth. "Now cut to the chase and tell me how you managed to get invited to walk the carpet, something I've wanted to do since I was a mere child. I'm so jealous I could scream," he admitted.

"I always love watching the Oscars, although I never pictured myself being there. Billy wrote the score for one of the movies nominated for Best Picture, and his music was nominated for best score and best original song. It's a huge honor for him and he said he wanted to share it with me because I'd always meant so much to him. Isn't that something?" she marveled.

"So who is this guy and why have I never heard of him before?"

"Because you're not a jazz buff, that's why. Billy Watanabe is *hot*, honey. His music is revered. He's considered one of the most respected jazz pianists in the world. His father, Akiro Watanabe, is also a world-known jazz musician and his mother, Juanita, is considered the best jazz harpist since Alice Coltrane as well as being an amazing singer. If you listened to something other than Nine Inch Nails and Siouxsie and the Banshees you might know that," she said with a wicked grin.

"The best part is that he's coming to Atlanta to work with Bump on a CD and he's going to be on *Paris & Company*. And I'm going to do a special on the Awards, since I'm going to be out there anyway. It's going to be a lot of fun, but a lot of work, too. We'll be taping out there for three days," she said happily. "This is going to do a lot for the show; it should give us a nice little boost in the ratings."

Aidan looked skeptical as Paris gave a big smile to the hostess approaching their table. "You haven't said what Lord Voldemort has to say about all this travel. Does he approve you going out of town? He may have to assign someone to go with you."

Paris made a sound of derision. "Titus is not my daddy, and he certainly can't tell me how to handle my work. I'm also going to a romance readers' conference. I wish he would try to keep me from going. I'd beat him like he stole something if he tries to curtail my traveling because I don't intend to miss that. If he wants to send someone with me that's his business, but he can't stop me," she said with a hard look.

"Miss Deveraux, this was left for you," a soft voice interjected.

Paris looked up to find the hostess holding out a long narrow box tied with a dark red ribbon. She thanked the woman and took the box, opening it before Aidan could stop her. "I wonder what this could be," she said, as curious as a child. The hostess shrieked as the tissue paper moved and a corn snake slithered out of the box, its tongue flicking in and out. Paris dropped the box and chaos erupted in the restaurant as the hostess fainted dead away while Aidan's chair fell over as he attempted to snatch Paris away from the table. A quick-thinking server came to the rescue by using the tablecloth to capture the snake. He grabbed the corners of the cloth and in seconds was holding a messy bundle consisting of partially eaten food, a broken glass, silverware and a very angry snake.

Aidan looked at Paris, who was visibly shaken, and said, "Check, please."

* * *

Now it was serious. Titus was, in a strange way, almost glad about the snake incident because Paris at last believed that someone was after her. Unfortunately, the police were also involved now, since the restaurant manager called them after the melee in the main dining room. The normally serene restaurant resembled a TV drama crime scene, complete with yellow "Do Not Enter" tape and forensics people milling about importantly. Paris sat to one side, glumly surveying the mess and Aidan remained close by, the look on his face daring anyone to approach her. Titus stood to one side, quietly talking to an old acquaintance from the Atlanta Police Department. The man was a detective and over the years he and Titus had formed a friendship based on *quid pro quo*; they had been known to help each other out from time to time.

The older man was named Luther Harris and he was not only a calm person, but also a highly intelligent one, one of the reasons he and Titus got along so well. "So you say the woman has gotten threatening mail before this? And you didn't think this was something we should know about?" he asked mildly.

Titus shrugged. "The idea was to get the culprit before things escalated. The letters stopped and I was basically waiting to see if the hate mail was going to get it out of the guy's system or if something else was going to jump off. And it seems I was right," Titus answered with his eyes fixed on Paris's wan face.

"Yeah, you were right, but at what cost? That corn snake was harmless, but it could have just as easily been a coral snake and I don't have to remind you how poisonous they are. The note that was with the snake read, 'Since you like snakes so much, this one is for you.' What do you think that means?"

Titus made a face. "She had somebody on her show from

the Atlanta Zoo or something and she was handling some snakes like they weren't anything. She's not afraid of things like that and it apparently enraged the guy enough he decided to go after her."

"And you said the *guy?* Do you think it's a man who's doing this?" Luther inquired, discreetly following the trajectory of Titus's vision to its target. His expression changed slightly as he watched Titus observing Paris.

"Actually, I'm not sure at all. The most obvious suspect is a woman, as a matter of fact," Titus answered. He made an involuntary movement toward Paris when he saw Aidan touch her cheek. He thought for a minute she'd been crying but he could see that she and Aidan were joking around and the sight relieved him greatly. Luther stared at Titus, and then looked at Paris again. He shook his head before speaking.

"Looky-here, hometown, you and I need to have a talk. I'm about done here. When you wrap it up get me on my cell phone and I'ma let you buy me a steak. We really need to talk, T."

Paris was hard at work a couple of days later. The snake incident was far from forgotten, but in an odd way the outcome of the situation actually took some of the load off her shoulders. For one thing, even though Titus had been kind enough not to lecture her about rashly opening the package she'd been handed, she felt an odd sense of calm now. She'd been given proof that it wasn't just paranoia. There really was a nutburger out there with an agenda that involved her. The information should have made her feel scared and squeamish, but somehow knowing that Titus was taking care of things relieved her anxiety. Plus, he had, at her suggestion, informed her staff about what was going on. The agents who'd been assigned to the case were introduced properly at a special staff meeting at which Titus explained the gravity of the situation and elicited a promise that no one would speak of the investigation outside the studio. She had to admit to a certain little thrill when she recalled how serious and handsome he'd looked while issuing the edict and she'd been truly gratified by the reaction of her trusted staffers, including her director, assistant director, the stage manager and everyone else.

At that moment her director, Twillia, was eying her with concern. Her pretty round face displayed a puckered brow as she asked the question uppermost in everyone's mind. "Are you sure you're safe? You know you can stay at my house, no one will think of looking for you there. Besides, I have an uncle who'll knock the crap out of anyone who looks at you wrong. He was a Navy SEAL and he'll not only find out who's doing this, but he'll take them out, too," she said in a serious voice.

Paris smiled at the gravity she saw displayed and reached across her desk to pat Twillia's hand. "Thanks for the offer, but I'm perfectly fine where I am. Aidan wouldn't let anyone get to me and Titus has someone posted outside at all times. I feel like I'm living in a fort sometimes, but that's okay. After the snake thing I decided it couldn't hurt to be careful so I stopped giving Titus grief and let him do his thing." She stopped talking to go over her notes again and Twillia jumped in.

"But you're being so cool and calm, Paris. I don't know how you do it. That snake would have sent me packing back to my mama in Flint, Michigan," she said with a shudder that wasn't at all phony. She really did fear snakes.

"It wasn't poisonous. It looked like a coral snake, but it was a harmless snake with similar markings. It let me know that creep isn't giving up, whoever he is. The note he put in there also let me know he watches the show," she mumbled, still going over the papers in front of her. The intercom was switched on so she could hear the sounds from the studio. A strain of soft, melodic music made her head come up and her mouth drop open in shock. The sound was one of her favorite songs, "Harbor Lights" by Boz Scaggs and only one person could play it like that. She leaped from her seat and raced out of the room with Twillia following her.

Paris careened into the studio and stopped stock-still, with her hands pressed to her cheeks. She screamed and then ran straight into the arms of a tall stranger who rose from his seat at the piano and held his arms out to her.

"Billy! Oh, sugar, it's been way too long," Paris sighed as she snuggled into his arms for a long hug.

The tall man didn't answer for a moment; he was too busy squeezing the breath out of Paris. When he finally let go, it was only to step away from her so he could see her better. "Damn, Paris, you're a knockout. I didn't think you could get any more gorgeous and look at you now. Come give a brother some love, girl," he growled as he pulled her into his arms again, this time for a big kiss right on the lips, which is what Titus saw when he entered the studio.

He didn't say a word, but his eyes turned to ice and his jaw was so set and tight he could have sliced something with it. Paris finally realized he was in the room and introduced the two men.

"Billy, this is Titus Argonne. Titus, this is my friend Billy Watanabe. We've known each other for years," she said hurriedly.

Titus gave a curt nod and left abruptly, without saying a word.

Billy gave a low whistle and stared down at Paris. "Whoa. Paris, baby, what did you do to that man? If looks could kill I'd be a dead man right about now."

Paris's face grew hot and she hastened to assure Billy that he was imagining things. "Titus and I are, um, friends. He has offices here in the complex and he's in charge of corporate security for The Deveraux Group. That's all," she said in a voice that lacked conviction, something Billy picked up on right away.

"Right. Tell that to someone who doesn't know you. You need to let me know if that's your man or what, because I don't intend to get shot over you," he said, laughing at the look on her face.

Paris frowned. "You're just sick and wrong, Billy. Sick and wrong."

"I may be sick, but I'm not wrong. Something's going on between you and the big man. What is it?"

I just wish I knew, Paris thought.

Chapter 12

Paris sat back in the comfortable plush seat of the private corporate jet and leaned into the headrest with her eyes closed. She was exhausted; there was no other word for it. Only a few weeks had passed since the nominations for the Academy Awards had been announced, but the weeks had been full of activity. With February being Black History Month there had been special programs going on all over Atlanta, many of which she had attended as an emcee or presenter or just as an enthusiastic supporter. There were Deveraux Group functions as well, not to mention special programs on *Paris & Company*. And on top of everything else, she had to find the perfect outfit to wear to the Oscars. Outfits, *plural*, since there were going to be numerous smaller events to attend with Billy and her own coverage of the weekend for the show. Right now she was merely grateful for the long flight to Los Angeles; at least she could get a little sleep. Or she could if her companions would shut up.

She was seated next to Perry Turner, the designer who'd created her dress in what seemed like no time at all. Danny Watley, her hairdresser and dear friend from Michigan, was seated across from her next to Billy, and all three men were talking nonstop, or so it seemed to her. She was so happy that Twillia had introduced her to Perry, she'd forgive him anything, but Billy and Danny were on very uneven terrain with her right now. She opened her eyes briefly and looked at Perry's face, handsome even in profile, and sighed with happiness; the man was truly a godsend. Well, a *Regina*-send, that was for sure.

When Billy told her she was coming to the Oscars, the perfect dress became an immediate necessity. Before she could begin to get frantic about it, Twillia made a suggestion. "My Aunt Regina lives in Texas, but her best friend, Perry, lives in Flint and he's a fantastic designer," she told Paris. "He especially loves to make fancy clothes like wedding dresses and evening gowns. If I ask her, she can have him down here in a heartbeat."

And sure enough, Twillia's aunt Regina was more than happy to oblige. After a long and chatty conversation with Paris she assured her that Perry would be delighted to create something fabulous for her. "I'll call him for you right now," she said in her unique voice. It was deep and sexy and gave the listener the impression that she was about to burst into song any second. Paris commented on this to Twillia, who laughed.

"She just might do that. She has a beautiful singing voice. My auntie is something else—she can sing, she has two master's degrees and a pilot's license, she's a gourmet cook and a preacher. There isn't much she can't do," Twillia said proudly.

Perry had agreed at once to create something magnificent and unique for Paris to wear and had come to Atlanta that very weekend to begin the fittings. Paris was totally taken with Perry; it was impossible not to be. He was six-two with warm brown skin, sexy eyes that slanted down at the outer corner, a firmly sculpted mouth and a nicely muscled body. His hair was cut close to his scalp and his moustache and beard were styled with meticulous detail. He worked full time as a plant manager for one of the Big Three automakers, but clothing design was his true passion and he was very, very good at it. He'd created something exquisitely beautiful for Paris so she could hold her head high on the legendary red carpet stroll. While she tried to sleep, he and Danny were talking about the best way for her to wear her hair. It was why Danny was flying out to California with her, something that she was very happy about, but if he didn't shut up soon she was going to try her best to throw him out of the plane.

"From what you told me about the dress, I think she should wear her hair down to make her look even more feminine," Danny said. "I said she should wear it up in a classic style and she said something about her butt being too big, which is ridiculous. Everybody's not meant to have a skimpy behind. I told the heifer she needs to get over it. She's always talking about losing twenty more pounds, but she needs to quit talking about it and accept her body the way it is. I hate to admit it, since my main job is to pick on her, but she looks damned good the way she is."

Billy chimed in, which made Paris vow to get him at her earliest opportunity. "Yeah, she really does. When we were in school she was bigger, just as pretty, but bigger. Now she's almost too skinny. I mean, where's she gonna take twenty pounds *from?* Not from the breasts—they look good just the way they are," he said fervently.

Perry agreed wholeheartedly. "Oh, definitely not the breasts, they're perfect. And not from the hips either, or the butt. I love a woman with curves and hers are all just right."

Billy laughed. "I know someone else who'd agree with

that—the big man. I'll bet he doesn't want her losing a pound. Not an ounce. He saw me giving her a hello kiss and he almost pulled a gun on me, swear to God he did."

All three men laughed, and then Perry had to tell his story of meeting Titus. "I was fitting the muslin shell for the dress the way I always do. I make up a dress in muslin and use it to fit the dress perfectly before I ever cut the dress fabric. I end up writing all over it with a special pen and quite naturally my hands are all over her body while I'm doing this. Well, we were in her office and I'm doing what I do and my hands were on her bust because this is what I was fitting."

Billy and Danny looked at each other and grinned. Perry had to laugh, too. "You can just about guess what happened then. There was a quick knock at the door and in he walked to find me touching his Paris. The big man is likely to have lost his mind up in there. I had my hands on his woman's pretty breasts and he wasn't having it. Before anybody could say a word he had an Uzi pressed against my temple and suggested I put my hands someplace else in a hurry."

Paris spoke without opening her eyes. "I can hear you, you know. I hear all those lies and exaggerations and all I can say is you need to quit. Titus is not my man, and it's just not that deep, so please cut it out."

Perry reached over and gave Paris's hand a squeeze. "Baby, the truth is the light and all we're doing is telling the truth. And it shall set you free, my dear."

Paris sat up and opened her eyes to look at her tormentors. "I'm telling you all, you're wrong. Titus and I are not a couple. He's doing his best to keep that freak from making good on his threats, that's all. I'm his charge, not his woman," she said crossly.

Billy smiled lazily. "Okay, sure. Fine. But if that's the case, why did he act like he did when you were in the accident?"

Paris stared at Billy's handsome bronze face with its mixture of African-American and Japanese features and frowned. His black wavy hair was worn long, down past his shoulders with the top part pulled into a ponytail and the rest flowing down his back. His exotically slanted eyes were merry, and so was his generous mouth, smiling over the stylized goatee he wore. He leaned forward and challenged Paris even more. "Go ahead, baby girl, and tell us why he acted like he did after your accident."

Paris leaned back again and closed her eyes. It didn't pay to have a friend as perceptive as Billy who knew her so well. There was no hiding anything from him.

The accident to which Billy referred had occurred two weeks before and the memory of it still made Paris wake up in the middle of the night covered with a fine sheen of perspiration. After the snake episode, the security around Paris had increased. She went from resenting the presence of Titus's agents in her life to welcoming them. There was one woman she liked particularly, a small blonde named Heide. She was tough and fearless and did her job efficiently and discreetly. She was also a good conversationalist and Paris found it easy to chat with her. One Friday night, Heide had confided that she was anxious to get home because her daughter had been running a temperature and Paris encouraged her to go straight home.

"Don't worry about a thing. You don't need to trail me. The weather is so rotten only a truly dedicated freak would try something tonight," she said, laughing. It was indeed a nasty night, with a thick sleeting rain and slick streets awaiting any drivers. Heide hesitated to go along with this idea but Paris insisted. "I'll be fine. You go on and see about your baby. I'm driving one of those granny-looking plain Jane corporate cars and I'll be perfectly safe. If it makes you feel better we can talk on our cell phones all the way home, how's that?"

Thus persuaded, Heide finally agreed to the plan and each woman went her separate way, staying in touch via cell phone. The roads were treacherous. The sleet was accumulating and turning into serious ice. In order to stay on the road Paris had to drive slowly and with great caution. She was a good driver but this was unnerving. There were too many people trying to drive too fast to get out of the storm and it created the perfect setting for an accident. Suddenly, the driver directly in front of her slammed on the brakes and the vehicle started spinning out of control. Her eyes widened and her hands gripped the steering wheel even tighter as she watched the car careen into another car. She registered the sickening squeal of brakes and the metallic crash, but her mind was on avoiding her own collision. Paris had no choice. She had to get out of the way and fast. She quickly put her foot on the brake and prepared to slow down to ease into a turn. Instead of slowing down, the car maintained its speed. It actually seemed to go even faster on the black ice of the pavement. She had the sickening realization that the brakes were gone as she repeatedly pressed the pedal, which pumped freely underfoot instead of catching and making the car stop. Pure, unadulterated terror took over as she frantically turned the wheel so she wouldn't rear-end the driver ahead of her. The car veered to the right and skidded off the pavement, hitting the guardrail and flipping over into the ditch that ran along the roadside. It was all over in mere seconds, with Paris mercifully unconscious and miraculously unhurt. Heide had arrived at her home by the time the accident occurred and called 911 immediately, then called Titus.

When Paris opened her eyes she was in the emergency room dressed in a hideous hospital gown. She was lying on an uncomfortable table being examined by a calm and competent resident doctor. Titus was there, too. To a stranger he would look calm and in control, but Paris could recognize his mood by the color of his eyes, which were the icy silver she'd come to know and dread. She cringed on seeing him. She knew he was furious with her, as he should be. This was all her fault. She should have done what she was directed to do and not involved Heide in her madness. Whatever he had to say to her, she'd have to bear it; whatever he dished out, she'd have to take because this was her bad and her responsibility.

To her utter surprise he didn't say anything at all to her; he just stood quietly next to her examining table, holding her hand while the doctor finished checking her over. She had a bump on her temple and a small cut on her cheekbone, and her neck was stiff and sore from the impact of her airbag. She was rather sore all over, something that would increase overnight. By tomorrow she would feel like crap and look it, too, of that she was sure. Titus and the resident helped her sit up and she leaned against Titus's comforting strength while the doctor looked into her eyes with his little penlight. She didn't wince when the doctor's surgically gloved fingers touched the cut on her face, but Titus did. She both heard and felt the sharp intake of his breath as the doctor touched her. Finally he spoke, his deep voice betraying his concern.

"Is it going to leave a scar?" he asked gruffly.

"Oh no, it's not deep at all. I'm not even going to put in stitches, just a butterfly tape, and it'll heal up nicely," the doctor said cheerfully.

"That's good. No one as beautiful as she is should have to wear a scar," Titus said quietly. He was holding both her hands and staring into her eyes as if she was the most precious thing in the world to him. She could see the warm blue color she loved returning. The doctor left, saying he would get her into a room because they wanted to keep her for observation. Now Paris was alone with Titus and she steeled herself for the harsh words she deserved. She squared her shoulders and began to speak.

"Titus, it's my fault, all mine. I shouldn't have told Heide not to follow me. I should have done as you've told me over and over again. I'm sorry—" His lips on hers silenced her words as he kissed her gently.

"Shh, baby, it's okay. Even if Heide had been right behind you, it would have happened. Your car was tampered with," he informed her. "In a bizarre way, this gives us a lead because it means whoever is behind this has access to the complex. Whoever did this was able to get to the parking structure in the complex and there's a good possibility we have that person on surveillance tape. In any case, the only important thing is that you weren't hurt," he said soothingly. "If something had happened to you, Paris, if you'd been killed…" Now it was Titus who had stopped talking and enfolded her in his arms, kissing her gently but with so much passion and tenderness that even now, two weeks later, she still got breathless remembering it. His words were as comforting as his arms around her.

"Don't be so hard on yourself, baby. This is my job. I'm going to take care of you, Paris. Nobody's going to do anything to you, not while I'm alive." She felt comforted to her very soul and knew at that moment that nothing could possibly hurt her.

The rest of the night was a blur. She was admitted to a room and Titus sat next to her bed, holding her hand until she fell asleep. When she woke up she felt the warmth of a strong male hand wrapped around hers and she smiled sleepily, opening her eyes to see Titus's warm gaze. Instead she stared into Julian's dark eyes and gasped. Glancing around, she realized they were all there, with Lucien sitting at the foot of her bed, Wade and Philippe at the head, and Julian sitting in the chair next to her. She grimaced and pulled the sheet over her head, or tried to, but Wade and Philippe were too quick for her and stopped her.

"None of that, now," Wade admonished her. Julian, who was holding her hand, agreed.

"We come in peace, Coco," he said. Tears sprang to her eyes when she heard the endearment only used by her brothers. It was a diminutive of her middle name, Corinna, and a play on the fact that she had adored cocoa when she was a little girl. "Titus called Judge last night to let him know what happened. And Judge finally let us know what's been going on with you and we got here as fast as we could."

Paris groaned. "Please tell me you didn't make a scene or start a fight with Titus or something. Did anybody have to post bail last night?"

Lucien laughed and squeezed Paris's foot from his post at the end of the bed. "Touché, Coco. But you can be proud of us. We all behaved like perfect gentlemen, believe it or not. We might have been marginally upset that certain information has been withheld from us regarding specific events in your life," he said in a voice heavy with irony. "And some of us may, in fact, have engaged in a physical demonstration of how little we liked being kept in the dark about our only sister being threatened," he added in a studiedly casual voice, suddenly turning away from Paris.

Philippe gave a harsh laugh. "What he means is that he took a swing at your boy and got popped."

Lucien raised his lip in derision at his brother. He faced Paris who could now see a slight swelling and redness along Luc's jaw. "Ignore him, Coco, you know how he lies. It's why he can't keep a woman."

Philippe quickly offered a repeat of last night's performance with him playing the Titus role, an offer that Lucien ignored. "Suffice it to say we were persuaded that no purpose would be served by our usual behavior and we managed to hold it down. In fact, we kinda like your boyfriend now," he added carelessly.

"You what?" Paris asked weakly.

"Your man, that Titus," Julian said. "He's a good man, Paris. He's got a good head on his shoulders and he has an outstanding reputation as well as an excellent credit rating."

Despite the pain in her head and the general achiness of her body, Paris rose up on her elbows in indignation. "You investigated him? Good God, what is wrong with you? Why in the world would you go snooping into his background? Are you all clinically insane and no one bothered to tell me about it?" she raged.

"Coco, calm down, little sis," Philippe said. "We only did it because he told us to."

Paris's head swiveled around painfully as she looked at each brother with her mouth open in shock. "He told you to investigate him," she repeated in a voice full of doubt.

"He did," Wade assured her. "He said if you were his sister he'd be equally inquisitive about anyone you were involved with and he couldn't blame us for being concerned. Then he said we could check him out to make sure he was legit and we did. Lucien had his laptop with him as always and we went online and checked him out."

Paris couldn't believe what she was hearing. "Are you telling me you actually went digging in the man's background, invading his privacy and snooping into his personal business? Are there no depths to which you won't sink?" Her voice was as hot as her face, which was flaming with anger.

Her brothers looked at each other, then at her, and answered in one voice, "No."

Julian elaborated. "Listen, sweet girl, when it comes to you, there's nothing we won't do to protect you, and Titus feels the same way. That gives us something in common. We may have gotten off to a rough start but he seems to be a pretty good guy. You could do a lot worse," he added. "He picked us up at the airport and we had a chance to really talk to him. He's cool with us."

This time, her brothers weren't able to prevent her from pulling the sheet over her head and moaning out loud. Having them despise Titus was bad enough, but having them develop a liking for him was infinitely scarier. With the sheet still protecting her, she asked where Judge was. "Where's Daddy? Didn't he come with you?"

"Of course he did, Coco. Actually, he had his own ride from the airport. A lady picked him up, believe it or not. He says you introduced them," Wade said. "Good work, baby sis, she is *fine*."

After spending the night in the hospital she went home. Aunt Ruth and Mac and the boys fussed over her all day and made sure she was comfortable and cosseted. But the thing that stood out in her mind the most was the loving care she'd gotten from Titus in the emergency room. Billy might be right—the way Titus reacted that night was indicative of something, but she was too gun-shy to speculate. Right then all she wanted to do was sleep.

Paris wasn't the only one with mixed emotions about her hospital adventure. Ruth had her share of memories to mull over, as well. She replayed the events of those days over and over and she still hadn't come to any satisfactory conclusions. While Paris was winging her way to sunny California, Ruth was also taking a trip, but she was going to Chicago to visit some girlfriends. And she had company all the way because she couldn't stop thinking about the days she'd spent with Mac Deveraux. She looked out of the plane window and the only thing she could see was his handsome smiling face. She leaned against the headrest and thought about the day they'd gone to visit Paris in the hospital. There were always cars available at Bennie and Clay's and they had taken one for the ride. With her eyes closed, Ruth could still smell the heavenly aroma of his special cologne and it was like being with him again.

Mac had looked over at Ruth, who was sitting in the passenger side of the Bentley. Her long legs were crossed, and she was once again thoughtful enough to wear a skirt so he could look at her legs all he wanted, and she smelled wonderful. He told her as much, thanking her again for picking him up at the airport and for accompanying him to see Paris. She gave him a sideways glance, then smiled and turned to face him.

"Julian, no thanks are necessary," she said sweetly. "It was my pleasure, as you should be aware."

Mac reached over to take Ruth's hand. "I love the way you say my name. No one has ever said it the way you do."

Ruth stroked the back of his hand with her free one. "Julian, if I didn't know any better, I'd think you were flirting with me."

He laughed and squeezed her hand. "That's what I thought I was doing. If you have to think about it I must be more out of practice than I thought." As he brought to car to a stop at a traffic light he looked into her captivating green eyes and gave her a sexy smile. "Are you going to help with that?"

Ruth lowered her lashes slightly and looked at Mac with a slight frown. "No. You flirt just fine, Julian. I'm not conducting a courting tutorial so you can attract even more women," she warned him.

He laughed out loud before leaning over to give Ruth a quick kiss. "Honey, there's no one in the world I want to attract other than you. You're more than enough woman for me, darlin'."

Ruth kissed him back with a smile. "You're really good at this, Julian. Just perfect, in fact."

An impatient horn behind them reminded Mac that they were still in traffic. Without a hint of shame he resumed driving. "You're a true distraction, Ruth. I'm glad you're with me because despite Titus's report, I really am worried about Paris."

Ruth sighed. "I am, too, Julian. Whoever this creature is that's after her isn't playing. For some reason he has a grudge against our girl and he's out to get her at any cost. Clay and Benita want her to move into their place for more protection, but she won't hear of it. She's really committed to this 'Living Without Fear' thing and she's determined to get through this crisis on her own terms."

"Tell me the truth, honey. Is Titus the man I think he is? Can I trust him with the most precious thing in my life, my only daughter?"

Ruth was touched by Mac's grave tone and hastened to reassure him. "You can trust Titus to take care of Paris, not because of *who* he is, but *what* he is, Julian. He's one of the best investigators in the country, he really is. When Ceylon Deveraux's brother stole all her money and left the country he tracked the man down and got every dime back. The man is still in federal prison even as we speak. He has the best investigators, the best resources, the best everything. If he says nothing is going to happen to Paris, he means it. Besides," she added in a softer voice, "Titus is madly in love with her and he'd give up his own life before he let any harm come to her."

Mac pounded the steering wheel. "I knew that young man had feelings for Paris. They looked so crazy about each other at the wedding and then something happened. I may be out of the game, but I'm not blind," he said dryly.

Ruth agreed. "They had a misunderstanding, a huge misunderstanding. Paris thinks it's a done deal, that there's no hope for them, but I think she's fooling herself. She's so in love she doesn't dare hope for anything. She's afraid to trust her heart."

"And now he's cast in the role of her protector so he can't reveal himself to her and maintain any professional integrity," Mac mused. By now they'd reached the hospital and Mac entered the parking lot. After securing a good spot, he got out of the car and went around to Ruth's side to open her door. He helped her out, pausing to look down into the face he was beginning to crave. He touched her lightly on the cheek with an unguarded look of longing. "Whoever said youth was wasted on the young was right. That's why love is lovelier the second time around. We don't like to waste time," he told her.

Ruth looked up at Mac and was momentarily terrified that she looked as open and yearning as he did. She was trying vainly to think of something to say, something light and witty when a booming voice called across the parking lot. "Judge!"

Thanking the good Lord for the arrival of Marcus Deveraux, she took in a deep breath. Life was about to get complicated again and she wasn't completely sure she was ready for it. And she still wasn't sure she was ready for that kind of life change, which is why she was taking refuge with her pals, the women who'd known her for years and who could help her figure everything out. A tremor ran through her as she recalled just how his lips made her feel. *This is ridiculous. I'm too old for this nonsense,* she thought sadly. A lone tear appeared in her left eye and she swiped it away hastily, trying to force herself to think of something other than that damnably wonderful Julian MacArthur Deveraux.

Chapter 13

Now it was two weeks later and Paris still didn't have an explanation for Titus's actions, other than to think he was just trying to reassure her. Despite Billy's teasing and her brothers, surprising acceptance of him, Titus was still an enigma. As soon as it was clear that she was going to be fine with no visible damage from the accident, Titus had apparently thrown himself into the investigation, because she saw almost nothing of him. She felt his presence in the increased measures taken to screen her phone calls, in the fact that she wasn't allowed to drive at all, and the fact that two of his people were stationed at her home at all times, but she had almost no contact with him personally. Now, jetting out to California, she still had no real clue as to what was going on in Titus's head, but she doubted seriously he was nurturing feelings for her other than those of a keeper for his charge. Still, she'd give a lot more than a penny for his thoughts. She slowly opened her eyes to look at Billy, frowning slightly at the smirk on his face.

"I'm taking you out of my will, I hope you know that," she said with a sniff. "For the last time, you don't know what you're talking about. Titus is not thinking about me, okay? So let it go. Just stop talking about it so I can get some sleep."

Billy looked at Perry with a wicked grin and advised him to move while he could. "Don't let her fall asleep on you, man. She drools and she's been known to snore like a Harley backfiring. It ain't pretty."

Paris didn't open her eyes. She merely held up her hand in Billy's direction. "Pick a finger, Watanabe. And don't make me tell what you do in *your* sleep, Mr. Noxious Fumes."

Titus was in no better shape than Paris. He wasn't getting enough sleep, primarily because his dreams were all the same. They began with Paris, they ended with Paris, and they were all about Paris. Night after night he was plagued with incredibly detailed erotic dreams featuring her; she had truly become the woman of his dreams. Touching her intimately, tasting her, feeling her incredible skin, smelling her uniquely feminine scent, all the images tumbled together in a heated explosion that made him wake up drenched in sweat and aching for her. And it wasn't just the sex, either; he wanted Paris, period.

He missed their long conversations, their dates; he missed her company and her laughter. He found himself spending more time working out, not to enhance his already superb condition, but to work off some of his frustration over Paris. The woman was driving him crazy. Since the threats had begun he was more aware of her than ever and his awareness of her heightened to the point where he was dangerously close to losing control. Running hard seemed to help, and that's what he was doing now, pounding away on the treadmill and thinking, as always, about Paris.

This assignment was one of his most difficult because of his feelings for her. Trying to behave normally around her was torture. When he was around her, he tried not to stare at her, but it was almost impossible. When he was in her presence his eyes were on her, drinking in everything about her. There was a tiny beauty mark near the outer corner of her right eye, for example. It was like a little magnet, drawing attention to her pretty eyes and making him want to caress her face and cover it with kisses. Then there was the way she smiled. He had to stifle a groan remembering that beautiful smile, the way it would light up her face, the way she gave that joyous smile to anyone and everyone, and the way that smile changed a little when she smiled at him. This time he did make a sound, a low growl of anger and desire. Every time he looked at her it was as if he were seeing her for the first time and the view was just amazing.

The sweat was pouring off his muscled frame freely as he ran mindlessly, trying to outrun the inevitable. He picked up his bottle of water from the holder on the treadmill's frame and took a deep swallow, smiling wryly as he put it back in place. He'd never thought of drinking water as an erotic act, but the way Paris did it…he had to wipe the sweat from his face as he recalled how she was always drinking twenty-ounce bottles of spring water. The brand she preferred came in a cylindrical bottle and while she was reading or talking on the phone her long fingers would stroke its surface, up and down, up and down, innocently mimicking the way a very sexy woman would stroke a very lucky man. Just when he couldn't take any more of watching her fingers caress the dewy moisture on the bottle she'd pick it up and drink deeply from it. There were times he'd be so aroused from the sight it was all he could do not to rip the bottle out of her hand. And it wasn't just the bottles of water; Paris always seemed to be eating something and turning the very act of nourishment into a carnal act.

It started with those damned bananas. Paris usually ate breakfast in the dining room in the office complex and she almost always had the same thing: fat-free yogurt, Grape Nuts or Kashi cereal, a cup of coffee and a banana. She liked bananas because they were sweet and chock-full of potassium, something he certainly didn't begrudge her, but the way she would peel the skin down and put the tip of the fruit into her mouth… Titus felt his stomach muscles clench and his groin tighten at the memory. He had actually considered buying up the dining room's stock of bananas to keep them away from Paris but he wisely rejected the idea. For one thing, it would have been nuts. And more importantly, it wouldn't have done much good. There were other things that looked equally enticing when Paris was consuming them. Sugar-free Popsicles were one of her favorite afternoon treats, for example. He'd sometimes see her licking one when he stopped by her office in the afternoon. The sugar-free fudgesicles were the worst; the way she could wrap her lips around one and lick it as if it were… This time he picked up the bottle and squirted himself in the face, wiping it off with the towel around his neck.

He hadn't felt this way in years. He'd only had this feeling two other times in his life, and both times had led to disaster, so why was he allowing these feelings to come back into his life, into his heart? An image of Paris's beautiful smile flashed into his consciousness and he smiled. He began to ease his body into a slowdown, preparing to end his run and head for the shower. He glanced at the clock on the wall and grinned. His internal clock never failed him and he was right on schedule. He had a date with destiny that he didn't intend to miss.

Chapter 14

Paris finally managed to get some sleep on the plane by moving away from the three men and taking another seat. She took two of the soft plush flight blankets stored on the plane and cocooned herself, drifting into a deep slumber almost immediately. She enjoyed a deep, dreamless sleep for the duration of the flight, undisturbed by the laughter of Danny and company in the back of the plane, or the conversation of her crew seated around her. She would have continued to sleep if Twillia hadn't wakened her.

"C'mon, Paris, we're landing in about forty-five minutes and you need to pull yourself together," she crooned. "Wake up, Paris. You can take a nap at the hotel, but you can't get off the plane looking like that."

Danny had made his way up to her seat and was much less gentle in his rousing. He reached down and palmed her head like a basketball, rocking it back and forth. "Get up, you hag, or I'll let you crawl off this plane looking like the Phantom of the Opera. You better be glad somebody's looking out for you, ya lazy heifer."

Paris grumped her way to consciousness, frowning and rubbing her eyes. "Who cares what I look like? I don't look that bad, do I?" She looked down at her charcoal-gray velour track suit. It wasn't wrinkled and it was stylish; a nice-fitting hooded jacket and properly fitting pants were timeless. She had on an expensive pair of Nikes and some good jewelry, so she didn't see what the big deal was.

Danny looked at her with disgust. "Do you want to end up on the front page of some tabloid looking like Fanny Frump? Or worse yet," he threatened, "as a fashion disaster in *InStyle*? You better get your butt in the bathroom and get changed if you know what's good for you. Unless, of course, you want to shame your friend Billy by looking like a hick. If that's the case, keep snoring until we land and crawl off this crate looking like a sea hag, see if I care."

Shamefaced, Paris scrambled out of her seat and hurried into the lavatory. She was surprised to find a pretty dress hanging there, complete with accessories. It was one of her favorite outfits, a V-necked merino wool jersey dress with long sleeves. It was the exact color of an American Beauty rose, a color she always favored. The dress was knee-length with a slit in the back and it accentuated her figure beautifully. She always felt she was looking her best when she wore it. She stepped out of the lavatory to put on the shoes she normally wore with it; they were the same shade of rose in suede with snakeskin accents. Their three-inch heel made her legs look longer and even sexier and the rose color of the dress did fantastic things for her skin. She knew better than to ask Danny to comb her hair, but it was still full of waves and the ends were still curled, so she was going to settle for brushing it away from her face when Danny surprised her completely by demanding that she sit down. She did so at once and he quickly fashioned a loose chignon at the nape of her neck and secured it with two big tortoiseshell picks.

"There. Now when you step off the plane you won't look like a Georgia bumpkin come to the big city," he said smugly.

"Excuse you, I am not a Georgia bumpkin. I'm a Louisiana swamp rat," she corrected him haughtily. She thanked him profusely before starting to touch up her face. Twillia came to her rescue, handing her the makeup bag Paris could have sworn was in her luggage.

"Twillia, bless your heart, I know you made sure I'd have something decent to wear," Paris said gratefully.

"Hey, it's what I do," she replied airily. "Isn't that why you pay me the big bucks?"

Suddenly Twillia's face paled and she grabbed the armrest. The plane was beginning its descent to LAX and it was evident that the young woman wasn't thrilled about it. Paris smiled sympathetically and put her hand over Twillia's. "Honey, you know what will cure you of that? Get your aunt Regina to take you for a plane ride or two. You'll feel much more comfortable, you really will."

Twillia got even paler at the thought. "I love my aunt Regina with all my heart but I'm never getting in a plane with her. The big planes are bad enough, but a little one like the ones she flies? Oh, no, not me. *Eww*," she moaned as the jet cut through the clouds and neared the landing strip.

It wasn't too long before the deplaning began and Twillia was able to put her feet on precious ground again. Billy Watanabe saw how wan she looked and put his hand to the small of her back to guide her off the plane. "You're fine, sweetheart, just lean on me a little," he said solicitously.

Paris strolled into the airport looking like a movie star, completely unaware that she was attracting attention. With every step she took more men were watching her with admiration and desire in their eyes. She was oblivious to their leering, as usual, talking to her field producer, Jamaal, and his assistant, Maury. She would have walked straight past the tall man with the placard if Jamaal hadn't nudged her.

"Umm, I think that's for you," he said with a smile.

She stared at Jamaal for a moment, and then looked in the direction he was pointing. There, dressed in a beautifully made suit and very expensive dark glasses, stood Titus with the rest of the hired drivers greeting passengers. Like the rest of them he held a cardboard sign, but his was in fancy script and read "Deveraux." Paris's cheeks turned almost as rosy as her dress and she just stared up at him. He removed his glasses and let the warmth of his gaze caress her for almost a full minute before saying, "Your chariot awaits."

No matter what happened to her for the rest of her life, Paris knew she would always remember the night of the Oscars with extreme pleasure. Everything about the weekend was wonderful and exciting, but nothing was going to top the night of the Academy Awards. She and Billy had been to pre-award dinners and parties and had a ball. She'd interviewed celebrities and movers and shakers, and enjoyed herself tremendously as she taped her show each day. It was wonderful being with Billy; she'd always adored him. They had been as close as siblings in college and their friendship had lasted all these years, something she assured Twillia of several times. Twillia was trying to be cool about it, but her interest in Billy was difficult to hide, especially from a die-hard romantic and matchmaker like Paris. They were in Paris's hotel suite finishing brunch. It was almost time for Paris to get ready to leave for the main event. It seemed incongruous, but the actual red carpet walk took place in the afternoon so she'd be in her fantastic dress for hours and hours.

She welcomed Twillia's questions about Billy and answered them all directly and honestly, laughing when Twillia asked her point blank if anything was going on between her and Billy.

"No, absolutely not. We were never a couple. We were always best friends," Paris assured her.

"So how does he know that you snore? And exactly what does he do in his sleep and how would you know that anyway?" Twillia persisted.

Paris laughed out loud. "First of all, that is a *rumor*. We do not know if I actually snore. I highly doubt it, being the perfect lady that I am. And I certainly don't drool," she said indignantly. "And we know about each other's sleep habits from taking road trips together, late-night studying, you know. We went to different colleges in the same city but we managed to hang out quite a bit. That's why you shouldn't eavesdrop. You get misinformation that way," she teased.

Twillia grinned unrepentantly. "You still haven't said what he does in his sleep," she reminded Paris.

"Oh, that. Let's just say no Mexican food after seven o'clock. In fact, make that no Mexican food on a date night, period, and just leave it at that."

A tap on the door sounded and Twillia went to answer it, coming back with both Danny and Perry. They looked at Paris lounging around in her robe and rollers and both of them began issuing directions to her and Twillia.

"Baby, we've got to make haste if we're going to get you ready in time. Get your makeup on so we can get going," Perry said in his deep, cultured voice.

Danny was more to the point. "Haul out that spackle and slap on a coat so I can get that hair done or you'll be going just like you are. And I know you don't want your 'chauffeur' seeing you like you're looking now, so put some foot in it, woman."

Aja, her makeup artist, had traveled with her, so she took over, making sure Paris would look her very best that afternoon and evening. Paris was too busy getting her makeup on to return Danny's sniping, but she had to contemplate what he'd said. She still couldn't get over the fact that Titus was waiting for her at the airport. She'd actually been feeling a little put out about him sending two of his agents with her instead of coming himself. It was just another indication that she was just another job to him. And when she was completely off guard, there he was with no warning whatsoever. It was a good thing Twillia had insisted on her changing clothes before… Paris's eyes widened in the mirror of the bathroom, then narrowed in suspicion. She called Twillia's name sweetly and gave her an equally sweet smile when Twillia came to her side.

"Sugar, why do I have the feeling that someone in this room knew I was going to be met at the airport? And since it wasn't me and it wasn't Aja, that leaves you, I think. Do you have anything to tell me, sweetie?" Paris cooed in a saccharine voice that fooled no one.

Twillia stared at the ceiling for a moment, and then looked down at the toes she was polishing in scarlet. Finally she came clean, sort of. Looking Paris in the eye with an innocent expression she said, "Okay, see, what had happened was…" only to collapse in laughter when Paris rolled her eyes and held up her hand.

Aja, who was normally quietly serene in demeanor, informed Paris that if she did that again she'd go out of there looking like Rocky Raccoon, so Paris went still at once, although she vowed to get revenge on Twillia at her earliest opportunity. Her makeup was finished and she looked utterly astounding, like a Creole china doll. Danny began the process of combing out her hair, but he didn't finish. He was waiting until the dress was donned. Finally it was time for her to put on the dress that had been so beautifully and skillfully designed and fitted by Perry. He made Paris stand on a white sheet procured from the housekeeping department and he slipped the dress over her head, and then began fastening it onto her body. It was by far the best-fitting dress she'd ever had on in her life, and she'd worn some truly expensive designer gowns.

The dress was made of silk duppioni and was completely lined with china silk in the same shade as the dress, which was an astounding shade of red. It was a red beyond all reds with a blue saturation that enhanced the depth of the coloring. Perry grinned when he told her the name of the color. "It's called Parisian Red. I thought it seemed appropriate for you." She couldn't answer him; she was too taken with what she saw reflected in the mirrored doors of the suite. Even to her own highly critical eye, she looked good. Better than good, actually, better than she'd ever looked in her life and it was all due to the dress. Perry had truly created something special, something no one would forget.

The neckline of the long-sleeved dress was a deep V, as was the back. The deep, wide neckline allowed her remarkable collarbones to show and opened up her face and neck, two of her most appealing features. The swell of her bosom was also visible, but not in a vulgar way. The focus of the dress went from the right shoulder to a point on the left side of her waistline. A medium-sized button in the same fabric fastened it in place, and directed the view diagonally down to the right knee. The dress fit snugly but not tightly through the bodice and waistline, and clung lovingly to the hips where it wrapped around her thighs until it flared out gently at the knee. Thanks to Perry's intricate and masterful fitting, the dress caressed Paris's body like a lover, but it was easily the most comfortable thing she'd ever worn. The design was simple and elegant with just enough detailing to make it memorable. All the edges of the dress, including the hems of the sleeves, were scalloped and the scallops were hand-beaded with Austrian crystals. Even the button at the waist was beaded, as was the small purse Perry had made as a finishing touch. When she put on her matching silk pumps and Danny finished combing out her hair into a cascade of shining black waves, Paris personified the kind of glamour that wasn't seen often these days.

"You do look good if I have to say so myself," Danny admitted. "If Rita Hayworth and Dorothy Dandridge had a child it would look just like you."

Paris was too busy trying to get rid of a necklace to pay attention to his nonsense. "Perry, I know you said this is the finishing touch, but I don't think so. I want people to see my neckline, not my necklace." She took off the offending piece and he promptly put it back on her, insisting that she needed more sparkle. Paris touched her ruby and diamond earrings, inherited from her grandmother, and said she was sparkling enough. The controversy might have gone on for some time but Billy came to the rescue by knocking on the door.

"Come on, woman, it's getting late and we need to…" Billy's voice died in his throat as he looked at Paris. He tried several times to speak but his ability to verbalize just deserted him. He was reduced to staring with his mouth hanging open helplessly and his eyes glazed over.

Perry was tickled to death at Billy's reaction. "I guess my work here is done," he said, slapping palms with Danny. Everyone agreed that Paris looked nothing short of amazing. Even she had to admit she looked quite lovely and it was all thanks to Aja, Danny and especially Perry. Twillia clicked her tongue impatiently. "You might want to take a little of the credit yourself, Paris. You're a beautiful woman, in case you hadn't noticed. Billy, you need to take her out of here before she starts working my nerves. We'll see you all after the festivities, I guess."

By the time they got to the lobby, discreetly accompanied by Titus's agents, Billy recovered his tongue. "Paris, honest to God, I've never been this close to anyone as beautiful as you in my life. If I wasn't afraid of losing my life I'd do what I've always wanted to do with you," he said honestly.

Her eyes, enhanced by the subtle and smoky makeup applied by Aja, were full of laughter as she gave him a sideways glance. "So who's stopping you?" she said in an I-dare-you voice as the elevator reached the lobby.

At that precise second the elevator doors opened and there stood Titus. He took one look at Paris and his eyes seemed to glow with the fire of a pair of London blue topazes. Everything dropped out of her view except the man standing directly in front of her, looking at her as if she held the mortgage on his soul.

The fact that Titus got through the afternoon and evening was a testament to his years of Special Forces training and the deep well of discipline from which he drew. From the moment the elevator doors opened Paris held him captive. He wanted nothing more than to take her away to a place where it was just the two of them and nothing between them but the scent of her incredible skin. The red dress made her complexion even more luscious than usual, her hair more lustrous and the way it fit her body was amazing. He could almost forgive Perry for putting his hands on her to make the dress fit the way it did. He would have been content to stare at her for several lifetimes, but they had to get in the limousine and proceed to the theater where the awards were being held. Titus reluctantly took his eyes away from Paris and stepped aside so she and

Billy could exit the elevator. He nodded to his two agents and they all walked out of the hotel to the car waiting for them outside.

Titus didn't really speak on the way to the theater; he limited his remarks to his two agents and even then he spoke to them via the discreet earpieces of their state of the art communication devices. He had to suppress an urge to smack the crap out of Billy when he took Paris's necklace off and fastened it around her wrist as she asked him to. It just seemed too personal, too intimate. If anyone was going to be doing things like that it should be him, no one else. Trying to keep his jealousy off his face was difficult, but he managed.

His stony mask almost slipped at one point, though. Paris was looking at Billy with great affection as he fastened the necklace around her wrist and she asked him a question that caused Titus's guts to knot in a fist of pain. "So what is it that you always wanted to do with me and why did you never do it?" she asked in a cheery voice as though Titus was invisible. Billy laughed in a self-deprecating way before answering.

"I was in love with you, Paris. I was crazy about you," he admitted. "I wanted to hit on you so bad I could taste it."

Her eyes got huge and her mouth fell open. "But…but you never said a word to me," she protested.

"Ha! That's because your brothers came to visit you one weekend and they took one look at me and I guess they knew I was up to something because they pulled me to the side and told me that if I laid a hand on you they would take my bony biracial ass and mail it back to my momma in Tokyo."

Titus almost choked trying not to laugh, but the look on Paris's face was priceless. "Billy, no they didn't! They didn't really say that, did they?"

Billy grinned and grabbed her hand. "The younger ones,

the twins, they said that. Your oldest brother, the quiet one, he was the scariest. He told me he had a shotgun and twenty-five acres of swampland and he said I looked like nobody would miss me. Him, I believed. I kept my hands in my pockets, baby, as much as I wanted you."

Paris sputtered and fumed and fussed, while Titus had to work even harder not to grin like a Cheshire cat. *That's why you don't have her now, and why you're never going to get her*, he thought. *I wish her brothers would come up in my face. I've got something for each and every one of them. Nobody's going to get between Paris and me when this is all over. Nobody.* Suddenly he didn't have to work to hide his amusement because he realized at that moment that he meant every single word and the gravity of the realization was anything but funny.

The long afternoon was surreal; it was distinctly unsettling to see the sheer number of people thronging the sidewalks hoping to get a glimpse of their idols. It was equally unnerving to realize that as unlikely as it might be, there could be someone in that very crowd who was after Paris. It might be overkill on his part, but Titus couldn't ignore the fact that someone had it in his or her mind to get to Paris, to hurt her in some way. The letters had stopped, but someone had cut the brake line on the company car she happened to be driving that fateful day. And that same person might have come to California to have another go at her; it was a distinct possibility. Titus's people had intercepted an e-mail message to that effect. It read: "*Going to Cali won't protect you. You can't escape me by going to La-La Land; I can get to you wherever you are. Go ahead and run, bitch, but you can't hide.*" It was mild, considering the vile and explicit nature of the first letters, but Titus had no doubt that the person meant every word of it and he was tired of playing cat-and-mouse games. He had a plan to bring the person out into the open and as soon as they got back to Atlanta, he was going to put the plan into action. He wanted Paris to be safe to go about her life unimpeded and in order for her to do that, the culprit had to be behind bars. The fact that Titus had a very personal agenda for wanting Paris out of his protective custody was another story altogether.

He hated admitting it, but Paris and Billy made a striking couple as they walked the red carpet. Even though he absolutely hated the fact that Billy was wearing a custom-tailored jacket made of the same fabric as Paris's dress, they looked like an exquisitely matched set and the photographers and interviewers seemed to think so, too. Every few feet someone was asking them to stop and pose and they were interviewed several times before they made it to the theater. Paris's eyes were as sparkling as the diamonds in her ears and her pretty mouth with the sexy red lipstick smiled radiantly. She charmed everyone she met and it seemed that most of the men there wanted to meet her. She was hugged and kissed and fawned over by most of the glitterati of Tinseltown and she was taking it all in stride.

Titus noticed that the first few times when someone would interview Billy, they would ask who the beautiful lady at his side was. "I'm Paris," she'd say with her beautiful, unaffected smile. In no time at all the other interviewers were greeting the couple as Billy and Paris, as word of his exquisite date spread. No one wanted to miss getting a picture of the most visually exciting couple at the event and their progress was slowed considerably as more and more people crowded around her, like she was a flame of pure radiance and they were love-addled moths seeking her light. Titus was amused greatly by the spectacle, although his face never once betrayed his emotions. He was the consummate professional, keeping close to her but so lowkey he was almost invisible. Indeed, everyone was so taken with Paris and the way she looked holding tight to Billy's hand that Titus doubted that anyone would even remember he'd been present at the event. And no one would be happier than he when it was all over.

Eventually, the evening was over and the little entourage was headed back to the hotel. Billy was triumphant, having won both the awards for which he was nominated, Best Original Song and Best Score. Paris was radiantly happy, flushed with the excitement of meeting so many Hollywood legends. They dropped in at several parties and were joined by Billy's parents at one of the soirees. When they finally returned to their respective suites, Titus entered before Paris to make sure it was secure and did a thorough walk-through before allowing her to enter. He looked at Billy, who was standing in the doorway with Paris, and it was all he could do not to toss the unsuspecting man out into the corridor. He did the next best thing, however, by holding the door open and nodding meaningfully at the door of Billy's suite across the hall.

"She'll be fine. Good night," Titus said tersely.

Billy gave him a slow grin and opened his mouth to say something, but the look on Titus's face convinced him this was not the time and he abruptly bade Paris good evening and crossed the hall to his suite. Titus closed the door and leaned against it, his eyes caressing Paris from head to toe. She looked at him with her eyes narrowed and crossed her arms tightly. "Well, that was just incredibly rude! What's the matter with you, Titus?"

Titus's eyes glowed with desire and he took a step toward Paris. "Don't play with me, Paris. What do you think is the matter?" he said in a low voice full of heat.

Her eyes widened and she stared at him mutely, and then

took a step backward. Titus smiled, and then took another step. "Aww, don't run, Paris. Why are you running away from me?"

Paris took another step backward, then turned away from him and walked into the middle of the sitting room, looking over her shoulder at Titus. "I'm not running, I'm… I'm… Why are you stalking me anyway? Can't you be still for a minute?"

Titus was right on her heels, so that when she stopped walking they practically collided, he was so close to her. "No, baby, I can't be still. I can't think, I can't breathe, I can't do anything unless I touch you right now," he growled softly. "Can I touch you, Paris, can I please touch you?"

They were standing an inch apart, close enough to feel each other's heat. Paris closed her eyes and sighed raggedly. "Touch me where, Titus?" she whispered.

He put his hands where he'd wanted them to be all night, placing his big warm palms on her curvy hips. "I want to touch you here, Paris," he said in a soft, compelling voice. "And here," he added as he slid his hands around to cup her bottom, flexing his fingers over the warm, firm mounds and pulling her even closer to his body, groaning when he felt her pressed against him. She hesitated about a nanosecond before putting her arms around his neck and rising on tiptoe so they could feel more of each other. They were trembling, shaking with need as he bent his head to hers, capturing her lips and tasting her honeyed sweetness with his tongue. The kiss went on for a long time as they greedily took their fill, each of them satisfying the craving that never went away. When they were finally able to break away, it was Titus who groaned again, the sound rumbling from deep in his chest.

"Paris, baby, I've wanted to do that for a long time," he admitted. "I'm not supposed to be touching you, but you look so damned pretty and I'm so crazy about you I can't—"

He stopped speaking when a thud on the other side of the door made him release Paris and set her aside, telling her to go in her bedroom and lock the door. He pulled his Beretta out of his jacket and pointed at the door with both hands. "Come out now. This is your only warning," he said in a cold, even voice. It was apparent he was prepared to shoot as the door quickly opened to reveal Danny, Perry and Twillia standing there looking sheepish. Twillia had a thick tumbler in her hand, which she'd apparently been using to try to listen at the door and Danny gave her a look of disgust.

"I told you that wouldn't work. Now we're busted and for what? We couldn't hear a thing," he said with a frown. "I can see you have a lot to learn from me, heifer. How are you going to spy on her if this is the best you can do?"

Perry was laughing so hard tears were running down his face, and Paris joined him. She had blithely ignored Titus's order to go to her room and she saw the whole thing, including the humor in the situation. Everyone was laughing now except Titus, who looked like he really wanted to use his gun; he just couldn't decide who to pop a cap in first.

Chapter 15

It was hard for Paris to admit it, but she was finally glad about her protection. Since the investigation had proven that her brake line was cut deliberately in an attempt to kill her, she'd been a lot more receptive to his security methods. Especially since her return from California when her tormentor made another move; after that incident she was not only cooperative but she welcomed the security. Aidan had joined her in California as they were taping segments for *Paris & Company*. They flew back to Atlanta on the corporate jet and ended up driving home together. Terry Patterson, a member of Titus's staff, trailed them. Terry was friendly, but intense and professional and Paris liked him a lot. She often had to tell him to slow down as he spoke so rapidly, but she had complete confidence in him.

"I'll be right behind you all the way and when we get to your house, I'll pull in first to make sure everything is secure, okay?" Terry looked at her intently as he leaned into the open passenger window. He had big light brown eyes, short curly hair and he wore little oval wire-rimmed glasses that made him look avant-garde instead of nerdy. Aidan was convinced he had a crush on Paris, something he teased her about as they drove.

"I'm telling you, the man is smitten. If he didn't work for Lord Voldemort he'd be hitting on you, no question about it," he said gleefully. "Let's face it, Paris, you're a hot chick. I was watching you out there in California. Those men were *drooling* over you. Perry, Billy, and every other man with two working eyes, they were all gaga over you. Girl, I saw Johnny Depp looking at you like you were a cherry lollipop and Sam Jackson was checking out your tushie, just to mention two of your admirers. And we won't even talk about the way Lord Voldemort was behaving," he added with a snort of laughter.

Paris made a face and ignored Aidan's remarks, although she had to ask him why he disliked Titus so much. Aidan frowned at the innocent question. "Are you kidding? Have you forgotten the night of bliss that turned into every woman's nightmare? You were there, I believe, on the receiving end of what had to be the lamest, most egocentric speech I've ever had the displeasure of hearing paraphrased. You may have forgotten all about it, but I haven't. I don't like the guy because he treated you badly and I don't forget things like that. I also don't forgive them. Who the hell does he think he is, treating you like some crummy one night stand? He has some serious issues, Paris, and he doesn't deserve a woman like you."

Paris was so surprised at the heated words from Aidan she couldn't think of a single thing to say. By now they'd reached the house and Terry tapped his horn to remind Aidan to let him in the driveway first. They waited until Terry reached the garage and exited the car. He walked toward the house, looking around alertly. Suddenly he stopped walking and began cursing, using a string of expletives Paris would have never associated with him. He turned to Aidan's car to indicate they should stay where they were, but Aidan was already out of the car. He ran to where Terry was standing and his skin turned even paler than normal. He tried to stop Paris but it was too late; she'd already gotten out of her seat and was walking toward the two men.

"What is it? You guys look like you've seen a—" Her words turned into a gasp of horror as she saw what they had already seen: a dead cat was hanging from the light fixture on the side of the house.

The next hour or so was a total blur, mercifully so because she was so sickened by what she'd seen. Titus had arrived on the scene in a very few minutes which would have made her suspicious if she hadn't been in a state of shock. As it was, he allowed him to seat her in his car while the Atlanta police and his agents went over the scene with precise attention to every detail. She was comforted only slightly by Aidan holding both her hands and telling her over and over that it wasn't Merlin.

"Merlin is fine, Paris, he's not even here. I took him to the cat sitter before I left for Cali. He's not here, that's not him, okay?"

Paris nodded numbly, although his words made her feel only marginally better. Merlin might be safe but the remains of a poor tortured animal were still on her porch. That animal died because of someone's obsession with her; how could she live with that? She didn't have long to contemplate her misery as Titus came to join her in the car. "You're coming with me, Paris. Everything is going to be fine," he promised and started the vehicle.

They arrived at their destination in about twenty minutes. Paris was so numb she didn't even question what was going on; she just rode with him in silence. When they arrived, he got out of the car to open her door and she allowed him to walk her to the door of what appeared to be a condominium. "Where are we?" she asked in a quiet, dull voice.

"We're at my place," he answered.

Without another word he led her into his living room and turned on the light. She looked around the room with great interest, suddenly eager to see where and how Titus lived. He led her over to a big black leather sofa and made her sit. He sat next to her and put his arm around her shoulder. "It's going to be fine, Paris. Believe it or not, every time something like this happens it gives us more to go on. This is all going to be over in a couple of weeks, count on it."

He was pleased when she relaxed against him and said, "I know it will, Titus. I know you're going to find out who's doing this and bring him in."

Titus pulled her into his arms and held her for a while, letting his strength comfort her. Then he surprised her with a simple question. "What makes you think it's a man, Paris?"

She pulled away from him and studied his face. "But it has to be," she murmured. A puzzled look came over her face and she looked deep in thought. She stared into the living room at nothing in particular, turning back to Titus. "Well, I guess it could be a woman, but what makes you think that?"

"Let me get you something to drink and I'll tell you," he said, kissing her forehead before getting up to go into the kitchen. Paris looked around the room with open curiosity while he played host. It was a big room, unremarkable in design but wholly adequate, or it would have been had it not been for Titus's décor or lack of it. There was, besides the big black leather sofa, a matching loveseat on the opposite wall, and a huge chair of the same design with an oversized ottoman in front of it. Aside from a floor lamp next to the sofa, there wasn't anything else in the room except for the biggest television she'd ever seen. The gigantic screen was parked in front of the wall with the windows and would no doubt block out most of the light during the day. The chair was positioned in front of the television, so it was obvious that this was where Titus spent much of his time. Paris had a sudden urge to test the chair out and rose from the sofa to go try it out. It was sinfully comfortable; she sank into its depths and sighed. However, its comfort didn't make up for the fact that this was a horrible-looking room.

Paris shook her head as she looked around the space. There wasn't a plant, a flower, a clock, a vase or a single picture to indicate that a human lived there. It was the most uninviting space she'd ever seen. There was a dining room off the living room and it was filled with exercise equipment. Where there should have been a table and chairs, there was a treadmill, a stationary bike, and a contraption she'd seen advertised on television touted to give the user a perfect physique in mere weeks. Again, nothing to indicate that this was anyone's home; she'd seen furniture store displays with more warmth. She was making a sound of disapproval when Titus came back with a small tray. It held a mug filled with some kind of hot concoction and a plate of butter cookies. They were the kind that came in the ubiquitous round tin available at any drug or discount store, but it was a sweet gesture nonetheless. Paris smiled as he set the tray on a small table next to the chair. She took a sip from the mug and said, "Mmm, that's delicious! What is it?"

If the idea hadn't seemed so incongruous, she'd have sworn the tips of his ears reddened when Titus answered gruffly. "It's warm milk. My grandmother used to make it for me."

Paris licked her lips with pleasure and continued to sip the soothing drink. It was laced with honey and had a touch of cinnamon and nutmeg. She also detected another subtle flavor, a little something extra. She gave Titus a teasing smile. "I don't think your grandmother put brandy in hers, now did she?"

Titus laughed out loud. "I refuse to answer that on the

grounds that it might incriminate a very sweet old lady. Now, let's talk about Gayle Rodgers."

He changed the subject so fast that Paris blinked. She cradled the mug in her hands and stared at him. "What about Gayle? You don't think she had anything to do with all this, do you?"

Titus had seated himself on the end of the sofa nearest Paris, leaning forward with his elbows on his knees as he returned her gaze with an intensity she knew all too well. "Paris, in the past weeks we've interviewed everyone involved with *Paris & Company*, everyone you work with throughout The Deveraux Group, your neighbors, friends and the people with whom you do business. We did it as discreetly as possible, of course, don't get upset," he soothed as he saw storm clouds gathering in her expression. "Here's the thing, though, everyone loves you," he said with a smile. "You have a lot of friends and admirers, Paris. No one had anything bad to say about you. In fact, they said some really wonderful things. But when we asked if there was anyone who might have a grudge against you or want to do you harm, one name came up time after time and that was Gayle Rodgers. We've been investigating her activities since she was terminated and guess what we found out?" he asked quietly.

"I don't know, Titus? What was it?" she said in a voice barely over a whisper.

"We found nothing, Paris. She seems to have vanished from the earth and unless she has some extraterrestrial contacts out there, that's not possible. She's hiding out, which makes the idea that she's up to something a possibility." He let that sink in for a moment, and then increased the intensity of his stare. "Tell me everything you know about her, baby."

Her eyes closed as she took the last swallow of the amazing elixir in the cup. With a little sigh she placed the mug on the tray and turned her gaze to Titus. "She's a very pretty woman, very smart, but not terribly disciplined. It was hard for her to take instruction or direction. She was definitely not a team player. She had this weird sense of entitlement, like she felt she should be able to do what she wanted *when* she wanted, which is fine if you're independently wealthy or self-employed, but that doesn't fly when you're working for someone else." Paris paused and put her feet up on the ottoman, then grimaced as she realized it was too far away for the length of her legs. Titus quickly pushed it into a better position and she smiled her thanks at him.

"She was from Philly and her family was quite well off. Gayle went to private schools all her life and she really was used to living the high life. She used to date a lot of NFL players, NBA players, record producers, anybody who was well known and had lots of bling," she said thoughtfully. "I really don't know what she did after she left *Paris & Company*. I'd heard she was going home to Philly, but that could just be a rumor."

Titus raised his eyebrows in amazement. In less than two minutes Paris had told him almost word for word what it had taken his agents a week to find out. During the course of his investigation, people had often remarked that Paris was an amazing repository of information. One person had commented that Paris knew more about what was going on at The Deveraux Group than anyone else because she was just naturally friendly and she talked to everyone. "And she never forgets anything. If she meets you once or twice she'll know your birthday, your mama's name and your favorite dessert. She's just like that," one of her staffers had said, and it was obviously true.

He brought his mind back to the present when Paris addressed him. "I just don't think it's possible that she'd be doing all this, Titus. She might try to ruin my reputation or steal my man, but cutting brake lines doesn't seem to be in her line of endeavor. And that thing tonight…" Paris shuddered and tears came to her eyes. "Why would she do that just to frighten me? How could I have that much significance in her life? I don't get it, Titus, I really don't."

Titus stood and scooped Paris out of the chair so that he could sit down with her in his arms. "Baby, there are a lot of sick and twisted people out there. Their motivations are complicated, but mine are very simple. I find them and I stop them. Period. And I'm going to find this person and make him sorry he ever decided to threaten you in any way. You got that, sweetheart?"

Paris relaxed into Titus's arms and inhaled the clean, masculine scent of his skin. "Got it. Now I have to go home and get unpacked," she said with a yawn. "I have a lot of work to do before next week and I need to get myself situated."

Titus didn't relax the hold he had on Paris. "Then you'll get situated right here, baby, because you're not leaving. You're staying here with me."

"I'm going home, Titus. Nobody is going to run me out of my house and have me living like I'm in the Witness Protection Program. I'm not going out like that. If they want me, they'll have to come and get me. And then I'll show them what my daddy showed me when I was ten years old and he taught me how to handle a gun. I'll blow a hole in them the size of the state of Louisiana. I'm tired of this mess, Titus. You do whatever you have to do to make the weasel come out of the hole, but I want this behind me so I can get on with my life," she told him with her eyes flashing and her face full of fire.

Then she smiled mischievously. "Besides, I can't stay here. I'm claustrophobic. I'm not staying in the Batcave with you. This place looks like a hit man lives here, Titus."

"It looks like *what*?" he said with disbelief.

"It looks like somewhere that a hired assassin would live. You could be out of here in fifteen minutes and no one would know you had ever lived here at all. There isn't one single thing that indicates a real person lives here. I've never been anyplace more sterile in my life," she told him honestly.

"Oh, come on, it's not that bad," he protested. Paris's answer was to get off his lap and demand a tour. He stood up with an air of defiance; he'd show her sterile. Taking her by the hand, he showed her the lavatory off the kitchen, the laundry room, the second bedroom, which served as his office, bedroom and bathroom. Everything was spotlessly clean and impossibly tidy and like the other rooms, there wasn't one bit of ornamentation anywhere to be found. Moreover, everything was black from sheets to towels to coverlet to throw pillows. There wasn't a speck of color anywhere. Paris pointed that out to Titus.

"You see what I mean? There aren't any pictures, any plants, nothing to suggest that the owner has a personality. And what's with all the black? Everything you own in here is available in a wide assortment of colors, you know. This looks so dark and forbidding," she told him.

"I like black," he said reasonably. "And this way everything matches."

"Yes, and everything depresses, too. This is actually worse than the Batcave. The Batcave is a virtual amusement park compared to this place," she said saucily, and then shrieked with laughter as Titus grabbed her around the waist and picked her up.

"Yeah, but the Batcave doesn't have a bed like this one," he growled as he tossed her into the middle of his California king-size mattress.

Paris let out a sound of surprise, a startled little yelp. She pushed her hair out of her eyes and looked at Titus warily.

He met her gaze with a sweet, sexy smile as he got on the bed with her. She scooted away from him to take a better look. He didn't move. He just watched her, his eyes warm and tender, the smile never wavering. He was wearing a denim shirt and a nice-fitting pair of jeans and he looked freshly shaved. Suddenly she looked shy, touching her hair with one hand and smoothing her top with the other. "I look a mess," she said softly.

"You look adorable," he countered, moving closer to her. She froze, looking like a fawn about to bolt.

"What are you doing?" she whispered.

"Nothing you don't want me to do, Paris. And anything you'll let me do," he responded in a voice as soft as hers. He held out his hand to her and she looked into his eyes for what felt like an eternity before she put hers into it. He was touched to feel it trembling just a little. "Come here, baby. Come closer to me, I'm not going to hurt you," he said softly.

Paris allowed him to put his arms around her and with a ragged sigh she wrapped her arms around his neck as he put her into his lap. "Oh, that's better, baby," he whispered. "That's much better." He caressed her face with his lips as his hands became reacquainted with her curves, starting with her breasts. He kissed her neck, burying his face in her fantastic hair, inhaling her fragrance and loving how she felt in his arms. He began to turn her body so she could lie with him on the bed and she stopped him.

"No, wait, I'm a mess," she said again. "I just flew in from California and I'm all rumpled and grubby and you look like a cover model for *GQ*. That's not fair," she said with a frown as she began batting his hands away.

"Aww, baby, you could never look bad to me," he assured her, putting his arms around her again and coming in for one more kiss. "But if you're uncomfortable, how about a bubble bath?"

Paris looked at him suspiciously. "Bubbles? In the Batcave? I'm not bathing in dish soap, Titus."

He laughed out loud, rolling her over on top of him. Giving her one more squeeze he assured her he could do better than that. "Come with me, Paris, I have a surprise for you."

Paris had to concede that Titus was right; he had something a little better than Dawn liquid to offer her. The rest of the condo might be Spartan and uninviting, but the bathroom was spectacular. There was a huge Jacuzzi tub with jets all the way around it and a separate glass-enclosed shower stall with showerheads on opposite sides. Each side boasted handheld nozzles with a variety of settings; everything from a soft mist to a monsoon setting was available. His towels were black, of course, but they were incredibly fluffy and soft, as well as being huge. A mini stereo on the vanity played an exquisite selection of jazz and Jon Lucien's incredible voice caressed her senses as she relaxed in the tub with bubbles up to her chin. Lovely fragrant bubbles, as a matter of fact. It seems that Titus had an affection for bath gel and he had several big bottles of Neutrogena Rainbath and Vitabath in supply. His ears reddened slightly as he explained that soap dried his skin too much. "I'm big but I'm sensitive," he muttered.

Paris sipped her goblet of sparkling water while she luxuriated in the warm, pulsating water. The force of the jets on her body was arousing, almost as arousing as the thought of being with Titus again. She emptied the glass and put it on the edge of the tub. She then stood, reaching for a towel. Stepping into the shower, she quickly rinsed the foam from her body and reluctantly turned off the shower. She wanted to play with all the settings, but there was time for that later. Right now, there was something else she needed to do. She had just wrapped the towel around her body when a tap at the door made her look around.

"Are you decent?" Titus's voice asked.

"Perfectly," she answered. He opened the door with a look of disappointment. "That's too bad," he said glumly. "I brought this for you to put on." He handed her a man's pajama top in heavy silk satin jacquard. It was luxurious, rich looking and completely unexpected, especially as it was a deep crimson. He pulled his earlobe and answered her unasked question.

"They were a Christmas present from my mother a couple of years ago. Don't ask me what she was thinking because I still can't figure it out," he said. Paris accepted the top with a smile and told Titus she'd be out in a minute.

And now she was ready, walking into Titus's bedroom trying not to appear as nervous as she felt. She padded into the bedroom in her bare feet, having no way of knowing how sexy and vulnerable she looked. All of her attention was focused on Titus, who was standing next to the bed setting a tray on the nightstand. He turned when he heard her enter the room. "I just thought you might be hungry. You had a long flight and a big shock and…damn, you're beautiful," he said hoarsely.

Paris kept walking until she was in front of him, and her trepidation vanished when she saw the way he was looking at her. He put one hand on her shoulder and touched her face with the other one. "I fixed you something to eat. Are you hungry?"

She slipped her arms around his waist and gave him a look of intense desire. "I'm hungry for you, Titus. Just you."

His eyes darkened to a velvety sapphire and he breathed her name reverently as he bent to kiss her. As their mouths met he picked her up and placed her on the bed with great care, their mouths still mated as he joined her. He knelt over her, kissing her over and over while he unbuttoned his shirt and removed it. He stopped only to get off the bed and remove his jeans, never taking his eyes off Paris. She gave him a shy smile and looked around the room. It was still utilitarian, but he'd done what he could to make it special for her. He had turned down the bed and lowered the lights to a dim glow. There was incense burning and John Legend was playing softly. She moved to the center of the bed and gasped in surprise. "Satin sheets, Titus? I never pictured you as a satin sheet kind of guy," she teased.

Titus made a face as he slid into the bed next to her. "I'm not, that's my sisters' idea of a joke. But the joke is on them because these things are really comfortable."

Paris wasn't concerned with bedclothes anymore; she was too mesmerized with the sight of his body and the way it looked in the soft light. She ran her hand over the bulging muscles of his upper arm, rising up on her elbow to get a better look. "I've never seen anybody with a body like yours," she said frankly. "I love the way you're put together, Titus." She blushed, afraid she'd said too much. He reassured her at once, taking the hand that was touching him and putting it to his lips.

"Thank you, baby. No one except you has ever said anything like that to me. And for the record, your body is perfect. I love the way you're made, Paris." He reached for her and took the top button of the pajama top in his long fingers. "Your skin is so soft and beautiful, it doesn't look real," he murmured as he undid the button. He kissed the tiny hollow at the base of her throat as he took another button. "You're tall, which I love because it makes it easier for me to kiss you without breaking my neck. And you're so graceful. When you walk you look like a queen. Your butt sways and your hips move and I get hot just from watching you," he admitted as he opened her top a little more. Now he licked the space between her breasts as he captured yet another button. "Your breasts are beautiful, Paris," he said as he opened the top even more, enough so he could move the fabric aside and expose one of her round, firm globes to his view.

He ran his palm across her nipple, smiling as it immediately responded to his touch. Cupping her breast, which was heated with desire, in his hand he brought his lips to its tip, surrounding her rosy, erect bud with his warm, wet mouth, circling it with his tongue while he gently kneaded and stroked the silken flesh. He finally pulled away long enough to expose the other breast as another button was undone. "I could do this forever, Paris. You taste so sweet and you feel just right in my hands, just right." He paid tribute to her other breast in the same way, until she moaned his name aloud. "I'm not finished, sweetness." He finally opened the last button, rubbing his hand over her rounded tummy with excruciating tenderness. "I love this part of you, Paris. It feels so soft, so sexy and it looks so good." He rubbed his face against it while his hand caressed her hip. He parted her legs gently. He didn't want to alarm her, but he was eager to find the treasure he knew awaited him. He touched her feminine mound, only to draw his hand back in confusion. He sat up and stared at her, unwilling to believe what he was feeling.

"Paris, what did you do?" His voice was hoarse with disbelief.

It took Paris a minute to answer. She was completely aroused by what Titus was doing to her body, yet totally relaxed. She was so into the sound of his voice and the feel of his hands and his mouth on her, she didn't want him to stop, she wanted it to go on forever, but Titus was insistent. "What did you do?" he repeated with growing anxiety.

"I had a Brazilian," she told him. "Don't you like it?"

"A *what?* What's a damned Brazilian? How could you violate the rose like that, woman?"

"A Brazilian is a bikini wax, Titus, so everything is nice and tidy. Doesn't it look cute?" She turned so she was completely on her back and he could see her pelvic area in all its glory. He didn't answer for a moment, but then he began to speak. "I'll tell you the truth, baby, I liked it the way it was. All that thick curly hair turned me on. But this is actually quite sexy, especially the little heart in the middle." He leaned over and kissed it, following the kiss with a caress of his fingers, which magically coaxed her legs into just the right position. He was so absorbed in his foray he almost didn't hear her question. "What rose are you talking about, Titus? You said I violated a rose, what rose?"

Instead of answering he moved over her body and settled into a kneeling position that allowed him access to that which he craved the most. Placing his mouth on her ripe womanhood, he used his lips and his tongue to explore her, to dissolve her into a sensual mass of bliss, to bring her to a level of pleasure she'd only experienced one other time. She rocketed to the edge of an abyss of sensation and careened over the edge with Titus holding her literally in the palms of his big hands. He held her hips in place while he sucked her and licked her into a sexual oblivion where there was nothing but the two of them. He devoured her, wringing every bit of inhibition out of her and leaving nothing but passion and desire. When he finally released her, it was with exquisite slowness, as he licked and kissed his way back up her body, stopping at her mouth as she struggled to breathe normally. "*That* rose, baby. Pink and pretty just like a rosebud. You're my rose," he whispered.

Paris sighed with pleasure. Her entire being was filled with the joy of being with Titus again. As he drew her into his arms for another soul-shattering kiss the words slipped out so naturally she didn't realize she was saying them. "I love you, Titus. Make me yours," she whispered.

Chapter 16

Titus glanced over at Paris as he drove through the streets of Baton Rouge, Louisiana. She was by far the most stubborn woman he'd ever met in his life, but she was no doubt the most captivating. He'd had a chance to witness more of her charisma at the conference they'd just left, an annual gathering of readers and writers of African-American romances. He had also gotten a real taste of her implacable nature after their encounter at his apartment. That was when he knew just how mule-headed Paris could be when she chose. They had made love all night like newlyweds and she still insisted on going home the next morning.

"This doesn't change anything, Titus. Someone is still after me and you and I aren't any better suited than we were before. That hasn't changed. You and I aren't destined to be together and we both know it. We gave in to the passion last night but it can't happen again," she'd told him with a sad maturity that made him want to kick something. The fact that she was completely correct notwithstanding, her calm demeanor and expressionless delivery put a wrenching pain in his gut he couldn't understand. How could she give herself to him so passionately and then act like it was no big deal the next day? How could she tell him she loved him over and over during the night and pretend they were mattress buddies the next morning?

Titus had to force his attention back on the road ahead of him. He couldn't drive and think about how sexy Paris had looked in his bed and the glorious love they'd made all night long. Every time he turned to her, she was waiting for him, welcoming his body with her loving embrace. She had delighted and excited him by initiating more lovemaking, too, turning in to his arms and whispering his name so sweetly it made his heart ache to hear it. She declared her love so naturally it touched him in a place he didn't know existed. And now she wanted to act like it was business as usual? *Fat chance of that*, he thought. She was right, of course, it would have been sheer madness for him to indulge his ravening appetite for Paris at the moment, but it sure didn't lessen his desire. *This is far from over, Paris, no matter what you think. I can show you better than I can tell you, so you're going to get a demonstration soon.* The thought made him impatient for her. But he had to wait until everything was settled. Until then, it was cold showers and professional decorum even though it was driving him crazy. And now she sat next to him in the car, as prim as you please, with no idea of the turmoil inside him.

She'd had her way; he'd taken her home and made sure she was safely settled inside with Aidan before leaving. A week later he had accompanied her to New Orleans for the romance conference, and it wasn't nearly as bad as he'd feared it would be. Paris was in attendance both as a fan and as a presenter; she'd been asked to give a talk at one of the luncheons. Titus was impressed anew by her speaking ability; she gave a speech that was amusing, insightful and laudatory. He was also amused by the fact that she was way more impressed meeting her favorite writers than she had been meeting all the Hollywood types at the Oscars. She was in a state of sheer delight for the two days she attended the conference, even more so since she got to spend time with her family. Her father was his usual gracious self and her brothers at least weren't trying to rip his head off, which was a pleasant change.

Now they were making a stop in Baton Rouge to fulfill a promise to her aunt Gertrude, her late mother's sister. Titus could tell her heart wasn't in it, but he knew better than to try to persuade her to blow it off. Her aunt had a book club and they wanted Paris to attend their monthly meeting. Paris was a huge proponent of reading and book clubs and she promoted local clubs on her show every week. She also featured writers regularly, especially romance writers because she loved the genre so much. Her aunt had more or less volunteered Paris's attendance when she found out that Paris would be in Louisiana and rather than disappoint the members of the club, she had agreed to attend. He looked at her again, her hands folded in her lap and her face set resolutely. He put his hand over hers and smiled when she clasped his hand tightly with both of hers. "You aren't nervous, are you, baby? Because no one can work it like you can, you know this. You're going to have them eating out of your hand in no time."

She gave him a faint smile in return. "Thanks for those kind words, but I'm not worried about those ladies, trust me. It's Aunt Gertrude," she said, her face looking sad without her normal sunny expression. "We've never really gotten along that well, so I don't know why she wanted me to come to this. She's going to start in on me about my weight, I know she is. And I lost seven pounds before I came to Louisiana because I can't resist home cooking while I'm here. Especially Aunt

Gert's cooking. She might be as mean as a black snake, but that woman can throw down in the kitchen," she admitted. "Oh, slow down, you need to turn here. Just pull up into that cul-de-sac—that's her house there in the center." Paris sighed deeply as Titus maneuvered the rental car into a parking space.

"You just have to walk me to the door and come back for me in two hours," she said for about the tenth time. He wanted to tease her, but he could see how nervous she was and he wanted to make it better. He squeezed her hands before getting out of the car to open her door. He looked down at her and told her how pretty she looked. She didn't give him her usual smiling thanks; she ran her hands over her hips and looked at him anxiously.

"Are you sure this outfit is okay? I don't look like a whale, do I?" Titus had to bite back some very uncomplimentary words about the woman he was about to meet for the first time. She must be some kind of cow to make his self-assured, confident Paris this uneasy. "You look exceptional in that outfit, baby. I don't know much about women's clothes but that looks really good on you," he told her, kissing her temple as he did so. She really did look fabulous, in a two-piece outfit consisting of a supple knit dress with a deep scoop neck and a matching jacket. The jacket had no lapels and it was long, coming past her hips. Both the dress and the jacket were in a deep shade of peacock blue with a subtle hint of green. The color contrasted with her beautiful black hair and the dress fit perfectly, showing off her figure. It was a little shorter than she usually wore her clothes and her long legs were a welcome sight to Titus, who never got tired of looking at them. He put his arm around her waist and told her again how good she looked. She didn't have time to reply as they had reached the front door, which was opened at once by an older woman Titus assumed was Aunt Gertrude.

She was medium height with brown skin, a puffy non-descript hairdo and an expression that managed to look welcoming and condescending at the same time. She wore half-round reading glasses perched on the end of her nose and stared at Paris for a long moment before speaking. "You've gained weight," she said with a smile that was eerily out of place on her haughty face with the harsh lines that emphasized her plainness.

Titus pulled Paris even closer and the look he gave Gert dared her to say another word. She seemed flustered for a moment, but recovered quickly. "Oh, come on in, dear, it's so good to see you," she said in a poor imitation of an affectionate manner.

They crossed the threshold into a house that was nicely decorated with antiques and looked very tasteful. The parlor was sunny and full of older women who all seemed to be thrilled to see Paris. Gert looked a little annoyed to see that the club members were already introducing themselves to Paris; she apparently had some grand speech planned. Sure enough, she cleared her throat loudly and called for silence. "I'd like everyone to meet my darling niece Paris Deveraux, who was kind enough to grace her dear aunt with her presence. And her...what are you, dear, her driver?"

Titus's eyes promptly turned the cold silver color that only Paris could interpret and he gave Gert a smile that was as false as her own leer. "I'm Titus Argonne, ma'am. I'm Paris's fiancé." A chorus of "oohs" echoed around the room and as his eyes met Paris's they turned almost the same color as her dress. Titus smiled in satisfaction. She was going to get him, no question about it, but it was worth it to shut that harridan of an aunt up. No matter what Paris did to him in retaliation, he could handle it. Nobody talked down to his woman and got away with it.

* * *

Paris was so startled by Titus's declaration she couldn't talk for a few minutes. It was just as well; there was no telling what she might have said. The morning actually passed rather quickly and pleasantly, with engaging conversation and discussion of books, even though Paris was so rattled by Titus's casual announcement she wasn't sure at all of what she was saying. She concentrating on not staring at him, something it was very hard to do. Titus had been prevailed on to stay; the ladies of the club were openly intrigued by his rugged good looks and unmistakable sex appeal. Paris was actually relieved that he was staying since it was apparent that he had the ability to keep the redoubtable Gert in check. It was an ability for which she thanked God when Gert started up with her again. It began when Gert's daughter, Charlinda, entered the room. Paris stifled a groan. She had nothing against the woman, not really, but she was hard to take. Compared to the slender and delicate Charlinda, Paris always felt like an ox, something Gert encouraged by her comments, which were constant and snide.

"Oh, there's my beautiful daughter now. Come on in, Charlinda, and say hello to Cousin Paris. You haven't seen her in such a long time. And you must meet her *fiancé*," Gertrude gushed in a voice that indicated her amazement at the situation. "She's managed to hook herself a big good-looking man, too. Come and say hello."

Paris kept her face from betraying her dismay; she made herself look serene and smiling as she greeted Charlinda. They were the same age, but bore no resemblance to each other. Charlinda was a model and wore a size four, even though she was almost as tall as Paris. She was very pretty in a delicate doll-like way and the two of them simply weren't close. They had nothing whatsoever in common. Paris dutifully returned Charlinda's quick hug and introduced her to

Titus. It gave Paris a secret thrill to note that Titus didn't have the poleaxed look that most men got whenever they caught sight of her cousin. The only woman Titus was looking at was Paris, something for which she would always be grateful. He was only pretending, but it was doing her all the good in the world.

She was startled and surprised when Charlinda seemed really glad to see her. Even when they moved into the dining room for lunch, Charlinda seemed attached to her. Paris found herself seated between Titus and Charlinda, which was rather weird but not unpleasant. She'd never had anything against her cousin; it was just hard to be constantly compared to an icon of beauty and found wanting. She really didn't know Charlinda that well, she mused as they chatted while lunch was served. Then something happened which Paris knew she'd never forget. Gert made a point of serving Paris herself, even though she had a serving staff to make sure everyone was served. Titus had a plate with smothered chicken, fluffy rice with gravy, sautéed squash and green beans cooked with smoked ham and pearl onions placed in front of him while Gert put a plate of cottage cheese and sliced tomatoes in front of Paris. "I made this just for you, dear, I know what troubles you have with your figure," she said in a whisper loud enough to be heard in Shreveport. Without hesitation Titus swapped his plate for Paris's while looking at Gert like he wanted her head on a spear. "Thanks, I'm a vegetarian," he said coolly.

A smart woman would have backed off, especially after her deliberately rude ploy was foiled, but Gert kept pushing. "I'm just trying to look out for you, dear," she said to Paris in that same saccharine tone. "After all, you landed this hunk. We want to make sure you keep him. I'm sure he wouldn't mind if you lost a few pounds."

Titus put his hand over Paris's, which was in her lap and, he was displeased to find, was trembling. "I love everything about Paris just the way she is," he said quietly, but with a deliberate force that the obnoxious older woman knew was serious. Titus looked deeply into Paris's eyes and smiled a warm and beautiful smile that no one but Paris ever saw. "She's the most beautiful woman I've ever seen in my life and I'm extremely lucky to have her in my life."

The women around the table sighed with pleasure at his declaration, but he wasn't finished yet. He turned to look directly at Gert. "Her remarkable beauty notwithstanding, I'm a big man. I have big hands, big feet and I drive a big car. What could I do with a little woman, besides hurt her?"

This time the book club exploded in laughter and applause as it was painfully obvious to everyone in the room that this man was totally in love with the woman at his side. Obvious to everyone except Paris, that is. She appreciated the fact that Titus was so protective of her but she wished with all her heart that he meant the words and he wasn't just playacting so she could save face.

Paris really tried, but she couldn't eat a mouthful of the meal. She was truly glad Charlinda was seated next to her because the other woman kept up a steady stream of chatter. Titus had his hand on her thigh under the table, which calmed her, but she wanted nothing more than to run out of the house screaming. *What an evil old bat,* she thought viciously. *How could my lovely mother have been related to this crone?*

Just then, Titus removed his hand and took his cell phone out of his pocket, glancing at the caller ID. He excused himself to Paris, saying it looked like an emergency. He spoke quietly in a rapid, low voice. Ending the call he turned to Paris again. "I hate to do this to you, but we have to go. There's an emergency and I have to get to Charleston right away."

In two minutes they were in the rental car and on their way to the airport.

Chapter 17

Titus would have felt like a fool, but he was past caring what anyone thought. Ever since he'd gotten the phone call in Baton Rouge he had one thing on his mind and that was getting home to Charleston. Embarrassment really didn't figure into the situation because he was with Paris and she wouldn't consider his actions foolish in any way. If he knew anything at all about Paris, he knew she was there for him. When he had tersely explained to her that she would have to go back to Atlanta alone because he had to get to South Carolina, she'd stared at him as if he was crazy, then calmly pulled out her own cell phone and instructed the pilot of the corporate jet to file a new flight plan that would take the two of them to Charleston, South Carolina. She then took the car keys from Titus and announced that she was driving and for him to get in the car and be quiet.

Bossy she might be but she was just what he needed. He told her the phone call was from his oldest sister to inform him that their grandmother was in the hospital. Paris reached over to take his hand, asking him what had happened to put her into the hospital. Titus pulled at his right earlobe and admitted he wasn't sure. "Nona, that's my sister's name, was so upset I couldn't really follow what she was saying, which isn't unusual. I just have to see for myself that she's okay. She means the world to me, Paris, I just have to make sure she's fine."

In a few hours they had touched down in Charleston. Thanks to Paris, a car was waiting for them and they got to the hospital promptly. Paris insisted that Titus get out at the front door and go in; she would park the car and find him. He was so rattled he agreed and got out of the car, not even waiting for Paris to get behind the steering wheel. He was directed to his grandmother's room and had to restrain himself not to run down the hall. He found her room number and took a deep breath before entering the room. When he entered he was relieved to find her sitting up and looking like her normal self with the exception of a cast on her left arm. Her eyes lit up when he came in and she greeted him with joy.

"Oh my goodness, look who it is! You look so handsome, baby, come give Mama a kiss," she told him. "What brings you to Charleston, sweetheart?"

Titus went to her bedside and gave her a kiss on the cheek. "What brings me here? *You*, of course. Nona didn't tell me exactly what was wrong, she just said you were in the hospital and it scared me to death. What have you been up to, Mama Sweet?"

Titus had been so focused on his grandmother he didn't notice his sisters were in the room, too, but they were in attendance and they hurried to answer his question. Nona, the oldest, went first. "She decided to make a cobbler and her big pan was on the top shelf of the pantry. So she decides to get it down and she gets on a stepladder," Nona reported.

Nicole, his youngest sister, took up the tale. "We've all told her not to do that, that we can come and get anything she wants off the shelves or out of the basement, but she had to try and be grown and get it herself. And she might have made it if that little dust mop of a dog of hers hadn't decided to help her. The little raggedy rascal ran up under the ladder and crash go boom, down they came," she said cheerfully. "But she's fine, she really is. She's going to be discharged tomorrow and she's going to go home with Mama for a while."

Mama Sweet, whose real name was Audrey Horne, made a sound of disgust as she listened to the last part of Nicole's narrative. "I don't know why I can't go home," she sniffed. "I'm perfectly capable of taking care of myself. I don't need Sarah fussing over me day and night."

Titus took Mama Sweet's hand in his big one and leaned down to kiss her again. "She won't fuss over you, she's just going to make sure you're comfortable. There's nothing wrong with that, is there?"

The elderly woman's petulant expression relaxed into a smile. Titus could always wrap her around his little finger, something his sisters often remarked on. Her eyes suddenly brightened in anticipation as she looked towards the doorway. "Well, hello, sugar, come on in. Are those for me?"

Titus turned to see Paris shyly entering the room with a bouquet of spring flowers purchased at the gift store in the lobby. She also had a magazine and a small stuffed teddy bear with a pink bow around its neck. "I hope I'm not disturbing you," she said softly.

He went to her at once, putting his arm around her waist. "Mama Sweet, I want you to meet someone," he began, only to be cut off by Nicole.

"Ooh, we know who this is! We watch your show all the time," she exclaimed. "Look, Mama Sweet, it's Paris Deveraux!"

"Nicole, I can see who it is, child. Hush that noise before the poor woman thinks we're all crazy," she said sternly. Giving Paris her best smile, she held out her good hand and invited her to come closer. "What a nice surprise this is. Are you Titus's young lady?" she asked archly, ignoring Titus's protest.

Paris ignored Titus as well, handing the flowers and teddy bear to him before going to the old woman and taking her hand. She bent to kiss her on the cheek, and then smiled radiantly. "It's so nice to meet you." She looked at Titus with mischief in her eyes and added, "And yes, I'm his girlfriend."

Paris decided at once the best course of action was to go with the flow. There was no use trying to make sense of all of it at once. Too much was happening right now and she could sort it out mentally when they got back to Atlanta. For now she was just going to be a gracious participant and amazed observer. She was stunned by what she'd seen when she entered the hospital room; there was Titus standing at the head of the bed, holding the hand of an elderly woman who had to be his grandmother. And there were two other women sitting in chairs on either side of the bed who had to be his sisters. The first time Titus had ever mentioned a single member of his family was the night he'd made hot milk for her and now here his family members surrounded her. *Literally surrounded,* she thought in amusement as she looked around the living room of Titus's parents, Sarah and Clifton Argonne.

She was sitting next to Titus on a comfortable sofa while his parents faced them from the matching love seat. Nona and Nicole were also present and everyone was wearing an expression of happy curiosity, except Titus, who was looking right addled. Unconsciously she moved a little closer to Titus, reaching for his hand as she did so. The gesture wasn't missed by anyone, especially Nicole, the sister Paris decided was the most outspoken. She was very pretty, too; she was plump with chocolate-brown skin and a head of thick black hair that came well past her shoulders. She had big eyes that were fringed with long lashes and a baby doll mouth, which she never seemed to shut. She was chattering away even now.

"We saw pictures of you in that red dress at the Oscars and you looked good in it, honey. You were working that dress, girl. Who did you say made that dress and can I get one like it?" she asked without pausing for breath. Paris laughed at her eagerness.

"You'll have to talk to Perry Turner about that. He lives in Flint, Michigan and he's the designer. I don't know how he feels about making duplicates of dresses," she cautioned Nicole.

"It won't be the same dress because I want mine in champagne. With gold beading," she said thoughtfully. "Let me go get that *InStyle* magazine, you know you were in it," she informed Paris.

Nona clicked her tongue as her younger sister left the room. "Nicole needs to let it go. Nobody's making that dress for her and if they did where would she wear it?" Nona looked amused even as she fussed at her sister's foolishness. Like Nicole, Nona was a striking woman with black hair, although hers was cut stylishly short. She also shared the deep rich cocoa color of her sister. It was, in fact, the color of their parents, too. Both Sarah and Clifton were brown-skinned. Clifton was a deep bronze and Sarah was regally ebony in hue. Paris held Titus's hand and thought what attractive people they were, although she also noticed that Titus didn't resemble a single one of them. Her thoughts were interrupted by a question put to her by Mrs. Argonne. "So tell us, dear, how did you meet our Titus?"

Paris ignored a groan from Titus and beamed at his mother. "A few years ago I was interning at The Deveraux Group complex in Atlanta. One morning I was in the cafeteria having breakfast with my friend Aidan and I looked up and saw Titus with my cousin Martin and that was it for me," Paris admitted.

Titus looked embarrassed but pleased at her revelation. "Don't believe a word of that," he said while smiling down at Paris. "It wasn't like that at all. She gave me a hard time. It was terrible, as a matter of fact. She wouldn't speak to me half the time. She used to ignore me," he said in a hurt tone of voice that fooled no one. Paris made a face and tried to poke him in the side but he was too fast for her. He wrapped his arm around her shoulders and told her to behave or he'd sic Nicole on her. Nicole returned to the living room with several magazines in time to hear his last words.

"Paris, girl, we can work something out. You get me that dress in champagne, and he's on his own," she promised.

Everyone laughed except Titus and Paris, who were smiling at each other as though they were alone in the room. Mrs. Argonne asked if they had eaten and Titus assured her they hadn't. She insisted on feeding them and she and Nona went to the kitchen to prepare something, leaving the couple alone with Nicole and Mr. Argonne. He was reserved, compared to his effervescent daughters, but warm and friendly. Paris enjoyed their conversation as she looked around the beautifully furnished room. There were tall multipaned windows with heavy matte satin draperies in persimmon. Mrs. Argonne had chosen an unusual color scheme of gray, citron and persimmon with chocolate brown and gold accents, but everything worked together to create a subtly harmonious environment. The highly polished antique furniture was mated with African sculpture and contemporary paintings on the walls and the total effect was a welcome haven from a busy world.

Paris commented on the attractive décor and Nicole happily accepted the credit. "Thank you! Mama was a little hesitant about these colors, but she finally had to admit I know what I'm doing. She even painted the pictures on the wall to help marry the colors. That's when I knew she really liked it," she said with satisfaction.

"I am in absolute awe of you, Nicole. How long have you been a designer?"

Mr. Argonne and Titus both laughed. "Since she was four," Mr. Argonne said. "The day she made the mural in the hallway with her crayons we knew she was destined to be an artist. No room was safe from her, she used to rearrange furniture like there was no tomorrow."

Paris had to smile at the image of an energetic little girl creating her own environment. Without thinking, she made a comment about Nicole inheriting her talent from her mother. "I can see Mrs. Argonne is a wonderful artist," she said warmly.

"Yes, she is," Nicole agreed. "She's the one who encouraged me to go to design school. A lot of parents want to discourage artistic endeavors, but my parents always let us choose our own path. Which makes sense since they chose us," she added cryptically.

Paris looked blank for a moment and Nicole elaborated. "They chose us, Titus and me. We're adopted."

At that moment Nona strolled into the living room and announced it was time to eat. She showed Paris to a powder room to freshen up and Paris was grateful for the brief solitude. Even for Paris, this was a lot to take in for one afternoon.

There were more revelations in store that day. After a delicious meal of she-crab soup, cheese straws, shrimp Creole and jasmine rice with a delicious green salad made from lettuce, tomatoes and cucumbers grown in Mr. Argonne's garden, Paris and Mrs. Argonne lingered in the kitchen while Titus and his father finished rearranging the room that would be occupied by Mama Sweet during her convalescence. The two women had taken the measure of each other and each was satisfied. Mrs. Argonne smiled gently at Paris. "Forgive me for staring at you, but you're so lovely I can't help it. You're the first woman Titus has brought to this house in twenty years. I know you're very special to him and I can see that he means the world to you. At least I hope that's what I'm seeing," she said frankly.

Paris didn't flinch under the older woman's calm scrutiny, meeting her gaze levelly. "I was never very good at hiding my feelings," she admitted.

"I'm going to ask your forgiveness again, but I want to know what made you fall in love with my son," Mrs. Argonne asked quietly. "Was it because he's so handsome and sexy?"

An embarrassed laugh escaped Paris before she could stop it. "I'm sorry, Mrs. Argonne, that was just a little unexpected."

"Please, call me Sarah. And don't be offended. I know it's unusual for a mother to admit that her child has sex appeal, but come on now, I'm not blind," she said chuckling.

"Yes, he is very handsome, I agree, but that's not why I fell in love with him. It was because he's so kind," Paris said thoughtfully. "I used to be utterly tongue-tied around him. Me, the woman who never shuts her mouth, couldn't say one word when I was around him. And he was always so nice to me, no matter how much I was stammering and stuttering. He was always courteous and polite and so sweet to me. And my little cousins just adore him, they think he hung the moon, they really do. They have a ton of uncles and they're all blessed with very loving fathers so they don't really have that much to do with people outside the family unit. But Titus they absolutely love, they think he's part of the family. My cousin Martin is his very good friend and Martin doesn't hang out with anyone other than his brothers. Titus is like a brother to Martin and that doesn't happen by chance, not with my cousin. Martin doesn't get close to anyone outside the family so I knew that Titus had to be someone really unique, someone I could trust. And I do, Sarah, I trust him with my life," she said earnestly, touching Sarah's arm as if to underscore her sincerity.

"I always knew he was a good person, because of how he behaved with my family and with me. And when I really got to know him, when we started talking to each other and going on dates, I *knew,*" she said simply. "I have four brothers and a very protective father. They always taught me to respect myself and to demand respect from any man with whom I was involved. And with Titus, I never had to demand respect. He always gave it to me freely. Once I stopped being a tomboy and the bully of the bayou, I found out I enjoy being treated like a lady and Titus treats me like one. He shows me the kind of care and consideration I get from my daddy and my brothers. They act like I'm someone really special and Titus does, too. He's a wonderful man, Sarah. He's just…wonderful." She sighed. Her eyes got big and she blushed hot red as she realized how revealing her words had been.

"Oh honey, don't do that," Sarah said comfortingly. "He truly is a very special person and I've always hoped he'd find someone who could recognize how loving he is. He started out in a hard place, Paris, and there were times I thought he'd never get over it, but look at him now." She put her finger on the corner of her eye. "I still get all watery when I think about what he's been through. He was an abandoned baby, you see.

He was found here in Charleston when he was just days old. There wasn't even a note, just Titus bundled up in a box on the front steps of a church." She shook her head, remembering the anger she'd felt when she read about it in the newspaper.

"He was such an adorable little baby. I saw pictures of him from when he was found and he was so pretty, with big blue eyes and curly blond hair. He looked like an ad for baby food or something he was so cute. A couple came forward to adopt him and it seemed like everything would be fine for him," she said with a faraway look in her eyes. "They were a well-to-do couple and they had the means to give him a wonderful life. He was about nine months old when they took him." Suddenly her eyes turned cold and flinty. "And he was almost three when they brought him back."

Paris gasped and covered her mouth with her hands. Tears sprang to her eyes, which were wide with shock. It was Sarah's turn to offer comfort, and she did, holding her hand out to Paris, who took it and held on to it tightly. "I can see you're imagining what it must have been like for him. They were the only family he'd ever known and he was old enough to know what was happening to him." She sat silently for a moment with her eyes damp from emotion. "Maybe he didn't know exactly what was going on, but he was old enough to know that one day he had parents and the next day he didn't."

"But why, Sarah? Why on earth did they do that?" Paris could barely breathe because she was so upset.

Sarah pursed her lips and made a face. "I've learned over the years to not bear them any ill will because, after all, they gave me a great gift when they brought him back to Child Welfare. If they hadn't I'd have missed out on the love of a lifetime, my beautiful son. So I don't harbor evil thoughts about them, although I did at one time," she admitted. "They brought him back because they thought they were getting a white child. They were a white couple and they didn't want a biracial baby. When Titus was an infant it was impossible to tell what he was, especially with that blond hair and those blue eyes. Nobody was trying to put anything over on the couple. Child Welfare just didn't know what he was.

"As he got older his hair stopped being curly and blond. It turned coarse and it darkened. His skin became more olive than porcelain and his eyes became the gray-blue color they are now. His features changed and it became obvious that he was mixed. Whatever he was, he wasn't one hundred percent Caucasian and the couple couldn't deal with it. They had no desire to raise a child of a different race," she said in a quiet voice that was still tinged with a bit of scorn for the couple.

Now tears were running freely down Paris's face, tears she didn't bother to remove. Her heart felt as if it were being twisted in a wringer and her stomach felt as if it were full of hot rocks. What a terrible thing to happen to an innocent child. She tried to speak several times before she could get the words out. "How…how did you…"

Sarah smiled and handed Paris a big soft cloth napkin from the drawer nearest her. "How did we get Titus? Oh, that part is wonderful, Paris. It proved to me that there really are miracles in the world. Before I met Titus, I was on the verge of suicide. I really was, and that's no exaggeration," she said as she watched the expression on Paris's face grow alarmed.

"Clifton and I had been married for about seven years. We had a beautiful family with our two girls, Nona and Natalie, the one you haven't met yet. We were all so excited when I was blessed with another baby, especially when it turned out to be a boy. The girls were thrilled with their little brother. They treated him like a doll baby. We named him Clifton and the day he was born was one of the happiest of my life. So you can understand that the day he died was the worst day I've ever known."

The tears started rolling again and Paris really couldn't speak this time. Sarah could see her distress and hastened to finish the story. "It was Sudden Infant Death Syndrome, and it was heartbreaking. I think my heart really broke, Paris, because I went into a depression I just couldn't shake. Clifton tried to console me, and the girls did, too, but I couldn't seem to break free of the despair. I was truly contemplating suicide. I simply didn't want to live anymore. I was the one who found him, you see, and I just couldn't get rid of the guilt, the idea that I was a terrible mother, that it was my fault. I didn't feel like I deserved my husband and my girls because I wasn't fit to take care of them. Oh, honey, my mind just went off in a billion different directions, all of them just awful. But my mother, bless her heart, was, and is, the smartest woman I'll ever meet."

Paris took her hand back and wiped her face thoroughly with the napkin. "What happened, Sarah? What did Mama Sweet do?"

"She was a registered nurse and she volunteered at the children's home. Titus was now a ward of the state and he was the saddest, angriest little boy anyone had ever seen. He was so miserable and confused he just struck out at anyone who came near him. His beautiful little face never smiled, and he couldn't tolerate contact with anyone, he couldn't stand to be touched. My mother knew in her heart that somehow he and I could heal each other. So she had me come down there to teach a crafts class. It took her a while to persuade me to do it, but I did. And that's where Titus and I found each other.

"I was teaching the little ones how to make some kind of Halloween craft and this adorable boy made his way over to me and wouldn't leave my side all afternoon. I made him my helper and we had such a good time! I found out later it was the first time he'd smiled since he came to the home. I couldn't stop thinking about him, so sweet and solemn," she said thoughtfully. "I didn't plan to but I came back the next day, and the next. I brought Clifton with me on the third day. The girls came with me, too. By now we were so familiar with one another, Titus and I, it was like we'd been together forever. It was relatively easy to begin the process to adopt him and by Christmas he was our little boy. It took some adjusting for all of us because he was still very shy of strangers and he needed constant reassurance. He would cling to me so fiercely sometimes all I could do was hold him, all day. I'd wash clothes, make dinner, vacuum and everything else holding him on one hip.

"He took to Clifton, too. When Clifton was at home, Titus would follow him everywhere like his shadow. Clifton would talk to him like he was talking to another adult, but Titus loved it. The sun rose and set just for Clifton as far as Titus was concerned," she said fondly. "He would only sleep with Clifton and me at first, and sometimes he wouldn't sleep at all, he'd lie there and look at us in turn to make sure we weren't going to leave him in the middle of the night."

Sarah looked at Paris's face, which was now mottled with red from sobbing. "Sweetie, you should go put some cold water on your face! Titus will think I've been giving you the third degree or something," she joked. She patted Paris's shoulder and insisted she go freshen up. Paris did as she was told and managed to come out of the powder room looking a lot less woebegone. She was still shaking her head at what had happened to Titus.

"I can't believe people could be that cruel. How on earth could they do that to a little baby, a baby they were supposed to love," Paris said with anger suffusing each word.

"Honey, try not to judge them so harshly. This is still the

South, after all, and it was quite a while ago. These people came from a very segregated world and in their own way they were doing what they thought was best for the child. I've come to believe they did love Titus, enough to give him back so he could have a life with a family who wouldn't have issues with his heritage." She paused and got a distant look in her eyes before she resumed speaking.

"A few weeks after he came to us we got a package in the mail. It was an album with all kinds of pictures of Titus from the time they adopted him until the time they brought him back. There was also a list of his favorite foods and the things he liked and didn't like. I really believe they loved him. They just couldn't handle the racial situation. And I can't condemn them for that. It was over thirty-five years ago and times were very, very different, very harsh. I can't judge them, I can only thank them. If they hadn't brought him back, I wouldn't have him now. He's been one of the biggest joys of our lives. And the girls loved him at once, they really did. Not to mention Mama Sweet! That's how she got that name, you know. Titus called her that when he came to live with us because she was so sweet to him. He fell in love with her and vice versa. They've been utter fools for each other for years and years." A noise from the back porch made both women look that way, just in time to see Titus and Clifton back from an errand.

Paris didn't stop to think about what she did next. She didn't consider or hesitate; she just went right to Titus and put her arms around his waist. He returned the embrace and kissed her forehead and her cheek before asking to what he owed this pleasure.

She couldn't answer him; her only response was to nestle even closer and hold on tighter. He stroked her hair and held her. They stayed like that for a long time, long after his parents discreetly left the room.

Chapter 18

Paris was consumed with embarrassment after the way she threw herself into Titus's arms. After what Sarah had revealed to her about his past, she'd felt her heart open up in a way she'd never experienced. The feelings she had for him were all consuming and she had to touch him; she had to be in his arms. He didn't seem to be bothered by her display at all; he simply accepted her tender embrace and returned it. His parents, bless their hearts, also acted as though nothing were amiss, they accepted the affection between the two of them as though it was the norm. They had no idea how things really were between their son and Paris. To be accurate, Paris didn't really know how things were, either, but now wasn't the time to question the situation. They were still in Charleston, having been prevailed upon to spend the night and despite the fact that the pretenses under which Titus's family were embracing her were slightly false, Paris had never felt more welcome anywhere in her life.

Nona and Nicole also spent the night and they had an impromptu slumber party. Paris had been given the guest room, another beautiful room decorated by Nicole. The furniture was mahogany, including a big four-poster bed on which they were all perched while eating Sarah's delicious teacakes and drinking hot chocolate. The walls were a feminine shade of green and the draperies were the exact same color, a pretty shade of sea foam. The bedding was a lighter shade of the same color in a raw silk with piles of pillows in various shades of pink. Nona referred to the room as the AKA palace, which was appropriate since Sarah was indeed a member of that sorority. A beautiful floral Oriental rug brought the colors together, as did the pictures on the walls, all of them framed in matte gold and all painted by Sarah. They talked for hours, giggling and gossiping and, in Paris's case, getting to know Titus even better as they regaled her with tales from his childhood. Nona was the better informant as she was older than Titus, but Nicole was the one who told about the ex-girlfriends. Paris was completely riveted by her colorful accounts.

"He wasn't one to mess around with a lot of girls," Nicole told her. "When he had a girlfriend it was just him and her and that was it. But honey, after what that heifer did to him over the junior prom, ooh, it still makes me sick to think about it," she said hotly. The flash of indignation in her eyes bore this out. Paris naturally wanted to know what she was talking about, and Nicole was happy to supply details.

"Titus had this girlfriend named Karen and he was crazy about her. Her folks weren't rich-rich, but they thought they were and they were pretty snotty, but she wasn't like that. At least that's with Titus thought. Anyway, he was going to take his girl to the prom and he went all out, honey. He didn't ask Mama and Daddy for a dime—he earned all the money himself. That boy worked like a slave for months so they would have a memorable prom night with a limo and dinner at the fanciest restaurant in town, all that. So the night of the prom comes and he rolls up to Karen's house all excited and happy and Karen's father met him at the door and told him his daughter wasn't going anywhere with some half-breed bastard." Nicole paused and handed Paris a fistful of tissues to stem the tide of tears that gushed from her eyes.

"I knew you were gonna spring a leak. I had these ready for you," Nicole told her. "Hurry up and blow so you can hear the rest."

Paris laughed and hurried to pull herself together. "Hang on a minute so I can wash my hands," she said as she slid off the bed and used the adjoining bathroom to splash water on her face and wash her hands, patting them dry on the soft towel. "You know something, this is amazing. I can't stand for anyone to see me cry and I've done nothing but boo-hoo all day. I'm pitiful," she said with a sigh.

Nona gave her a wise look. "That's because we're practically family. A few tears here and there don't matter."

"Both of you need to hush so I can finish telling the story," Nicole said sternly. "Get back on the bed so I can conclude this tale of heartbreak." She spoke flippantly, but Paris could tell Nicole felt this as deeply now as when it had actually happened. She climbed back onto the bed and waited for the end of the narrative.

"There really isn't much more to tell, except that he was heartbroken. I was in middle school when he was a junior in high school and I can still remember how humiliated he was over it. And that heifer Karen, ooh, girl, I can't stand her to this day." Nicole made an angry face and rolled her eyes. Nona tried for a more temperate approach. "Now, Nicole, she was just a kid—it's not like she could control her parents," she said.

"Oh, please. That heifer knew her father was gonna go ziggety-boom because he'd been telling her for weeks to get rid of the yellow boy and she didn't do it because he was like a prize or something. All the little girls wanted to go with Titus because he was so fine and so sweet and since she was the one who had him, she wasn't giving him up. She knew her father was gonna go ballistic when Titus came to pick her up and she could have avoided all of that if she'd been straight about the whole thing. Hmmph, havin' my brother come up there and make a fool out of himself for her sorry butt." Nicole's fury was plain in her face.

Nona sighed. "Yeah, it was pretty foul. The killing part is that the little wench still went to the prom. It turns out she had a backup date. You're right, Nicole, she was a selfish little cow. But she was nothing compared to that chick he almost married. That's the one I can't stand," she said moodily.

Paris looked from one sister to the other and demanded to know the story. "You can't just keep me in suspense. What happened?"

Nona told this one, and a sorry tale it was. "Titus had just graduated from West Point and there was some girl he'd met in Texas where he was stationed who was supposed to be a real sweetheart. She was smart and pretty, blah, blah, blah and she was supposed to be crazy about Titus. Julie was pretty, I grant you that, but I couldn't see any of those other positive attributes. But I have to say, I really think he was in love because this was the first woman he'd been serious about since that wench Karen. Julie was always so prissy and perfect when he was around but there was something about her I just didn't like. Anyway, Titus heard her talking on the phone about how he was going to give her some pretty babies and that's why she was hooked up with him. She wanted him because she'd been looking for a good-looking light-skinned man to get some pretty kids like her sister had, can you believe it?" Nona looked as angry as Nicole.

Nicole laughed wickedly, and nudged Paris with her elbow. "Yeah, but this time we had his back, didn't we, girl? We were visiting him in Killeen when this all came down and we waited until he went on duty and then we got that witch good. Natalie was with us and we went down to the mall where Julie worked and waited for her to come out to her car. Honey, we chased that little bee-atch down like a dog and caught up with her in the Piggly-Wiggly parking lot. We beat her down, girl, we really did. Mess over *my* big brother like that? I don't think so!" Nicole snapped her fingers in the air and looked totally self-righteous.

Nona hastened to assure Paris it wasn't as bad as it sounded. "We shoved her around a little and called her lots of names and then we took her engagement ring back. As much money as he spent on that thing, if she thought she was going to keep it she had another think coming. We made her write a note telling him she wouldn't feel right about keeping it and we gave that ring back to him that very night. Miserable wench," she said with a haughty sniff. Then she burst into embarrassed laughter. "I still can't believe we did that, though. If Mama and Daddy knew what we'd done...shoot, if *Titus* ever found out what we did, we'd be dead meat."

Nicole was unrepentant, though. "Screw that noise, that heifer made my mama cry. She was so upset over the situation she just broke down and nobody makes my mama cry and gets away with it. Just don't mess with my family, period. That way you get to keep breathing," she said fiercely and Paris absolutely believed her. But she was stunned by the stories and said so.

"I just don't get it. Why wouldn't they want to be with Titus just for Titus? He's everything a woman could possibly want in a man, he's like a dream come true," she said. "He's smart and handsome and hardworking," she said dreamily. "And he's sexy and successful and brave and…"

"And he's nosy and sneaky, too," Nicole said, pointing to Titus who was standing in the doorway with a big cheese-eating grin on his face. "How long have you been standing there, ya sneaky rascal?"

"Long enough" was all he would say. "So why don't you two get out of here so I can say good night to my baby? We have a long day tomorrow and she needs her rest," he said while his eyes caressed Paris.

Nicole and Nona got off the bed, gathered the plates and cups left from their cocoa and cookies party and headed for the door. Nicole couldn't resist a dig though, making a face as she walked past her brother. "Why don't you fasten that shirt up? Nobody wants to see all that there," she said, gesturing at his broad and muscular chest.

Nona laughed and pushed Nicole out of the room. "Speak for yourself. I think Paris likes the view."

Paris was indeed enjoying the view of Titus standing in the doorway wearing old faded jeans and an equally ancient cotton shirt, which was completely unbuttoned so she could see the smooth golden expanse of his body. She touched the corner of her mouth to make sure she wasn't drooling, and then remembered she was wearing pajamas. They were cute, to be sure, but they weren't sexy or slinky, just pale pink classically cut menswear pajamas covered in tiny rosebuds. She was barefoot and also makeup-free, having showered and scrubbed her face before the slumber party. She looked at Titus filling up the doorway looking sexier than she could remember seeing him and wished with all her heart that she could crawl under the bed. Titus moved suddenly, crossing the threshold and pulling her into his arms.

"I needed a good-night kiss," he said softly. "You look

cute, baby. You're really gorgeous, aren't you?" Before she could answer he bent to her lips and took the kiss he'd been craving. When his lips touched hers she melted into him, her hands moving up his chest, touching him the way she'd wanted to for days. Their tongues mated hungrily and their mutual caress went on and on until Titus finally pulled away with great reluctance. "Thank you, Paris."

Paris rubbed her face against him until she found his heartbeat and she rested against it, contentment and arousal warring within her. "For what, sweetheart?"

"For coming here with me to see about Mama Sweet, for pretending to be my girlfriend," he teased, kissing the top of her head. "Just for being your own sweet self."

"I think I should get another kiss if I'm that sweet," she said with a serious look on her face.

"You can have all the kisses you want any time you want them," he told her, then proceeded to demonstrate.

Down the hall, Nona and Nicole watched with avid interest, nudging each other in the side. "Girl, we're going to have some nieces and nephews pretty soon," gloated Nicole.

Nona smiled broadly, and then caught herself. "You know Titus always said he was never having children and you know why."

Nicole raised one perfectly arched brow as she looked at the couple locked in each other's arms. "If that's the case he needs to cut that out 'cause that's where babies come from. You know that, right? That definitely makes babies and lots of 'em."

Titus looked down at the sweet armful of woman cuddled into his side and smiled. Paris had fallen asleep shortly after takeoff and the way she relaxed into his arms was deeply gratifying to him. They'd had a pretty eventful two days, especially this morning. He had to smile when he thought about how the day started off, with breakfast. Sarah had insisted on fixing them a traditional repast and while she was waiting for the hot biscuits to come out of the oven she innocently asked Paris if she'd like some fruit. Paris had naturally reached for a banana, a selection that caused Titus great pain. He'd taken it from her and gone to the counter with it. In a few minutes he placed a small glass dish in front of her with the banana sliced neatly. He'd drizzled heavy cream and sprinkled a bit of cinnamon and nutmeg on top. Paris stared at it for a moment before thanking him and picking up her spoon to taste it. Her eyes closed in bliss and she made a sound of pure enjoyment. "This is delicious, Titus, what made you think of doing it this way?"

He'd given her a strained smile and said he'd tell her later. The rest of the meal went well and Paris had pitched in with his sisters to get the kitchen cleaned up while he went with his mother to pick up Mama Sweet from the hospital. It hadn't taken long to get her settled comfortably in her room, and it also hadn't taken long for her to start interrogating Paris. Titus had steeled himself for almost anything when he realized it was Mama Sweet's intention to find out everything there was to find out about his so-called girlfriend. Mama Sweet was sitting in the middle of the bed, propped up on big fat pillows looking like a delicate wind could blow her down. Her snowy white hair was beautifully styled as always and she was wearing a pretty bed jacket Sarah had given her. She'd insisted that Paris sit next to her on the bed so she could get to know her better. And Paris had obliged her at once, talking animatedly and answering any question the dear old lady asked.

Titus had sat in the big armchair between the two big windows and watched Paris, enjoying the play of expressions on her face and the sweet way she talked to his grandmother. Mama Sweet's yippy little Pomeranian, Pumpkin, was in his lap. This was the holy terror who'd caused the accident and as far as Titus was concerned the dog was a menace and a nuisance. For some reason Pumpkin adored Titus and assumed the feelings were mutual. Titus pretended he could barely tolerate the fluffy little creature, but he was actually quite fond of the furball. He'd almost drifted off to sleep when he heard Mama Sweet asking when the wedding was going to be. "Because my grandson has a strong nature, baby, and he's not going to be able to hold out much longer. You all had better make this a summer wedding because my boy can't keep his hands off you. I can see it in his eyes, sugar, he needs you bad. That poor boy might lose his mind if you don't do something soon," Mama Sweet said pertly.

Titus's eyes had flown open at the same time his mouth did. "Mama Sweet, you can't say things like that!"

Mama Sweet had waved a hand at him. "Hush, baby, don't interrupt me. Now Paris, how many babies are you two planning on? Two big good-looking people like you and Titus are going to make some beautiful ones. Do you want a big family, honey?"

Titus had turned bright red and almost choked when he heard that. "Mama Sweet! You can't ask her those kinds of things," he roared. "You can't be getting all in her business like that!" He almost dislodged Pumpkin in his agitation and she barked her displeasure in high-pitched yelps.

His grandmother had looked at him with pity in her eyes. "Button, baby, are you bound up? Have you been getting enough fiber in your diet? You know how you are when you're not regular," she said sweetly. She had then turned to Paris and suggested cooking Titus greens at least three times a week. "I started calling him Button because he was as cute as a button when he was little. But he has to eat right, you know. He's prone to being constipated if you don't watch his fiber," she said in a stage whisper.

Now safely on the plane and away from those who would render him a child in front of his woman, Titus could see the humor in the situation, something he'd been hard put to find at the time. Paris stirred in his arms, moving closer to his body and murmuring his name softly. "Titus?"

He stroked her shining hair with gentle fingers and kissed her forehead before answering. "Yes, baby, what is it?"

"I love your family, they're all so wonderful," she said sleepily. He tilted her face up to his and kissed her nose, her cheek and her lips, inhaling her precious scent.

"They think you're pretty special, too. Too bad you didn't get to meet Natalie, but she was out of town on business. But I have a feeling they'll be coming to Atlanta for a visit soon," he said with a wry smile. If he knew his family they wouldn't be able to stay away, they were too taken with Paris, especially Mama Sweet. He found the prospect didn't make him uneasy in the least, which was a surprise. For some reason it was okay with him, it really was. What wasn't okay was the fact that Paris's stalker still hadn't been caught. It was way past time for the whole thing to be over. He had a plan, though, a plan he would put into action as soon as they got back to Atlanta. He only hoped that Paris would see things the same way he did.

The flight to Atlanta was short and the deplaning was easy. Titus collected his Hummer and their luggage and they arrived at Paris's house in short order. While Titus brought the bags in, Paris went to the refrigerator to get something cold to drink. She always felt dehydrated when she got off a plane. Titus found her standing in front of the refrigerator with a look of utter horror on her face. He dropped her bags and took her by her shoulders. "What is it, baby? What's the matter?"

She pointed at the refrigerator with a shaking hand. "He's been in my house," she whispered. "He's been in here, Titus."

He turned and looked where she was pointing. The magnetic

poetry squares had been arranged in a threat so explicit and vile it was all he could do not to swipe them all away so she couldn't see them anymore, but he couldn't do that because this was evidence. He did the next best thing; he held her tightly and assured her it would all be over in a few days.

The next day Paris thought her eyes would never focus properly again. She'd spent the day in her office at the complex, watching surveillance tapes until she feared she'd go blind or stark raving mad. Titus had come to her that morning with news. He'd entered her office and closed the door behind him, giving her a smile that melted her heart. His words, "You look very pretty, Paris," warmed her all over. He'd joined her on her long sofa and they exchanged a tender kiss before he got down to business. "We found Gayle Rodgers, Paris. And you're never going to guess where."

Paris had indeed been surprised to find out that Gayle had been in rehab for her drug addiction. "She'd made a huge mess of her life and your firing her was the impetus she needed to get herself together. She went home to Philadelphia and her parents put her into a private hospital. She'd been given Vicodin after a root canal and one thing led to another and she got hooked on it. It got to the point where no doctor would write her a prescription for it and she started buying it online. She maxed out all her credit cards and was beginning to pawn her belongings to sustain her habit. She did quite a few other things, too, to support that habit," Titus told her. He shook his head slowly, and then got to the point. "Here's the thing, baby. It can't possibly be Gayle who's been doing these things to you because she's been on lockdown. But there remains the possibility that someone could be acting on her behalf. Someone might be trying to get to you because of her," he said slowly.

While Paris was trying to get her head around that concept

Titus pressed on. "I need you to look at all the surveillance tapes and see if you can detect anything odd or recognize anyone. For a lot of people it might be a shot in the dark, but I have a feeling you'll be able to see something we've missed."

And so it had begun, with Paris sitting in her office staring at tape after tape, trying her best to follow Titus's instructions to observe everything. Terry Patterson was with her to make note of anything she found unusual. Now her eyes were burning and she was beginning to get goofy. Suddenly she sat up straight and stared intently at the screen while she pressed the Pause button on the remote control. She reached over and grabbed Terry's arm, pointing at the television. "Terry, I think I have something," she said, her eyes fixed on the frozen image. "Call Titus."

Soon they were in the video lab that was a part of Titus's operation. Paris looked around the big room with awe; she'd never seen that much television equipment outside of an actual television studio. "Wow, Titus, you use all of this?" she asked him as she mentally cataloged all the professional and highly expensive gear.

Titus nodded as he waited for one of his skilled technicians to edit the tapes. "We do all kinds of investigative work. Most of it's corporate security, but we also look for missing children. We've handled kidnappings, insurance fraud, identity theft, internet fraud, you name it, we've done it all. Political scandal, custody battles, missing heirs, *fake* heirs, dognapping—I can't think of too much we haven't investigated," he said offhandedly. Paris was amazed that he just tossed it off as though it were of no importance. She knew for a fact that Argonne Investigations, as his firm was known, was one of the top detective organizations in the world. His reputation was impeccable in the U.S. as well as several other countries. Titus was a man of respect in his chosen career and she suddenly felt humbled that he was taking the time to personally oversee her situation.

"Paris, we're ready. Tell me again what you saw in these tapes. We played around with them a little so you can see the images better. So what was it that made you pick these tapes?" Titus sounded all business as he asked the question, even though his hand was on her elbow as he led her to a seat at the conference table in the center of the room. She looked at the tape being played on the nearest TV screen.

"That man is George Wilson. The tall one with the bald head and the sunglasses. He's a chef and he used to work in the dining room here at the complex. He left about a week after Gayle did," Paris said.

"Did he know Gayle, by any chance?" Titus again sounded nothing but professional.

"Yes, he knew her. He knew her quite well, actually, because he was also from Philly, I believe. It was quite a coincidence that they ended up working in the same building because they also went to college together at Carnegie-Mellon, I believe. They lost track of each other when he went to culinary school, but then they both found their way to Atlanta. I think he had a little crush on her because he was always fixing her special dishes, things like that."

Titus nodded his head, and then asked her what else she saw. She looked at the next screen and pointed at the date in the corner. "Okay, George had been gone a couple of weeks before this was taped and yet there he is in the parking garage, big as day. And he's wearing coveralls with the Deveraux Group logo on it, as if he worked there. So he could have had access to the company cars. If he's been hanging around there he might even have known which cars I was going to drive…" Her voice faded off and her face was shadowed by dismay. "If he's the one who was doing it, he could have been tampering with every car out there, Titus. Everyone who drives those cars could be in danger because of me."

His face turned fierce and tender at the same time. "Look, Paris, don't you ever say that again. It's not your fault. It was never your fault. People who do things like this have their own agenda, usually one that none of us can understand. But it has nothing whatsoever to do with your behavior. It's an outgrowth of their sickness, that's all it is."

"But George is such a nice, normal-acting guy," Paris said sadly. "I can't believe he'd do things to me, that he would suddenly hate me and want to do me harm. It just doesn't make sense, Titus."

"Then why was he hanging around here, Paris? How did he get those coveralls and why would he want them?" Titus asked patiently.

"I don't know. I just don't know. But it's going to take more than a couple of surveillance tapes to make me believe that a perfectly nice man has suddenly turned psycho and has decided to make me his pet project," Paris said wearily. "I'm certainly not trying to tell you how to do your job," she added quickly, "but that's a whole lot for me to swallow, Titus."

Chapter 19

Titus gave a knock on the door of Martin Deveraux's private office. It was strictly a courtesy as he was expected. "Come on in, man, and sit down. You're a hard man to catch," Martin said in his deep voice.

Titus shook Martin's hand before taking a seat in one of the big leather chairs that flanked Martin's desk. He gave Martin a weary smile and said something about his business keeping him running twenty-four seven. Martin returned the smile with a sincere one. A big grin, as a matter of fact. "Man, you can't let your life be all about business. You have good people working for you. Let them do their jobs. I love my work, but I love my family more," he said looking at the newest portrait of his wife, Ceylon, and their three children that held pride of place among all the awards and honors given to the music division of The Deveraux Group. "I can't think of anything I'd rather do than be with my woman and our babies.

You need a wife, man, that's no joke." Martin leaned back in his huge chair and gazed at the beautiful likeness of Ceylon, the woman who'd stolen his heart so long ago.

"Don't hold back, Martin, how do you really feel?" Titus said with dry wit. Martin chose to ignore his wry tone and answer him seriously.

"I feel blessed, that's how I feel. Ceylon is pregnant again," he said with evident pride. "She's excited and so am I, although she's having a little more trouble with this pregnancy than the others. Elizabeth was a piece of cake and even the boys were a snap, which was great since they're twins. This one is a little harder on her. After this one we're done, no more. I don't like to see her uncomfortable."

Without considering his words Titus asked if she was going to have her tubes tied. Martin frowned and shook his head. "I'm getting fixed, man. Ceylon will have given me four babies and I'm damned if I'll ask her to do that. And she shouldn't have to fool with birth control, either. Snip, snip and I'm in the no-baby zone. Simple."

Whoa. That's what you call devotion, Titus thought. "How are the kids, anyway? How's Miss Elizabeth? Still large and in charge?"

Martin gave a shout of laughter. "We can't thank you enough for starting that Miss Elizabeth thing. She not only introduces herself as 'Miss,' she makes her brothers call her that now. You've created a diva, thank you so much for that. Really. I just can't wait until you have some little divas of your own so Uncle Martin can spoil them rotten."

A shadow passed over Titus's face so fast it was as if it never happened. He segued into another topic, the real reason he'd come to see Martin in the first place. "Everything is set. I had her watch some tapes so I could make sure this was the guy and she picked him right out. I've been investigating him for about six weeks now. Once we isolated the name Gayle Rodgers, we started looking for people with ties to her and his name came up repeatedly. Paris thinks he's just a nice innocuous guy who wouldn't hurt a fly, but it seems he has a pattern of inappropriate behavior with women. There are at least six counts of stalking and sexual intimidation on file in New York State and a few juvenile counts in Philly. And here's the beauty part—he's obsessed with Gayle Rodgers."

He leaned back in his chair before continuing. "They knew each other in college and he was crazy about her. They dated briefly and she dropped him like a hot rock when someone better came along. The real reason he went to culinary school is that he had a nervous breakdown. He couldn't get over his busted affair with Gayle and he went off the deep end. He tried going to graduate school but he couldn't handle the pace or the stress so he opted for his culinary studies. He did really well and the irony is he might have been a huge success as a chef if he hadn't run into Gayle again.

"He pretended like everything was cool, but seeing her again here in Atlanta tripped his trigger and he went cruising on the dark side again. He was content to exist on the fringes of Gayle's life, trying to work his way back in, but when she got terminated, it blew his mind. He blamed Paris for her absence in his life and decided to get revenge on her, thus the escalating program of harassment."

Martin frowned deeply. "How the hell did we end up hiring a nut job like that? We screen everyone we hire and we do a background check as well. This shouldn't have happened, Titus."

"Well, for one thing, he wasn't an employee of The Deveraux Group. The dining room is staffed and managed by Gourmet Dining, Incorporated. They actually lease space in office buildings and hotels. The chefs and service people they use are their employees. The Deveraux Group doesn't employ them. Their screening process is completely different than the one used by your company. Their screening consists of reading their resume and checking their references, that's all. If they'd dug a little deeper they might have found out a lot more about George Wilson. Some of the records were sealed," Titus said with a cold, lethal smile, "but I managed to circumvent that little obstacle."

Martin gave Titus a deeply serious look of his own. "So what's the plan? How are you going to run him to earth?"

"The same way we let him get in while she was out of town. We allow him to think he's disabled the security and that the house is vulnerable to entry. We deliberately left the inner garage door that opens into the house open and he found it. What he didn't realize was that the house was not only being surveilled, there were agents inside as well as outside in the trees and on the roof. When my people don't want to be seen, they're invisible, trust me." Titus gave Martin a pleasant little grin that was totally at odds with his icily silver eyes. "We're going to use Paris as bait to lure him in. Don't worry, I'll be on site, as will twelve agents. It will look like she's alone, but nothing will be further from the truth. There will be an agent inside the house as well as a phalanx outside and he'll be able to get in, but he'll never get out."

Martin leaned back in his chair and propped his elbows on the armrests, steepling his fingers. He stayed that way for a few minutes, obviously deep in thought. "I don't like it, Titus. I just don't like the idea of Paris being in jeopardy, even for a few minutes. She's like our sister, man, we love her that much. I can't have anything happen to her, I'd never forgive myself."

Titus leaned forward, eyes blazing. "You have to understand, Martin, nothing is going to happen to Paris while I'm alive. *Nothing*. If you're concerned we can just call in the police and let them handle it. They'll go to his home with warrants and writs and he'll be thrown into jail and a good lawyer will have him out in a day or so, then he'll disappear. Or he'll get some jail time if we can get a competent prosecutor on the case. He'll behave himself inside and be out in six months to pick up where he left off. I want him caught in the act so we can put an end to it once and for all. If he's apprehended in the act, we can make sure the charges stick and he'll get a stiff sentence. It's up to you and your brothers. Just say the word and I'll call the officer in charge of the case."

Martin looked at Titus for a long moment before answering. "I wasn't trying to say I don't trust you, I have every confidence in you and your ability to get the job done. But I have to say it again—Paris is much more than a cousin to my brothers and me. We love her and if anything happened to her, anything at all, we wouldn't be able to live with it. And I can see you feel the same way," he said, gratified to see the color surge to Titus's face. It was the first time he could ever remember Titus showing so much emotion.

"You have some very strong feelings for my cousin. I've known it for a long time, a real long time. I know you and I trust you so I haven't gotten all up in your business about it, but I have to say I'm curious. What's going on with you two? You seemed like you were on your way to something lasting for a while, and then it was all over. What's up?"

Titus again acted in an uncharacteristic manner, this time he made a face in which all his chagrin showed. "You Deverauxes don't hold back, do you? You sound just like her father did when he asked me the same question."

Martin gave a low whistle. "You mean Judge pinned you to the wall, too? And you lived to tell the tale?" He chuckled. "Either Judge is mellowing in his golden years or he likes you. Time was he'd take off your head and hand it to ya, partner. Look, if her daddy's already been there I'm not going to belabor it. I do have one piece of advice for you though. Just what you need from a friend—unsolicited advice, right?" He laughed, and Titus joined in. "Seriously though, my advice to you is to get it done. You need to let her know you love her and get a ring on her finger. You know you're never going to find anybody like her in the whole world so why drag it out? Handle your business, bro. I'm always available as a best man and my calendar is open," he said cheerfully.

Just then his office door opened and his identical twin sons raced in, followed more sedately by their older sister, Elizabeth. Ceylon was last, admonishing the little ones as she entered. "What have I told you about that? We can't just come racing in the door whenever we get ready. Daddy might be very busy," she told them firmly but lovingly.

Titus and Martin were both on their feet as she entered. Martin wore the smile that was for her alone and Titus had a bemused expression on his face. He watched as Martin came around his desk and embraced his wife, looking into her eyes with love and concern. "Come sit down, baby. What are you doing out by yourself with the Too Live Crew? I don't want you overdoing it," he said as he led her to the sofa. Ceylon was a raving beauty with smooth brown skin and big hazel eyes fringed by long lashes. Her short brown hair was always fashionably styled and even now, in the throes of a difficult pregnancy, she glowed with happiness. She barely got out a greeting to Titus before Martin was questioning her about why she was out with the children sans nanny or any other help.

Ceylon laughed gently at his concern. "Sweetheart, we just went to the doctor's office for their checkups. I'm fine," she insisted.

In the meantime, Elizabeth made a beeline for Titus, whom she considered her personal property. He smiled down at her, taking the hand she offered him and bending way down to put a kiss on her fingertips. "Hello, Miss Elizabeth, how are you today?"

She was so much like both her parents it was hilarious. Elizabeth had Martin's thick black hair, sweeping eyebrows and creamy skin. But she had her mother's hazel eyes, dimpled smile and perfect skin. She looked like a perfect little lady, all dainty and sweet, but she was a real tomboy and could hang with the rowdiest boys on the block. Today she was all girl in a pretty little dress and she was full of smiles for Uncle Titus, as she called him. "I'm just fine, thank you. When are you coming to see us? You haven't been to see us in a long time," she pointed out. The twins agreed, asking when he was going to come play football with them again.

Titus promised to come soon, but explained he had to get going. He exchanged greetings with Ceylon and noticed how beautiful she looked. Incipient motherhood really agreed with her; she was radiant. While he was leaving Martin's office he had time to wonder why his friend's words regarding marriage didn't strike terror in his heart or freeze the marrow of his bones or something. There was a time when the mere mention of the word *marriage* would wrench his gut in hot agony, but that time seemed to have passed. Instead of brooding over what Martin had said he found himself singing under his breath, something he hadn't done since he'd sung in the church choir back in Charleston.

Paris was sitting cross-legged on her bed, writing in her journal as she did every night. *I'm trying not to freak out over this. Titus says this is going to work and I have to believe him. Titus is very smart and very careful and I know he won't let anything happen to me. I'm just not completely convinced that George is the one doing this, but I want my life back. This has to work, Titus wouldn't put me though it otherwise.*

She looked up to see Aidan in the doorway with a bottle of water in one hand and his car keys in the other. Merlin, who bounded onto her bed without waiting for an invitation, accompanied him. "Well, don't mind me, come on up," she said absentmindedly as she stroked Merlin's ears. "Where are you off to?" she asked Aidan, although she already knew the answer.

"I'm on my nightly prowl to nowhere, driving aimlessly around while we wait for the perp to show," he said blithely. Suddenly he looked glum. "I just said 'perp.' I'm starting to pick up the vocabulary of all those ghoulish detectives or PIs or whatever they call themselves. I'm going to lose my sardonic edge and start sounding like a rerun of *Cops* pretty soon." He came all the way into her room and surprised her with a kiss on the forehead. "Be careful and sleep well. Throw Merlin out if he starts fooling around," he advised and abruptly left the room.

Paris looked at Merlin, who'd made himself quite comfortable on the mohair afghan at the foot of the bed and sighed as she closed her journal. Her keeper for the night was Heide, who was in the downstairs den, which was lit by one dim light only. She felt sorry for her because her job was to remain out of sight and perfectly still until George or whoever it was made a move. Then it was her job to signal the men outside and they'd come barreling in and grab him. It was a simple plan but in Paris's experience nothing was that simple. Nothing had happened over the past two nights and she had no reason to believe anything would happen tonight. Oddly enough though, a part of her wanted tonight to be the night; she'd had enough of the whole ordeal. And she'd had enough of being away from Titus.

She said her prayers as she always did, kneeling next to her big bed. Then she slid under the covers and turned off the light with a sigh that started at her toes and ran through her whole body. And then the little shiver that always preceded her fantasies about Titus would assail her and the memory of being in his arms would take her off to dreamland. They always started at the same point, the night she'd spent with Titus in his condo, the night he'd cared for her so tenderly and made her feel like the most desirable woman on earth. She'd actually bought a huge bottle of Neutrogena Rainbath because the delightful fragrance of the gel was now a permanent part of her memory. She'd never smell it again without thinking about that night.

She tossed restlessly in the big bed, wishing with all her heart that Titus were there with her, to touch her, to say the sweet things he'd said that night, to teach her more of the erotic pleasures he'd shown her that night. Her body flamed with desire and as always she was choked by the passion she felt for him. Titus. Despite everything she'd vowed in the past, she loved him. There was no point in trying to fool herself, nor was there any reason to believe that he could return her feelings in the same way and they'd live happily ever after. It wasn't in the cards for them because he'd never be able to love her in the same way. But he did desire her. That much was plain and it gave her an odd sort of comfort. And for now, desire was all she had. She drifted off to sleep, unaware of the tears rolling down her face.

A short time later, Paris's eyes flew open and she winced in pain. Her heart leaped to her throat, pounding madly as she became aware that someone was pulling her hair. Then she heard the yowling and hissing and realized it was Merlin. "Cat, have you lost your mind?" she asked sleepily. "Cut it out or you'll be banished to the garage." She was about to close her eyes again when Merlin hurled himself against her, emitting a low whining growl she'd never heard before. Just then she heard a sound on the steps and she knew why Merlin had gone mad—there was someone in the house.

Wishing with all her heart she'd taken Lucien up on his offer of a gun, she got out of bed as quietly as possible and looked around for a weapon. There was a pair of Georgian silver candlesticks on her chest of drawers and she was inching her way toward them when she heard a voice, a strange yet oddly familiar voice. "I've got you now, bitch."

Titus wasn't feeling it that night. Something was wrong. All his instincts and training were on red alert and he knew with a certainty that things were going wrong. He spoke quietly into his mobile unit, "I'm going in. Wilson triggered the silent alarm but Heide didn't give the signal. Something is going down right now."

"I got your back, T." That was all the assurance he needed, coming from his best field agent. Paul Brown was as cool of head and as fearless as Titus and he had Titus's complete trust. Titus entered the darkened house and silently made his way into the den where his worst fears were realized—Heide was unconscious on the floor. Something that looked like a tranquilizer dart was in her back. She was definitely alive though, and that's what mattered. A sudden crash from the second level made him move with the speed of a jungle cat and he was upstairs in three bounds. The lights suddenly came on and what he saw froze his blood: Paris was being held by her neck and a gun was being pointed at her temple by the man from the videotape, George Wilson. He was anything but calm; his eyes were wild and his nose was running like a crackhead's. His lips were ashy and dry and he was laughing, a weird staccato giggle like a madman in a second-rate horror movie.

"Well, well, well, what have we here? Come to rescue Miss Priss, here?" he cackled. "It's not gonna happen, not tonight."

Titus could feel his rage reaching a dangerous point as the man locked his arm around Paris's throat more securely and pulled her body, clad in only a silk nightshirt, closer to him. "Let her go. Let's talk about this," Titus said soothingly. "You don't want to die, and I don't want to kill you. Just let her go, and you can leave, simple as that," he said, hoping with all his heart that he sounded sincere. Apparently he didn't succeed in convincing Wilson.

More maniacal laughter was his response. "Let her go? I don't think so. This is the first time I've seen her up real close and I have to tell you, she looks better in person. This is a fine piece of woman here. I might decide to just keep her, what you gonna do about that? Huh? What can you do, big man? I got a gun and you got a gun and I got your woman, so what you gonna do?"

At that moment Merlin flew through the air, launching himself at the man's face. Wilson's gun went off and so did Titus's, but Titus was the better shot and it was all over as Wilson slumped to the floor. Paris almost went down with him, but Titus caught her. She choked back a sob and started laughing. Titus was dressed all in black with a hooded spandex jacket and pants. He also had black camouflage paint on his face and he looked rather odd. Entirely beautiful to her relieved eyes but totally odd. He scooped up Merlin, who licked him in the face. "I'm buying you a case of caviar, cat. You deserve it," Titus mumbled. Paris's laughter continued as Terry Patterson, also in blackface, arrived on the stair landing. She was so relieved she didn't realize how close to hysteria she was. By now sirens were wailing and the house was flooded with light as all kind of floodlights were turned on to aid the police.

Paris was still clinging to Titus, loving the feeling of his strong arms around her. Suddenly she laughed again. "I'll bet the neighbors are loving this," she said. A pitiful meow made her take Merlin from Titus's arm. "Aww, Merlin, you poor kitty,

I didn't thank you, did I? You're a hero, did you know that?" She stroked him comfortingly, then gasped as she felt something wet and sticky. "Merlin, you're bleeding! Oh my God," she cried as she took him into the bathroom and used her expensive pink hand towel to wipe him. "Hold still, kitty. I don't see a wound of any kind—where did you get the blood from?"

The answer was only too obvious as Titus suddenly slumped forward and called her name before falling. She was there to catch him, though, as best she could. "Terry, help me," she shouted. "Hold on, baby, I've got you, I've got you, baby. It's going to be fine, Titus, I've got you."

Of course you do, Rosy. You've always had me in the palm of your hand.

Chapter 20

Titus came awake slowly, his eyelids heavy from the effect of the sedative he'd been given. Unbelievable as it seemed, he'd really been shot. It was a minor wound, but the way Paris had carried on you would have thought otherwise. His lips turned up in a faint smile as he remembered how Paris had yelled at Terry, the ambulance driver and anyone else who stood between Titus and instant medical treatment. She had ridden in the ambulance with him, refused to change clothes or put on a coat and stayed with him in her bloodied night-shirt, holding onto to his hand as she gave him all the comfort she could. He'd thought at the time that she was the one who could have used some comforting because she looked so stricken by his injury, but she was a Deveraux after all, and she could take it. She was definitely the woman to have on your side; she'd be there come hell or high water.

There was a soft pressure around his right hand and he

flexed his fingers slightly and was comforted to feel that pressure returned. He opened his eyes to find Paris sound asleep in a very uncomfortable looking position. She was sitting in a hard chair pulled up next to the bed and her head was pillowed on his shoulder. Someone had provided her with a sweat suit to wear and she looked utterly exhausted, even though she was asleep. She'd never looked more appealing to Titus, however. He moved his head so he could kiss her, just a gentle caress on her forehead. She barely stirred but she squeezed his fingers gently and murmured his name. It was more than enough for Titus, who drifted right back to sleep.

Paris sat cross-legged on the floor, cradling Merlin in her arms. He was purring happily while she told him again what a brave, superlative cat he was. He accepted her homage as his due, although every time her hand would stop stroking him, he would emit a sharp yowl and bat at her hand until she continued the cuddling. Aidan looked amused at the two of them and told her she'd brought it all on herself. "You know you can't dote on him. He's so rottenly spoiled he mistakes every gesture of goodwill for voluntary servitude." Merlin looked insulted and gave a lazy hiss in Aidan's direction, but he didn't move from his seat on Paris.

"He deserves every accolade. He's a wonderful, brave and resourceful cat and he saved me. I love him and he can do no wrong."

Aidan continued to put the last of his belongings into a canvas valise and glanced at Paris. "That's sort of the way I feel about Titus," he admitted.

"What? You mean you're not referring to him as Lord Voldemort anymore? I can't believe it! What changed your mind about him?"

Aidan closed his suitcase as he spoke. "Because even I, the

permanently cynical and jaded, can see the change in him. He's not the same person. Looks like the Tin Man has been given his heart," he said as he lifted the heavy valise off the bed. Paris stared at him as she set Merlin off her lap and stood clumsily. Pushing her hair out of her eyes she tried to look casual and unconcerned. "And what does that mean?"

"Don't be coy—you know what it means. Come on, Merlin, we're heading back to the homestead." He left the guest room and went down the stairs with Merlin scampering ahead of him. Paris followed more slowly, looking at the freshly papered wall of the landing. Aidan knew some people who had come out the morning after the scene had been released by the Atlanta Police Department and put the upstairs back in order. They had removed the bloodstains from the wall and replaced the wall-paper. They also stripped the floor and refinished it and every-thing looked the way it should, although Paris wasn't sure she felt the same way about living here. A part of her could never forget that this was where Titus had been shot while he was rescuing her. And she could never, ever forget that a man had broken in here and tried to kill her. A shudder passed through her body and she shook it off to follow Aidan down the stairs.

"Aidan, just say it outright. I don't have time for your cryptic nonsense," she said in a voice that was dangerously close to a whine. She stopped dead in her tracks, however, when she realized Aidan wasn't alone in the room. Titus was there, too, looking handsome and healthy with a stern look on his face. Paris's eyes got huge and Aidan grinned wickedly on his way out the door. He had the valise in one hand and the other hand held a carrier containing Merlin, who was making his distress known at the top of his lungs.

"It's been lovely, we'll have to do it again sometime, stay in touch, and, Titus, it's good to see you upright and taking nourishment. Buh-bye!"

Paris narrowed her eyes at Aidan as he winked and took his leave. She closed the door behind him and turned around to face Titus, who looked as forbidding as he had when she entered the room. He looked perfectly well, though, that was what was important. He was wearing a blue oxford cloth dress shirt opened at the neck with the sleeves rolled up. It was tucked into his faded and precisely pressed jeans and it enhanced his eyes, which despite his cool demeanor, were the warm shade that meant he was relaxed and happy. It suddenly hit her that he wasn't supposed to be here at all.

"Titus, why aren't you in the hospital? When were you released?"

"They turned me loose this morning, as you would have known had you been there with me. You left me, Paris," he said with a frown. "Why did you leave me?"

"I—I—I," Paris stammered. She looked as flustered as she felt, then something snapped. "I left because I felt I was getting in the way of your treatment. I was trying to make sure you got the best possible care and I was just in the way. And I needed a shower and a decent meal, thank you very much for asking. I've done nothing but worry about you and be there for you and I called every single member of your family and made sure they wouldn't worry and—"

She was so caught up in what she was saying that she didn't realize she was walking toward Titus as she made her points, or that he was walking toward her. He stopped directly in front of her and stemmed her tirade by putting his lips on hers. After a long and tender kiss he pulled away slowly and kissed her forehead and her temple.

"Baby, I know what you did and why you left. I was just teasing you," he said softly. Taking her by the hand he led her over to the sofa where he made her sit down on his lap and held her closely, kissing her neck and whispering her name.

"I'm fine, Paris, I really am. I'm made out of granite. Bullets bounce off me. I'm concerned about you, though. How are you doing, sweetheart?"

"I'm okay, Titus, I'm fine, in fact. I'm bracing myself for the invasion of the overprotective Deverauxes because my brothers are on their way, along with my daddy. I made them promise to wait until my birthday to come, but I wouldn't count on their cooperation. They're not going to be happy until they see for themselves that I'm in one piece."

"I don't blame them one bit," Titus said solemnly. "You're precious to them, just like you are to me. If I were a couple of states away from you, I'd be on my way here too, to make sure you're okay. You went through a lot, baby, and you need someone to watch over you."

Paris was touched and surprised to hear those words from Titus, but she had to make a point. She nestled closer to his uninjured side and stroked his face while she kissed him, little sweet kisses that she bestowed between her words. "I'm fine, Titus. I don't need a nursemaid. And besides, I didn't go through that much. Don't make it sound like I was a suffering maiden in a tower," she told him in a teasing voice. "Besides…" Her voice faltered a little. "It's all over now."

It was indeed all over. George Wilson had been taken into custody by the Atlanta Police Department but he'd tried to escape and had been shot for his efforts. He'd died on the operating table of the same hospital where Titus was treated. Paris stared at Titus with stricken eyes. "I still can't believe he was after me because he was so obsessed with Gayle. If he was going to start a vendetta with someone, why didn't he go after the ones who got her hooked on drugs, who kept taking her money to buy those prescription drugs online and sent her into bankruptcy?" she asked angrily.

Titus silenced her by taking her lips in a kiss. "Come on,

Rosy, don't get all upset. It's impossible for us to ferret out other people's motives for aberrant behavior, especially when they're as disturbed as Wilson was. He's gone now, really gone, and he can't bother you again," he said quietly.

They were both quiet for a moment, until Titus broke the silence. "I have to tell you, Paris, when he had his hands on you, when he was touching you with that gun in his hand, I wanted to kill him. I never wanted anything in my life more than to see his brains splattered on the wallpaper. God forgive me, but it's the truth. If anything had happened to you…" His voice trailed off and he kissed her again and again with growing need and passion. "If anything ever happens to you the person who does it better be long gone before I get there, because hell will be a party for them compared to what I'd do."

Paris was speechless. "Titus, I don't know what to say."

He gave her a slow, sexy smile. "Well, Rosy, maybe you'd better show me if you can't tell me. Let's go upstairs."

A low, throaty giggle escaped her throat and she tried to look scandalized, but she was already heating up from Titus's touch. "Why am I never looking seductive and sensual at these moments? Look at me—I'm so not sexy it's ridiculous," she said resignedly.

Titus looked at her from her hair, which was still damp from the shower and a mass of natural curls, to her toes, which were adorned with pink cashmere socks. She was wearing a pale green cotton knit outfit consisting of a long-sleeved top with a V-neck and matching leggings. She wasn't wearing a speck of makeup, but she smelled really good. "You don't get it, Rosy. You're always beautiful to me and you always look sexy. I think about making love to you all day, every day. And you smell fantastic, too. What's the name of that perfume? I don't want you to ever run out," he said with a lust-filled smile.

"It's called Stella," she said in a soft, sweet voice. "And if you come upstairs I'll show you the bottle so you'll know what to buy."

"Oh, yeah? And what else will you show me?" he growled.

Paris got off his lap and stood with her hand extended. "What would you like to see?" she countered playfully.

Titus loomed over her and suddenly gave her bottom a light smack that ended with a squeeze. "I want to see this hot, naked and ready for me. Am I going to get my wish?"

Paris's mouth was a perfect O of surprise but she recovered quickly, removing her top with lightning speed and tossing it at Titus. "You'll get your wish if you can catch me. Are you up to it?" He barely got a glimpse of her sexy green half-cup push-up bra before she dashed up the stairs.

Even a brief hospital stay hadn't slowed Titus down. He caught her before she got to the door of her bedroom and grabbed her around the waist, making her burst into laughter. "You'd better be careful, mister—you're still in a weakened state," she reminded him.

"Don't even try it, baby. Where you're concerned I have superhuman strength. Come here and let me show you what I mean," he said, taking her hand and pulling her through the doorway.

Paris made him sit on the big bed while she slipped out of the knit pants. She stepped out of them and folded them neatly, placing them on the slipper chair in the corner of the room. She looked at him over her shoulder, enjoying the expression on his face as she disrobed. She walked over to the bed slowly, putting seduction into every step. "As soon as I take these socks off, it's your turn," she purred.

Titus was already unbuttoning his shirt. "Leave the socks on for a minute, they're cute. They look sexy on you for some reason."

Paris did as he asked, but she stopped him from undoing his shirt. She stood in front of him, between his long legs that were spread wide. "That's my job. Let me undress you for a change." Titus took his hands away and allowed her to undo the buttons, although he was hot and moaning when she was done because she was licking his ears and sucking his earlobe while she worked. When the shirt was open, she slid her hands under it, caressing his shoulders as she changed ears. While she was taking the shirt off his body, the erotic teasing of his ear was really getting to Titus. A fine sheen of perspiration formed on his forehead and as soon as he was free of the shirt he put his hands on her butt and began to massage it, caressing and stroking and taking full advantage of the fact that she was wearing a thong panty. He pulled her closer, scooting closer to the edge of the bed so they could feel each other better.

"Kiss me, baby, I need to taste you," he groaned. Paris was more than happy to oblige; she loved kissing Titus. They tasted each other, their tongues moving in a sensual dance as they gently sucked each other's lips.

"Take off your pants, Titus." Paris made a soft noise when Titus unexpectedly undid her bra. She cupped her hands protectively over her breasts but there was no point to the modest gesture. Titus quickly stood and unzipped his jeans, then sat back down while he kicked them off the rest of the way. He took the straps of the bra off her shoulders with his teeth and pulled the delicate garment away from her body, moving her hands while he did so.

"Don't hide from me, Paris. Don't ever cover yourself around me. I love to look at you too much." He kissed her again while massaging both of her breasts in his big warm hands, kneading and caressing them with just the right amount of pressure to yield maximum pleasure. His lips trailed down her throat, lingering at the sensitive spot at the base, just above her collarbones. He kissed the silken skin all the way down her chest, licking the space between her breasts before releasing her left breast and taking it in his mouth, applying a deep pressure to the hard, erect nipple that made her cry his name. He moved the thong aside so he could access her wet femininity and give her even more pleasure. His long fingers sought and found her jewel, hot and moist, yearning for his touch. Paris moaned his name again and parted her legs to get the gift he was offering her. She undulated against his hand, holding on to his broad shoulders as the waves of release washed over her. His loving caresses left her shaken and breathless, leaning on Titus and moaning his name. He relented in his loving assault on her and wrapped both arms around her, kissing her neck and shoulder. "Come on, Rosy, let's get in the bed and you can show me how you really feel," he crooned in her ear.

She touched his injured side gently, looking at the neat gauze bandage that covered his wound. Titus turned her suddenly sad face to his, kissing her gently. "It's not as bad as it looks. No vital organs were involved. It was practically a flesh wound, baby. Don't look like that," he entreated her. She kissed him back and gave him a good imitation of her usual bright smile. When they were under her six-hundred-count sheets and she was snug against his good side, she teased him right back. "By the way, sugar, this is what a bedroom is supposed to look like. This is a lot different than the Batcave, isn't it?"

Titus tickled her under the sheets before admitting that yes, it was a far cry from his Spartan digs. The walls were the same peony pink color that Vera had painted them when she lived in the house. Paris's queen-sized head and footboard were antique replicas, and she'd put on the linens she liked to use in the springtime, ivory eyelet pillow shams and dust ruffle, and a handmade quilt that was an antique, and had been made by her great-grandmother on the Deveraux side of the family. It was a wedding ring pattern in red and pink flowers with a muslin backing and she had added accent pillows in various shades of pink and red to bring out the print of the quilt and make the bed even cozier.

She had an antique washstand on one side of the bed as a nightstand, and there was a small chest that matched her dresser on the other side. The dark cherry finish of the dresser, chest of drawers and nightstand contrasted nicely with the pale walls. Her curtains were also ivory eyelet with tiebacks that were clusters of silk flowers and she had French impressionist reproductions on the walls. It was a soft and feminine room, inviting and warm. Titus wasn't terribly fascinated by his surroundings at the moment, however; Paris had him in hand and was stroking him into a frenzy of passionate desire. At that particular moment they could have been in a tent, the back of a pickup truck or marooned on a desert island; all he cared about was the fact that they were together and her touch was exactly what his body had been craving for what seemed like his whole life.

Paris suddenly pulled the sheet away from his body and stared at the place her hand was manipulating with her newly acquired sensual skill. "You had a Brazilian?" she asked in a dumbfounded voice.

Titus laughed at her expression. "No, Rosy, they shaved me when I went into surgery. It feels kinda weird," he admitted.

Paris continued to inspect the hospital handiwork as she continued the firm, gentle strokes that were making him hotter and harder than he'd ever been before. She treated him to the same kind of loving torture he'd bestowed on her, sucking the most sensitive part of his chest and teasing it with her teeth while she explored all of his masculinity with her questing hand. He was so enthralled by her touch he almost didn't notice when she kissed her way down his body and put her lips where her hand had been. Now the torture began in earnest and his body responded with a volcanic surge of yearning. He called her name hoarsely, one hand tangled in her hair and the other twisting the linens as he fought for control. "*Paris*, oh baby, stop, Rosy, damn, baby, please," he groaned and she finally relented as he forced her to come back into his arms for a long, satisfying kiss.

"Feel my heart, girl. Are you trying to kill me?" He kissed her smiling face all over and tried to roll over on top of her, wincing as he did so. Paris was immediately concerned and began to fuss over him. "Listen, beautiful girl, I'm just fine. I'm a little sore, but that's all. We'll figure out a way to do this with no pain because I'm not finished with you, not by a long shot. I've missed you so much, baby. I want to make love to you the rest of the day and all night long." His voice was deeper than usual; it always was when they made love.

How about making love to me the rest of your life? The words were on the tip of her tongue, but Paris managed to bite them back. She would have died of embarrassment if he could have somehow guessed what she was thinking, so his next words were startling to say the least.

"I think we need to make a change in your living arrangement, Paris. I think I need to move in with you."

Chapter 21

Paris would have spent the next few days wallowing in the angst caused by Titus's suggestion that they live together, but something else took up all her attention. Yes, Titus had suggested they live together, and for what she considered the most prosaic of reasons: because he was concerned about her. She was used to having Aidan in the house with her and he didn't want her to be lonely or frightened so he proposed that they stay together for a while. She managed to say "no" rather airily, acting as if it were of no real importance when in reality her heart was crushed. If he wanted to be with her because he had to see her every morning and every night, because he wanted to build a life with her, because he loved her and wanted to be her husband, that would be one thing. But because he wanted to be her guardian with sex benefits? Oh, no way was that going to happen. She would have had a boatload of misery to deal with but the tabloids gave her something else on which to focus.

Some beady-eyed little sneak had managed to get pictures of her standing next to the EMT vehicle in her bloodied night-shirt and what a pretty sight it was; she was screaming at the attendant like a fishwife. There was also a nifty shot of her asleep on Titus in the hospital; it looked like she was sprawled across a dead man. Oh, they were just peachy stories, really they were. Her phone hadn't stopped ringing as each one of her brothers checked in separately and in groups; they were fond of yelling over the speakerphone. As expected, concern over her reputation was leading them to litigation. They planned to sue the tabloids and everyone connected with the stories for lots and lots of money. Her father was concerned, Aunt Ruth was concerned, Angelique and Donnie were concerned and it seemed all of her fans were worried, too, to judge by the enormous amounts of e-mail she was receiving. At one point the entire telephone system of The Deveraux Group had to be shut down due to the influx of frantic phone calls. Finally Paris called a meeting with all her cousins and her staff. She also invited Titus to attend.

They converged on the largest conference room in the complex and when everyone was assembled, Paris got right down to business. She directed her first remarks to Clay, Malcolm, Martin and Marcus as the principal governing board of the corporation. "I want to apologize personally for all the hysteria that has plagued us as a result of the George Wilson situation. Obviously I wish it could have been handled differently, but if wishes came true I wouldn't have thighs like the ones everyone in North America has now had the opportunity of viewing," she said dryly. "I suggest there's no reason whatsoever to let this go on. We need to take control of this at once and I suggest counteracting their coverage by telling the truth on my show."

She let that sink in for a moment before continuing. "I say

I do a show that explains what was happening and how it was handled and let that be the end of it. You know what they say, 'if you can't hide it, paint it red and put it on the porch.' So let's just put it out there and be done with it. Part of the thrill of stories like this is the speculation and rumor. Once the truth is told the already dubious credibility of the tabloids is shattered and the little ferrets go on to the next victim. It's not a perfect plan, but it's all I've got right now. What do you think?"

The silence that followed was deafening in its intensity. Paris's heart was beginning to sink into her shoes when Clay's deep voice drawled, "It's a brilliant idea, Paris. Doing this will show you as a smart, level-headed woman who managed to live without fear even when she was being stalked by a crazy man."

Martin agreed as well. "He's right, and you're right—you need to confront this and put it behind you. You can't pretend it didn't happen and this is the best way of handling your business. We're all behind you on this, Paris."

Malcolm and Marcus added their enthusiastic support, too, as did her staff. Twillia was taking notes and adding it to the week's production schedule. They decided to do the show on Friday so they'd have a week to publicize it. Titus didn't have much to add to any of the proceedings, but he shocked Paris down to the toes of her expensive shoes when he said he'd be happy to participate in any way that he could. The meeting was dismissed and Paris and her staff went to work on the segment. Titus had to go out of town for a couple of days, but he assured her he'd be back in time for the broadcast. As everyone was leaving the conference room he stayed behind to give her a long hot kiss before departing. "I'll call you tonight," he promised.

The day of the live broadcast arrived and Paris was as calm as she could be under the circumstances. A lot was riding on what she did today and she intended to do very well indeed. She had to present her side of the story in a calm and non-sensational fashion and she only had one chance to do it. She was looking her best in a fabulous red jacket with black wide-legged trousers that had a deep cuff. Her hair was looking its best as Aja had shampooed and set it that morning. She checked her reflection to make sure the clasp on her pearls was in place and her teeth were free of lipstick. She could hear Twillia doing the preshow audience warm-up and prepared to take the stage. It was showtime.

"Hello! How is everybody today?" Paris said with her usual warmth. She waited for the audience response and then smiled mischievously. Suddenly the two back walls, which doubled as screens when a movie clip or video was being pre-viewed, displayed the two most embarrassing tabloid photos of Paris. "So," she said slowly, "what's new?"

The audience laughed as Paris turned to the screens with a raised eyebrow. "I'm sure that by now most of you have seen these lovely photos. You may have heard some things regard-ing the story and read some other things and I thought you might like to hear the truth of the matter. So I'm going to take a little time from today's show to set the record straight, if that's okay with you. What do you think?" she asked the audience, which exploded in applause and shouts of encouragement.

"First of all, those are not my thighs," she said with a straight face. "They obviously doctored that photograph with someone else's thighs because those can't possibly be mine." More laughter resulted from her tongue-in-cheek delivery. The rest of the show went very smoothly as she explained the facts behind the situation and fielded questions from the audience. Everything was going perfectly until someone asked the inevitable question, "Who is the mystery man in the pictures?"

For the first time, Paris hesitated, and then answered with confidence. "He owns the investigation firm that handled the case. He's not able to be here today," she said smoothly, only to be interrupted by the voice she heard in her dreams every night.

"I'm late, but I made it," Titus said as he walked onto the set. He went over to the sofa where Paris was sitting and sat right next to her, draping his arm across the back of the sofa and giving her a warm smile that made the women in the audience go "ooh" on a long drawn-out note. To Paris's grateful surprise, he explained his firm's role in the case and made it sound very matter-of-fact and low-key. He also complimented Paris for her bravery throughout the ordeal. "You were a real trouper, Paris. You kept it together under some very stressful circumstances and to a large extent that's what helped this situation along. I've worked on a lot of other similar cases and when the target panics and goes off on a tangent, it complicates everything."

He patiently answered more questions, right up until someone hit on the one thing Paris hoped to avoid. "So are you and Paris involved?"

She gave her best enigmatic smile, the one meant to convey absolutely nothing. "We're very close," was all she would say.

Titus had his own take on the question, however. He turned to Paris and planted a kiss on her cheek. "We are definitely involved," he said firmly. "Very *seriously* involved."

Paris looked bemused as the audience erupted into applause and Titus's only response, other than a truly smug grin, was to lean over and kiss her soundly.

A few hours later, Paris still wasn't sure how she felt about the kiss. Was he declaring himself on national television or just making a grand gesture to save both of them from embarrassment? After all, he'd presented himself as her fiancé in Baton

Rouge, and she'd said she was his girlfriend in Charleston. Until they could straighten those little white lies out he probably decided to go along with the general assumption. It was pure Titus logic, she figured. There was nothing romantic or impulsive about it, although it would have been wonderful if there had been. Everyone thought the show went well, and Paris was just pleased to have it behind her. Her birthday was coming and she was going to have fun; after all, this was a milestone. She was going to be thirty years old and that deserved a celebration. She glanced at her wristwatch and realized why she was so tired. It had been a long day and she was going home. She had almost reached the elevator that would take her to the parking garage when Titus appeared next to her.

He smiled down at her, using his index finger to brush a lock of hair from her face. "You look tired, sweetheart. If you don't have any other plans for the weekend, I want to do something special with you." It sounded like a wonderful idea to Paris and she allowed him to escort her into the elevator as their adventure began.

Paris looked at Titus with her heart in her eyes. Her cheeks were still pink from what had happened a few hours before and she didn't quite believe him when he said everything was fine. "I'm really sorry," she said for the tenth time. And for the tenth time he assured her that all was well.

"Come here Rosy, and let me tell you once again that it doesn't matter in the least. All that matters is that we're here together. That's the important thing. The other thing, well, that couldn't be helped. I just wanted to be with you and spend the weekend helping you relax and I think we can accomplish that quite nicely right where we are, don't you?"

Paris leaned into Titus and let him hold her even closer.

They were sitting on big pillows in front of a crackling fire at the Deveraux weekend home on St. Simon's Island. Titus's plan for the weekend involved taking Paris to an exotic "couples only" hotel in Atlanta. It was set up to cater to all kinds of erotic fantasies and each suite had a theme, like Arabian Nights, or A Night in Tunisia, whatever suited the taste of the customer. Titus had booked a suite with a Garden of Eden theme and like all the suites it was exquisitely decorated. It included an indoor swimming pool with hot tub, Jacuzzi and every creature comfort imaginable. Paris had looked around the suite with a big smile of anticipation on her face, a smile that faded when she failed to see something essential, something she had to have in order to enjoy anything about the weekend. She had turned to Titus, biting her lower lip with concern. "Umm, where are the windows?"

And that's how they ended up driving to St. Simon's with Paris apologizing about every twenty-five miles or so. "Titus, I'm so sorry. I know you went to a lot of trouble to make this weekend special for me, but I'm so claustrophobic I can't even go into a closet without getting choked up. I just hate small spaces, closed-in spaces, even big places with no windows. I have to be able to look out a window, preferably one that opens. I'm not too crazy about those hotels where you can't open the windows, either," she'd told him with her cheeks crimson from shame.

He'd taken her hand and kissed it. "Mmm, you have the softest skin in the world. Please stop apologizing, beautiful girl. It's completely understandable. If I'd had any idea that you were afraid of closed spaces I'd never have booked the suite. I just want to be with you, that's all. I just want to spend some time with you," he'd said with such sweetness it won her heart all over again.

And now they were alone in the comfortable weekend

home everyone in the family used. Since it was only April, it was still early enough in the year that no one had planned on coming that weekend so they were guaranteed privacy. The Deverauxes tended to flock to St. Simon's in the warmer weather. Although April in Georgia is warm enough for outdoor activities like a long walk on the beach to be plea-surable, Titus didn't have a long walk in mind.

After they arrived at the house, Titus got the bags out of the car and they unpacked and put away the groceries they'd brought with them. Then Titus said he was going to take a shower and suggested Paris take a bubble bath if it suited her, which it did. She found a big bottle of Pink Peony bath gel by Perlier, something that Vera used. She always kept it at St. Simon's and it was understood that it was community property. All the Deveraux women kept the place supplied with bath gels and soap, shampoo and other necessities. In next to no time the big claw-footed bathtub was full of fragrant bubbles and she sank into its depths with real pleasure. She was basking in bubbles when a tap at the door made her open her eyes in time to see Titus, clad only in a towel sarong, enter the room with a steaming mug in his hand. "I thought you might like something to drink," he said, offering the mug to her.

She accepted it with a smile and took a sip. It was the same delicious warm milk concoction he'd made for her before. "Thank you, Titus, this is just what I needed."

"I know something else you need," he said and knelt on the bath mat. "You need to have your back scrubbed very, very gently, that's exactly what you need."

Paris didn't offer a single protest; it sounded too wonder-ful to her. She handed him the mug, which he placed out of harm's way on the bathroom vanity. She then leaned forward so he could have his way with her back and it was heavenly.

"Scrub" wasn't the right term for what he did to her back but she couldn't think of the right word for what he did. His strong hands applied more bath gel and he used a terry bath cloth to rub her in small circles from the nape of her neck to the base of her spine and from shoulder to shoulder. He did this over and over until she was purring with contentment, then he used his fingers to massage every square inch of her back, leaving her limp from sheer enjoyment. She was so relaxed she almost fell asleep in the tub as Titus discovered when he helped her lie back again. He kissed her and suggested it was time she got out.

"Okay. Let me finish my drink and I'll get out," she said sleepily.

He handed her the mug and she sipped the rest of the milk. "Mmm," she sighed when it was gone. "Now I need to rinse these bubbles off," she said with a delicate yawn.

Titus did the honors, helping her to stand and supporting her while he directed the hand held shower over her body until the foam was all gone. He wrapped her in a towel and carried her into the great room in front of the fireplace. And now he was ready to relax her even more, or he was until she started fretting. But his words finally got through to her, his words and the incredible bath she'd just taken. Now it was time for another level of release and he had just the thing. She was sitting in front of him, resting against his chest. He reached for a flat bottle labeled Sole Impressions and opened it, inhaling the pretty fragrance of the thick emollient lotion. He rubbed it in his hands for a moment to warm it, and then spread it across Paris's shoulders and down her arms. The exotic fragrance permeated the room as he worked and the soft music that was playing intensified the heady atmosphere. He finished with her arms and shoulders and reached in front of her to loosen her towel, letting it slip down around her waist.

He applied more of the scented emollient cream, this time to her breasts.

Paris's long lashes fluttered and she trembled under his sensual touch, arching her back and leaning against his warm, broad chest for support. Titus didn't stop; he kept rubbing her already sensitized breasts in circles, manipulating the tender, erect nipples that blossomed under his care. Her hands clutched his thighs as the sensations he was creating built a fire in her that spread to all her erogenous zones. She breathed his name over and over but he didn't relent, he continued the massage, squeezing and caressing her with his hands while his middle fingers stroked her hard nipples that were bigger than he'd ever seen them, engorged from his stimulation. Her breathing grew erratic and her moans became cries of release as he brought her to a shattering orgasm. He finally relented long enough to kiss her neck and whisper in her ear, "That was just the beginning, baby. I have more for you."

She wanted to answer him, but she could only manage the softest whisper imaginable. "I love you."

Chapter 22

Paris was extremely happy about this year's birthday for several reasons. First, it was a real milestone. She was having her real adult birthday by turning thirty, which she saw as a cause for celebration, not panic. Second, she was having the party to end all parties and her whole family, with the exception of the evil Aunt Gert, would be there. She loved her father and brothers dearly and despite the fact that they babied her something awful, she loved to be with them and missed them terribly when she was away from them. The third reason was also a very important reason: Aunt Ruth would be in town and Paris had been dying to see the older woman. There was something about confiding in Aunt Ruth that made her feel so much better, so much more at ease with herself. With the exception of her cousins' mother, Lillian, Paris hadn't had a mother's influence in her life since she was a small child and from time to time she felt that absence keenly. She couldn't wait to see Ruth and get her take on all that had been going on in her life since they were last together.

Her face got flaming hot and she picked up a manila folder to fan herself. Okay, maybe she couldn't tell her everything that had been going on; the incredibly hot sex life she and Titus shared wasn't anything she wanted to confide. She put the folder down and went to the small refrigerator in the corner of her office and made a sound of relief when she found several bottles of her favorite spring water and a plastic container of ice cubes as well. She took out a bottle of the water and a couple of cubes of ice and went to her sofa to sit down. Placing the bottle on the long coffee table in front of the sofa, she bent her head forward and held her hair up off her neck with her free hand and ran the ice cubes up and down her neck in an effort to quench the burning inside. She was so wrapped up in what she was doing she didn't hear the knock at her private office door.

"You're a little too young for personal summers so it must be that man who has you so hot," said an amused voice.

Paris dropped the ice and tossed her head back in disbelief. "Aunt Ruth! Ooh, I'm so glad to see you," she exclaimed as she leaped to her feet and ran to embrace her. "What's a personal summer, by the way?"

Ruth gladly accepted the hug before stepping away from Paris to give her a good long look. "A personal summer is a euphemism for a hot flash, honey, and I know you're not having one of those. What's been going on around here that you want to share with me? You have that I-want-to-talk look on that pretty face of yours."

Paris sighed and shook her head and led her over to the long rose-colored Ultrasuede sofa. "To tell you the truth, I don't even know where to begin," she said as she curled her legs up on the sofa pillowed surface of the couch.

Ruth's eyes were alight with curiosity and she followed suit. "Well, just begin at the beginning, that's always seemed like the best place to me."

Paris finger-combed her now messy hair and gave Ruth a genuine smile, not a wan imitation. "You'll never know how glad I am you walked in that door. Well, this is how it all started," she began.

Meanwhile, Titus was having an uncharacteristic reaction to Paris's upcoming birthday: indecision. He was having difficulty deciding what to get her for a gift because he had very little experience in gift giving. Outside of his mother, grandmother and sisters, he'd only given gifts to the high school sweetheart who dumped him and the color-struck fiancée who used him. After those experiences, he'd shut down emotionally. He'd meant every word he said to Paris the first night they'd made love. His relationships were finite; they were about sexual gratification and nothing else. Paris was the one exception to that rule. He had an inkling of the depths of his feelings the night he'd brought her flowers, the first flowers he'd sent anyone other than his mother and Mama Sweet. At some point, between the first time he'd laid eyes on her, the first time he kissed her and the first time they had become as one person, wrapped in each other's arms with nothing between them but passion, the rough, heavy bricks that made up the wall around his heart came tumbling down. That's the effect Paris had on him. And that's why he wanted to get her something really special, but he had no idea what to get.

He was in his private office, leaning back in his oversized leather chair with his arms behind his head staring at the Romare Bearden print on the wall. He supposed he could get a clue from the women in his family, but he didn't want Nicole up in his business, he reflected with a smile. He loved his youngest sister like crazy and that's just what she could do to him, drive him absolutely mad. He was distracted by the sound of the intercom. "Titus, there's someone here to see you. Mr. Clayton Arlington Deveraux would like a few minutes of your time if that's possible."

Titus raised an eyebrow as he told his secretary to send him in at once. He was about to stand up when the heavy oak door opened and Trey stuck his head in. "Yo, T. Got a minute?"

"Of course, man, come on in," Titus invited. Trey was at the complex often; he loved nothing better than hanging out with his father and his uncles. While the young man took a seat across the desk, Titus remembered a time the previous summer when Martin had asked him to come with him for a ride. They had gone to the summer camp where Trey and his younger brothers, the unruly twins Martin and Malcolm, were spending three weeks. As they drove, Martin had confessed he had no idea why they were going.

"Trey called me and asked me to come as soon as possible. And he wanted me to bring you, too. I have no idea what this is about. I asked if he wanted me to bring his father and he said no, just you and me. So brace yourself, there's no telling what we're getting into," Martin had said.

Titus still got a smile when he remembered that afternoon. They had found Trey in his cabin with his two brothers, who were rather subdued, compared to their normal behavior. Trey had shaken the hands of both men and gotten right down to cases. "They said Marty and Mal did something they didn't do and they won't listen to me. It's one thing to discipline them for rule infringements, but to make an assumption and act on it is egregious and specious reasoning," he said with real anger in his voice. "That's why I wanted you to come, Uncle Martin, to act as counsel. And T, I want you to be our investigator."

Both men had to sit down after Trey made his pronouncement. Who knew he knew that much legalese? Trey was a true Deveraux, that much was plain. Nobody messed with his brothers as long as he was around. It seemed that the young twins had been the usual suspects when a snake was placed in the bed of the camp bully. But Trey knew for a fact they couldn't have pulled this prank because they didn't like snakes. They disliked them to the point that neither one of them would have dared pick up one. "If it had been a frog or a lizard, sure. But not a snake," Trey said passionately. "None of the counselors or the director will listen to me. You have to present our case, Uncle Martin, and T, you have to find out who did it. And you have to get our money back because I don't want my dad paying for us to go to a place that calls us liars."

Titus disciplined his face to keep from smiling as he looked at Trey sitting across from him with all the insouciance of a man three times his age. Everyone who knew him agreed he was the image of his father in looks and demeanor, and he was. Tall for his age with the same Creole coloring, thick, wavy black hair and piercing eyes under thick eyebrows, Trey displayed none of the gawky awkwardness of the normal preadolescent. He was a very old soul, Trey was. And Martin had indeed left Camp Wildwood with three nephews, three weeks worth of camping gear and a check. The red-faced camp director had decided it was better to forfeit the money than risk the lawsuit Martin assured her would ensue.

"So what's up, T? Are you getting geeked up for Paris's birthday party? It's going to be a good time," he said with a smile. "Have you gotten her a present yet?"

Titus confessed he had not and was amused to see Trey's look of dismay. "What are you waiting for, T? Her birthday party is next week. You should have it wrapped and ready by now," he said disapprovingly.

Titus had to confess. "Well, part of the problem is I don't know what to get her," he admitted. Trey shrugged. "That's not a problem. What was the last present you gave her? You don't want to give her the same thing," he said.

"Umm, I've never actually given her a present," Titus said, and winced at the Trey's expression of utter disbelief. "You've never given her *anything?* But you've been her boyfriend for a long time, T. Do you send her flowers?"

This was one Titus could answer confidently. "Yes. I brought her some flowers once, I got them from…"

Before he got the words out, Trey was on his case again. "*Once?* Just *once?* Do you send her cards?"

"Uhh, no."

"E-cards?"

"No."

Trey was stunned into silence. Finally he spoke with real concern for Titus's welfare in his voice. "T, you got no game, man."

Titus promptly threw a staple remover at him, which Trey ducked, laughing. "Hey, man, don't blame me because your game ain't tight. You don't know how to treat a lady, that's all. It's not my fault if you lack skills."

Titus burst out laughing at Trey's cocky assumption. "So you know all about women, do you? Have you got a girlfriend?"

"I bet I know more about know more than you do about women," he muttered. "And yeah, I have a girlfriend," Trey said casually, as though it were no big deal.

"What's her name? Is she pretty?"

"Her name is Paget. And she's my best friend. She's real pretty, on the inside. The outside is okay," he said offhandedly as he inspected various objects on Titus's desk. "But she's gonna be real fine in a few years."

Titus raised his eyebrows. "You sound pretty confident about that, Trey. How do you know what she's going to look like?"

Trey gave him a slow grin. "I told you, she's pretty on the inside. She's really smart, she's funny and she's nice to everybody. And," he grinned even wider, "Her mama is *fine*. Her big sisters are both *fine*. Even her grandmother is fine. So it's just a matter of time before her outside catches up with her inside."

While Titus was thinking that Trey was the single coolest kid he'd ever encountered, Trey was deep in thought. He looked at Titus without cracking a smile. "T, you need some help. You need a few guidelines for dating in the new millennium and I'm going to help a brother out. Can I use your computer?"

Titus moved his chair away from the desk and invited Trey into the space. "Go for it, dude."

Paris was about to spill the contents of her soul to Ruth when she realized it was getting late. "Let's get something to eat and we can go to my place and talk, if that's okay. There's a deli near here that has really good chicken salad and crab salad, and I have a couple of perfectly ripe avocadoes at home, and some good wine," she said thoughtfully. "We can get the salads and some good bread and chill out at my place."

Ruth nodded, but had one stipulation. "Throw in some cheesecake and I'm all yours."

They did just that, stopping at the deli for provisions and enjoying the impromptu but delicious meal that resulted. They shared avocado halves filled with crab salad, a salad of mixed field greens topped with marinated artichokes, black olives and grape tomatoes with red wine vinaigrette dressing, whole-grain sourdough rolls with goat cheese and for dessert, *dulce le leche* cheesecake with a cinnamon-pecan crust. They were in the living room enjoying the cheesecake with coffee as they eased into the night's conversation.

Paris unburdened her heart, starting with the part when the threats started and Titus began his investigation and protection. She covered the trip to California for the Oscars, and the trips to New Orleans, Baton Rouge and Charleston. She hesitated a moment before sharing what Sarah told her about Titus, then grew resolute. "She didn't tell me not to tell anyone, so I'm not betraying a confidence. And *he* didn't tell me, so I'm not betraying him. But this is so key to what makes him tick," she said earnestly. And she related what Sarah had told her about Titus. Ruth's face was full of concern for both Titus and Paris.

"That's some story," she said, shaking her head. "My God, what that young man went through. I can see where he would have issues with intimacy and fears of abandonment. It makes it a lot easier to understand why he's been such a loner."

Paris nodded unhappily, and gave Ruth the rest of the story about his disastrous loves. "So he got dumped by one girl because he was too light and he was about to marry a woman who only liked him because of his light skin. Can you imagine? I just don't understand the color game we play with our own people." She frowned and shook her head again. "But that's why I know it's hopeless, Aunt Ruth. As much as I love him, I have to keep telling myself that it won't last forever because he can't commit to anything long term. And now I understand why," she said with a poignant sigh.

Ruth stared at Paris and reached over to take her dessert plate, which still bore a sizeable piece of the lusciously rich cake. "You don't deserve this," Ruth said crisply. "If you really believe what you just said you need your head examined, dear. Is there any more coffee?" Paris picked up the thermal carafe and poured Ruth another cup while Ruth continued to take her to task.

"Paris, sweetheart, men and women are very, very different. If a woman says something you can take it to the bank because we're very verbal and that's how we express ourselves. If you want to get a clue about a woman all you have to do is listen to her because she'll tell you everything you need to know. Men aren't like that," she said, taking a swallow of hot black coffee and cheekily offering Paris the last bite of her portion of cheesecake. Paris refused and Ruth looked slightly contrite. "I shouldn't have just bogarted that piece, but I was trying to shock you. And I'm greedy. I only eat dessert once or twice a month and this is my weakness," she confessed.

Paris smiled warmly. "I didn't mind. To tell you the truth I'm not much of a cheesecake fan. I don't really have that much of a sweet tooth except for fruit and sorbet and Popsicles, things like that. But quit stalling and tell me what you mean about men and women. You can't leave me hanging like that."

Ruth swallowed the last bite and followed it with coffee. She daintily blotted her lips and placed the napkin next to the dessert plate on the coffee table. "Okay, if you're really ready to hear this, here we go. Men communicate in a different way, Paris. It's actually not good for some of them to talk too much because they say some really stupid things, like the night you made love for the first time. You remember that soliloquy, of course. You'll be able to recite it from memory on your fiftieth wedding anniversary, but that's not the point. The point is you have to watch what a man *does,* and not count too heavily on what he *says* because they don't express themselves as easily as we do. And when you meet a man who can express himself with a lot of ten-dollar words and poetic phrasing, watch him. There's a good chance he's lying through his teeth or on the down-low," she said briskly.

"Now you've convinced yourself that Titus is incapable of committing to a relationship because of what he told you over six months ago, right? Let's forget that he was stuck on Stupid that night and let's fast-forward a bit. How does he act toward you? How does he treat you? What has he done to show you what you mean to him?" Ruth paused while her words sank into Paris and she could see the younger woman recalling specific incidents that apparently brought her great joy in the recall.

Her cheeks flushed and her eyes sparkling, Paris looked genuinely happy for the first time that evening. "You're a very smart woman, Aunt Ruth. Thank you for pointing that out to me, although I should know it already, growing up in a house full of men. It really doesn't matter what they say, the bottom line is what they do. And no matter what he says or doesn't say to me, Titus treats me like I'm the most incredible thing in his life. He really does," she said softly, her eyes growing all misty. "But sometimes I wonder if I even deserve to be in a relationship with him."

"Paris, what are you talking about? Why on earth shouldn't you be with Titus?" she demanded.

"Because in all the time I've known him I never knew anything about his past. I claim that I fell in love with him because he's so wonderful, but I didn't know one single personal thing about him until we went to Charleston together. Doesn't that make our relationship seem really shallow and phony? I'm like the nosiest person in North America. I always find out everything there is to know about a person," Paris said sadly. "I really missed the boat on Titus."

Ruth looked at Paris with great affection. "You really are far gone, aren't you? Sweetie, if a man doesn't want to tell you something no power on earth is going to drag it out of him. I'm willing to bet that you asked him the usual questions and he ignored them or changed the subject so smooth you didn't even know he was doing it. Stop stressing about what he told you or didn't tell you and just enjoy the love. Just think about how he looks at you, how he makes you feel and how he treats you. Those are the important things."

Paris looked at Ruth and suddenly her eyes sparkled again, this time with mischief.

"So tell me, Aunt Ruth, how does my daddy treat you?"

Ruth raised one eyebrow and gave Paris a smile that was more mysterious and provocative than the Mona Lisa's. It was so enigmatic and deliciously feminine it actually surpassed that famous look and set a standard of its own. If she'd been a cat, Ruth would have been purring out loud. "He treats me like I'm the Queen of Sheba, honey, that's how he treats me. Like royalty."

Paris had her mouth open to say something when Ruth's cell phone played a jazzy little tune. She answered it quickly, saying, "Hello, Julian." Her smile got even more beguiling and adorable as she chatted. "I'm just fine, and you? No, I'm not too busy to talk to you. I'm having dessert with your lovely daughter, actually."

Surmising it would be a good time to give Ruth a little privacy, Paris discreetly left the room with the dessert plate and coffee paraphernalia on a tray. She rinsed everything off before filling the dishwasher, humming the whole time. Her phone rang and she answered it with a lilt in her voice. "Hello?"

"Hello, yourself. Just wanted to hear your voice."

With a big smile she sank onto a tall stool. This was the perfect way for her evening to end.

Paris would always remember this as her best birthday ever. It was held at Bennie and Clay's house because it was the biggest. Everyone she loved was there and everyone was having a wonderful time. It was the first weekend in May and it was warm enough to grill outside. The Summers sisters were catering the affair, but to her amusement, her father and Bump Williams, Lillian's husband, took over the grillwork and dared anyone to try to usurp their territory. They kept referring to themselves as the Grillmasters and made a huge production out of the process, although the result was absolutely delicious. They grilled ribs, steak, chicken and fish and there were hot dogs and hamburgers for the smaller children, as well as Boca burgers for Aidan and any other vegetarians.

The music was supplied by Trey and a couple of his schoolmates and they were surprisingly accomplished DJs. They kept the music varied and constant, not too loud but loud enough to create an air of festivity. Since Clay and Bennie had purchased the house next door for a guesthouse, they'd added a big pavilion between the two homes, which was perfect for big outdoor parties like this one. It served as a dance floor as well as overflow seating and there were colorful little golf carts available to travel back and forth. Paris was so busy hugging and kissing everyone she didn't have time to get really nosy, but she made notes. There were a couple of people she wanted to question carefully once this was over.

Billy Watanabe was still in Atlanta recording with Bump, who was also a world-famous jazz artist. And there he was with Twillia, holding hands and acting as though they'd gotten to know each other very well indeed since the weekend of the Academy Awards. Paris didn't say anything but she gave Twillia a look that said "Gotcha" and Twillia just grinned at her without a hint of guilt. She finally relented when she hugged Paris and whispered that she would give up the details at work on Monday.

Angelique had come all the way from Detroit with Donnie, Lily Rose and a big announcement: she and Donnie were expecting again. That made two babies on the way, with Ceylon and Martin also expecting. While she was hugging Angelique and exclaiming over the news, Paris had an opportunity to see the look on Bennie's face as she congratulated her youngest brother Donnie. It was a look of longing and intense desire that Clay also picked up on, apparently. She wasn't trying to eavesdrop, but she heard Bennie and Clay talking later in the evening.

"You wouldn't want another baby, would you?" His tone of voice clearly indicated, at least to Paris, that he certainly wanted one. "You already have so much on your plate with the rowdies we have now. And having another baby would add to the madness, Peaches, not to mention the physical effects on you," he said.

A momentary silence told Paris they were probably kissing right then and she felt terrible for listening, but then Benita replied.

"I know, Clay, I know. It's such a crazy idea I wasn't going to say anything. But I really would like just one more," Bennie said sadly. "I love you so much and I love our children so much and I don't know how to explain it, but I love carrying your babies. I feel so close to you and so much more desirable when I'm pregnant. I really do want to have one more baby," she told him with a deep sigh.

"Then that's what we'll have, Peaches. I want one, too, but I didn't want you to think I was nuts. I love you so much, baby. When you're pregnant it's so beautiful and sexy it drives me crazy, it really does. You bring me more joy than I ever thought was possible and I'll never be able to tell you how much I love you," he told her.

"Then show me, Clay. Show me right now."

Paris sped out of the kitchen, which was one of her best listening spots. The sexy giggles she'd heard from Bennie in the dining room needed no interpretation and no audience. She was in such a hurry she ran smack into Julian, who'd come looking for her with Lucien in tow.

"There you are. Come look at your present so we can take it to your house and set it up," Julian said.

Paris followed him out to the driveway with a puzzled look on her face. "Why do you have to set it up? I don't get it."

Her brothers and her father gave her the same thing every birthday and that was jewelry. Paris had an extensive assortment of really fine pieces, all genuine and all expensive. Her father wanted her to have lovely things and her brothers wanted to give her things that she could pawn if things got rough. And as Wade put it, if she were used to fine things she wouldn't let some punk bribe her with something shiny. Loving to the end but always practical, that was her brothers to a tee. This was different, though. She waited until Wade opened the door of his SUV, since he and Julian had driven from New Orleans. There on the backside was a box that contained a state-of-the-art plasma TV, something she never would have expected to get from them. She couldn't decide whether to be pleased, surprised or hurt, but the look on her face told it all, at least it did to Wade, the most perceptive of her four brothers.

"Look, *cher,* we didn't get you jewelry this year because you don't need us to do that anymore. Things have changed, baby girl, and we have to change with them," he told her with a look of great affection.

"I don't get it," she said fretfully.

Julian tried again to explain it. "What he means, Coco, is that we won't be the ones buying your jewelry anymore," he said gently. He turned Paris so she could see Titus, making his way up the driveway with a gift bag in one hand and a beautiful bouquet of roses in the other. "No man wants another man buying jewels for his woman, even if that other man is kin."

Paris would have sworn he gave her a little push in Titus's

direction, but she would never be sure. But she was in Titus's arms in seconds and everything else fell away from her consciousness, the way it always did.

"I'm sorry I'm late, Rosy. I had a little delay in Kansas City." He handed the bag to Julian and the flowers to Wade so he could give her a proper hug. They looked at each other and shrugged before departing.

"I missed you," Paris whispered.

"I missed *you*," he returned. "Happy Birthday, baby. I hope you like your presents."

"You brought me presents? What did you get me?" she demanded. Paris loved surprises of any kind. "You'll get a couple of them here," he said, kissing her neck and her ear. "And you'll get another one at home," he added, finally capturing her lips for the long, juicy kiss he'd been dying for. "And if you keep kissing me like that, you'll get even more when it's just the two of us," he promised.

Paris stood on her tiptoes, pressing to get even closer to Titus. "Let's go right now," she whispered. "Everyone's having such a good time, no one's going to notice if I'm here or not. Let's go."

He laughed gently at her eagerness. "We're staying right here. Nobody's going to accuse me of corrupting you. Besides, you look so pretty I want to get a chance to look at you for a while. Because once we get to your house you're not going to keep that on for very long."

Paris stepped away from his embrace and modeled her dress, a red silk jersey wraparound with a full circle skirt that came to midcalf. The bodice had a halter neck but Paris was wearing a matching red shrug to cover her shoulders. On her feet were pretty Chinese Laundry embroidered flats, which she had chosen because she planned on dancing a lot. Seeing Titus had changed her mind somewhat, though; she really couldn't have cared less about dancing at the moment. All she wanted was to be in his arms and boldly, she told him so. She looked shocked and then aroused, when Titus gave her bottom a smack, then grabbed it and pulled her to him almost roughly.

"Don't tease me, Rosy, or I'll haul you out of here so fast people won't know what hit them. Let's go back in and behave."

Paris gave him a mock pout and then returned the gesture, smacking his hard, sexy butt and then grabbing it hard. "Okay, if you insist," she said cheekily, laughing when Titus groaned.

"Damn, Rosy, you're really trying to kill me, aren't you?"

Her only answer was a very seductive smile.

Chapter 23

really was a memorable and happy birthday. Titus was
ased that Paris was so happy and he was also pleased that
·y was so astute, although he wouldn't have said so earlier.
us stretched his long arms and legs and gave a huge yawn.
hadn't slept this late in years and it felt really good. He
tled himself more comfortably on the pillows and chuckled
he thought about the list Trey had typed up for him in his
ice. The young man had pulled it off the printer and handed
o Titus with a flourish, saying this was all Titus needed to
arantee a happy relationship. Titus had read it over and
ked at Trey, who'd given him a look of supreme self-
urance. "Trust me, T, this works."
He thought about the list.
1. Send flowers
2. Give her a nickname
3. Buy jewelry

4. Cook for her
5. Take her on a trip
6. Make her laugh
7. Kiss her a lot
8. Be nice to her family
9. Talk to her
10. Buy her a pet

Titus had looked over the top of the list, clearly uncon
vinced. "Buy a pet? This works?"

Trey had nodded enthusiastically. "We like animals in ou
family. My mom had a cat, Aretha, and she had gotten really
old. She was way older than me, even. Anyway, when she die
my mom was really sad and Dad went out and got a black kitte
like Aretha and left her on the patio for Mom to find. She wa
so happy. She said it was like Aretha had sent Della to her s
she wouldn't be sad anymore. She didn't think she wante
another cat because she had told Dad she didn't. But he go
Della anyway because he knew she would like her and not b
so sad about Aretha." Trey studied his fingernails for a moment
and then looked at Titus with solemn eyes. "Aretha was the bes
cat in the world, T. You can't go wrong with a pet."

Titus had initially rued the day he'd gone along with tha
advice. He did pretty well with his main gift selections; Pari
had been delighted with them. She had insisted she didn'
want gifts, but people brought them anyway and she was a
excited as a child. She let Vera and Marcus's son Chase hel
her open the packages. Chase was a handful but he love
Paris devotedly and would do anything she asked. Titus wa
very pleased that Paris liked her gifts. He was more tha
pleased; he felt like king of the world at the joy on her face
I'm going to have to do this all the time, he thought. He'
bought her a set of fourteen-karat gold bangle bracelets, eac
one with a different gemstone, since he noticed she favore

olorful stones. There was a pair of matching hoop earrings
hat had each of the gemstones attached as a little dangler. She
as totally taken with them and put them on at once. He also
ought her perfume. He was going to get her "Stella," but one
alled "Paris" that was made by Yves St. Laurent caught his
ye. He smelled it and decided it would be perfect for her; it
as very feminine and smelled like roses. He bought every-
ing the store had in that fragrance from bath gel to eau de
arfum to dusting powder and she was very pleased with it.
wasn't until he brought her home and gave her the last
resent that his confidence wavered.

He brought her into the living room and had her sit down
hile he got the gift. "Close your eyes, baby," he'd said and
he held her left hand out, palm side down. Then she jumped
s Titus set her present in her lap. She opened her eyes and
tared down at a tiny…dog. The dog had stared back without
oving, and then its tail wagged. Her eyebrows had flown up
nd she picked it up and turned it over on its back.

"What are you doing, Paris?"

"I'm trying to see where the batteries go. This is a toy,
ght?" The little dog had squirmed and barked and she had
en at once that it was a real live dog. "Oh, you bought me
puppy," she said in an odd voice. "Something that has to be
alked and fed and housebroken and no doubt eats shoes. A
al puppy."

Titus could still remember the dismay he'd felt as he made a
ental note to get Trey as soon as possible. "He's half Pomera-
ian and half cockapoo. I got him from a breeder in Kansas City
I've been calling him K.C., which you can change if you
ant." Paris had insisted that she liked the puppy, which she
dn't put down the rest of the night, but Titus was just not sure.
e thought he'd made a dreadful mistake until Paris called him
e next morning at an ungodly hour weeping uncontrollably.

"He's gone, Titus, he's disappeared! I think he got out when I got the newspaper and he ran out into traffic and he's probably killed and it's all my fault," she sobbed. Titus had soothed her as best he could and broke every speed limit in the city getting to her house. She was still crying and distraught as he looked all over the house. She was overcome by joy when he found the puppy sound asleep in the bedroom snuggled under the afghan, which had slipped off the foot of the bed. "Kasey! Oh you found my baby! Why did you do that, you naughty doggie? You can't scare Mommy like that, you scared me half to death, you know that?" She hugged the little dog while it eagerly licked her all over and was plain that the little dog meant a lot to her. The three of them ended up on the sofa with Titus holding Paris and Paris holding Kasey. Paris rubbed her head against Titus's shoulder and sighed with contentment.

"I would have died if anything happened to Kasey," she said. Titus finally said what was on his mind.

"I didn't think you were that crazy about him," he admitted.

Paris had smiled sleepily and given Titus a gentle kiss. "This is the cutest doggie I've ever seen in my life and I'm going to spoil him rotten. I admit I was hoping he'd be something in eighteen-karat gold with a big stone for my engagement finger, but just because I was surprised doesn't mean I don't love him. He's from you—how could I not love him?" She nestled closer to Titus and closed her eyes. "I love you so much, how could I not love anything you give me?"

Titus hadn't followed her into slumber; he had too much to think about.

Now as he lay in her bed, waiting for her to come back to his arms, he thought some more about his master plan. A lot of women wouldn't like what he was going to do, but a lot of women weren't like Paris. She loved surprises and she loved him, so he had every reason to believe this was going to work.

Kasey scampered in the door before Paris, who was carrying a tray with Titus's breakfast. In the weeks since her birthday he had gone from being a cute puppy to being unbearably adorable. He was a pretty buff shade and his fur was thick and wavy and he didn't shed. His ears stood straight up, perfectly inverted Vs, and his dark eyes were shiny with good health, as was his heart-shaped little nose. He always looked like he was smiling, especially when he'd done some mischief. As Paris predicted, he did have a fondness for chewing her shoes and every time he did it she'd make Titus replace the pair. He had no idea how much a woman's shoes could cost, but he didn't care. He had plenty of money and all he cared about was her happiness. He just hoped she truly felt the same way about him, considering what he was about to do.

"You're going to spoil me, bringing me breakfast in bed. I haven't had this since I was about five and I had the measles or chicken pox or something," he said as he eyed the pretty and appetizing meal she'd brought him: crisp waffles with apple butter, smoked sausage, scrambled eggs and grits, plus a carafe of coffee and a glass of orange juice. "You're so wonderful, Rosy, that's why I love you so much," he said quietly.

She was curled up next to him by now and he was touched to see her eyes fill with tears. "Baby, please don't cry, what's the matter?"

"That's the first time you ever said that to me," she said, wiping the tears away with the corner of the sheet. He held out his hand and pulled her closer to him for a kiss. "That's just the first time you heard it," he said softly. "It doesn't mean that's the first time I said it, or that I just this minute realized I love you like no one else in the whole world, Paris. I had no idea I was capable of feeling like this. I adore you, Rosy."

The tears were running freely by then and she insisted that he eat. "I slaved over that, those aren't Eggos, you know. Eat your breakfast and then I'm going to have my way with you for the rest of the day, how's that sound?"

It sounded fine to Kasey who barked agreeably, making both of them laugh.

A few days later, Paris was about to do the audience warm-up in Twillia's place because Twillia had a sore throat. Every day before taping, Twillia would come out and chat with the audience and get them primed for the show they were about to see, but today it would be impossible. She sounded like her throat was lined with sandpaper. In her now-raspy voice, Twillia told her there was a man in the audience who wanted Paris to read a special note to the woman he loved and Paris's eyes lit up. There was nothing better than romance and she was always happy to help it along. She looked her absolute best that day for some reason. Her hair was especially lustrous and arranged just so, her makeup was flawless and she was wearing a new suit in lipstick red with a sexy skirt and a jacket that showed off her curves beautifully. She went out to do the customary sound checks and engage in chitchat with the audience, and then announced that she had something to read to a very special viewer.

"It's so special, in fact, that I'm going to read it on the air. My director tells me it's the most beautiful thing she's ever read and if Twillia says it she means it because she takes her romance seriously. So we've got a lot to look forward to in about two minutes!"

Once the musical introduction played and the show began, Paris turned to the camera and smiled the 100-watt smile everyone in the country associated with her. "This is probably the most romantic thing I've ever participated in," she told her viewers. "One of our audience members has something to say to his sweetheart and I'm going to help him. She turned to the

udio audience and began reading the letter. "My beautiful
irl, this is long overdue. I've known how I feel about you for
long time, but I was afraid to tell you, afraid that I'd wake
p one morning and realize our relationship has all been a
ream. I've been guarding my feelings the way a miser guards
is money and I can't do it anymore. Your sweetness makes
le world a sweeter place to be. Your kindness makes me
ant to be a better man for you. Your laughter makes my heart
ar and your smile outshines the sun. I don't know what I
id to win your heart, but I will be forever grateful that you
iink I'm man enough for you. With all my heart, I'll love you
ntil I take my last breath. I am yours, now and forever."

The audience was sniffling and ooh-ing and aah-ing after
le beautiful declaration and Paris was having a hard time
ontrolling her own emotions. "Twillia was right. That's the
lost romantic thing I've ever read in my life." She looked out
ito the audience and asked if the gentleman who wrote it
ould please stand.

"I'll be happy to, if you'll answer a question for me. Will
ou marry me, Paris?"

Paris's head jerked up and she stared into Titus's eyes as
e stood in the back of the audience. He was smiling as he
epeated the question. "Paris Corinna Deveraux, I love you
lore than my life. Will you marry me?"

The audience was screaming for her to say yes and as soon
s she could remember how to speak English, that's just what
le did. "Yes! Yes, I will, Titus!" she answered as tears of joy
olled down her cheeks.

By now he'd reached the stage and they were locked in a
ght embrace, kissing for all they were worth. When they
nally broke free, she looked into the camera with teary eyes
lat glistened like black diamonds. "We'll be right back," she
iid happily.

Only then did she notice two things. One, the audience was full of people she knew and loved: Mama⬤⬤⬤⬤, Mac and Ruth, all of her brothers, Bennie and Clay and most of the Deverauxes, Sarah and Clifton, Nona and Nicole and another pretty woman who had to be Natalie. The other thing she noticed was the beautiful ring Titus had slipped on her finger. It was an oval cabochon stone of at least eight carats and it was a deep red with an undertone of pink. On either side of the stone there were six brilliant-cut diamonds that caught the light and sparkled so brightly Paris was blinded by its beauty. "It's a ruby, Paris. I was on a case in Brussels about a year ago and I bought it. I knew in my heart it was for you when I saw it," he told her. "I just didn't know if I'd ever have the nerve to give it to you," he admitted.

Paris took one last look at the ring and looked back into Titus's eyes, which were bathing her with the warmth of his love. "I love you," she told him. "I love you so much, Titus."

"I know. And I love you, too. I can't wait to be your husband."

"I won't make you wait very long. I love you too much."

Titus had another surprise for Paris, something that she got to see after the show and the huge buffet lunch that Twillia arranged to be served after the show. They managed to slip away from the teeming mass of happy friends and relatives and got into Titus's Chrysler 300. "Let's get out of here, baby, I have something for you I hope you'll like." He drove for about a half hour, heading back into the city.

Paris looked puzzled. "Are we going to my house? Is that where the surprise is?" she asked curiously.

Titus wouldn't answer; he just smiled at her mysteriously. Finally they reached the place he'd been seeking, a stately residential district with big brick houses and lushly landscaped lawns. He turned up a driveway that wound up a slight hill and finally brought the car to a stop at the top. He got out of the car and opened Paris's door, holding his hand out to her. "Come with me, Rosy."

Paris stared at the big house. "Who lives here, Titus? Is it someone we know?"

Titus smiled and put his arm around her waist. "Yes, baby. We live here."

The house was magnificent; it had everything Paris wanted in a house. There was a deep bungalow-style front porch, a large screened-in back porch that opened off of the kitchen, as well as a solarium. There was a huge gourmet kitchen, a breakfast room, dining room, butler's pantry and study on the first floor, as well as a big sunny living room. There were five bedrooms upstairs with three baths, and the master suite was on the first floor with its own sitting room and full bath. Paris was astounded. "When did you do this and how on earth did you know exactly what I wanted?"

"Nona's in real estate, baby. And I know what you like because I listen to you. And Twillia and Angelique, too," he confessed. "I wanted us to have a real home right away and I wanted it to be a place you'd love. Do you love it?"

"Not as much as I love you. Let's go make love in our bedroom right now," she said. "Come on, let's go."

"Not unless you want to have Mama Sweet and Judge walk in on us. They should be here any minute. Everybody is on the way over," he informed her.

She laughed and said, "Okay, that could be ugly. Oh, Titus." She sighed, putting her arms around his waist. "You're the most wonderful man in the world. This means so much to me. I can't tell you how happy you've made me."

He kissed her and smiled. "Then you'll just have to show me tonight, won't you?"

Chapter 24

Paris peered at her directions again and glanced at the road in front of her. She slowed down and looked for the landmark she was told would be there and smiled in triumph when she found it. She wasn't that familiar with Augusta, Georgia, which was where she was now driving, looking for the place she would meet the man who might have the answer she was seeking. She'd been working on this for a couple of weeks and even though a part of her said leave it alone, another part of her, the pushy part, wanted to forge ahead. *I know this is the right thing,* she said to herself. *Mama Sweet wouldn't have given me the information if it weren't the right thing to do.*

The day she and Titus had become engaged, she and Mama Sweet had a long talk and the old woman had confided that she always thought it was a shame that Titus had never looked for his own family. "He always said he'd never have children because he didn't know how they'd come out. He didn't know if he was carrying some disease gene or if he came from criminals or what. I always thought it was a shame he never tried to find his birth parents," she said thoughtfully.

Paris looked at Mama Sweet with new respect for her insight. "The thing is, Mama Sweet, where would he begin? He was found in Charleston on the steps of a church. Where in the world would you begin a hunt for his parents?"

Mama Sweet had leaned towards Paris with an intent look. "I don't think he was from Charleston. The clothes he was wearing and the blanket he was wrapped in came from a department store in Savannah. If I was going to start looking, I'd start there," she said wisely.

Paris hadn't acted on the information right away. It wasn't until she talked with Titus one night about his family that she decided to move forward. They had been lying on his gigantic sofa supposedly watching a movie on his giant screen, but what they were really doing was necking and feeling each other up. Kissing Titus was one of her most favorite things to do and she did it as often as possible. They lay facing each other with their arms and legs entwined. Kasey was in the big chair taking a nap and everything was perfect and peaceful. After another long and arousing kiss, Paris rubbed her face against his neck and asked him if he ever thought about his birth family.

He didn't answer right away; he looked at her with loving eyes and kissed her again. "I do and I don't, Paris. The first family that adopted me, well, that was trauma. As little as I was I knew something was wrong. Mommy and Daddy just took me somewhere and left me and I didn't get it. It was days and days before I stopped running to the door or window every time I heard a car. I was really messed up by that, you know? But then Mama came into the children's home one day and everything was better. From that first day, everything was better. I think it was her voice," he said thoughtfully. "I loved the sound of her voice. It sounded like love to me. And she came back again and again and she and Pop took me home and that was it. I was loved and protected again. They're the ones who made the most impact on my life, my first adoptive parents who brought me back to the children's home and my second adoptive parents who kept me, who loved me and gave me everything. The people who tossed me away? Nope, can't say I spend a lot of time thinking about them," he said but his eyes told a different story.

"The thing is it's so typical. Black father, white mother, can't deal with the disapproving parents so they just get rid of the baby. I'm glad they didn't abort me, I'll say that much for them. And I'm glad they put me where I could be found instead of putting me in a Dumpster or in the river somewhere," he said in a quiet, dead voice.

"The thing is I just recently realized how much I want to have a family." He kissed her again. "That's your doing, you know. I want to give you babies, Paris. I want to come deep inside you and make a beautiful baby for us to raise together. A lot of babies, Rosy, as many as you want to have. I want to fill our house with noisy little boys and pretty little girls and I want you. I want you now as a matter of fact," he said with cheerful lust.

"I'll tell you the truth, Paris. The only thing I want from my birth parents is my medical history and then we can call it even. But that's never going to happen, so I'm over it." He had rolled on top of her and moved his hips in a way that let her feel how aroused he was already. "If I didn't have you in my life, I don't know how I'd end up, Paris. But you're here and you're mine and I'm happy. I love you, baby."

Paris sighed with happiness every time she remembered those beautiful words. And because she couldn't forget the look on his face when he was telling her how he felt about his birth parents, she decided she had to do something. She got with the best researcher on her staff and explained what she was looking for, medical records from the time of his birth in what she assumed was Savannah. She reasoned that if Titus was born healthy the mother had to have gotten some kind of prenatal care. What she was after were women who had prenatal care, probably from a free clinic, who had given birth but had no children. Ellen, her researcher, had looked at her with dismay. "If this child was abandoned there's a good possibility it wasn't born in a hospital," she pointed out.

"You're right, Ellen, and that will complicate things. But I have a feeling this was a hospital birth. Don't ask me why I think so, I just do," Paris had told her.

Thanks to Ellen's meticulous digging and the help of Terry Patterson, Paris had come up with several likely leads and she was following one up now. Even though this trail led to Augusta, she felt it was worth checking out. She found that which she was seeking, Chancellor Mortuary. And when she entered the cool, quiet interior of the well-appointed building she could almost hear her heart pounding as she caught sight of the man she had come to meet. He was older, he was shorter and heavier, but he was an almost dead ringer for Titus. This was more than she ever expected.

Titus was getting upset. He didn't like to admit it, but by now he was so attached to Paris that he actually resented the time they were apart. He couldn't wait until they were man and wife and they slept in each other's arms all night, every night, when they shared their lives together and brought forth some healthy babies into the world. He couldn't wait until the wedding and he didn't see why it had to be in December. As far as he was concerned they could get it done that night and he'd be perfectly happy. But he knew that Paris wanted a big fun wedding and he wanted her to be happy, so that was it. He was getting ready to leave the office and he called Paris again. He'd been trying to get her on her cell phone all afternoon, as well as calling her office and her home. They were supposed to go furniture shopping tonight and he couldn't understand where she'd gotten to. He decided to go to her place and wait. Besides, he could take Kasey out for a jog. He and Kasey were great pals, even though the dog was costing him a small fortune in replacement shoes.

Walking out of the office he tried again to get Paris on the phone. *Woman, where are you?*

"I'm Colby Chancellor, so nice to meet you," the older man said. He offered Paris a seat in his private office and her choice of beverage.

"I'd love some iced tea if you have it," she said with a smile. "Forgive me for staring at you," she said with a charming smile, "but you resemble my fiancé so closely, it's remarkable. I have a picture if you'd like to see it," she offered.

"Let me get your tea, my dear, and I'll do that." He left the room, leaving Paris to gaze around. She saw a picture on the wall that had to be a family portrait and went to examine it closer, which was what she was doing when Chancellor returned to the room with a glass of iced tea on a small china plate. He put the glass and the plate down on the corner of the desk and joined Paris at the portrait.

"Forgive my nosiness," she said disarmingly, "but the resemblance is remarkable. Who is the older man?" she asked.

"That's my uncle, Charles Chancellor. His father founded Chancellor Mortuary and was quite successful with it. We also have an insurance company and a real estate company. We have several branches of the real estate company and the mortuary."

By now Paris had sat down again and she took a long swallow of her iced tea. It was strong and sweet, very tasty but with a slightly bitter edge. She reached into her purse for the picture of Titus she carried with her at all times and passed it to Chancellor who looked stunned to see it. He sat down at the desk rather heavily and stared at the picture. Paris wondered at his reaction and prodded him a little. "Don't you see the resemblance?" She drank some more tea and blinked her eyes; it was getting stuffy in the office.

The look on Colby Chancellor's face was distinctly odd and furtive, something Paris didn't notice. He took a minute to answer her, but finally began speaking in low voice that was almost a monotone. "Yes, Miss Deveraux, I do see a resemblance. He looks exactly like my cousin, Charles, Jr. Charles moved away from here years ago after he disgraced the family."

Paris was trying hard to follow the older man's words, but it was so hot and stuffy everything sounded like a singsong, almost like an irritating buzz. She took another swallow of the iced tea as he continued to drone. She set the glass down on the desk and watched through bleary eyes as he rose from the desk and began to move around the office. She wanted to tell him to sit down, he was making her dizzy, but she was too polite. He kept on talking as though he had to unburden himself or something.

"Charles got a girl pregnant, you see, and he refused to do the right thing."

"He refused to marry her?" Paris mumbled.

Chancellor's voice rose and he said, "No, he refused to do the *right* thing. The right thing would have been to get the little bastard aborted. We are Chancellors. We don't have little insignificant bastard children running around underfoot. Charles wouldn't have anything to do with it. He defied his father completely. So Uncle Charles had to take care of things and then he turned his son out of the house. You see, we are people of class and character, as well as money. These mortuaries, the real estate, the insurance agencies, all of them belong to my uncle and since he disowned his son, he no longer has an heir, other than me," he said with an ominous smirk.

"Uncle Charles is getting weak in his old age. He regrets what he did to his son and he wishes he had it all to do over again. So I know that if his long-lost bastard grandchild shows up here on his doorstep, he's going to change his will. But that's not going to happen because I've worked too hard for too long to lose everything to a bastard stranger. You're just too smart for your own good, Miss Deveraux. You were right, you dug up just enough information to let you know your fiancé is related to us, but you should have kept your nose out of it. You should have kept your big butt in Georgia and everything would have been all right," he said with a strained, high-pitched laugh.

I know he just didn't say my butt is big, thought Paris. She wanted to call him a crazy old loon, and tell him that no power on earth could make her keep her mouth shut, but for some reason she couldn't talk. She looked at the glass of iced tea and suddenly understood what was happening to her. Her head rolled forward and her body slid out of the chair on which she'd been sitting. Everything went black as she lost all consciousness.

Titus went from being perplexed to panicky as the day began to wane. Paris was nowhere to be found and he knew that something was wrong. She wasn't answering her cell phone, she'd left no note with any kind of explanation, and she hadn't shared with him any plans to do anything except furniture shopping with him. Something was wrong and he knew it in his gut. The sooner a problem was recognized, the

oner it was solved. The police department wouldn't act on
missing person report until twenty-four hours had passed,
Titus wasn't about to waste that kind of time. He had to
ure out who the last person was to see her at the complex
l try to reconstruct her day. Then the hunt could begin.

He was still at her house where he had remained after
lking Kasey. He picked up the small dog and put him under
e arm, gathering his lead and a scarf that Paris often wore.
ome on, pooch, we're going to get your mama," he told the
ppily panting dog. He put Kasey in the car and he imme-
tely began trying to sniff every inch of the car. Titus gave
harp whistle and told Kasey to sit, and he did immediately,
pping into the passenger seat. Reaching over him between
ears, Titus stared straight ahead and asked "Where is she,
sey? Where can she be?" Kasey whined softly, as if to say
didn't know.

By the time he reached his office, Titus had put in calls to
r of his best operatives. Three of them were already on their
y. The only one he hadn't heard from was Terry Patterson.
'd also called Twillia, Aidan and Jamaal and they were also
eting him at the complex. Kasey was on his lead, scam-
ing importantly ahead of Titus as they entered the building.
nan of Titus's size would have looked more appropriate
h a large dog, a bull mastiff or something, but right now
could have cared less about appearances. He'd barely
ched his offices when Twillia walked up with Aidan, both
hem looking somber and concerned. Titus picked up Kasey
l handed him to Twillia, who took him gladly, although she
led a cautionary statement. "I'm not Paris—you can't be
sing me in the face, hear?" While Kasey gave her several
wet ones on the chin, Titus turned to Aidan.

'Paris is missing. I've been trying to get her on her cell
ne all afternoon and she doesn't answer. She hasn't been

home and she didn't make any arrangements for Kasey's care, so I know she intended to come home this evening. Besides, she and I were going furniture shopping and those plans were never changed. I'm convinced something has happened to her and I need to retrace her steps today. Where was she and what was she doing most of the day?"

Titus took a seat at his desk, looking intently at Aidan. He was wearing a blue dress shirt that normally would have been the color of his eyes, but his eyes were a dark and stormy gray right now. Aidan dropped into a chair across from Titus's desk and tried to remember the last time he'd seen Paris. "She was working on a project with Ellen, one of our research staff. I heard her thanking Ellen and telling her how much she appreciated the information." Without waiting for a directive from Titus he said he would call Ellen and find out what they'd been working on. As Aidan left the office to go back to the studio, Twillia said she'd look through Paris's planner.

"She keeps everything in her BlackBerry, but she had one tank on her and she really doesn't trust them. She has everything written in a planner, too, as well as keeping a schedule on her computer, but I don't know her password. She usually keeps the planner with her, but let's see if she left it in her desk. I'll be right back," she said as she turned to leave with Kasey.

Titus could hear her warning the little dog to behave. "I don't love you like she does, so if you pee on anything I'll spank that hairy little bottom of yours. And that goes double for poop, hear me?"

Just then Terry Paterson strolled into the office and asked what was going on. Titus tersely informed him that Paris was missing and he needed Terry's help. Terry's eyebrows were much lighter than his dark curly hair and he often looked surprised when he wasn't. This time, though, his blond brows climbed to his hairline when Titus made his announcement.

He stared blankly at Titus for a moment before saying "I thought she was going to Savannah." His words had the echoing effect of a single stone being dropped into the bottom of a tin pail.

"Sit down and tell me everything you know," Titus said in a low voice while his eyes frosted over to silver.

Paris's head was splitting open from pain. She didn't get headaches often, but when she did it seemed like they were making up for lost time. This one was a doozy; she could feel the pounding all over her skull. She tried opening her eyes, slowly, so the bright light didn't make the pain worse. Odd. It was dark, very dark. She wasn't on her own bed, that much was certain. Her bed was comfortable and supporting; whatever she was lying on was hard and unyielding. The air was musty and close. She tried to detect a stirring of the air somewhere that would indication air-conditioning or a fan, because it was hot where she was. She could feel a tiny trickle of perspiration near her hairline and her first instinct was to wipe it off. She tried to move her hand and realized both hands were tied together. She jerked them up sharply and they hit against something, which led her to another discovery, a terrifying one. She was in a box of some kind; she couldn't move her arms, her legs, or her head...she was trapped. She wanted to cry out, and then realized her mouth was taped shut. With a sickening rush of clarity, she knew where she was and why she couldn't move. She was in a coffin.

Chapter 25

The small caravan held a motley-looking crew as it sped along I-20 east to Savannah. The lead SUV held three of Titus's best agents along with Ellen Smith, the researcher from *Paris & Company*. It had been decided that she would come along with her laptop in the hope that she could shed more light on the situation. In Titus's Hummer, Terry and Twillia were in the backseat with Kasey. Titus was in the passenger side poring over Paris's journal. Once Terry explained what he'd been doing for Paris it became clear that she'd taken off to do some investigating of her own. It was Aidan's idea to read her journal in case there was something of importance in its pages.

"She writes in it every night, sometimes in the morning, too. There's a chance she might have jotted something in the journal that can help."

Twillia agreed. "I tried to check her planner, but it wasn't

n her desk, she must have it with her. But there's probably
omething in the journal that can help."

Titus felt an idiot for not thinking of it himself when he was
t her house. Wasn't he supposed to know everything there was
o know about Paris, know her better that she knew herself?
Yet he ignored something that could prove to be the only thing
hat could lead them to her. Cursing himself inwardly, he had
driven the Hummer to her house in Ansley Park and dashed
nside, running up the stairs to her bedroom. He opened her
ightstand and sure enough, there was a pear green leather
ournal inscribed with her monogram. He snatched it out of
he drawer and pounded back down the stairs. He was about
o get back into the driver's seat when Aidan stopped him.

"Even you can't do two things at once, chief. I'll drive,"
e said, getting behind the wheel.

They'd been on the road for an hour while Titus pored over
he pages of her innermost thoughts. This was something he
would never have done under any other circumstances, but it
ouldn't be helped. He felt his heart stop for a moment when
e read an early entry.

*This was the best day of my life, and the worst. I found out
wo things today that I'm never going to forget. One is that
aking love is the most wonderful, most intimate experience
wo people can share. And the other is, when your heart breaks
ou can actually feel it. There's a horrible sharp pain and then
little "pop" that feels like something ruptured. Then there's
 gush of hot agony like someone spilled acid into your blood-
ream, and you know you'll never feel anything again.*

A hot acrid taste came into his mouth and he was awash
 shame. He'd done that to her, no one else. He had almost
estroyed her that night with his selfishness. And yet she was
oman enough to give him the one thing he didn't deserve,
other chance. He was so humbled by the notion he could

barely focus but he forced himself to concentrate. His eyes fell on another entry, this one dated the weekend of the Oscars.

I never really understood desire before I met Titus. It's like a hunger that can't be appeased, like a punishment meted out in Greek mythology where some transgressor is forced to devour something delicious all day and still suffer hunger... He touched me tonight, he put those beautiful hands on me and I was on fire from the very top of my head to the soles of my feet and everything in between. His lips touched mine and I couldn't remember my own name. All I knew was hunger, the urge to devour, to satisfy the most primal appetite I've ever known. I wanted him so badly I would have gone with him anywhere, done anything to have him. But the Three Stooges next door put an end to that; an end to the kiss, but never the desire. I still hunger for him... I will always hunger for him.

He closed the book roughly and stared blankly out the window as Aidan drove with speed and skill to Savannah. Aidan was wise not to let Titus drive because with the way he was feeling right now he'd get them all killed. *What in the hell have I ever done to deserve her? Who decided I was worthy of a prize like Paris?* He brooded in silence for a moment, and then turned back to the book, deciding to stick to the very latest entries.

I can't even picture the look on his face if he knew what I'm doing. But it's not about some family reunion; it's only about getting his medical history. He has a fantastic family already. His parents and his sisters are wonderful and I love them all. Maybe I love them because they love him so much, I don't know. They're so crazy about him and that makes me very happy because no one deserves it more than my man. But he also deserves to know who he comes from so we can make a bunch of babies. Big healthy babies, just like him. I can't wait to be pregnant! I probably won't turn up anything and

*I don't I'll let it go. I know it's a long shot but I'm going to
y this once for Titus's peace of mind.*

He couldn't take anymore. Abruptly he handed the book
Twillia. "Check the last couple of entries, please."

"Sure. Take your little friend here. He doesn't seem to un-
erstand that I don't like kissing dogs," she said as she gladly
wapped Kasey for the journal.

Titus was drawing a small measure of comfort from scratch-
g Kasey's ears when Twillia let out a shout. "She's not in
avannah, she went to Augusta! Aidan, we need to change di-
ctions, she went to Augusta," she said triumphantly. "Look
re, Titus, read this entry, the very last one."

*This is weird. I was pretty sure he was born in Savannah
ut there's this strange connection I need to check out in
ugusta. At least I was able to talk to someone who can give
e information. His name is Colby Chancellor and I'm going
meet him at six tonight at his place of business. A mortuary,
hat fun…NOT! Oh well, maybe this will pay off and I can
rop the whole thing. I should probably let Titus know what
m up to. I'll call him when I get to Augusta.*

It was daylight when they pulled into Augusta. They had
ade a four-hour drive to Savannah, then had to make a three-
our detour to Augusta. They'd stopped a couple of times so
asey wouldn't disgrace himself and they stopped once for
eakfast and to plan their strategy. Now it was still very
rly, but Titus wanted the element of surprise on their side.
hey drove directly to the mortuary, as Titus wanted to size
e place up. They circled the building slowly, looking for
mething that seemed out of place. Titus found it at once, in
e parking lot of the Chancellor Real Estate office across the
reet. In the parking lot there was a pink Thunderbird that
uld belong to only one person. There was a luxury car

parked on the side of the building, something that indicated the building was occupied. Everyone stared in silence as Aidan parked next to the vehicle. The only sound was of Titus checking his gun.

"Terry, you come with me. We're going to go in and ask a few questions. I hope he gives us the right answers," he said with a grim smile.

The two men got out of the Hummer and walked to the front entrance, while his other agents made themselves invisible around the perimeter of the area. Ellen Smith was more than happy to stay in the car and wait until it was all over. The door was locked, but it took Terry all of three seconds to open it. Lock picking was something he'd mastered in his feckless youth and a skill that came in handy quite often. After the two men entered the building, Twillia had a mission of her own. "I have to pee and so does Junior here. As much as Titus dotes on this fur-bearing insect, I doubt he wants puppy pee in his Hummer. We're going to take a stroll," she said. Her eyes never left the building and it was evident that she was a mass of nerves.

Aidan, in the meantime, had an idea of his own. "I'm going around back in case somebody tries to slip out. If you hear anything weird coming from back there, you go in the front and find Terry. I'd stay away from Titus if I were you."

It was a wise assessment on Aidan's part. At that moment Titus was looming over Colby Chancellor with a barely controlled fury in his eyes.

"What…how the hell did you get in here? That door was locked," the older man sputtered. His face was pasty and sweat was springing out all over it. "Who are you people and what do you want with me? I'll call the police if you don't get out of here now," he said loudly.

Titus gave the cowering man another grimace that could

have been loosely interpreted as a smile. His eyes silvered over as he introduced himself. "I do apologize for our impromptu entry," he said suavely, although his eyes betrayed his rage. "My name is Titus Argonne and this is my associate, Terry Patterson. We came here to look for my fiancée, Paris Deveraux, and I happen to know that this was the last place she was seen yesterday. Where is she?"

"I'm sorry, I don't know who you're talking about. I... can't say I've met the young lady. From Atlanta, you say? No, I don't think so, I have lots of appointments, I see lots of people, and I, uh, don't recall anyone by that name," he said weakly, mopping his face with a large handkerchief.

"Is that right? Then how did you know she came from Atlanta? I didn't mention where she was from, did I, Terry?"

Terry looked from the cowering older man to his boss, who was vibrating with fury. The physical resemblance between the two men was obvious but that's all it was, a similarity of coloring and features. "No, Titus, you sure didn't mention Atlanta. I wonder how he knows that's where Paris is from?"

"And how did my fiancée's car end up parked across the street from this building, the building where she had an appointment with you? Can you explain that to me, or would you rather wait for the police so you won't have to tell your lies twice?" Titus's harsh voice resonated in the office.

Incredibly, Colby Chancellor didn't seem to realize the extent of his peril and actually attempted to reach for his desk drawer. Whether it was to get a weapon or some sort of medication wasn't clear because Titus had had enough of the man. Without warning he reached across the desk and grabbed the older man by the throat, yanking him across the mahogany surface.

"Do not," Titus said in cold measured tones, "mistake my calmness for patience because I don't have any." He pulled a gun out of his shoulder holster and pressed it against the man's temple. Drops of sweat rolled down Chancellor's face and touched the barrel of the lethal-looking weapon. "If you've been a big enough fool to do something to my woman you're going to be your own customer in about two minutes so you need to think twice before you tell me another lie. Where is she?" Titus ground out.

The actual order of the next events was somewhat confusing because several things happened at once. There was a deafening crash from another room, coupled with a scream and then the unmistakable sound of Kasey's barking. Titus kept his hand tightly around the man's throat as he dragged him in the direction of the disturbance, which seemed to be coming from the showroom where the coffins were displayed. A most unlikely sight greeted Titus; there was Paris, trying to extricate herself from a smashed coffin. It had fallen off its stand and the impact made the top shatter, surprising for something that was supposed to be fine cabinetry. Twillia was standing there with her mouth open and Kasey rocketed to Paris, barking his joy at seeing his mistress.

Titus threw Chancellor at Terry and said, "If his ass moves, shoot him."

Terry grinned and replied, "No problem, boss."

While Paris was trying to pull the last of the duct tape off her mouth, Titus grabbed her and held her as tight as he could, breathing her name over and over. He could barely stand to let her go but he had to set her away from him to make sure she was all right. He hair was a mess, her clothes were rumpled and she was covered with chips of fiberboard from the crappy coffin, but she never looked lovelier than she did right now.

"Paris, when we get you home I'm putting a tether on you. Woman, you have no idea what this did to me, none at all," he told her, none too quietly.

"I'm sorry, baby, I can explain, I really can. But I need to do something right now. Is there a ladies' room around here?"

Titus kept his arm around her as he led her out of the showroom. She looked pale and weak until they got nearer to Terry and Chancellor. She stopped her weary walk and turned on the prisoner, calling him a name Titus had no idea she knew while she drew back and knocked him smooth out with a tight right hook. She wasn't finished, either. She drew back her foot and kicked him several times, still using some truly colorful language. She had snatched Terry's gun and had drawn a bead on the semiconscious man, preparing to blow a hole in him, when Titus took the gun back.

"Rosy, baby, calm down! The police are on the way here. He's going to be dealt with. Come here, baby, and let me make sure you're all right," he said soothingly.

"I'm not calming down—you can cram that crap," she said angrily. "That joker took my engagement ring! He'd better give it back or I'ma stomp the life out of him. I'll bet he steals everybody's jewelry, the thief. And he took my good shoes, too. If I don't get those shoes back I'm going to tear this place down," she raged. "I come here for some simple information and that fool has to try to go Edgar Allen Poe on me. I think that dummy was going to try to bury me," she sputtered indignantly.

The police burst in at that point and all was chaos for a few minutes. Finally Paris had availed herself of the ladies' room with Twillia's help and now she was sitting in the office with a police blanket around her shoulders and Titus standing next to her, stroking her hair. She was answering the detective's questions as concisely as possible, but given the sheer rage that dominated her emotions right now it was impossible for her to stem the editorial comments.

"That has to be the dumbest man on the face of the earth,"

she said, her disgust evident in her voice. "He doped up my drink and I passed out. When I came to he had me tied up and gagged, ghetto style. There was duct tape on my mouth and he tied my hands together in front of me with some cheap twine. Any fool knows you don't tie somebody's hand in front, unless you want them to get loose. I grew up with four brothers in Louisiana. If I couldn't get out of that lame mess I needed to suffocate, which apparently was his intention." She looked at Chancellor like she wanted nothing better than to pound the life out of him with her bare hands.

"I admit I was terrified at first," she said, looking at Titus for strength. "I'm very claustrophobic. But when it started getting light outside I could tell because of the raggedy coffin he put me in. I could actually see daylight coming through the cracks! Those things are incredibly shoddy," she added. "For some reason it pissed me off that her would put me in a crappy piece-of-junk coffin and then I remembered I had gravity on my side. What's the point of being a thick sister if you can't work it, right? So I started rocking back and forth to see if I could make the thing move. After I did it a few times the piece of junk rolled right off the stand it was on and broke wide open. And the rest is history. Like I said before, that's a real big dummy over there." She glared at Chancellor again and refused the offer of a glass of water with a look of horror. "I'm not drinking anything in this joint. Can we leave, please?"

The detective, a lieutenant named Hunter, was having a hard time keeping a straight face. "In just a few minutes, Miss Deveraux." He turned to Titus, who was stoically silent. "From what we can gather, Mr. Argonne, the story Colby Chancellor told your fiancée is true. It appears that you are the long-lost grandson of Charles Chancellor. He's on his way here now." Just then another detective stuck his head in the crowded office and beckoned to his superior. Lieutenant

Hunter excused himself and went into the corridor. In minutes he was back, with a sober look on his face. "Mr. Argonne, Mr. Chancellor just arrived," he said slowly. Titus's expression didn't relax, if anything it became more forbidding and stern. The lieutenant repeated himself, adding, "Would you like to meet your grandfather?"

Without hesitation, Titus said, "No." Just one word, spoken without any inflection but it revealed volumes about the man who uttered it. Without another word he removed the blanket from Paris's shoulders and replaced it with his arm, leading her out of the office. They walked past a tall, white-haired man with gray eyes and a chin just like Titus's own. Titus didn't even look in the man's direction.

Chapter 26

The events in Augusta seemed like a distant memory to Paris now. She and Titus spent a long weekend on St. Simons to rest and recuperate and now they were moving into their new home. They were taking a break from unpacking, sitting in the sunny solarium enjoying each other's company and anticipating their impending marriage. At least one of them was. The other one was deep in turmoil to judge from the look on Titus's face. Paris was straddling Titus's lap, facing him. His hands were around her waist while he looked deeply into her eyes. He was getting better, but the strain of the last week was showing. For the first few days after her rescue he couldn't stand to have her out of his sight. Paris could sense the tension in him and she wanted nothing more than to ease it. She rested her forehead against his and rubbed her hands over his shoulder, squeezing them gently. "How about a massage, baby? You feel so tense," she said softly.

"I am, a little," he admitted. "I don't know if I can do this,

Paris. It's too much for me to take in right now. Maybe if we weren't trying to plan a wedding I could deal with it better, but right now I'm just not feeling it. I don't see what the point is, that's all."

Paris wrapped her arms around his neck and cradled him to her, trying to ease away his nerves with her love. Ever since the story had come out about Titus's biological parents, he'd been like this. They now knew of his existence and wanted to meet him and Titus wasn't convinced it was something he needed to do. His adoptive family assured him they weren't threatened in any way by the meeting. They were, in fact, encouraging him to meet the people who'd created him. Paris tried to be as supportive and reassuring as possible, but it was difficult to know exactly what to say to him. She gently released him from her loving embrace and pulled away so she could cup his face in her hands and kiss him.

"I love you so much," she whispered. "All I want is your happiness. If you don't want to meet them right now, I'll call them and postpone it for you. Maybe you're right. Maybe it's too soon. It's not like you're on a schedule, you know. You can do this anytime, you know."

Titus tightened his grasp on Paris and leaned into her comforting warmth. "I love you, Rosy. You are the most amazing thing that's ever happened to me and I'll love you for the rest of my life. Ten days after I'm dead I'll still be in love with you," he vowed. "And I don't want anything to be hanging over us when we start our life together. I want it to be just you and me and nothing else. So thank you for the offer, but I'm going to meet the parents," he said dryly.

Paris's heart melted again at his tender words of love. She could see the strain and tension in his face even though to everyone else he looked like his usual calm and collected self. She whispered in his ear that they should go lay down.

Yes, there was a sea of boxes everywhere, but Titus's huge bed was in place and she had a feeling that a little afternoon delight might be just the thing. It would be pleasurable for both of them as well as helping to remove some of the tension from Titus. He smiled his agreement and moved his hands to her butt, palming it and moving his hands in slow circles. He was about to take her up on her offer when the doorbell rang. They both jumped at the sound and stared at each other.

"They can't be here already," Paris whispered. She smoothed her hair and looked down at her outfit, which consisted of old jeans and a *Paris & Company* denim shirt. She didn't look her best, but they were moving, after all. Titus was similarly attired but he looked good in anything, darn him. Holding tight to each other's hand, they went to the front door and Titus opened it to a most unexpected sight. A man of Titus's complexion and nearly his height was standing there with two younger women who looked to be identical twins. The man had a hand on the shoulder of each young woman. He smiled grimly when he saw Titus and Paris standing there.

"These are for you," he said. "Good luck."

"Listen to him, good luck," one of the young women said. The other one clicked her tongue in disgust. "He thinks he's funny—don't pay him any attention."

"He's just trying to be a comedian," the first one said.

"Yeah, but there's a problem with that—he's not funny," the second one chimed in.

The women were tall and slender and each had close-cropped natural hair the color of Titus's. Their eyes, which were full of laughter, were gray. They kept right on talking as though this were an everyday occurrence.

"Nope, he's about as funny as a toothache, that's why we were really happy to find out about you," said one.

"Yes, we have a brother now," gloated the other one.

The man finally spoke up, sounded more amused than in-
dignant. "So what am I, chopped liver? I'm also your brother,
or did you forget that little fact?"

"No, we didn't forget, we just don't like you because
you're mean to us," they said in unison.

Titus and Paris were looking at each other and at the specc-
cle on their porch. Finally Titus addressed the man. "Do they
ever stop talking?"

"Not that we're aware. Look, I'm Justice Chancellor, your
brother," he said extending his hand to Titus, who shook it
warmly without realizing what he was doing. The younger
man smiled at the bemused expression on Titus's face. "These
two are your sisters, Jamie and Jodie. I can send their stuff if
you want to keep them," he said hopefully.

"See what I mean," Jamie said shaking her finger at Justice.
"You're not funny." The twins ignored Titus's outstretched
hand and each one gave him a big hug and a kiss on the cheek.
They also introduced themselves to Paris, since Titus's ability
to speak seemed to have deserted him. Paris gladly returned
their hugs; she was thrilled to meet them. She was also the
only one who realized they were still on the porch.

"Please come in and make yourselves at home," she
invited. "I'll get some iced tea for you. Come sit down. It's a
mess, but you're more than welcome." She got a puzzled look
on her face and asked the question Titus was afraid to voice.
"But where are your parents?"

Justice's face softened into a gentle smile, so much like
Titus's it was eerie. "They're in the car. Mama was too
nervous to get out."

Titus took Paris's hand again and they walked to the edge
of the porch, descending the stairs together. They approached
the late model car parked in the driveway, watching as a tall,
ruddy-haired man got out, his bluish eyes damp from emotion.

It was easy to see where Titus got his looks; the older man had probably looked exactly like Titus when he was younger. The two men shook hands solemnly and the handshake became an embrace as father and son connected for the very first time. Titus was smiling as he looked into the eyes of his birth father. "So what do I have to do to meet my mother?"

His father laughed. "She's too scared to move, son. You'll have to go get her, I think."

Titus approached the car and opened the passenger door. He smiled down at the woman inside. "Aren't you going to say hello? You came all this way to meet me," he said softly.

A middle-aged woman with green eyes and rich caramel skin got out of the car. Her hair was dark brown and tears were running down her face. Titus put his arms around her and gave her a big hug. "Come on now, I'm not that ugly, am I?" Her only answer was to burst into unchecked tears of joy.

Her loving husband shook his head. "I've known this woman for forty-five years and she's been doing that for every single one of those years. I don't know where she keeps all that water." He turned to Paris who was watching the touching scene with tears of her own falling. "You must be the charming and beautiful fiancée I've heard so much about. I'm Charles Chancellor," he said with a smile. Paris didn't hesitate; she gave him a big hug.

"I'm so pleased to meet you," she said. "Why don't we all go inside and get acquainted," she suggested.

In a short time they were all seated in the solarium, at least everyone but the twins were seated. Jamie and Jodie were exploring the house. They already knew the story and they were, by their own admission, just nosy. They wanted to see the new home. Titus was sandwiched between his mother and Paris on the wicker sofa, while his father and Justice each had a comfortable armchair. Paris had brought out iced tea and a plate of teacakes from Aunt Sisters, although everyone but Justice was much too keyed up to eat. He commandeered the plate and was devouring the cakes with gusto while his father cleared his throat and began telling the story of Titus's life.

"Mattie and I are both from Savannah. We went to the same high school, and I guess you could say we were high school sweethearts, in a way," Charles said with a fond look at Mattie.

"I wasn't allowed to date," Mattie said shyly. "My parents were very strict and old-fashioned and I couldn't have company. But we still liked each other," she added with a look of love directed at her husband. He took up the story from there.

"We went to the same college and we were able to date openly at last. I always knew that Mattie was the one for me, no matter what. She was so sweet and loving, she was like my other half. When we found out we were going to be parents, we were thrilled. We were scared, of course, because we were still in school and we knew our parents wouldn't approve of us getting married, but the love we had for each other was so strong we knew everything would be all right. We came home to tell our parents and get their blessing for our marriage," he said.

Mattie stopped dabbing her eyes with her handkerchief long enough to chime in. "Well, that just shows you how young and naive we were," she said with a trace of bitterness. "They treated us like criminals. My parents were bad enough, they were so angry and disappointed in me they just turned me out of the house," she said sadly.

Titus squeezed her hand and Paris tightened her grip on his hand when they heard those words, but there was more to come. When Mattie saw their stricken faces, she smiled wanly. "Well, that's how things were back then. Especially in a household as strict as mine was. My parents were just crushed by my pregnancy, they were. They eventually got over it and we reconciled, but it was a very hard time. Especially after what…" Her voice trailed off and she looked at Charles as the tears gathered in her eyes once more.

An awkward moment of silence ensued, broken by Charles's voice, heavy with emotion. "My parents were much worse than Mattie's. My father wanted me to have nothing to do with Mattie because she wasn't the girl they wanted me to be with. We were supposed to be big shots in Savannah because he owned a few businesses and Mattie's people were regular working folks. He expected me to marry someone of what he called 'class' and he wanted me to break it off with her even before we knew we were to become parents. When he found that out, he went crazy and I mean that literally," he said sadly. "We didn't understand the full range of his anger then. We really didn't understand it fully until we found out about you. I still can't believe what he did. It's still almost impossible for me to comprehend it," he said with a deep sigh.

Titus looked from his father to his mother, whose hand had grown cold in his own. "I'm sorry, I'm not following you," he said gently. "What did he do?"

Mattie answered him in a low voice that was nonetheless filled with anger and pain. "He took you away from us, that's what he did. He had one of his people take you away from the hospital and we were told that you had died."

Paris gasped and her hand tightened on Titus's. "He did *what?*"

Mattie took a long, tear-filled breath. "I know, it's inconceivable, isn't it? He actually paid someone to steal our baby and make it seem like he died. He was that powerful. He had people who could do those kinds of things. From what we were told, the idea was to get rid of you altogether but the man he hired couldn't do it. He ended up driving you to Charleston and leaving you on the steps of a church. We were heartbroken, son, just devastated. Losing you was like a punishment from God. It was as if we deserved to be heartbroken because we'd sinned," she told him.

Titus put his arm around her shoulder and held her closely. "My God, how could anyone be that cruel? Why would he torture his own son like that?"

Charles shook his head. "Because he was a ruthless man, determined to have his own way in every aspect of his life, and in my life because I was his only son. He tried to force us to abort you and we refused. And when he could see that we had no intention of giving you up for adoption, either, he took matters into his own hands. But it didn't work. As soon as Mattie was able to leave the hospital we left Georgia and went to Virginia to start our lives over. We got married and we worked our way through school. I got a degree in theology and became a pastor and Mattie became a teacher. We had Justice, Jamie and Jodie. We've had a good life, son, but we never forgot you, our first child. The pain of losing you never went away completely. And when found out you were still alive, it was like God's greatest miracle."

By now Mattie and Paris were sobbing and even Titus had to blink back moisture. Justice was looking touched, as well, and it was a deeply tender moment, broken by the sudden reappearance of Jamie and Jodie and Kasey. He dashed into the room and jumped into Paris's lap to see what was distressing her.

"We love your house," the twins said as one. Jamie looked at all the emotional faces and nodded. "They told you all about it, didn't they?"

Jodie said, "Daddy's father did a terrible thing, he really did. But this is the good part, everybody, the part where we get to live happily ever after. We found each other, that's what's important."

"Well, that and us being in the wedding. Can we be bridesmaids, please?" Jamie asked winsomely.

Paris hastily wiped away her tears and gave a huge genuine smile. "Of course you can! What a wonderful idea," she said.

Justice helped himself to the last teacake with a laugh. "That's what you think. If you knew what those two are capable of you wouldn't think it was such a hot idea. Chaos and panic are their middle names," he said dryly.

"Oh Justice, don't be silly," Paris admonished him playfully. "This is going to be the happiest day of our lives and we have so much more to celebrate now. The more the merrier, I say."

Those words grew to be her mantra as the days raced by. The wedding was going to be huge; there was no way around it. Paris had Angelique and Ruth as her matron and maid of honor. Her bridesmaids were Nona, Natalie, Nicole, Jamie and Jodie, in addition to her oldest friend Chastain from New Orleans, Twillia, Nina Flores and Lisette Alexander. She also had her young cousins, Amariee, Jilleyin and Jasmine as well as Heide. The only person to turn her down was Aidan, who flat out refused to contemplate standing up with her.

"But you're my friend," she said. "I want you to be in my wedding."

"As what, woman? I'm a little to old to be a ring bearer, don't you think?" Aidan laughed at the very thought.

"No, as a…a bridesman, I guess. You can just come down the aisle with the bridesmaids," she said firmly. "I want you in my wedding," she said stubbornly.

"I can be an usher or a groomsman but there is no way I'm sashaying down the white carpet with the girls. I really think being in love has fried some of your brain circuits," he said grumpily, but Paris didn't care as long as she got her way.

It was going to be the Cirque du Soleil of weddings but Paris didn't care. She had a flock of adorable flower girls and three ring bearers instead of one, just because there were so many small cousins to include. Even moving the wedding from December to August was a piece of cake because Paris had the world's best wedding planner working with her. And it was essential that they get married as soon as possible because Titus had cut her off. The day after his reunion with his birth family, Titus had made an announcement. "I'm a preacher's son, you Jezebel. No more sex until after we're married."

He was smiling when he said it, and he was also holding Paris tightly, having just kissed the life out of her. He laughed at the look on her face but insisted he was serious, which made her get just as serious. They were getting married with lightning speed because she couldn't go until December without her man. Titus was pleased, although he'd only been teasing when he said no sex until they were man and wife. He just loved the look of consternation on her face when he told her he was saving himself. The joke was on him when she took him up on it. Now it was hard to say who was the most needy, Titus or Paris.

Twillia's aunt Regina knew, though. She had, at Twillia's request, arrived in Atlanta to take charge of the planning. In addition to her other talents she was an ex-marine who brooked no nonsense from overly anxious brides and grooms. She took one look at Titus's glazed expression every time he looked at Paris and shook her head. "Sweetheart, I have a cattle prod in my bag and if you two don't cut it out I'll use it on you. The only way we're going to pull this off is precision planning so there's no time for fooling around."

She and Aunt Ruth got along like a house afire and between the two of them Paris had no worries. It might be the speediest wedding of its size in the known world, but it was still going to be beautiful and meaningful, especially since Titus's father was officiating. Paris and Titus had hosted a dinner where the two families met, his birth family and his adoptive one and it was a spectacular success. Mattie had once again dissolved into happy tears when Sarah and Clifton presented her with a huge album of pictures from the time they adopted Titus to the present. Mattie said it was like getting a glimpse of him growing up and she couldn't thank them enough. And Mama Sweet was happy to supply them with every anecdote she could recall of his childhood antics, regardless of how embarrassing they were to him. All in all it was a typical family party.

In one of their increasingly rare minutes alone, Paris and Titus were in the solarium, trying their best to behave. Paris was curled up next to him on the sofa and they were kissing, little sweet kisses that weren't meant to arouse, but did anyway. Paris held her hand up and stared dreamily at her ring. "We're getting married in three days," she said softly. "I can't believe this is happening, Titus. This time last year I was just miserable. It was after John and Nina's wedding, remember? After..."

"After I made a huge fool of myself," Titus said ruefully. "I'll never stop regretting that, Paris. You were so sweet and so sexy I think I really lost my mind for a minute or two. I've never had an experience like that with a woman and I really put my foot in my mouth. I'll be apologizing to you for that for the rest of our lives, I think."

"I think not," Paris said indignantly. "Yes, I wanted it to turn out differently, but it really was a beautiful way for me to learn what lovemaking is all about. And if it hadn't happened just the way it did, we might not be sitting here now," she reminded him. "Everything happens for a reason."

"That's where you're wrong, Rosy," Titus said, pulling her into his arms for a long, soulful kiss. "We were always meant for each other. No matter what, we were intended to be with each other. You're mine and I'm yours and that's forever," he vowed.

A voice from the doorway made them jump. "If you don't want to see how well my cattle prod works I suggest you step away from the bride and get busy unloading my car. In three days you can do anything you want to with each other but right now, what I say goes." Aunt Regina stood there with her arms crossed and brandishing the cattle prod so Titus could get a good look at it. Titus kissed Paris once more and dashed out the door to do her bidding. The older woman had pity on Paris, who sighed deeply as she watched her beloved's retreating figure.

"Sweetheart, it's just three more days and he's yours for a lifetime. You waited your whole life for true love, so what's seventy-two more hours?"

Paris smiled brilliantly, thinking about the wisdom in Aunt Regina's words. "You're absolutely right. I'll have the love of my life for the rest of my life, so I think I can wait just a few more days."

Chapter 27

The day of the wedding arrived and none too soon for Titus, who was about to expire from his longing for Paris. He didn't think it was possible to love her any more than he did, but the self-imposed abstinence he'd unwittingly imposed on them made him realize how much he needed her. His life had been so arid and sterile before Paris, and now it was happy and fulfilled. His heart was full and his soul was at peace since he had been reunited with his birth parents thanks to Paris. Any tiny little bits of bitterness at being a cast-off child of uncertain racial origins were gone, once he met Mattie and Charles, his very loving and very African-American parents. He also got a charge out of being the oldest, for a change, as his two older sisters never let him forget that they were older and wiser than he.

From looking stern and serious most of the time, Titus smiled all the time now, something that Trey was happy to point out to him as the men of the wedding party got dressed in their tuxedoes. "Man, you smile twenty-four seven, don't you T? I told you those hints would help, didn't I? Now you're marrying Paris and you're gonna be my cousin for real," he gloated.

"You're wise beyond your years, Grasshopper," Titus said with a grin. He made as if to ruffle Trey's hair and Trey ducked away from him.

"Don't mess with my 'do, man, I have to look good for the ladies," Trey protested.

All the men laughed as Trey dashed to the mirror to make sure he was still perfectly groomed. There was an army of good-looking men getting dressed, as Titus had to dig up a corresponding number of attendants to Paris's bridesmaids. Martin and Justice were his best men, and all the Deveraux men were included. Both Paris's brothers and her cousins participated, but that wasn't enough. Trey was a groomsman too—there was no way Titus was leaving him out. Donnie and Adam Cochran were also in the party, along with the other Cochran brothers, Alan, Andre, Andrew and John Flores. Paris got her wish, as Aidan was also in the wedding party, but on Titus's side of the altar. Terry and Paul were also pressed into service as ushers. It would probably go down in the record books as the biggest wedding the old church had ever seen, but it was going to be beautiful. Titus couldn't wait to see his bride and looked at the clock in the dressing room one more time, which brought a shout of laughter from Martin.

"Relax, man, you're worse than I was at my wedding to Ceylon. In a few minutes you'll be standing by the altar ready to take your vows, so try to chill out, man."

Titus took him at his word and sat down for all of thirty seconds before he was up and pacing again. Martin shook his head in amusement. There was no holding back an eager groom.

* * *

In a very short time the men were assembled at the front of the church and Titus's fondest wish came true. The brides-maids entered the church wearing very pretty gowns of deep pink, followed by the maid and matron of honor in rose-colored gowns. They all carried bouquets of roses in soft pink. Everyone went "aww" as the ring bearers marched solemnly down the aisle, concentrating on their awesome task. There were more coos from the guests as the flower girls came next, sprinkling rose petals over the white runner rolled out by Marty and Malcolm. Then the church doors closed and a murmur of anticipation rippled through the sanctuary. Everyone turned to the doors, looking down the aisle bordered with rose topiary trees. Blossoms by Betty had provided all the flowers and she had done a fantastic job of creating a romantic setting for the wedding.

Vera and Marcus Deveraux sang "All I Ask of You" from *The Phantom of the Opera* and the lyrics took on a whole new meaning as Titus meditated on the start of his new life with Paris.

The music swelled to signal the arrival of the bride and Titus could feel his heart pounding in his throat. The doors finally opened to reveal his beloved looking like a princess from a fairy tale. She was utterly radiant in the gown Perry had created for her. It was strapless with a tight-fitting bodice that extended below her waist. The bodice was simple and un-adorned except for a row of pearl buttons down the back. The skirt more than made up for its simplicity, however. It was silk organza and it was gathered into a full skirt so delicate and ethereal Paris looked as if she was floating in a cloud. The skirt was embellished with tiny silk rosebuds that were white at the top of the skirt. As they inched down the length of the garment they turned a baby pink, ending in a soft rosy pink near the hem. The toes of her shoes were also adorned with ilk rosebuds, and she carried a cascading bouquet of roses n various shades of pink and ivory.

Even her sheer veil couldn't mask the sparkle in her eyes. The love she felt for Titus was a palpable thing, as was his for her. They looked into each other's eyes and the wedding became a mere formality as they pledged their hearts forevermore with one burning look. Paris was so taken with the ardor she saw on Titus's face she didn't notice her brothers shedding tears. She did see a suspicious moisture in her father's eyes as he placed her hand into Titus's. It was hard for her to keep tears from flowing from her own eyes until she felt the warmth of his hand on hers. She was fine after that. Reverend Chancellor performed the ceremony beautifully and with deep meaning. If it hadn't been for the unexpected response to the question "Who giveth this woman to be wed" she might have made it through the ceremony dry-eyed. But the chorus of voices from her brothers, Lillian and Bump and her cousins made her heart swell with love and dampened her eyes.

Titus sensed her reaction and tightened his gentle grasp of her hand, bringing it to his lips for a kiss. "I love you, Rosy," he whispered. Soon it was all over and Titus was lifting her veil to salute his bride. They had promised each other they wouldn't make a spectacle of themselves in front of the church but it was a hard promise to keep. Their lips met and mated, but it was a sweet and tender kiss that promised a future of nothing but happiness.

Their reception was truly festive. An outdoor venue in a formal garden provided just the ambience Paris had hoped for. It was hot and sunny and flowers were everywhere, just the way she'd envisioned it. The food, courtesy of the Summers sisters and Aunt Sister's restaurant, was sublime. The guests dined sumptuously on Creole and Low-country specialties while the music flowed and laughter rang out joyously. Trey took the microphone to announce that in order to see the new-lyweds kiss, each table had to stand up and sing a song that used the word love in it. "You can't just tap on your glass with your fork, you have to stand up and sing if you want to see them smooch," he said. He looked at the blissful pair who were at that very moment engaged in a long kiss. "Okay, maybe we should change that. If you want to see them come up for air you can stand up and sing," he said with a wicked grin.

It was a long, happy and very musical reception. Everyone's mouth dropped open when Titus stood up and serenaded his bride with "This Very Moment." There was hardly a dry eye among the ladies when he finished pouring out his soul to her in song. Their first dance was memorable for two reasons. One, because they looked so absolutely beautiful in each other's arms, and two, because something that had never happened in the annals of Deveraux family history occurred. Titus and Paris had their first dance to "The Closer I Get to You" sung by none other than Bennie and Clay Deveraux. Like the other members of his family, Clay had a fine voice but no one outside his wife and children ever heard it because he never sang in public. But for his favorite cousin and his beloved wife, who was carrying his child, he could never say no.

Paris felt as if she could dance all night, she was so happy. There were a few tears as she danced with her daddy to "Someone To Watch Over Me," tears that she joined in when Mac graciously handed her over to Titus, the man who would watch over her for the rest of their lives. Titus shook his father-in-law's hand solemnly to assure him that he would take care of Paris forever. Mac nodded with equal gravity, but his face broke into a smile when Ruth came to claim him for a dance. They spent the rest of the evening dancing and enjoying each other's company to the fullest.

It was hard to say who enjoyed the reception more, the bride or the groom. Titus shed his tuxedo jacket and danced with both his mothers, with everyone in the bridal party, with his sisters and every other family member and friend he could find, but all the slow dances belonged to Paris. It was the best party anyone had ever had, but after the dancing and the cake cutting and the toasts and serenades, it was time for the most important part of the evening when they would depart to begin their honeymoon. Paris tossed her bouquet straight to Aunt Ruth, which brought a burst of surprised laughter from her. Next came the tossing of the garter, which meant that Titus had to get it off his blushing bride.

The music changed tempo and became a sultry African drumbeat. Paris was seated in a chair and her skirts billowed around her. She looked innocently virginal but exotically seductive at the same time as she looked at Titus. Titus stood there looking like a conquering hero come to claim the fair lady, and then he began walking toward his beloved. Then he resembled a jungle cat, stalking his mate as his movements matched the rhythm of the African drums. Suddenly he dropped into a crouch directly in front of Paris, a movement so sinuous and full of intent every woman in the room sighed. He grasped her ankle and slid his big hands slowly up her leg, his eyes fastened to hers the whole time.

He knew she didn't really like this tradition, where so many men made a big show of diving under the bride's dress and pulling the garter off with their teeth. She found the practice embarrassing and he thought it was stupid, so he made sure to discreetly remove the garter without exposing her beautiful legs to anyone. They had no idea how sexy they looked as they looked into each other with eyes made hot with desire. When Titus's questing hands discovered his wife was wearing a garter belt under all her finery, his eyes glazed over and he was barely able to remove the garter without throwing her over his shoulder and hauling her out of there. Several women were fanning themselves rapidly during the ritual, which was over quickly as Titus tossed the garter over his shoulder in no particular direction. He didn't even see it land on Mac Deveraux's shoulder. In minutes they were in the limousine that would take them to the airport where the Deveraux corporate jet was waiting.

Titus looked at Paris; the other half of his heart—no, his *whole* heart—and wondered again what he had done to deserve her love. He bent his head to hers and kissed her hard and long. When he was through she was dazed and breathless.

"Wow," she murmured. "I don't know what I did to deserve that, but I'll take as many of them as I can get."

"All you did was love me unconditionally, even when I was being the biggest jerk in the world. I love you, Paris, and I'm going to love you a little more every day for the rest of our lives. Is that okay with you?"

Through her tears of happiness Paris managed to nod her head and say yes. "Only if I can love you right back."

Epilogue

After spending the night in a luxury hotel in New York City, Titus and Paris flew off for their honeymoon to the place Titus felt was most appropriate for his bride. They landed in Paris, France for a weeklong honeymoon that was the beginning of a lifetime of passionately profound love. Titus looked down at Paris, who was cuddled into his arms as they lazed in bed. They'd had breakfast and a long shower, but they didn't feel compelled to move out of bed.

"I think you wasted a lot of money bringing me to Europe, baby." Paris's sleepy voice had an amused lilt to it. "I don't want to get out of this bed to see any sights. The only sight I want to see is you."

Titus laughed and Paris could feel his big muscles rippling under her cheek. "No amount of money I spend on you is ever wasted, Rosy. If we want to stay in bed the entire week that's our business, and just for the record, I don't want to move, either. I love feeling you next to me. I could do this for the rest of my life and not complain."

Paris sighed with happiness and looked at her fantastic rings again, smiling at the amazing sight. "It was a beautiful wedding, wasn't it? And the reception was a lot of fun. I think people really enjoyed themselves," she said with a little yawn.

Titus chuckled. "I think everyone enjoyed themselves thoroughly, especially Corey. I have to admit, Rosy, your plan worked really well. I had my doubts, but as usual you were right."

Patting his chest for emphasis, Paris insisted that she was always right about these matters. "When Perry and I went to Chicago to look for fabric for my gown and I saw her, I knew I had to do something. Believe it or not, Julian is my most reasonable brother and I knew he would do what I asked him to do. And he did, didn't he?"

"Yeah, he did. So what happens next?" her sleepy husband asked.

"We'll find out when we get home, I suppose. One thing about my family is we're never, ever boring," she said with a soft giggle.

"You're right about that. I'm glad we're here right now, though. I love this honeymoon, even though we haven't gotten out of bed yet."

"I love it, too. And thank you for bringing me to Paris. I'm glad we're not in the tropics right now." She yawned and kissed his chest.

"So am I, Rosy. What's the name of that storm again, that big one?"

"Katrina," Paris said softly, and went to sleep in the arms of the man she'd always loved.

Dear Reader,

Thank you for accompanying me on Paris and Titus's journey. I know that a lot of you have been waiting for their story and I hope it fulfilled your expectations. Paris waited for her man for a long time, and I know I kept you waiting, too. Thanks for being patient with me.

I am full of thanks these days, for all your love and support during this very trying time. Your prayers and your good wishes meant so much to my mother and to me. We appreciated and cherished each and every one of them.

I'll see you again in 2006 with two full-length novels. And yes, you will find out lots more about those Louisiana Deveraux men, starting with the two Julians, father and son. Until then, thanks again for your prayers and your support.

Stay blessed,

Melanie
I Chronicles 4:10
MelanieAuthor@aol.com
P.O. Box 5176
Saginaw, Michigan 48603